Stephen McCranie's

SPACE
BOY

VOLUME 13

Written and illustrated by
STEPHEN McCRANIE

DARK HORSE BOOKS

President and Publisher **Mike Richardson**

Editor **Shantel LaRocque**

Associate Editor **Brett Israel**

Assistant Editor **Sanjay Dharawat**

Designer **Anita Magaña**

Digital Art Technician **Allyson Haller**

STEPHEN MCCRANIE'S SPACE BOY VOLUME 13

Space Boy™ © 2022 Stephen McCranie. All rights reserved. Dark Horse Books® and the Dark Horse logo are registered trademarks of Dark Horse Comics LLC. All rights reserved. No portion of this publication may be reproduced or transmitted, in any form or by any means, without the express written permission of Dark Horse Comics LLC. Names, characters, places, and incidents featured in this publication either are the product of the author's imagination or are used fictitiously. Any resemblance to actual persons (living or dead), events, institutions, or locales, without satiric intent, is coincidental.

This book collects *Space Boy* episodes 196–210, previously published online at WebToons.com.

Published by Dark Horse Books
A division of Dark Horse Comics LLC
10956 SE Main Street | Milwaukie, OR 97222
StephenMcCranie.com | DarkHorse.com

To find a comics shop in your area, visit comicshoplocator.com

First edition: June 2022
ISBN 978-1-50672-876-6
10 9 8 7 6 5 4 3 2 1
Printed in China

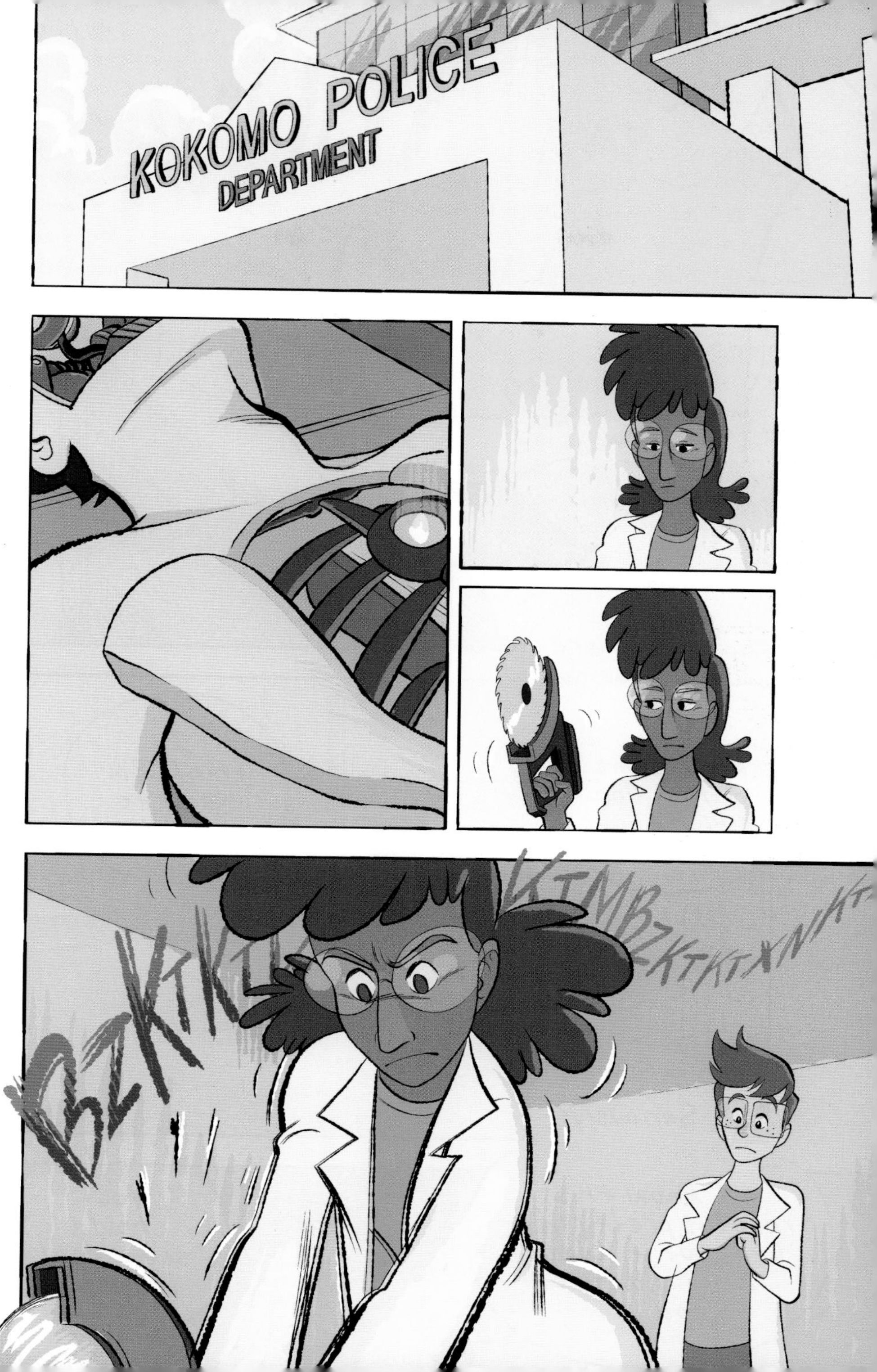
KOKOMO POLICE
DEPARTMENT

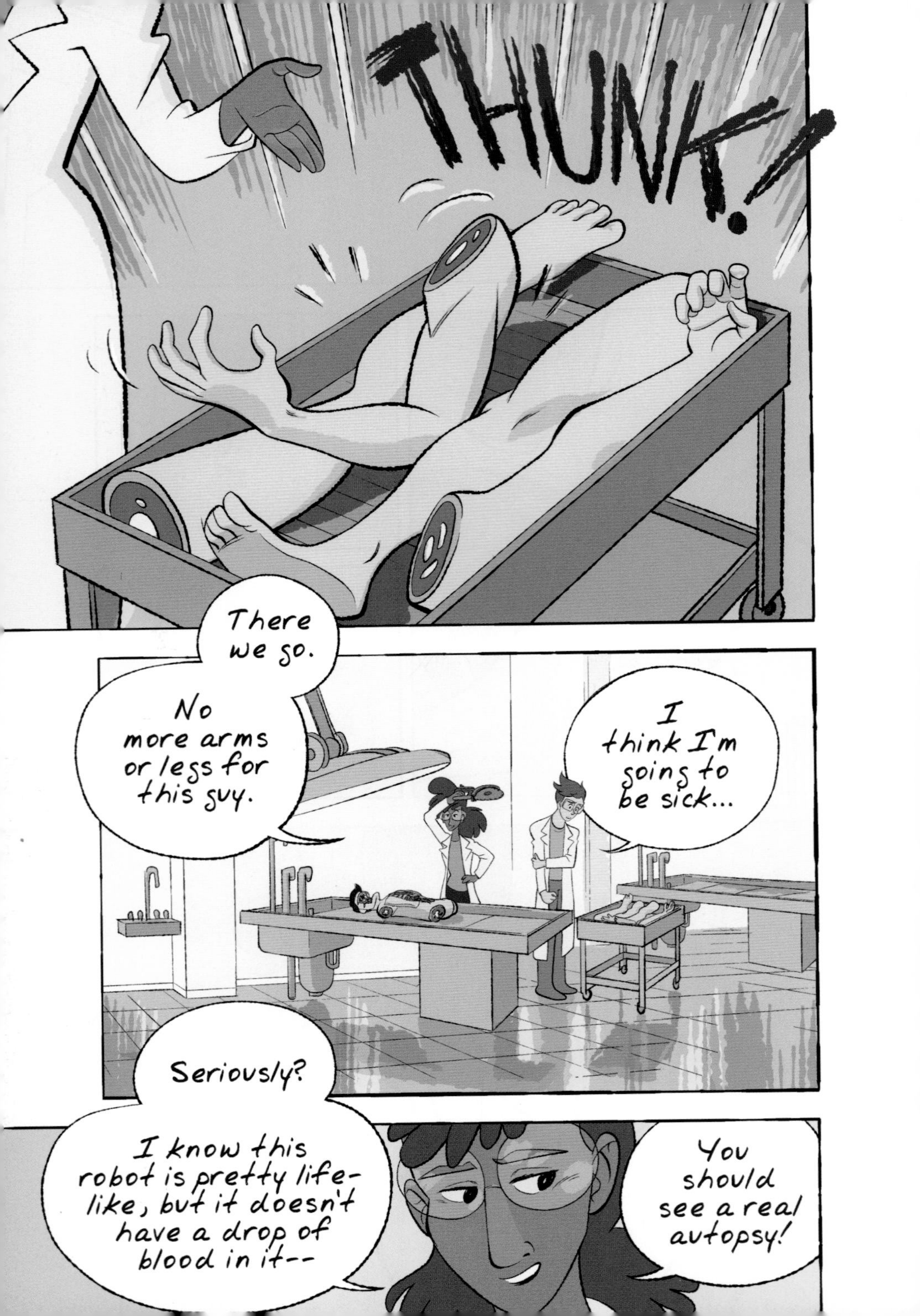
THUNK!!
There we go.
No more arms or legs for this guy.
I think I'm going to be sick...
Seriously?
I know this robot is pretty life-like, but it doesn't have a drop of blood in it--
You should see a real autopsy!

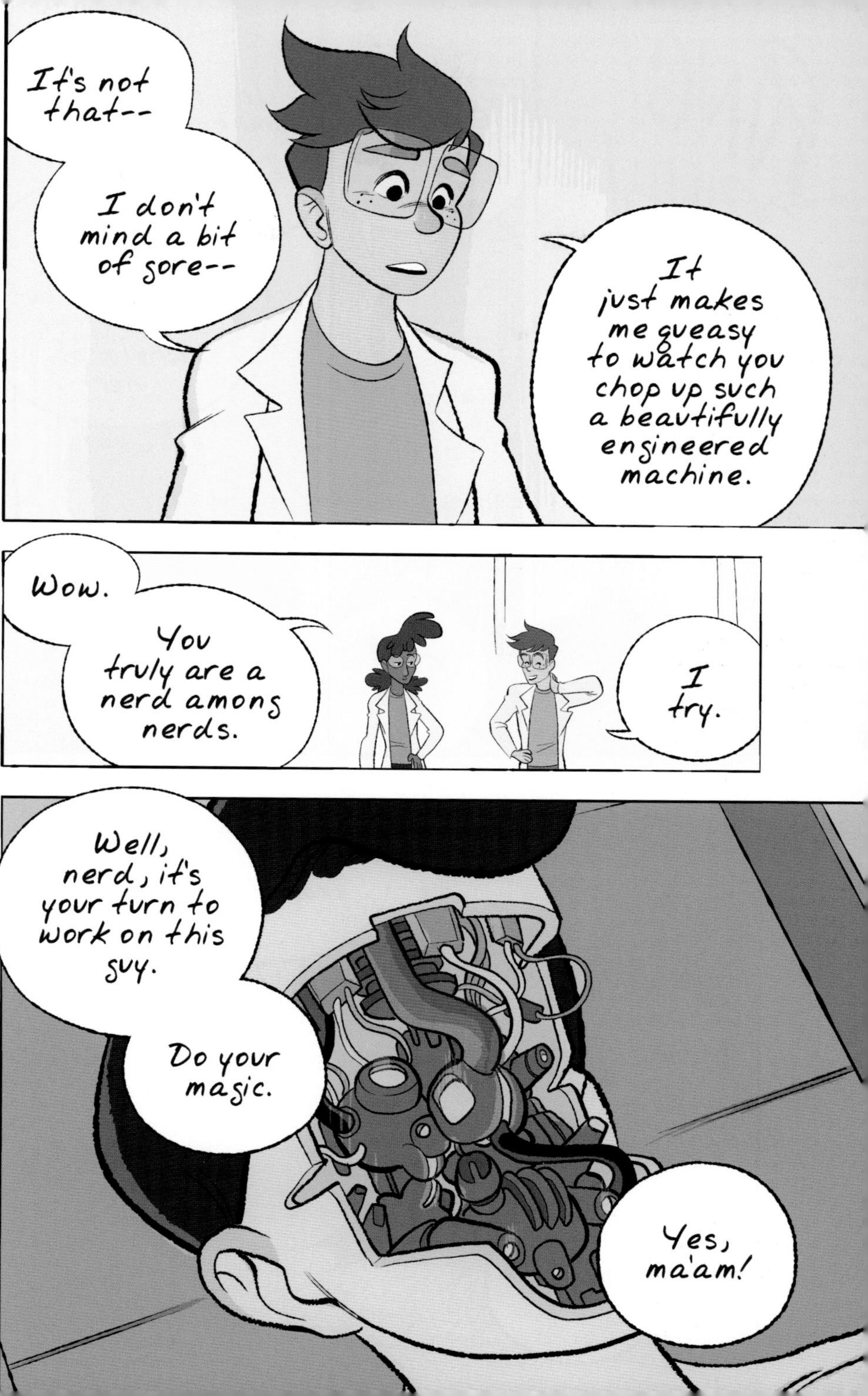
It's not that--
I don't mind a bit of gore--
It just makes me queasy to watch you chop up such a beautifully engineered machine.
Wow.
You truly are a nerd among nerds.
I try.
Well, nerd, it's your turn to work on this guy.
Do your magic.
Yes, ma'am!

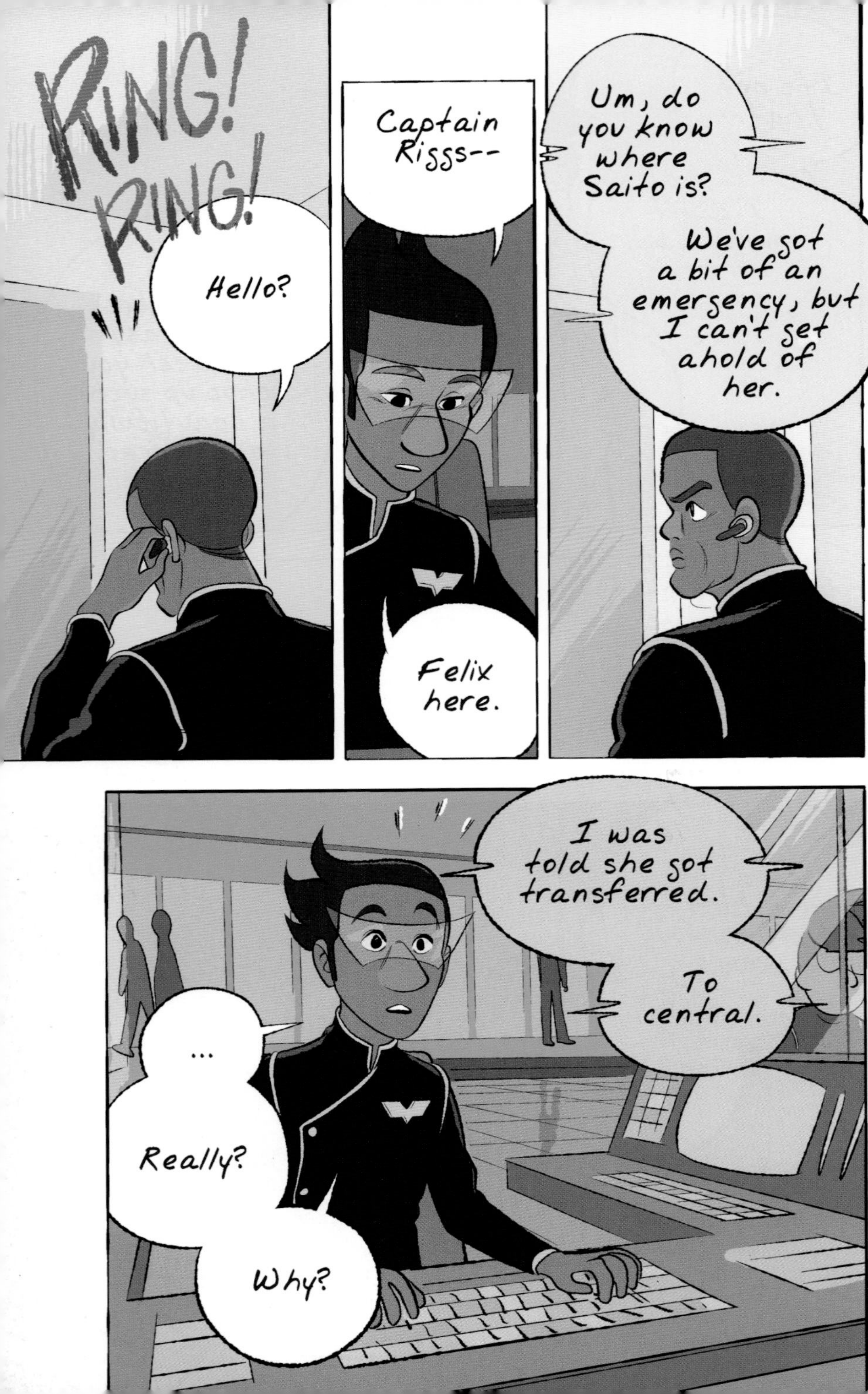
RING! RING!
Hello?
Captain Risss--
Felix here.
Um, do you know where Saito is?
We've got a bit of an emergency, but I can't get ahold of her.
I was told she got transferred.
To central.
...
Really?
Why?

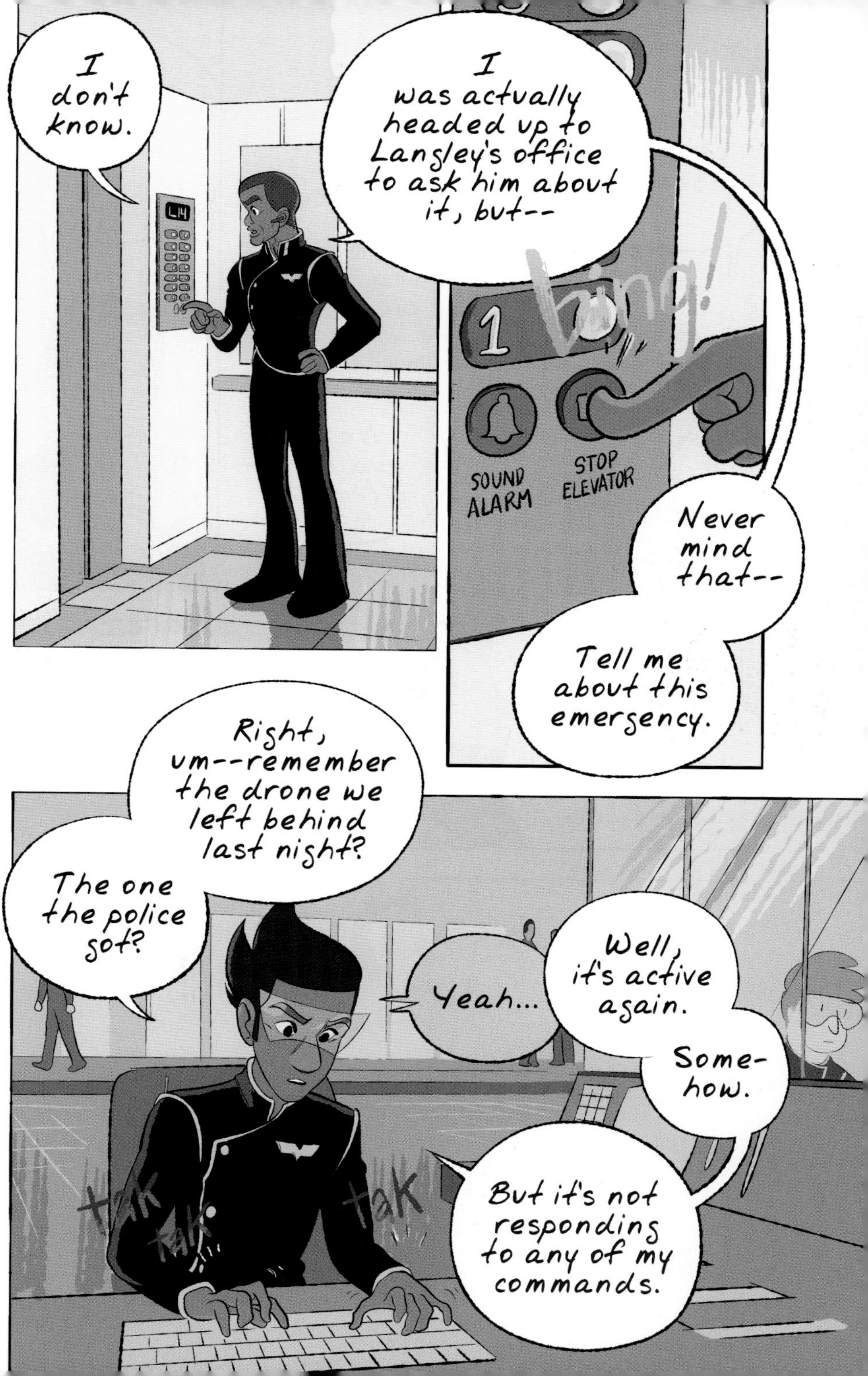
I don't know.
I was actually headed up to Langley's office to ask him about it, but--
L14
bing!
1
SOUND ALARM
STOP ELEVATOR
Never mind that--
Tell me about this emergency.
Right, um--remember the drone we left behind last night?
The one the police got?
Yeah...
Well, it's active again.
Some-how.
tak tak tak
But it's not responding to any of my commands.

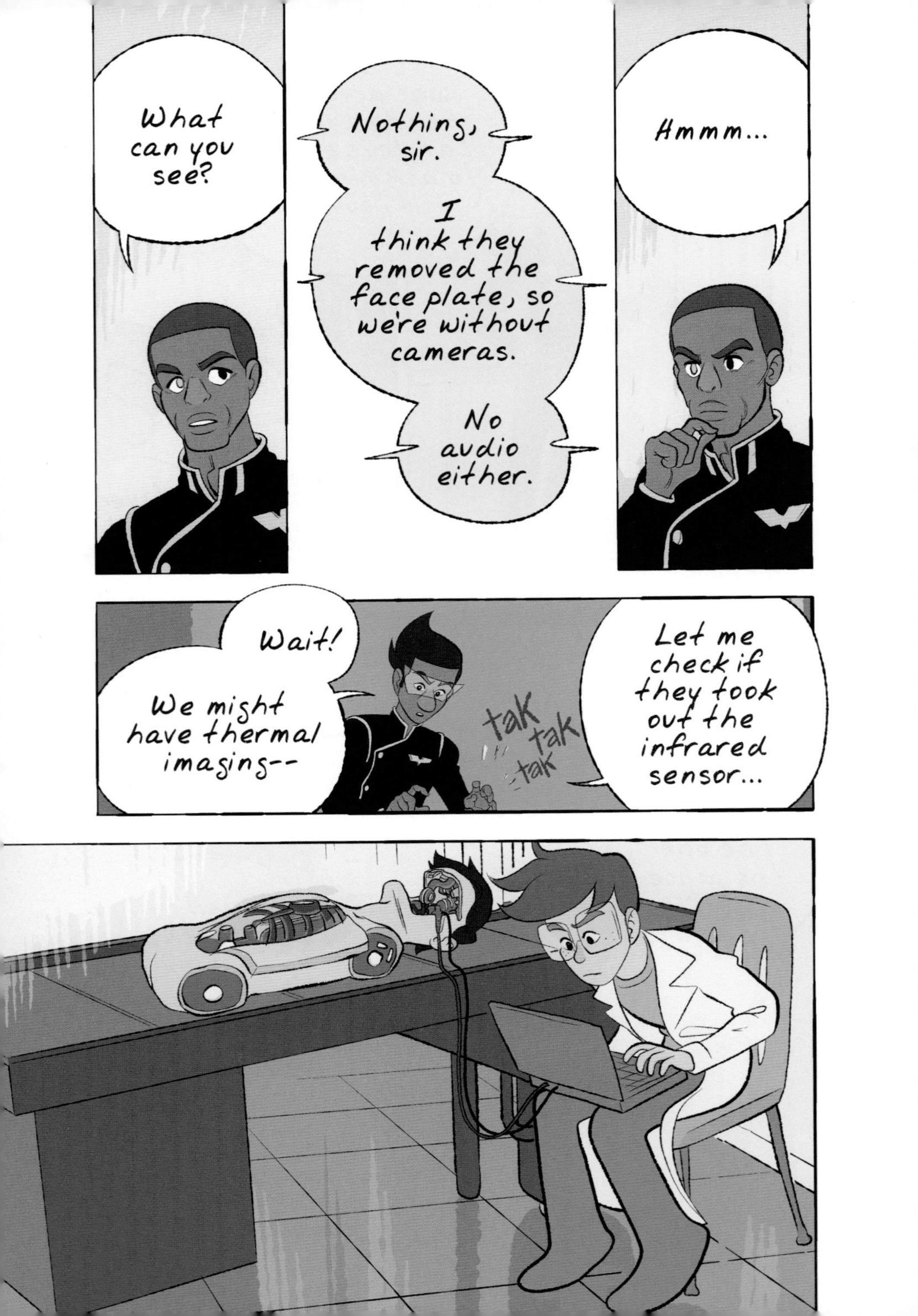
What can you see?
Nothing, sir.
I think they removed the face plate, so we're without cameras.
No audio either.
Hmmm...
Wait!
We might have thermal imaging--
tak tak tak
Let me check if they took out the infrared sensor...

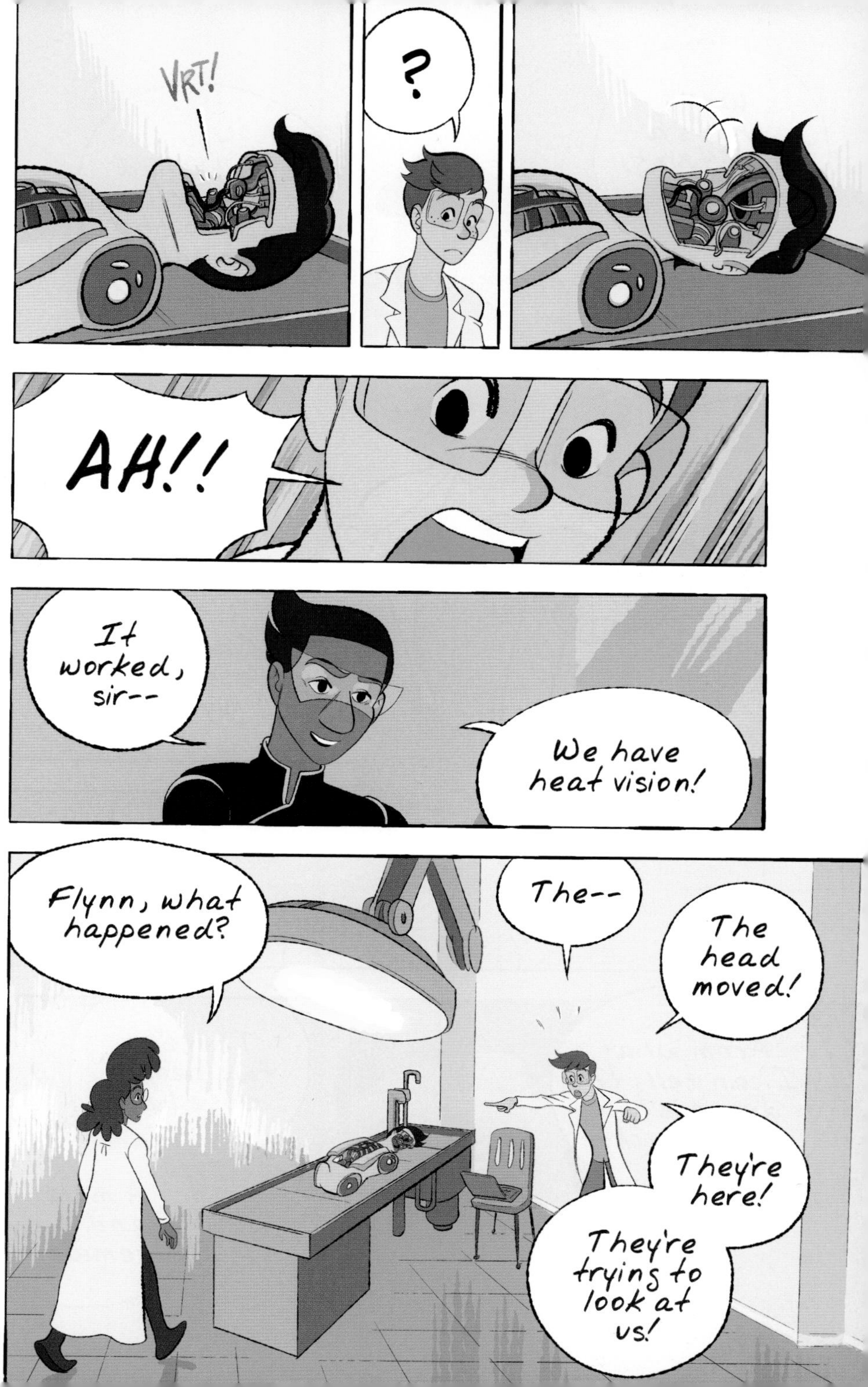
VRT!
?
AH!!
It worked, sir--
We have heat vision!
Flynn, what happened?
The--
The head moved!
They're here!
They're trying to look at us!

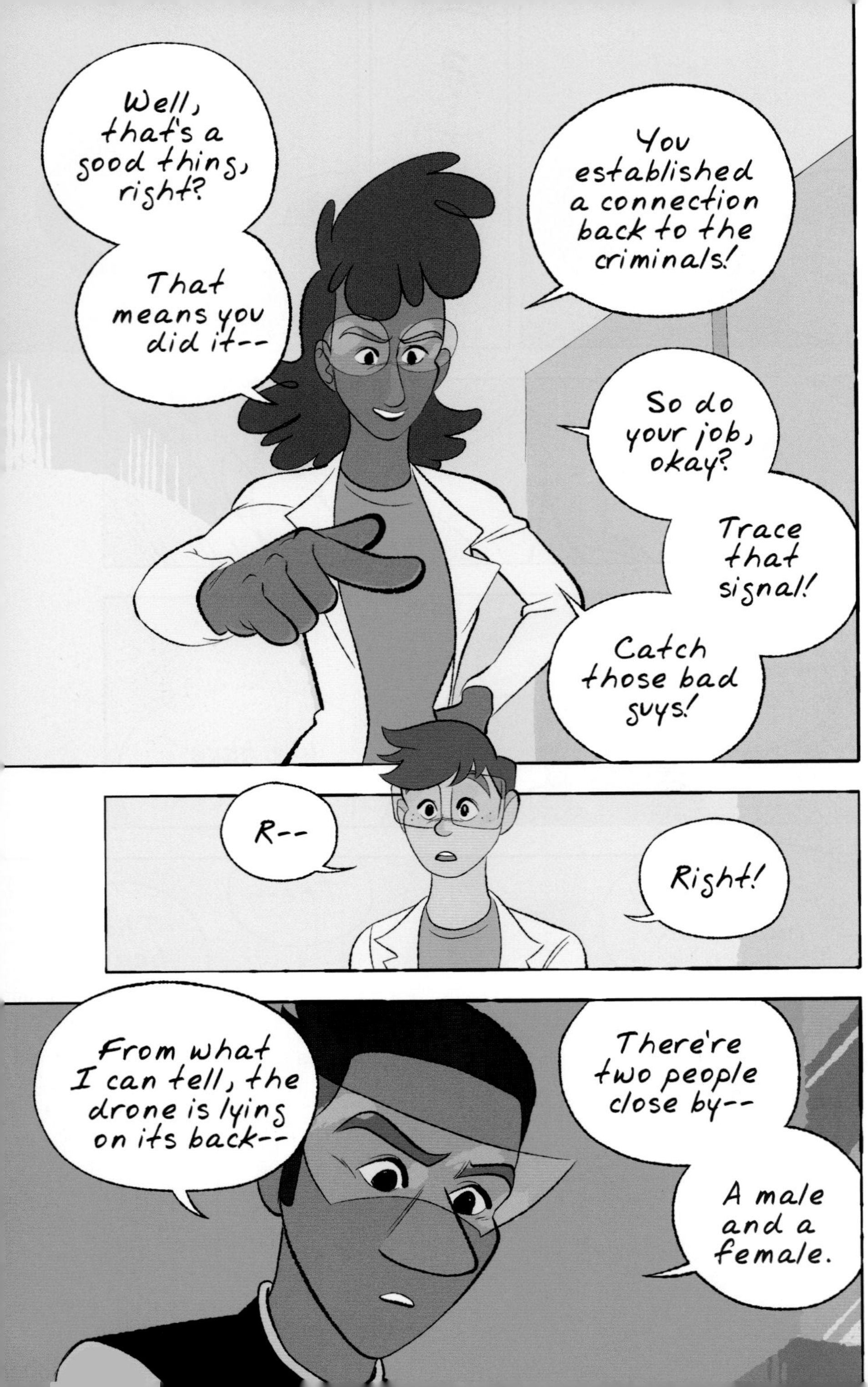

Well, that's a good thing, right?
That means you did it--
You established a connection back to the criminals!
So do your job, okay?
Trace that signal!
Catch those bad guys!
R--
Right!
From what I can tell, the drone is lying on its back--
There're two people close by--
A male and a female.

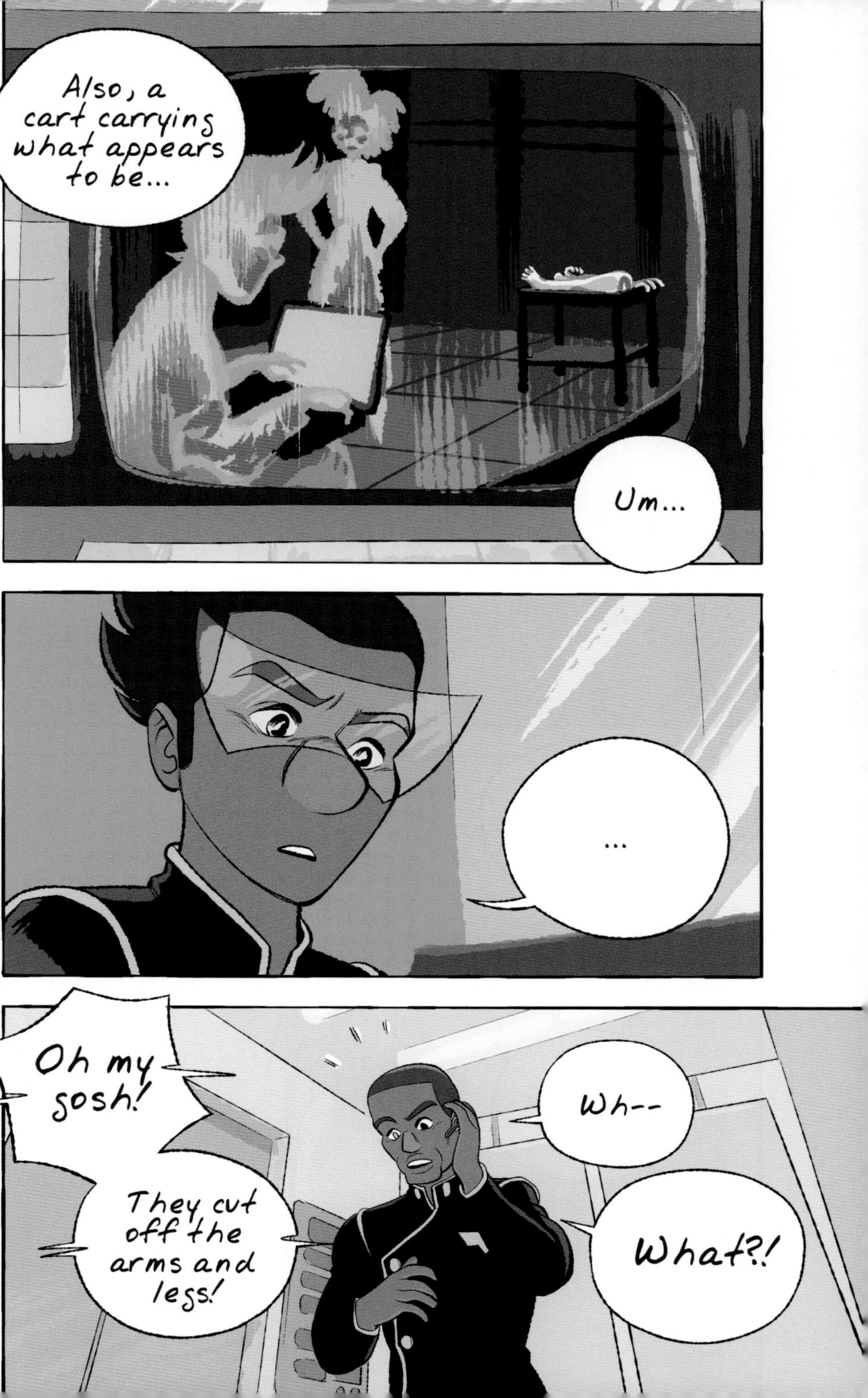
Also, a cart carrying what appears to be...
Um...
...
Oh my gosh!
Wh--
They cut off the arms and legs!
What?!

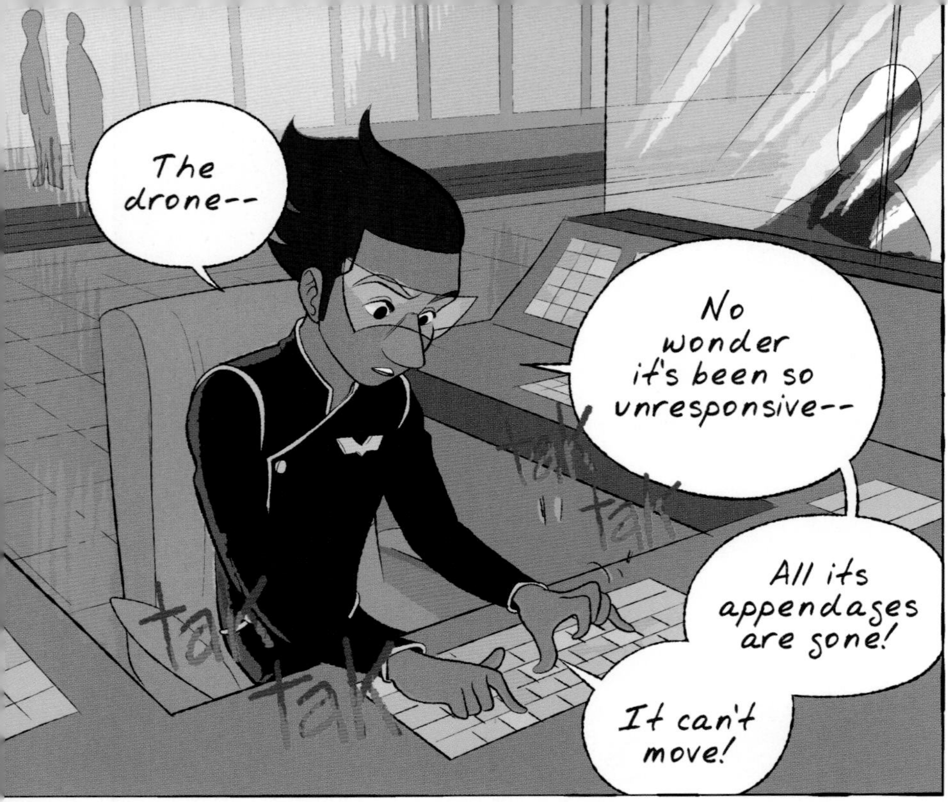
The drone--
No wonder it's been so unresponsive--
talk talk
talk talk
All its appendages are gone!
It can't move!

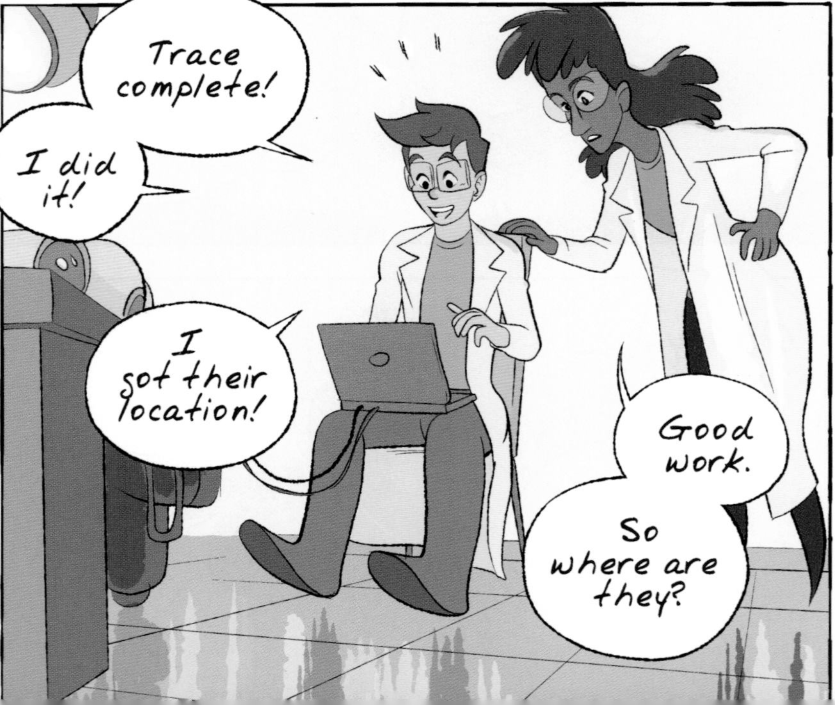
Trace complete!
I did it!
I got their location!
Good work.
So where are they?

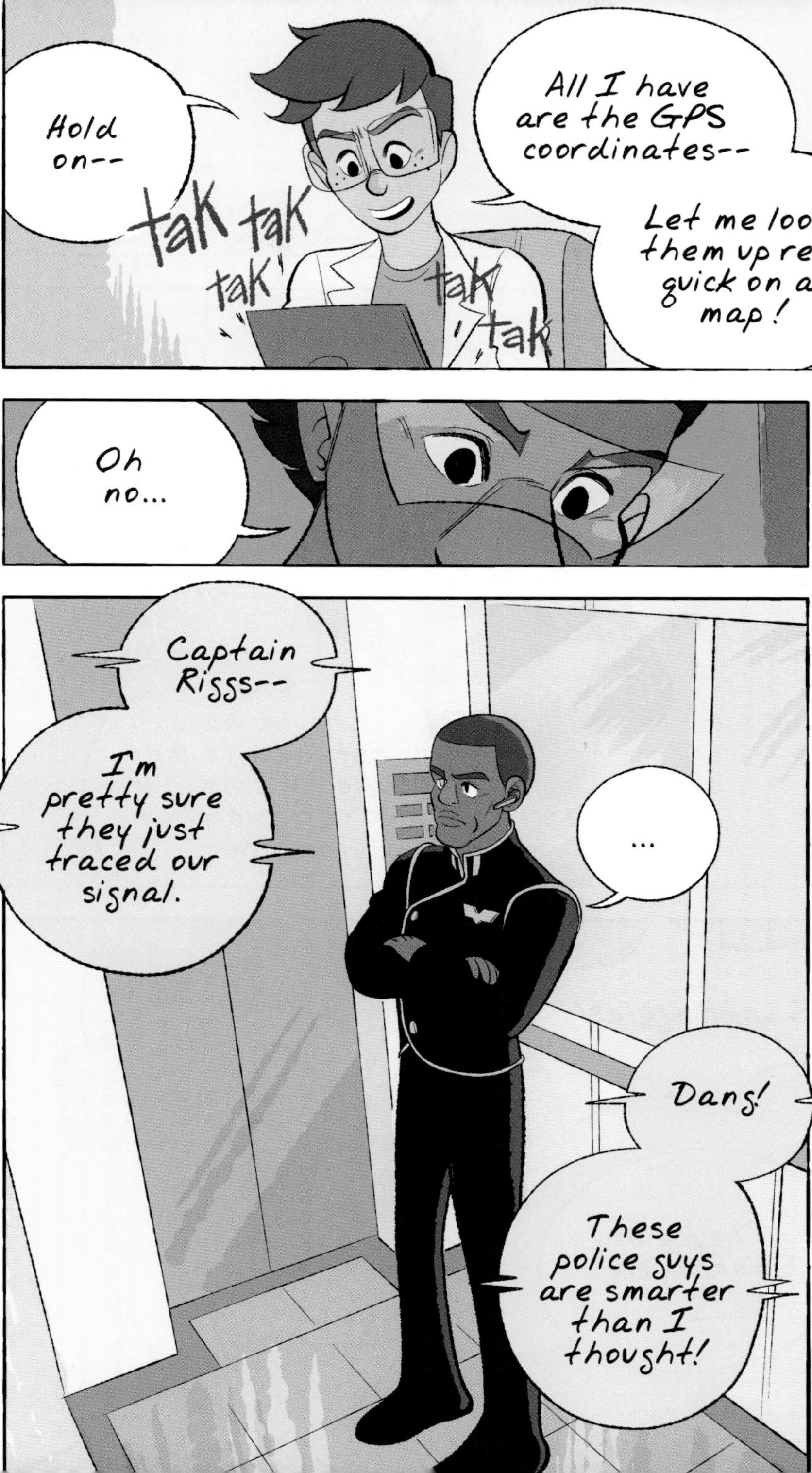
Hold on--
tak tak tak tak tak
All I have are the GPS coordinates--
Let me look them up real quick on a map!
Oh no...
Captain Risss--
I'm pretty sure they just traced our signal.
...
Dang!
These police guys are smarter than I thought!

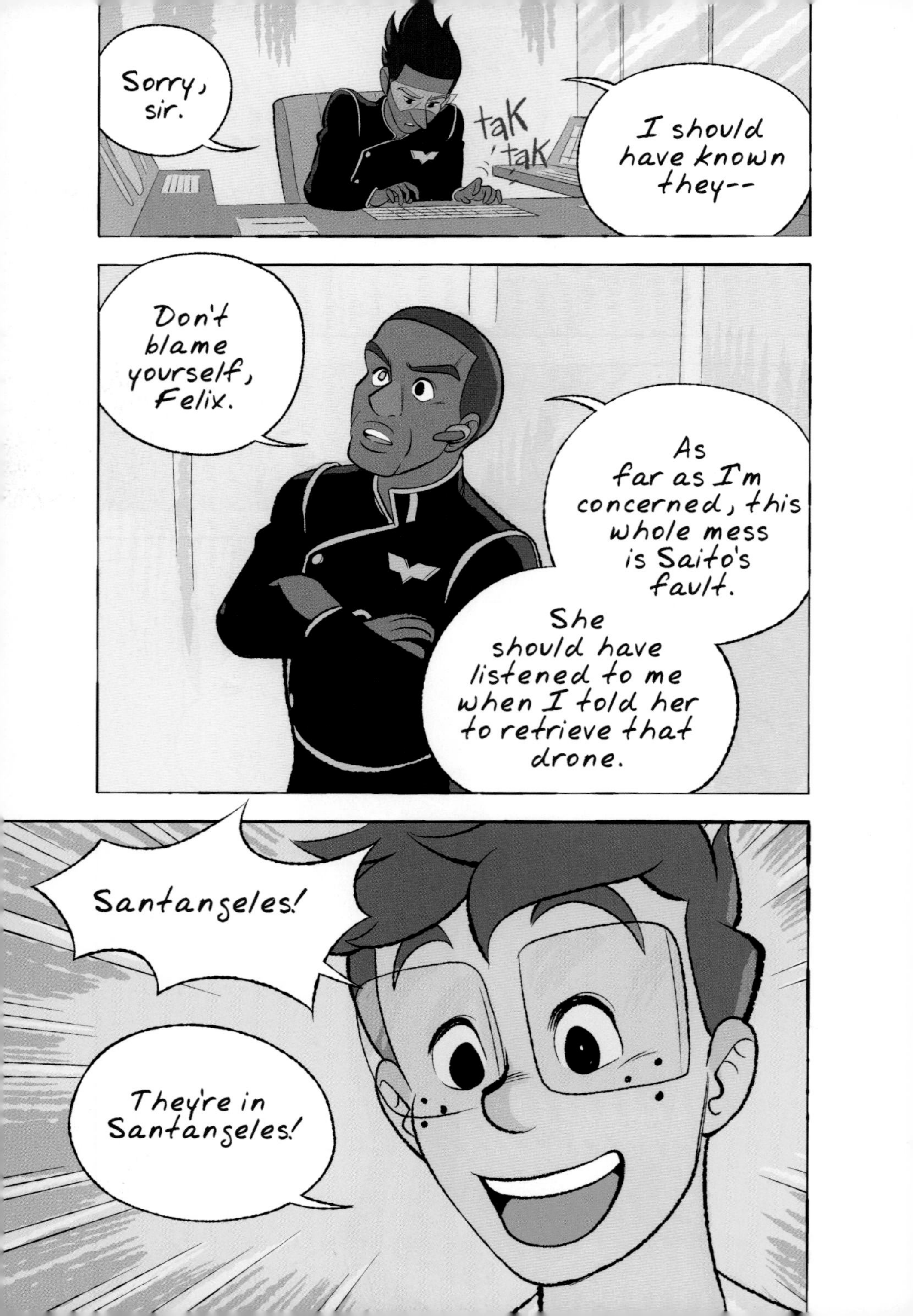
Sorry, sir.
taK taK
I should have known they--
Don't blame yourself, Felix.
As far as I'm concerned, this whole mess is Saito's fault.
She should have listened to me when I told her to retrieve that drone.
Santangeles!
They're in Santangeles!

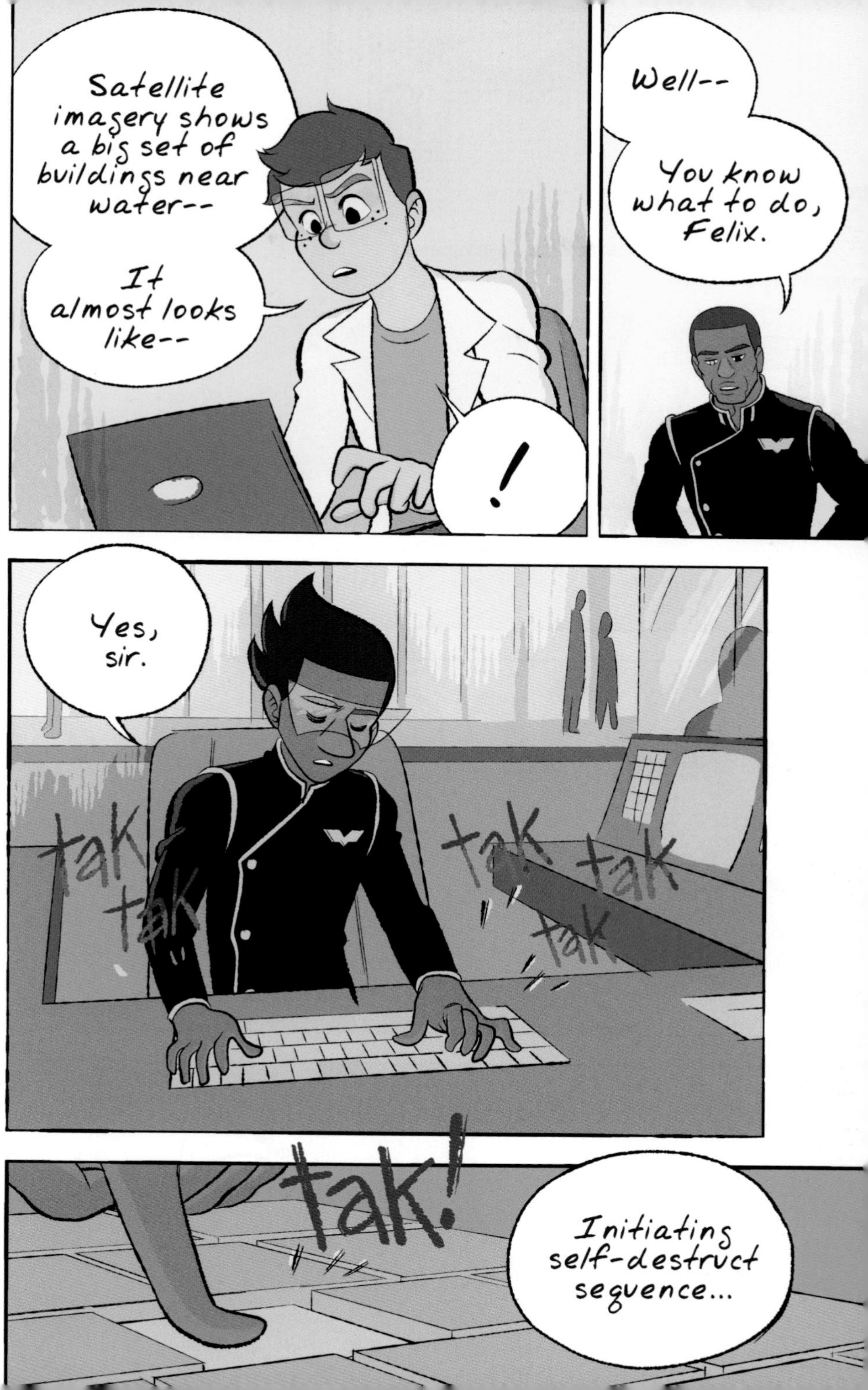
Satellite imagery shows a big set of buildings near water--
It almost looks like--
!
Well--
You know what to do, Felix.
Yes, sir.
tak tak tak tak tak
tak!
Initiating self-destruct sequence...

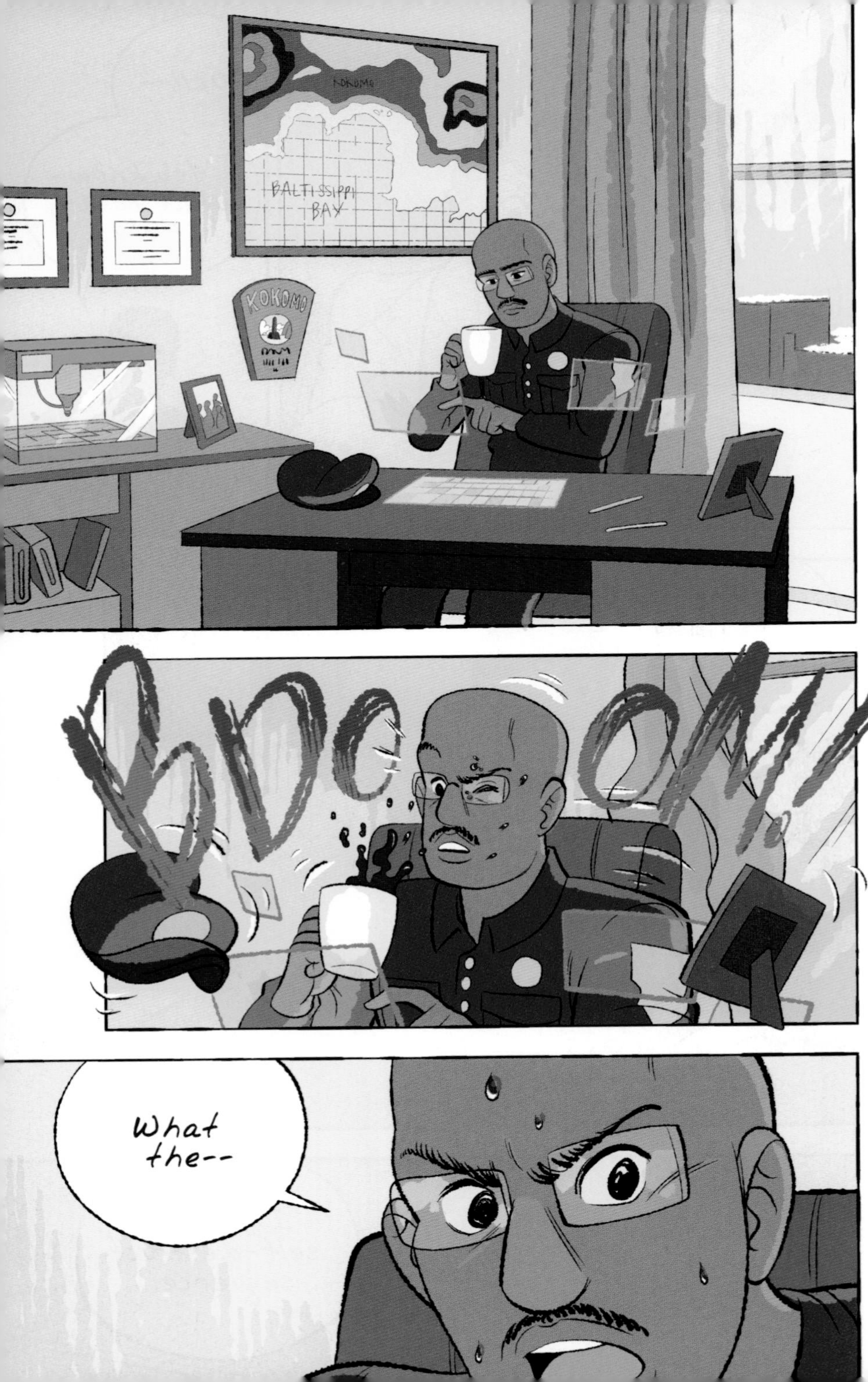
KOKOMO
BALTISSIPPI BAY
KOKOMO
BOOOM!
What the--

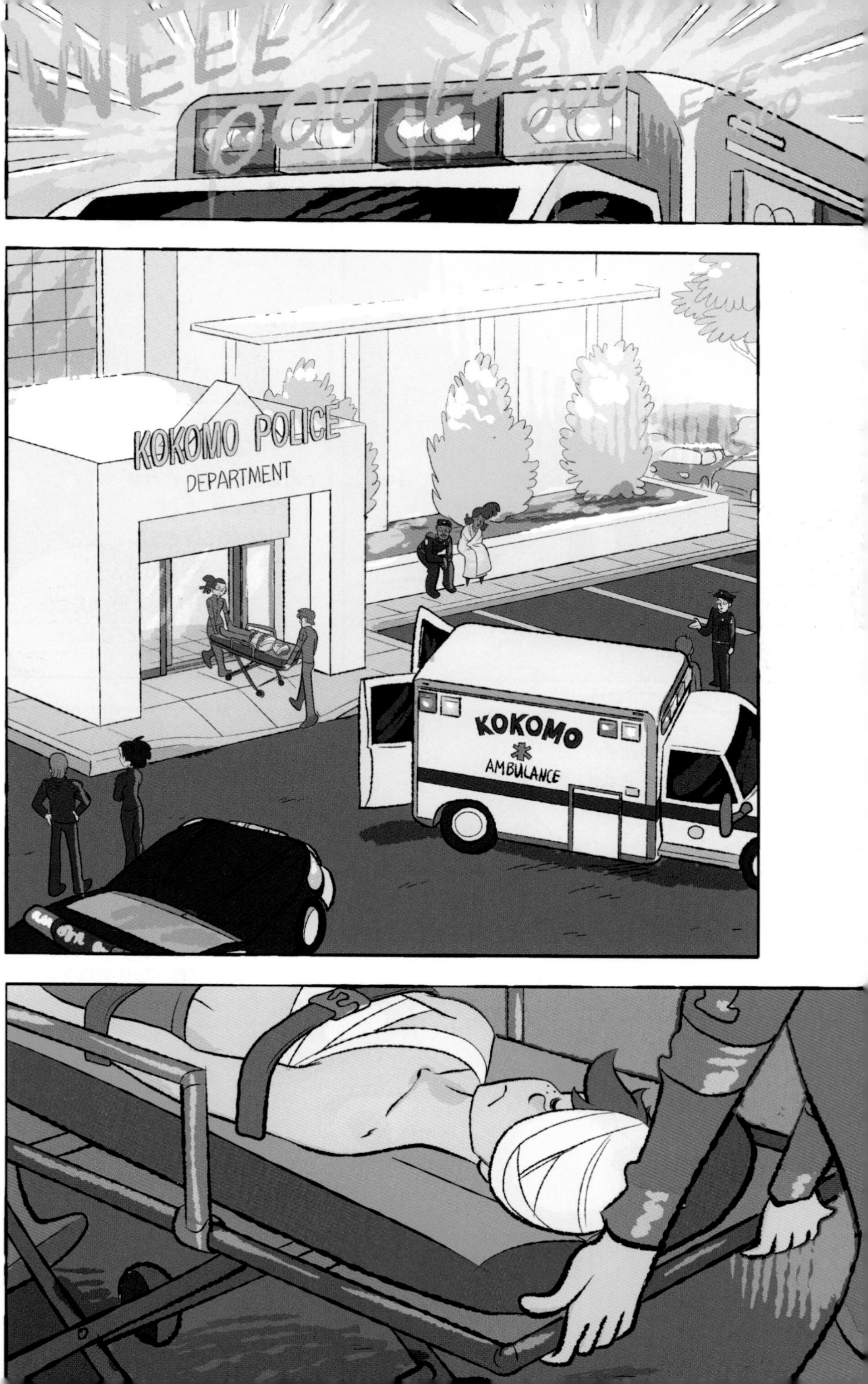

WEEE
OOO EEE
OOO EEE
OOO
KOKOMO POLICE
DEPARTMENT
KOKOMO
AMBULANCE

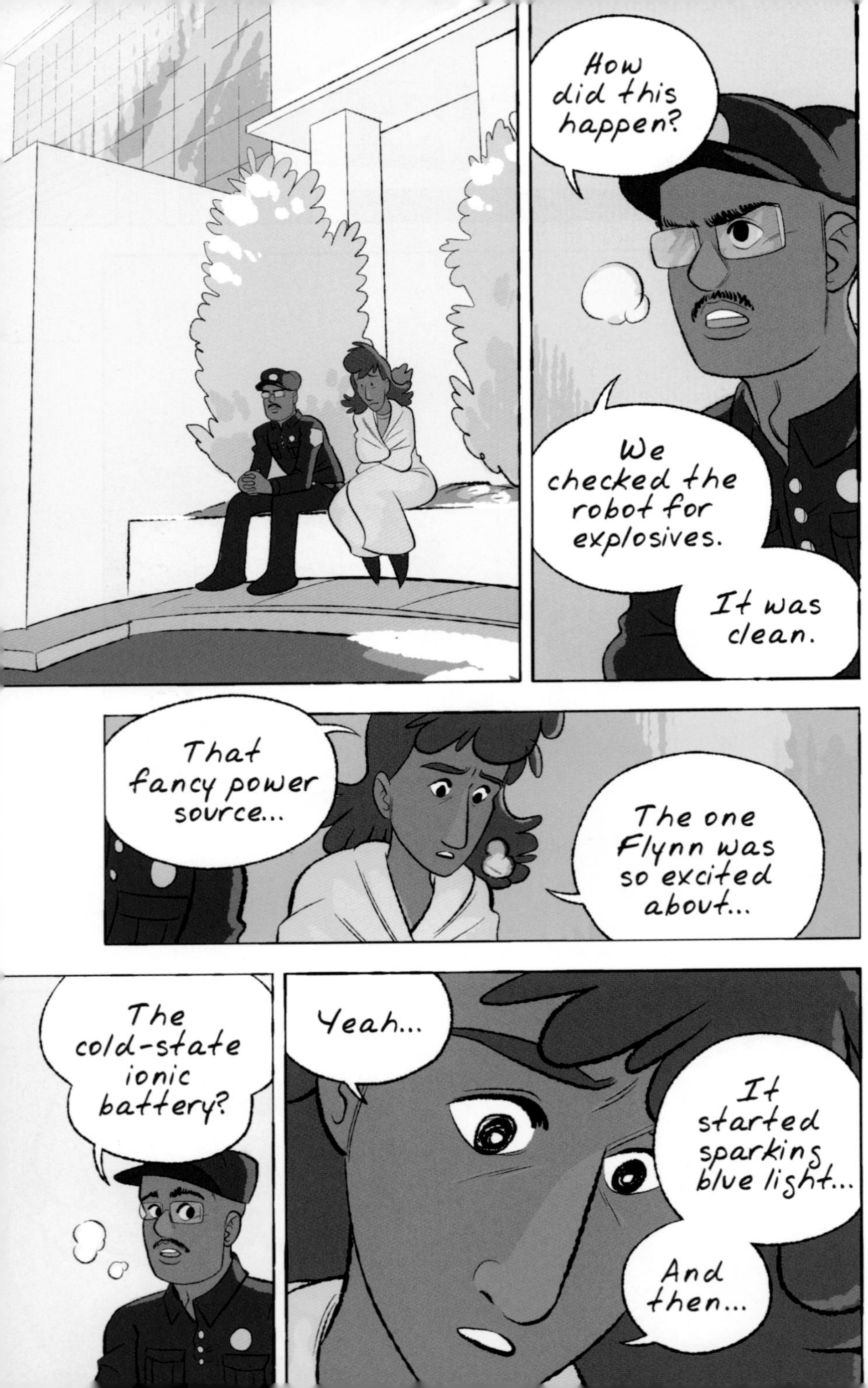
How did this happen?
We checked the robot for explosives.
It was clean.
That fancy power source...
The one Flynn was so excited about...
The cold-state ionic battery?
Yeah...
It started sparking blue light...
And then...

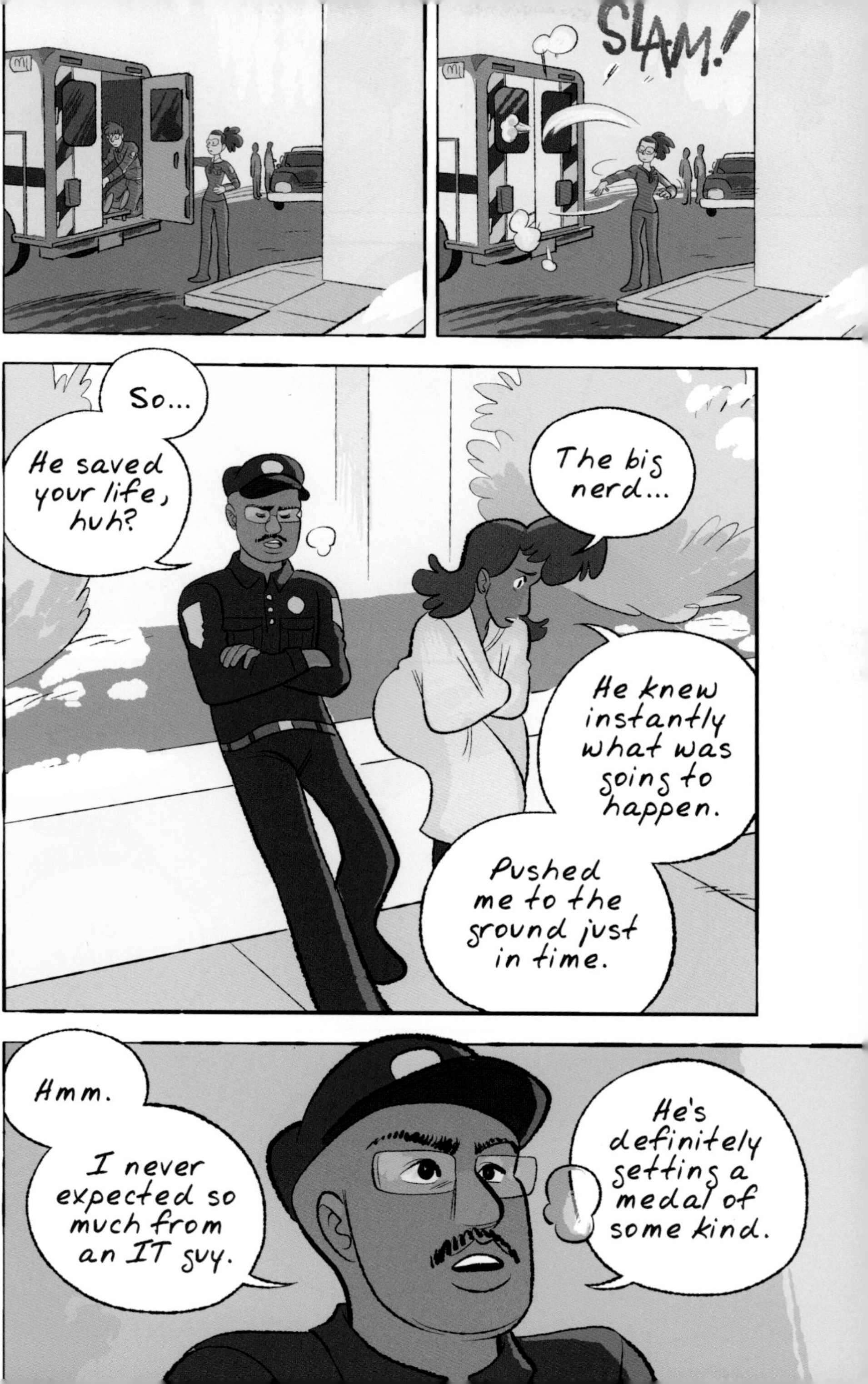
SLAM!
So...
He saved your life, huh?
The big nerd...
He knew instantly what was going to happen.
Pushed me to the ground just in time.
Hmm.
I never expected so much from an IT guy.
He's definitely getting a medal of some kind.

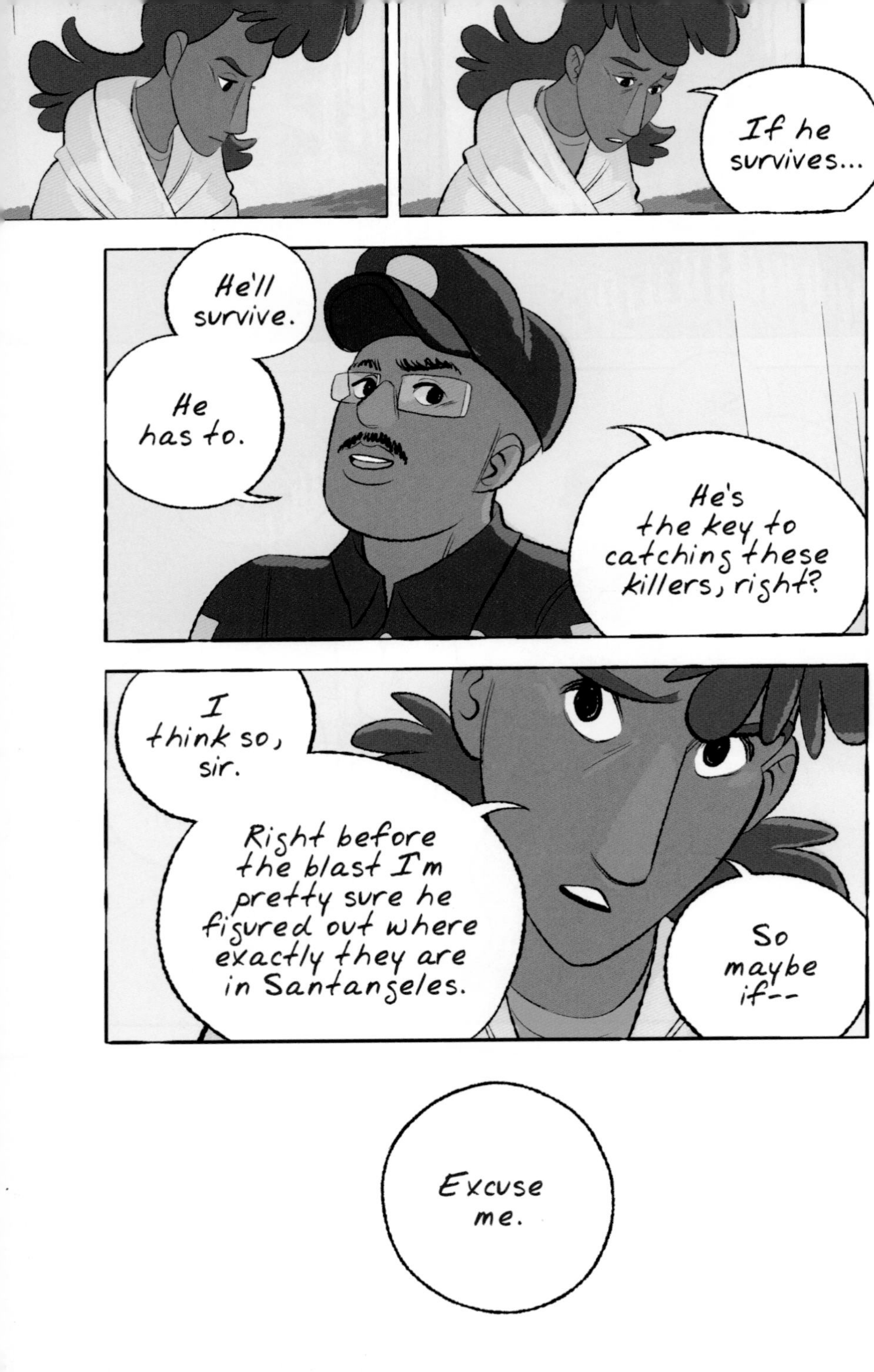
If he survives...
He'll survive.
He has to.
He's the key to catching these killers, right?
I think so, sir.
Right before the blast I'm pretty sure he figured out where exactly they are in Santangeles.
So maybe if--
Excuse me.

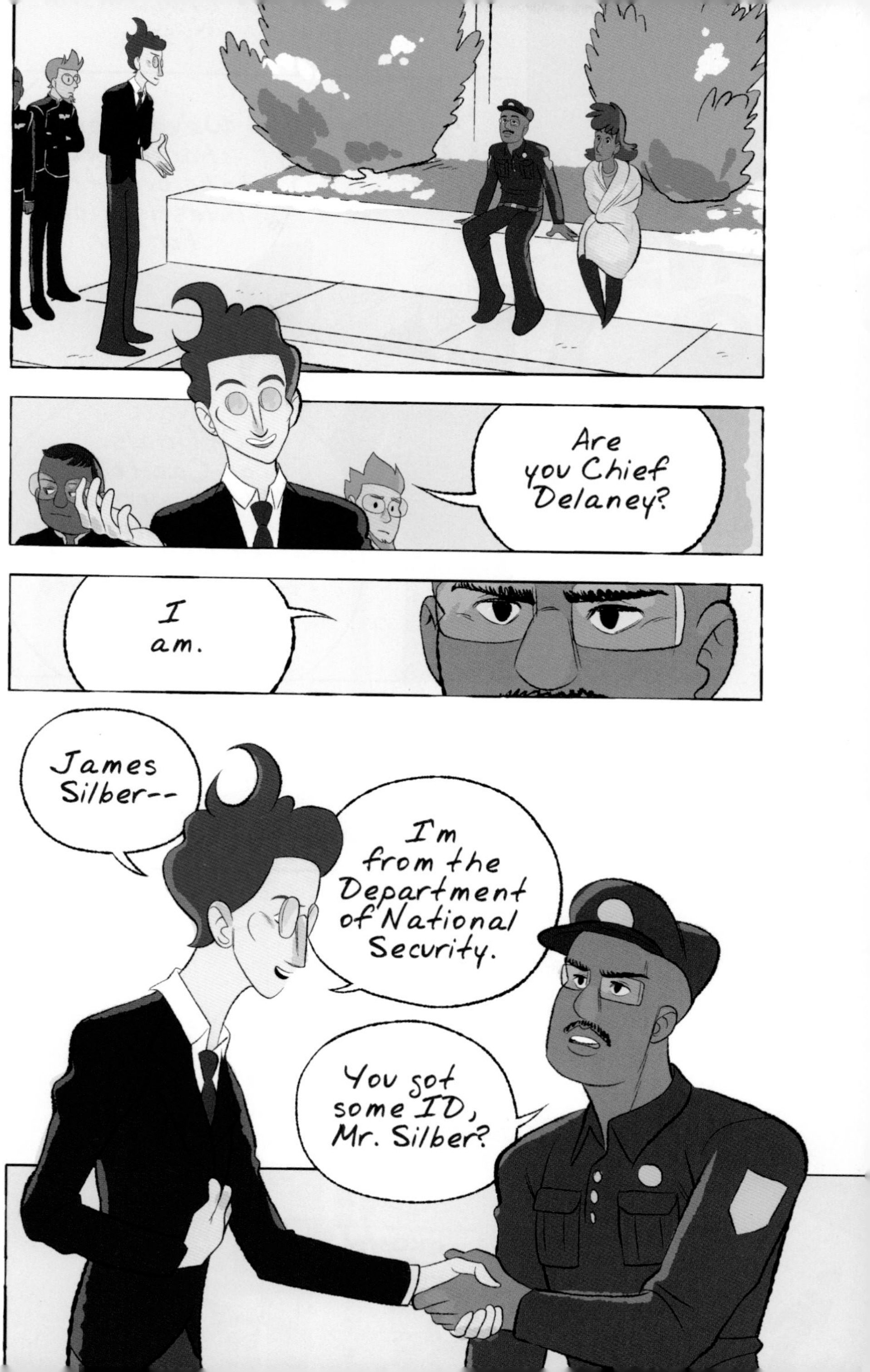
Are you Chief Delaney?
I am.
James Silber--
I'm from the Department of National Security.
You got some ID, Mr. Silber?

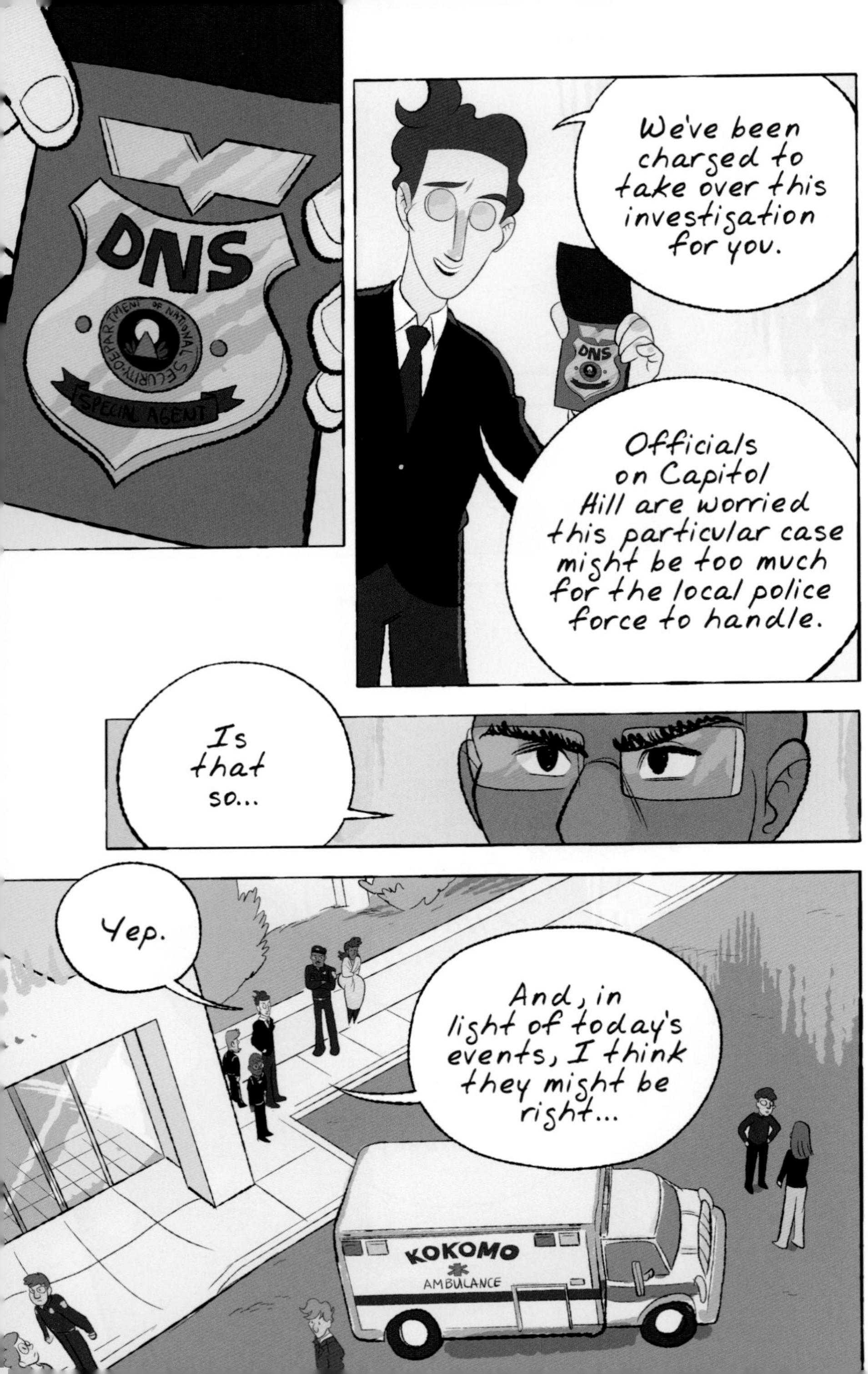
DNS
DEPARTMENT OF NATIONAL SECURITY
SPECIAL AGENT
We've been charged to take over this investigation for you.
DNS
Officials on Capitol Hill are worried this particular case might be too much for the local police force to handle.
Is that so...
Yep.
And, in light of today's events, I think they might be right...
KOKOMO
AMBULANCE

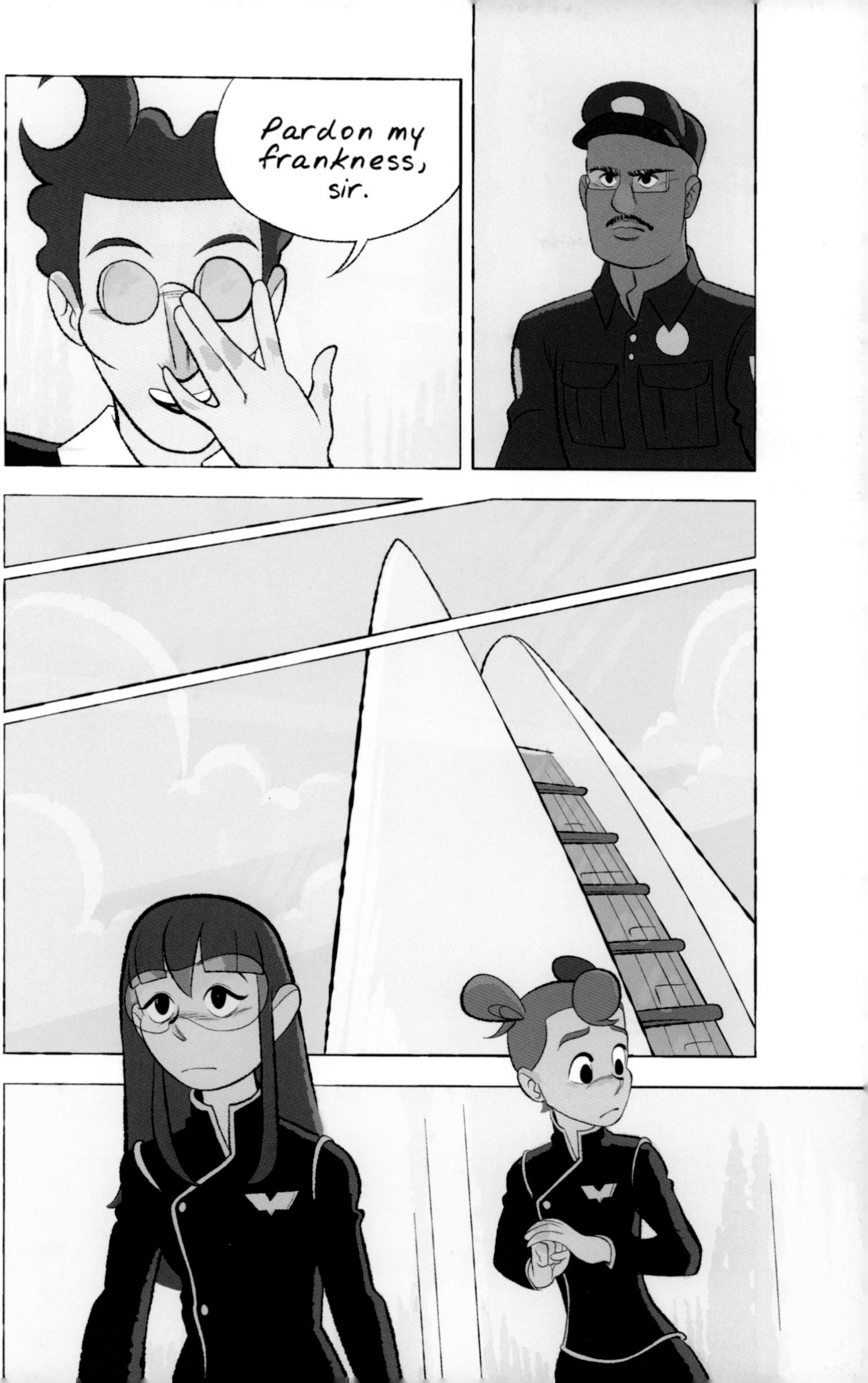
Pardon my frankness, sir.

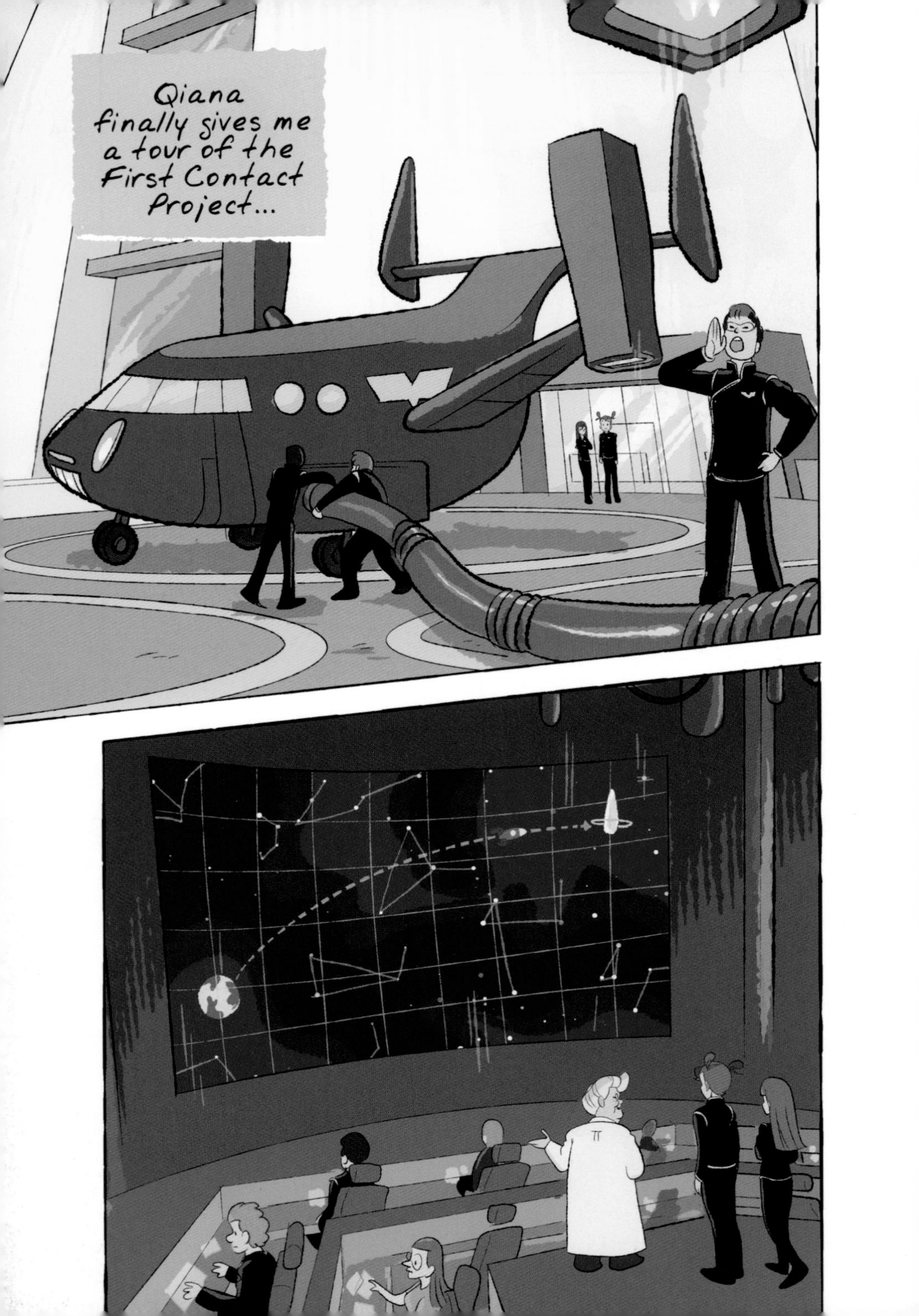
Qiana finally gives me a tour of the First Contact Project...

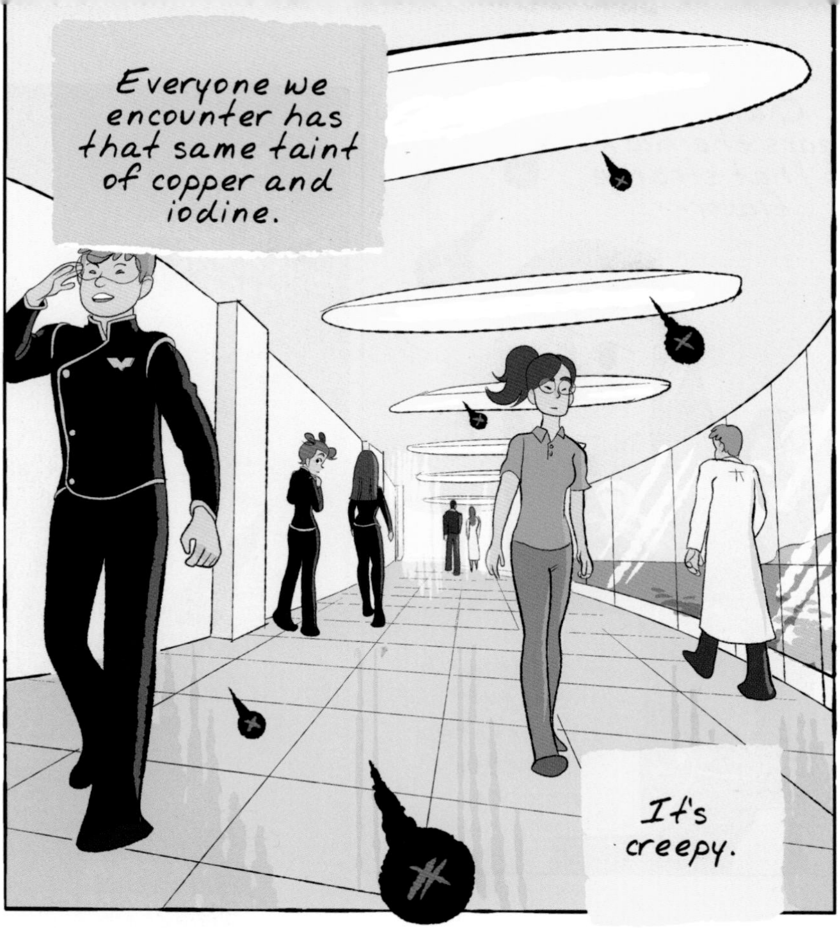
Everyone we encounter has that same taint of copper and iodine.
It's creepy.

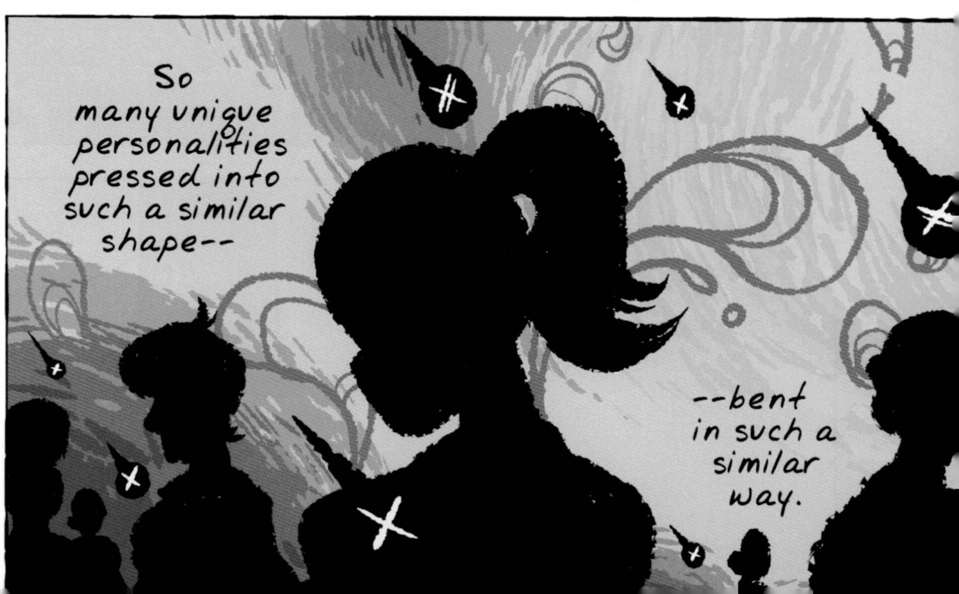
So many unique personalities pressed into such a similar shape--
--bent in such a similar way.

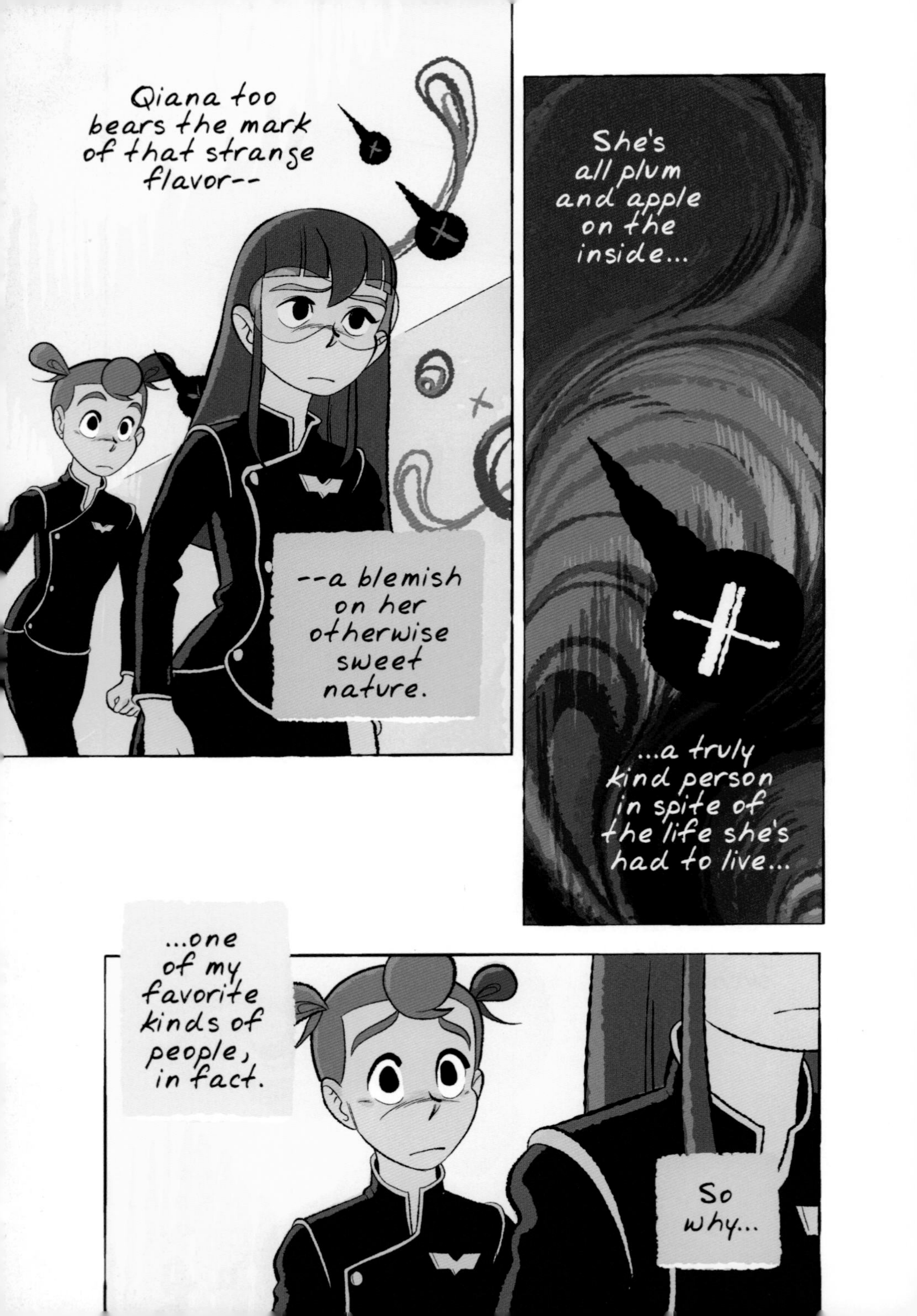
Qiana too bears the mark of that strange flavor--
--a blemish on her otherwise sweet nature.
She's all plum and apple on the inside...
...a truly kind person in spite of the life she's had to live...
...one of my favorite kinds of people, in fact.
So why...

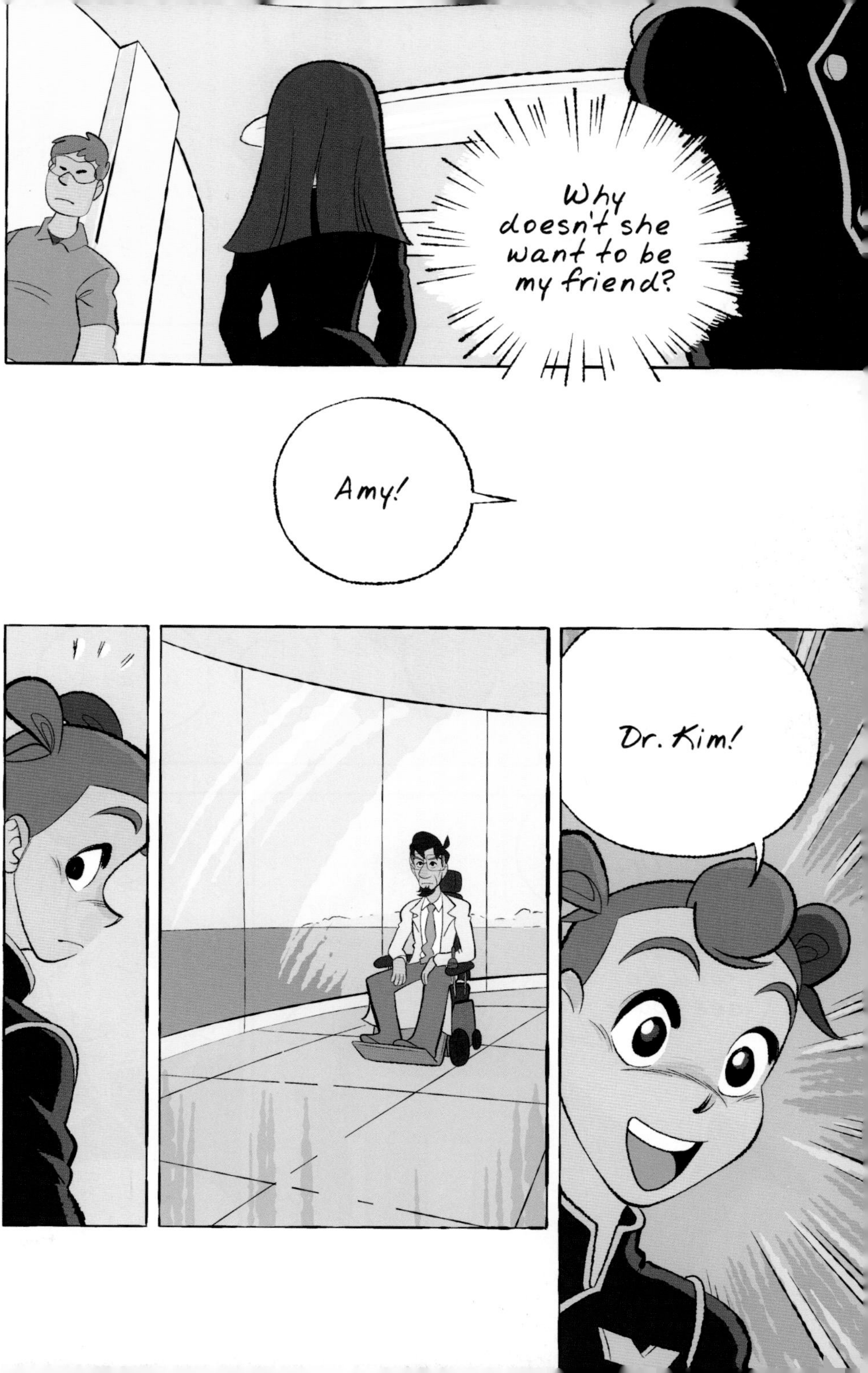
Why doesn't she want to be my friend?
Amy!
Dr. Kim!

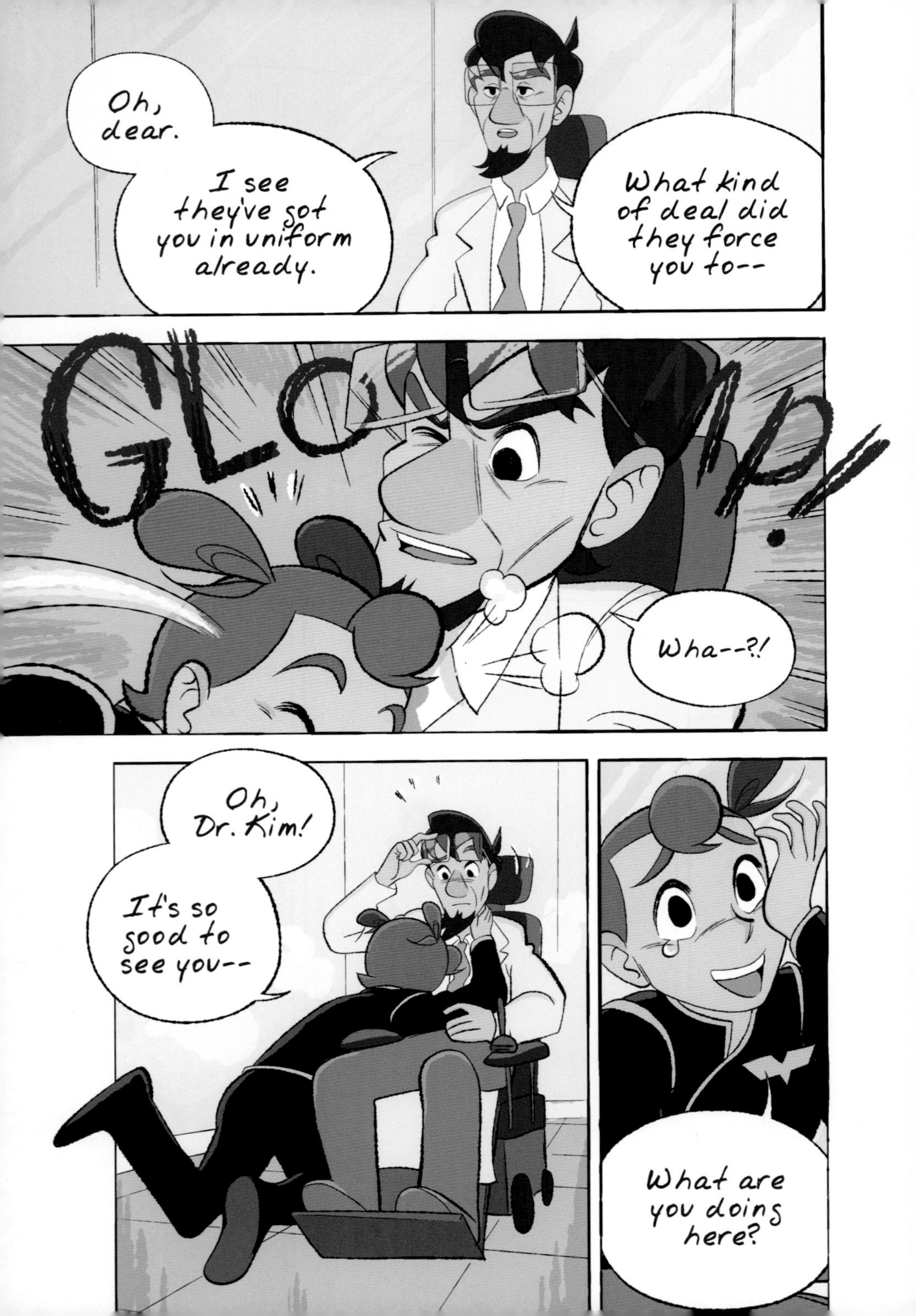
Oh, dear.
I see they've got you in uniform already.
What kind of deal did they force you to--
GLOMP!!
Wha--?!
Oh, Dr. Kim!
It's so good to see you--
What are you doing here?

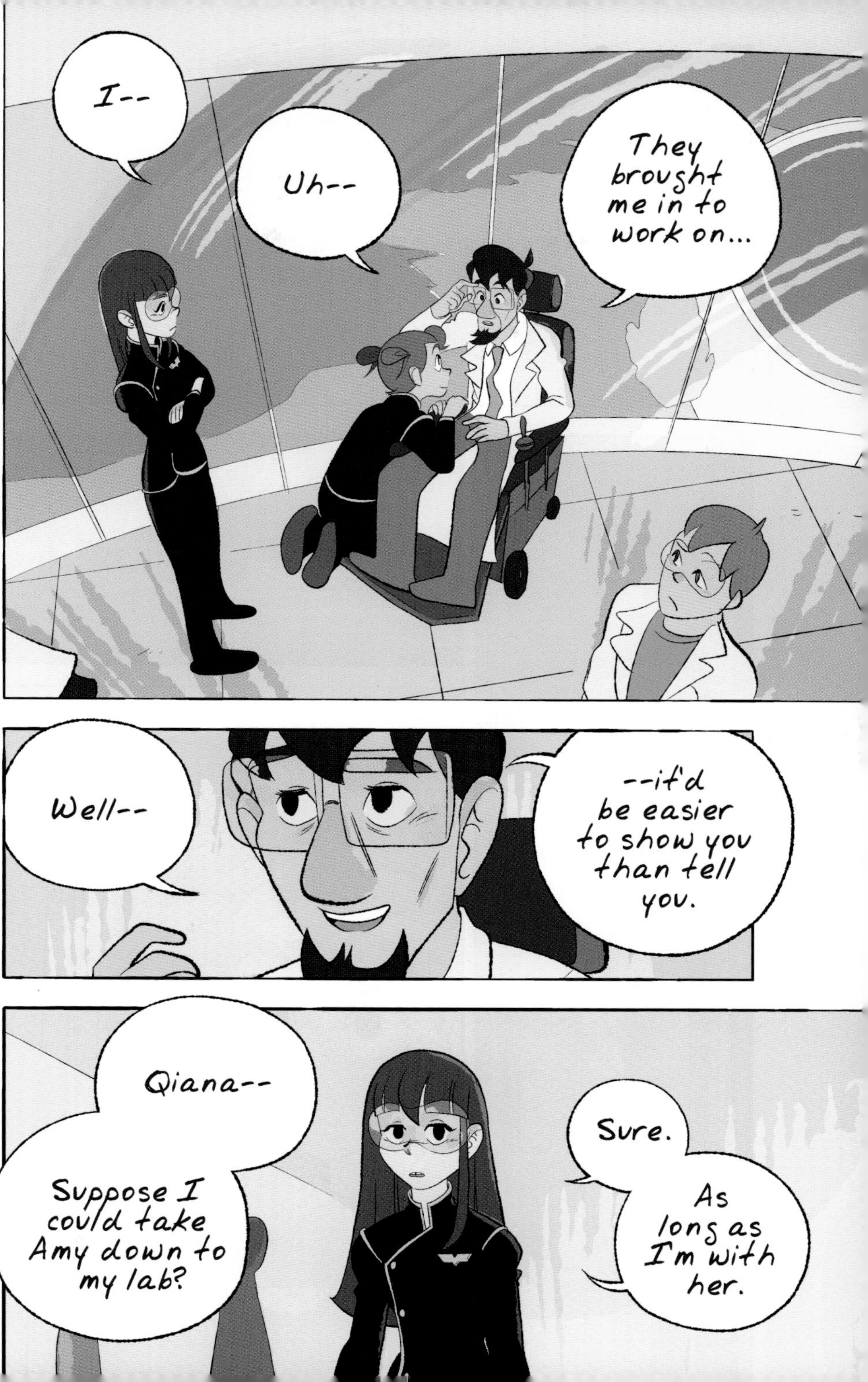
I--
Uh--
They brought me in to work on...
Well--
--it'd be easier to show you than tell you.
Qiana--
Suppose I could take Amy down to my lab?
Sure.
As long as I'm with her.

Dr. Kim guides us to the elevator and we descend down to the first floor, then the basement, and then beyond that...

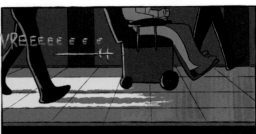

bing!

B 06

Six floors underground, we stop.

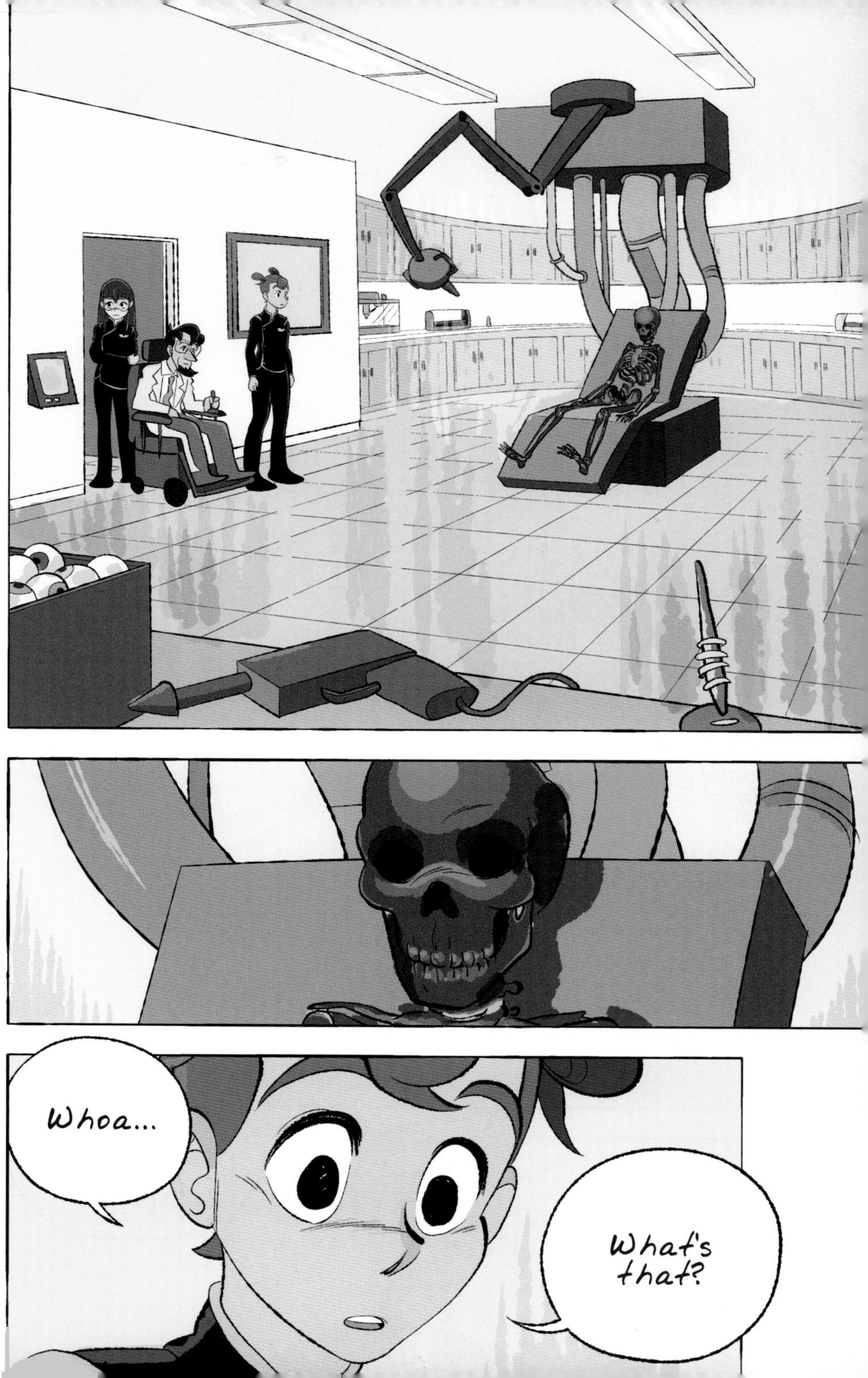
Whoa...
What's that?

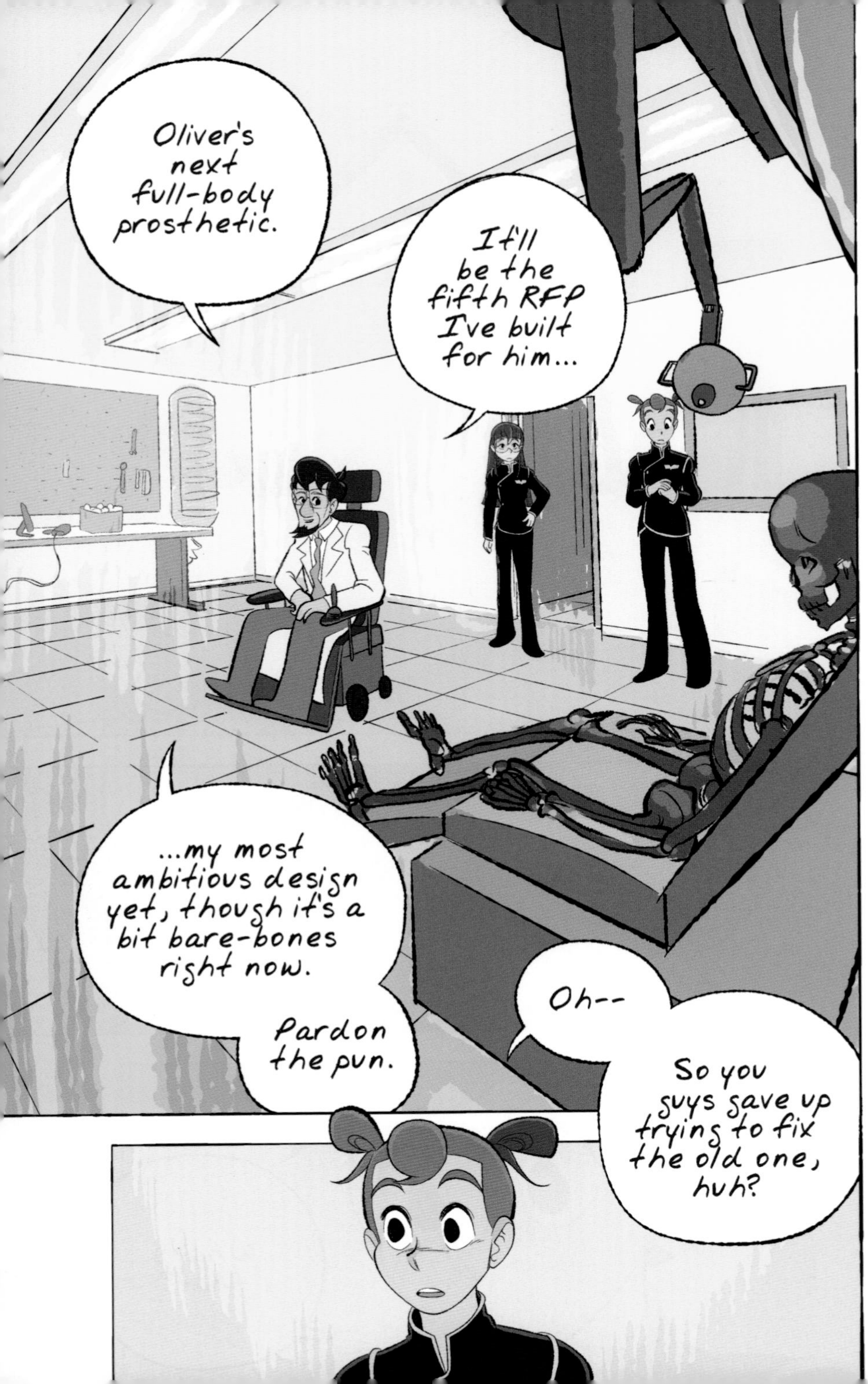
Oliver's next full-body prosthetic.
It'll be the fifth RFP I've built for him...
...my most ambitious design yet, though it's a bit bare-bones right now.
Pardon the pun.
Oh--
So you guys gave up trying to fix the old one, huh?

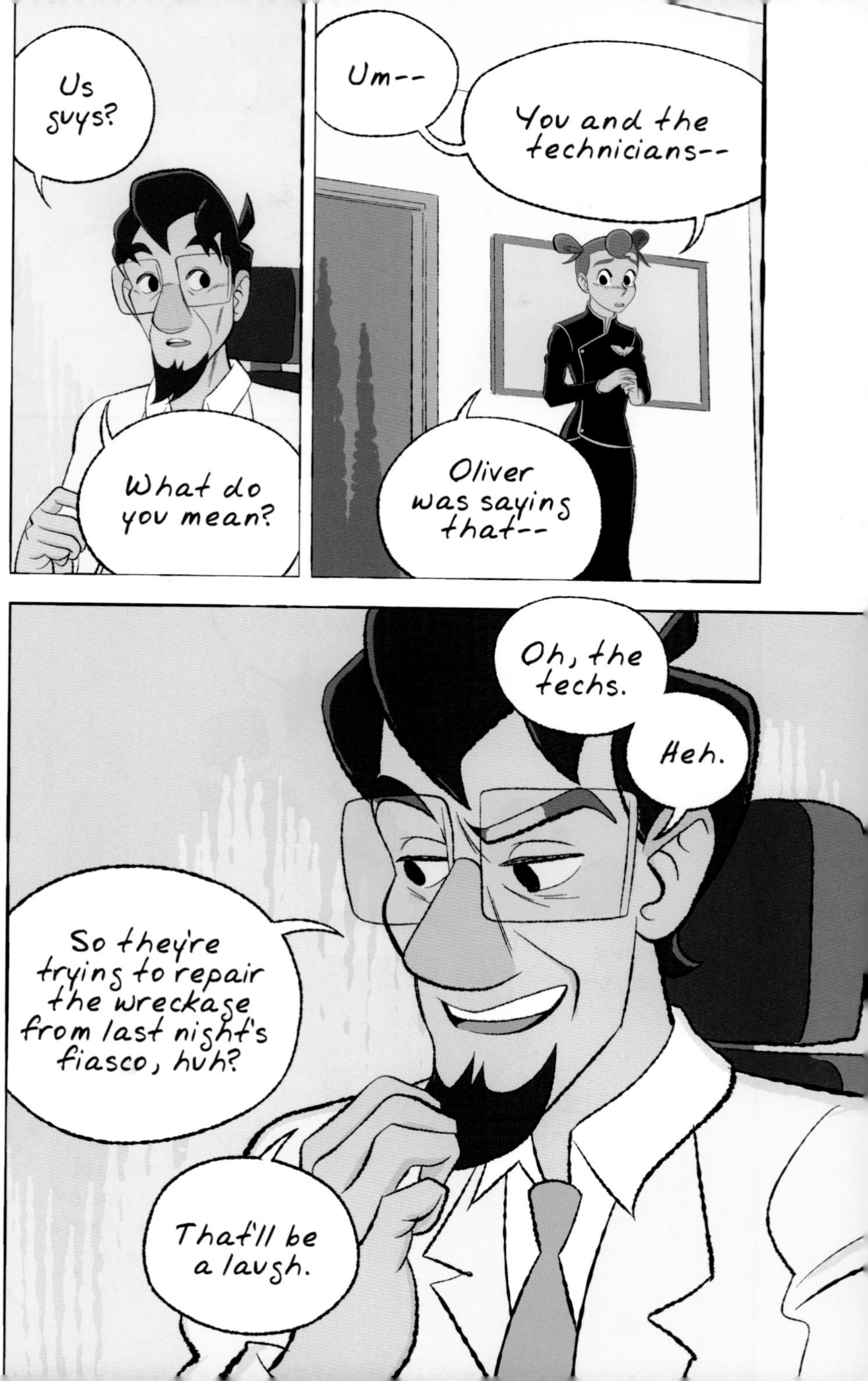
Us guys?
What do you mean?
Um--
You and the technicians--
Oliver was saying that--
Oh, the techs.
Heh.
So they're trying to repair the wreckage from last night's fiasco, huh?
That'll be a laugh.

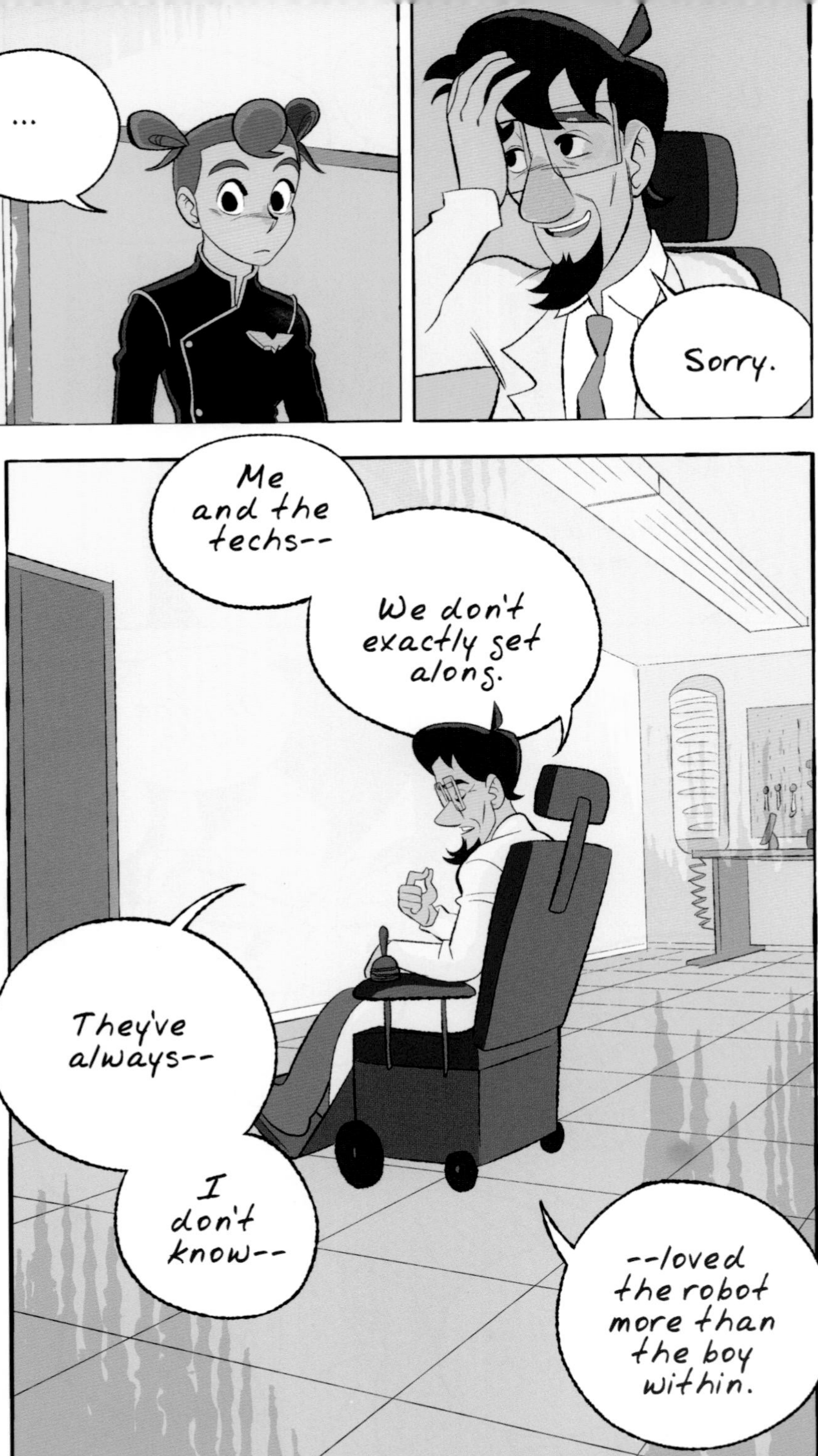
...
Sorry.
Me and the techs--
We don't exactly get along.
They've always--
I don't know--
--loved the robot more than the boy within.

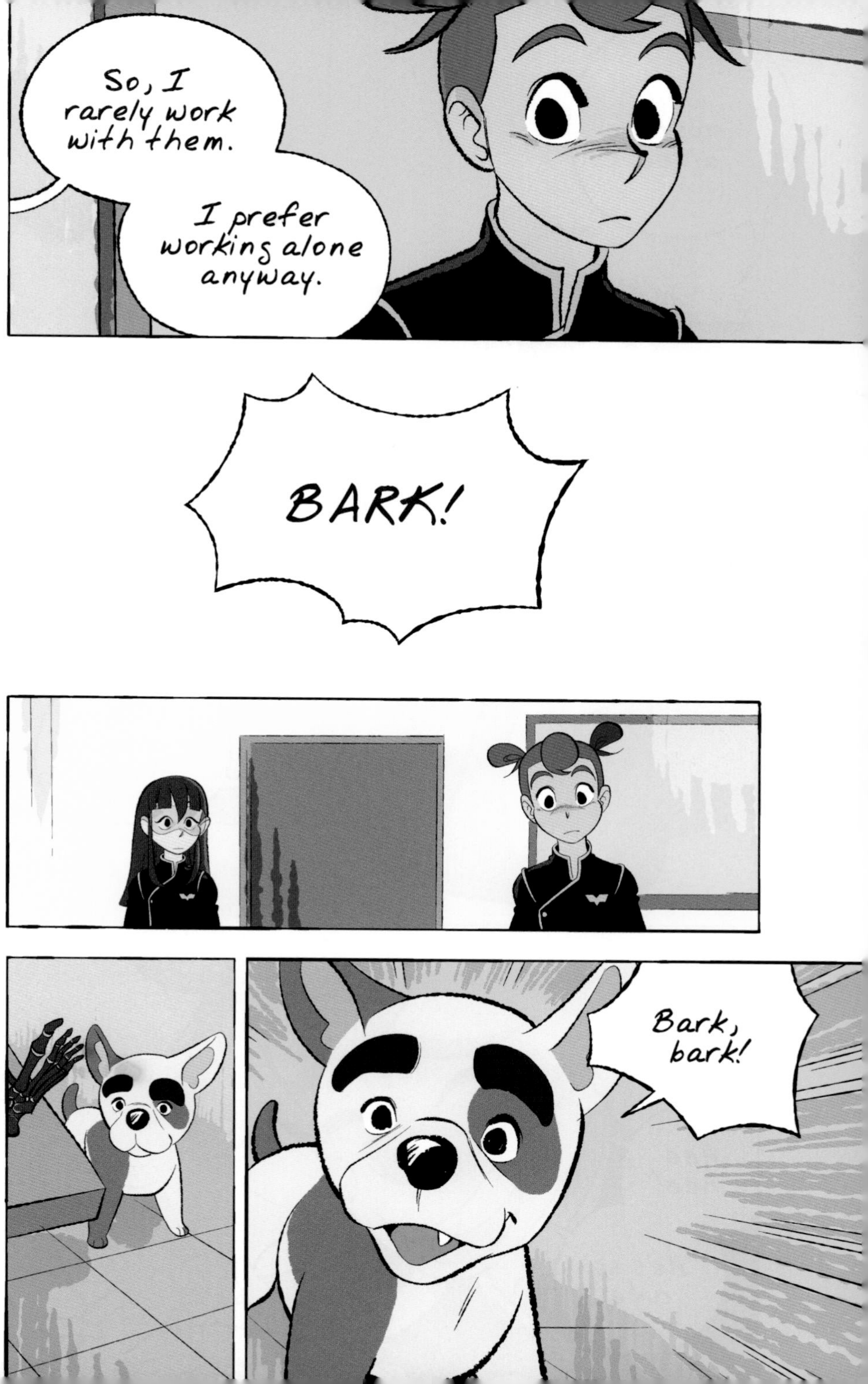
So, I rarely work with them.
I prefer working alone anyway.
BARK!
Bark, bark!

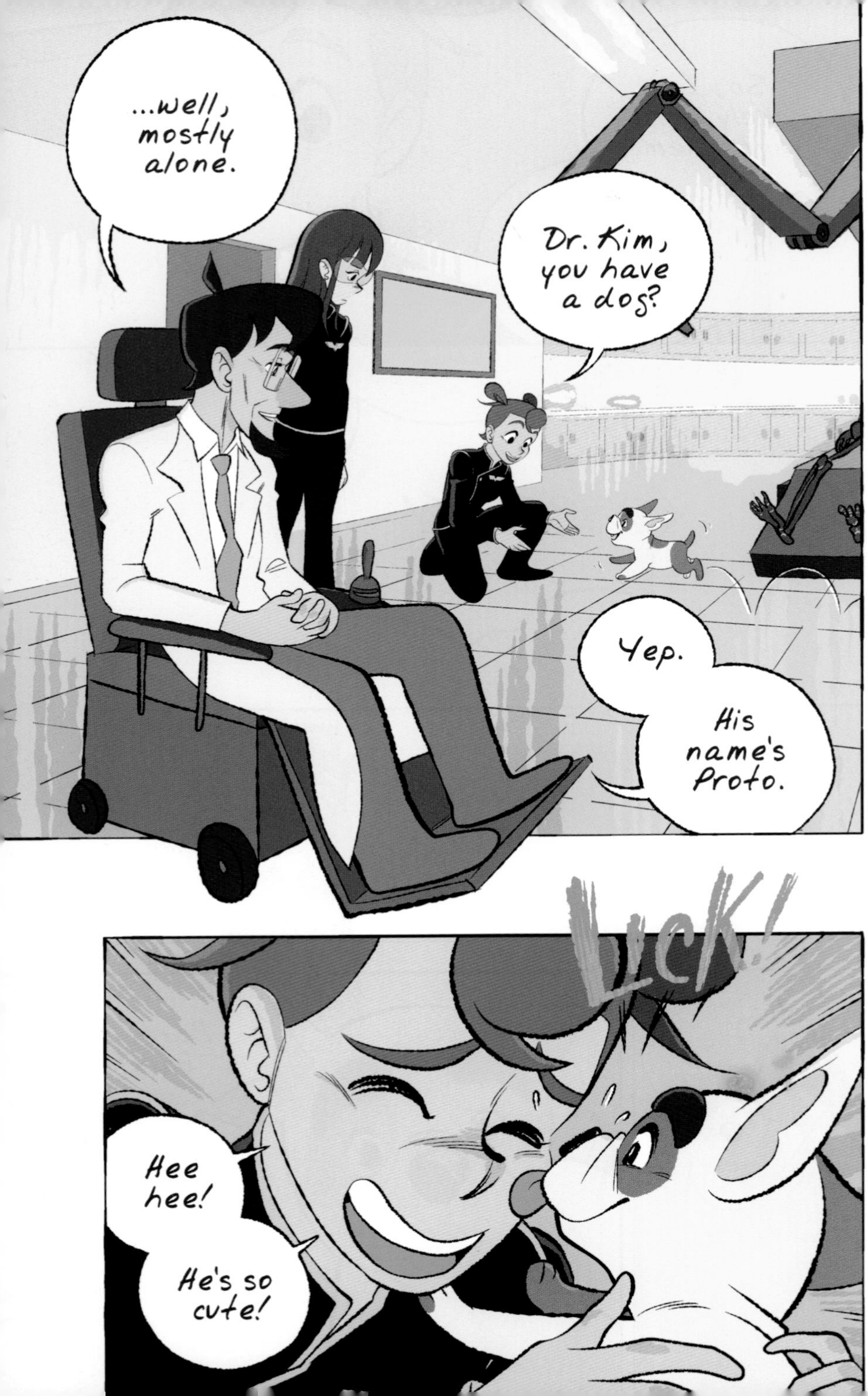
...well, mostly alone.
Dr. Kim, you have a dog?
Yep.
His name's Proto.
LICK!
Hee hee!
He's so cute!

I've always wanted a dog..

I have a virtual one, but he's--

--you know, not real.

Well, Proto's not exactly real either--

--not in the way you mean it.

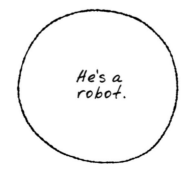

He's a robot.

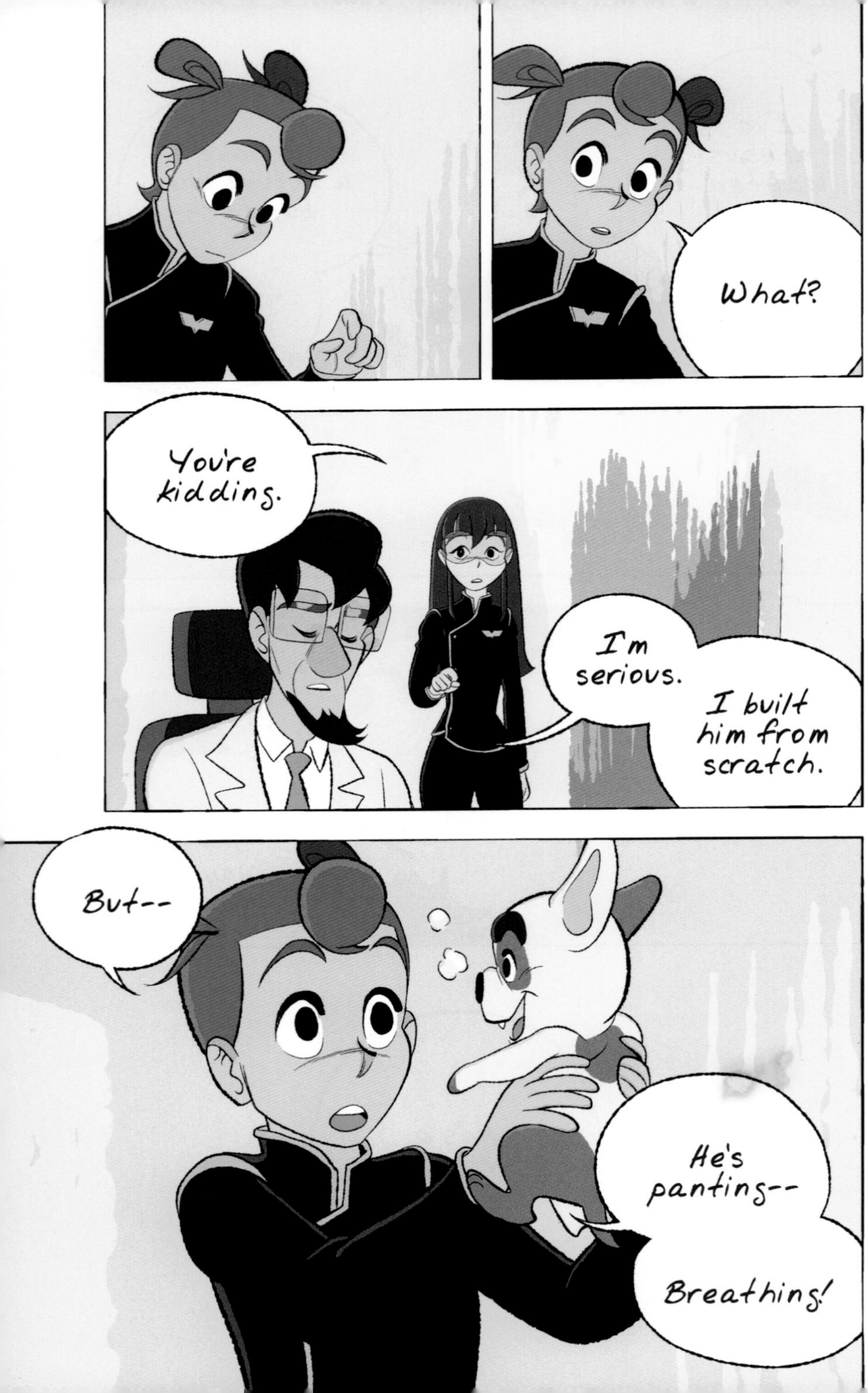
What?
You're kidding.
I'm serious.
I built him from scratch.
But--
He's panting--
Breathing!

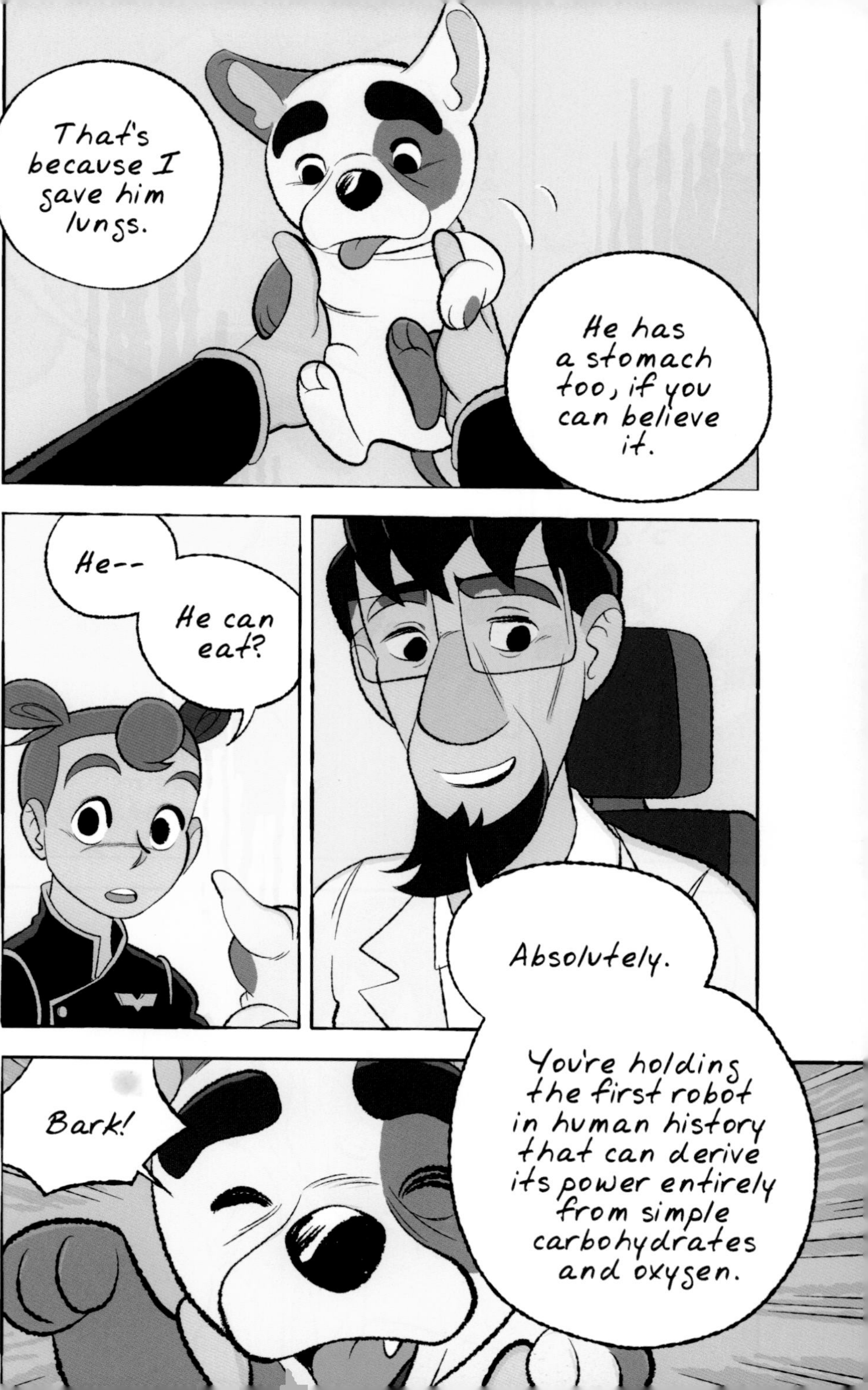
That's because I gave him lungs.
He has a stomach too, if you can believe it.
He--
He can eat?
Absolutely.
You're holding the first robot in human history that can derive its power entirely from simple carbohydrates and oxygen.
Bark!

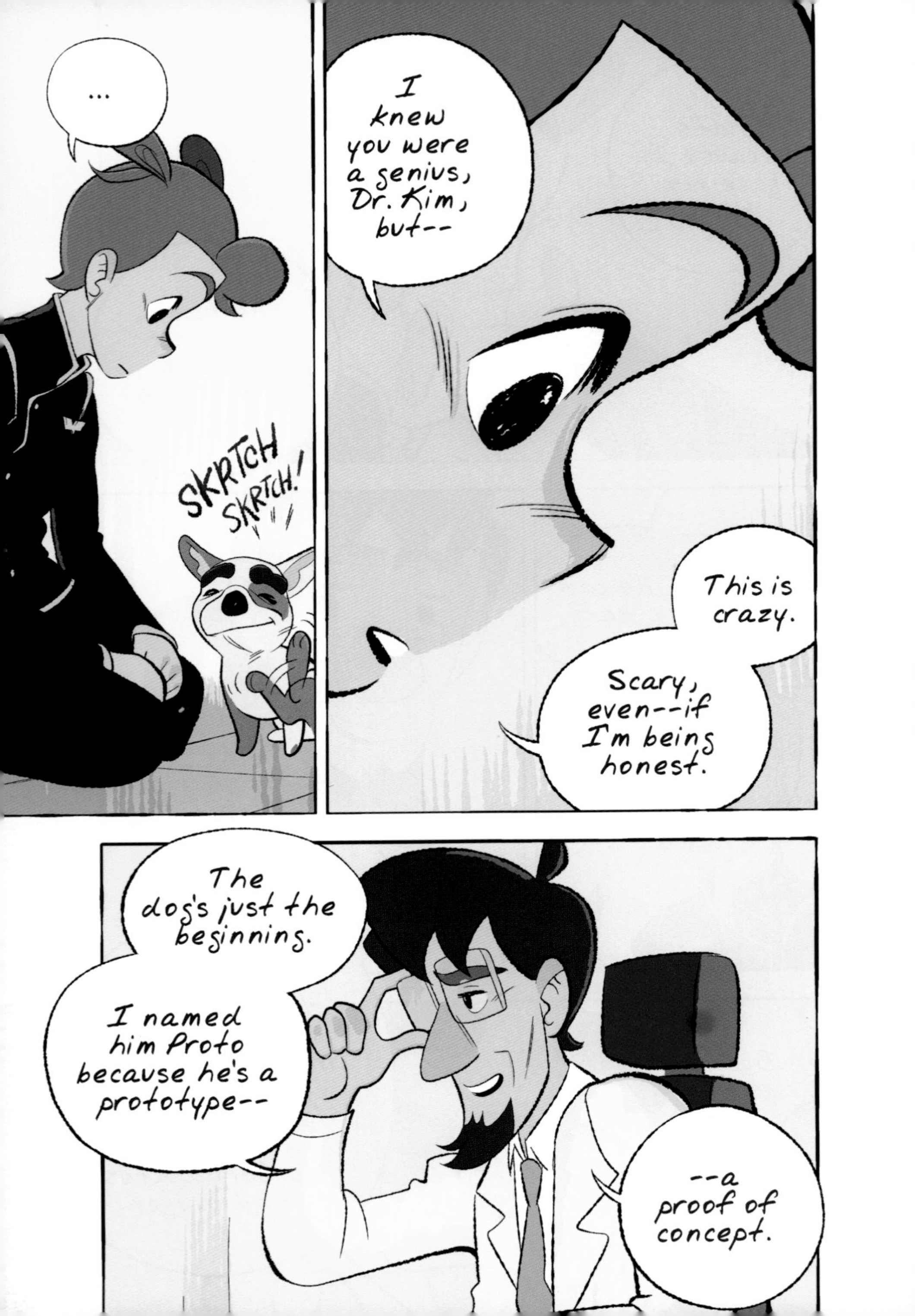
...
I knew you were a genius, Dr. Kim, but--
SKRTCH SKRTCH!
This is crazy.
Scary, even--if I'm being honest.
The dog's just the beginning.
I named him Proto because he's a prototype--
--a proof of concept.

He's the foundation I need to build Oliver the RFP he deserves.

One that can taste and smell and feel.

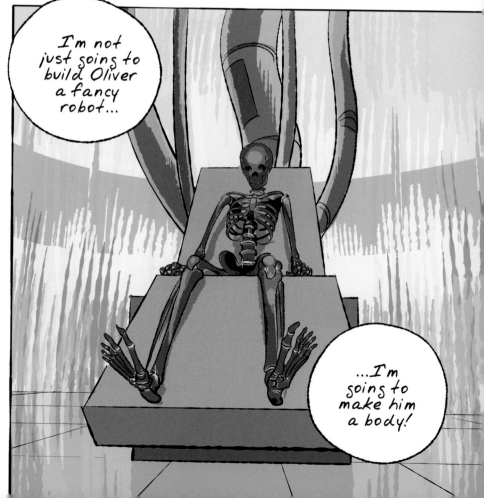

I'm not just going to build Oliver a fancy robot...

...I'm going to make him a body!

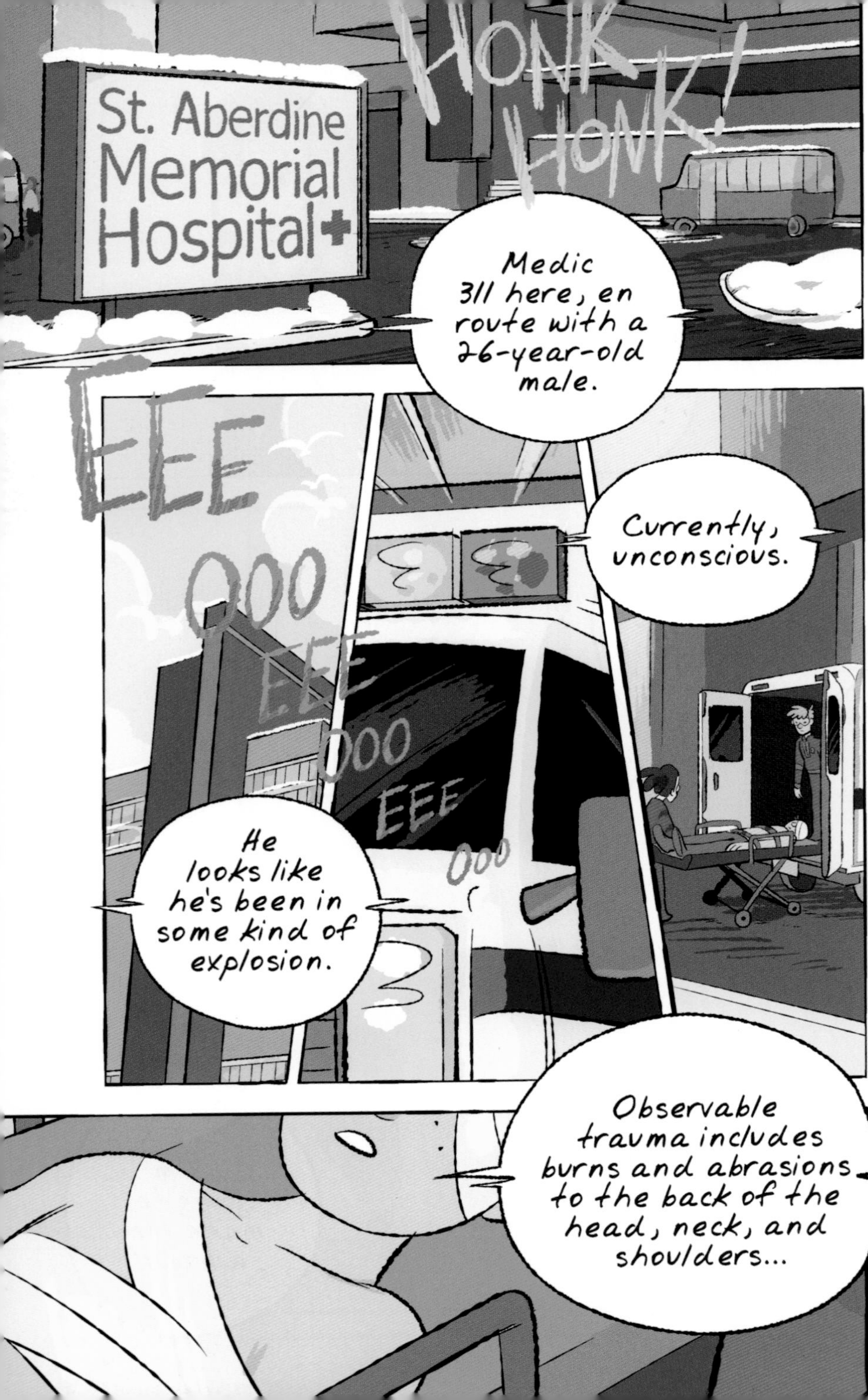
St. Aberdine Memorial Hospital
HONK HONK!
Medic 311 here, en route with a 26-year-old male.
EEE OOO EEE OOO EEE OOO
Currently, unconscious.
He looks like he's been in some kind of explosion.
Observable trauma includes burns and abrasions to the back of the head, neck, and shoulders...

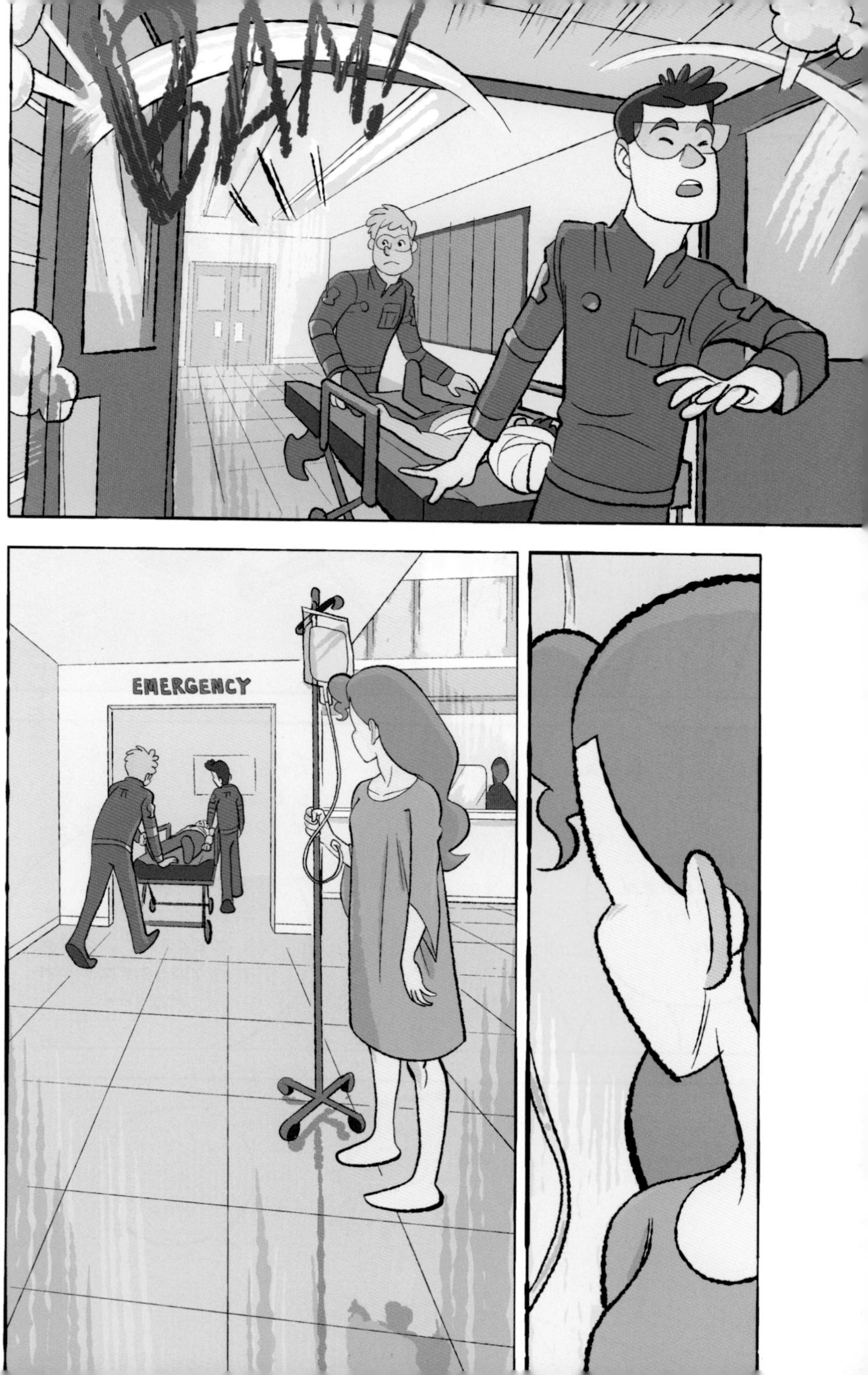
BAM!
EMERGENCY

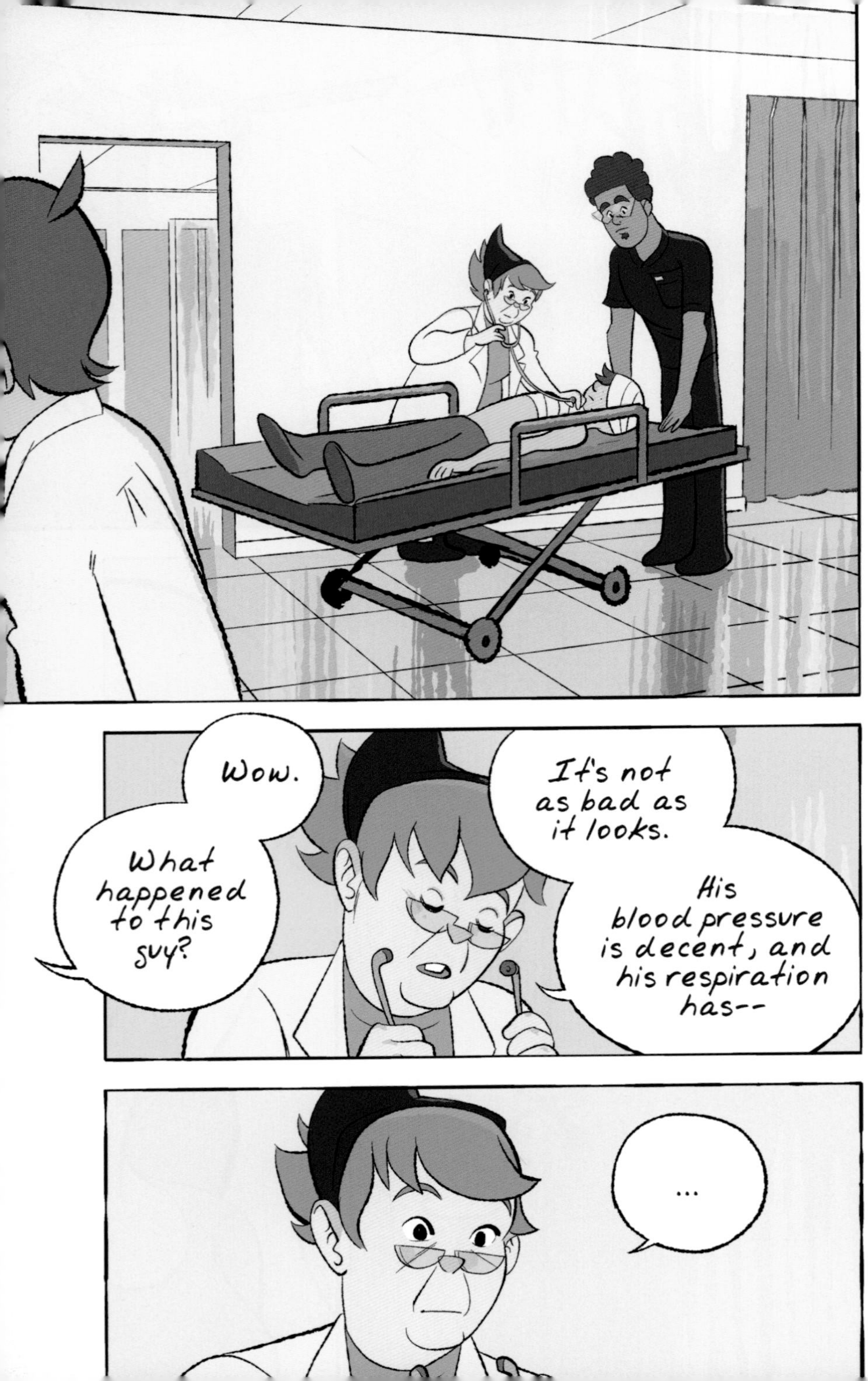
Wow.
What happened to this guy?
It's not as bad as it looks.
His blood pressure is decent, and his respiration has--
...

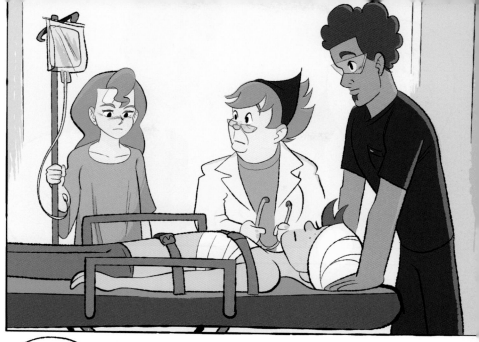

Cassie!

What are you doing here?

Looking for you.

I wanted to know when I can go home.

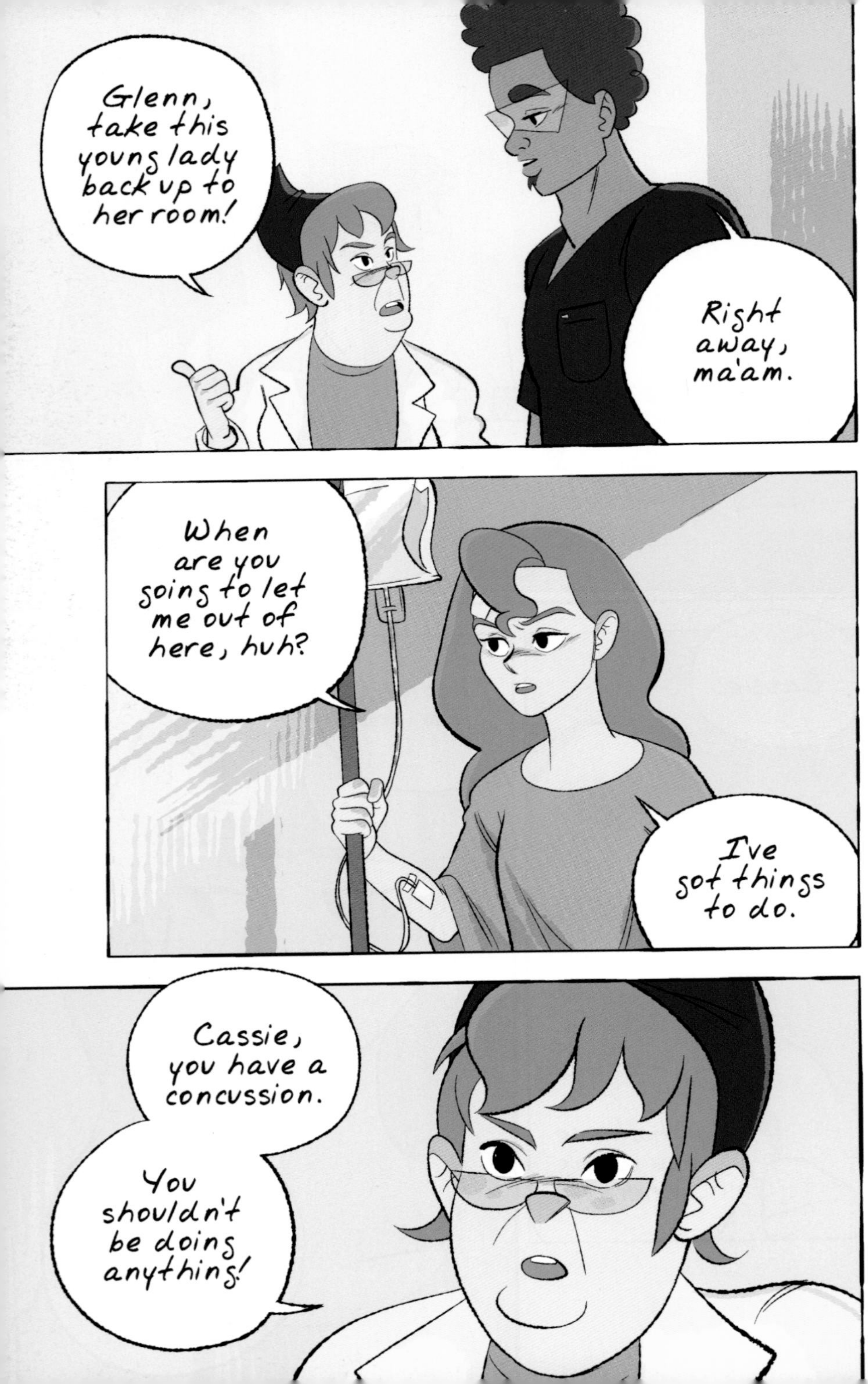
Glenn, take this young lady back up to her room!
Right away, ma'am.
When are you going to let me out of here, huh?
I've got things to do.
Cassie, you have a concussion.
You shouldn't be doing anything!

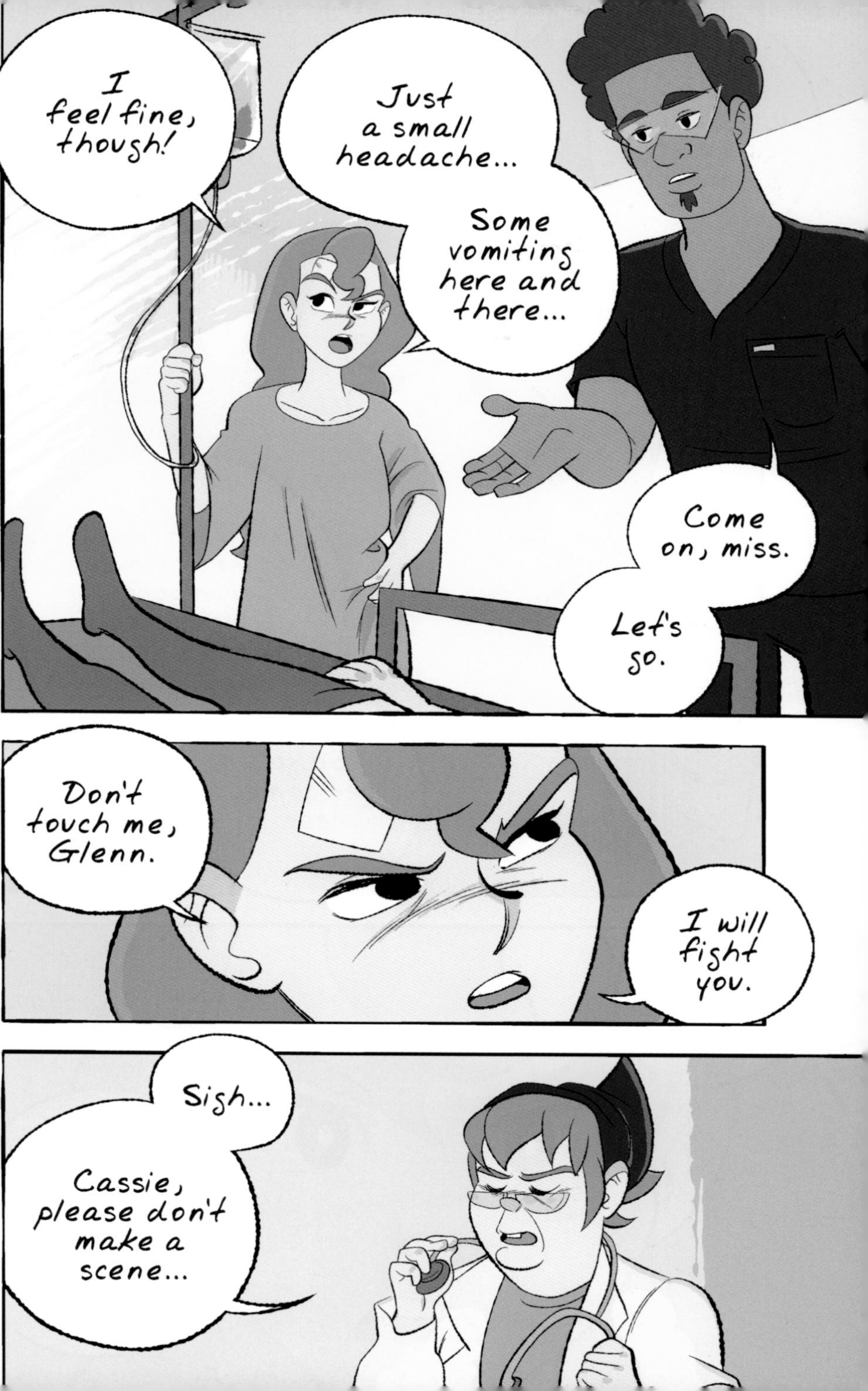
I feel fine, though!
Just a small headache...
Some vomiting here and there...
Come on, miss.
Let's go.
Don't touch me, Glenn.
I will fight you.
Sigh...
Cassie, please don't make a scene...

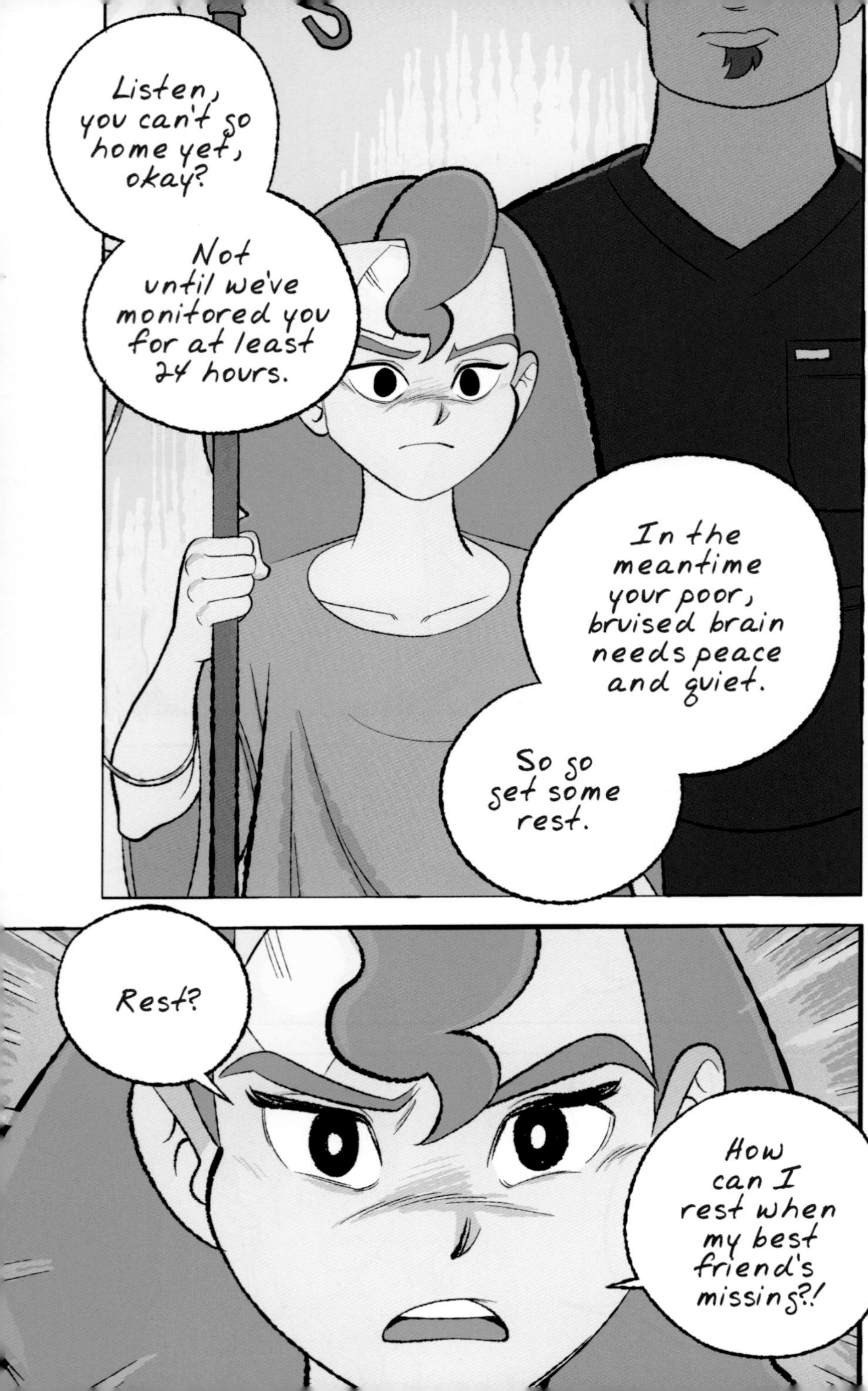
Listen, you can't go home yet, okay?
Not until we've monitored you for at least 24 hours.
In the meantime your poor, bruised brain needs peace and quiet.
So go get some rest.
Rest?
How can I rest when my best friend's missing?!

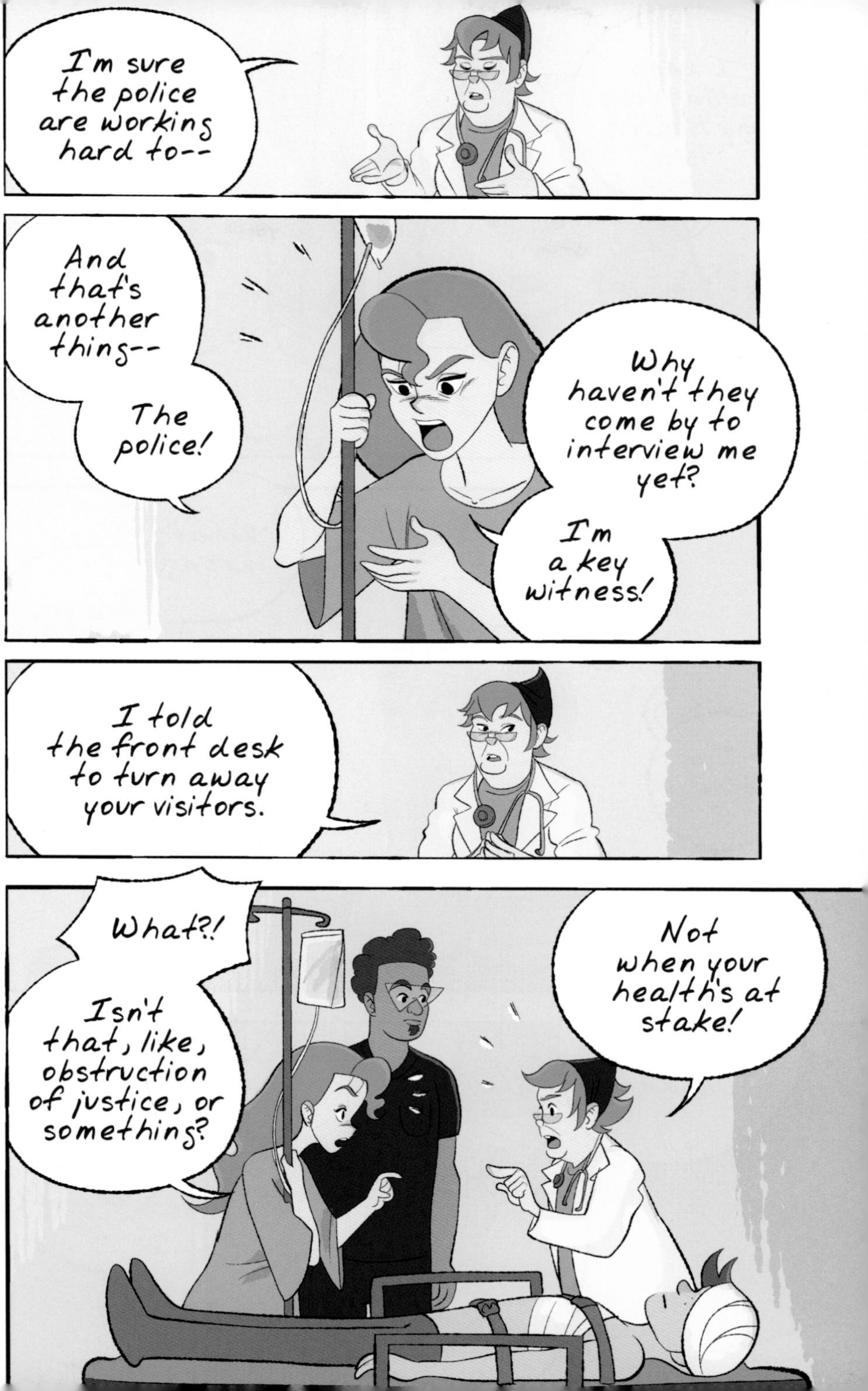
I'm sure the police are working hard to--
And that's another thing--
The police!
Why haven't they come by to interview me yet?
I'm a key witness!
I told the front desk to turn away your visitors.
What?!
Isn't that, like, obstruction of justice, or something?
Not when your health's at stake!

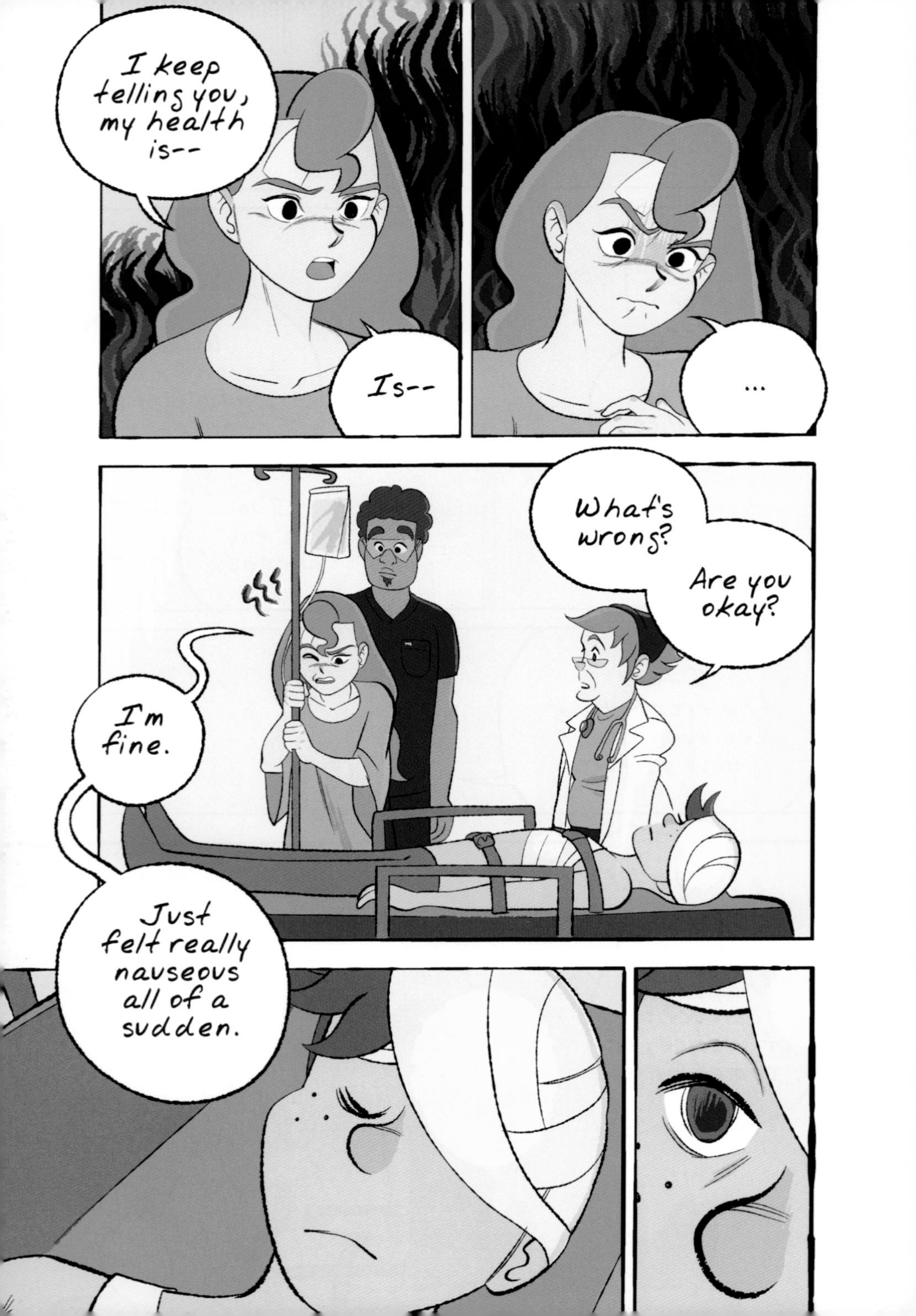

I keep telling you, my health is--
Is--
...
What's wrong?
Are you okay?
I'm fine.
Just felt really nauseous all of a sudden.

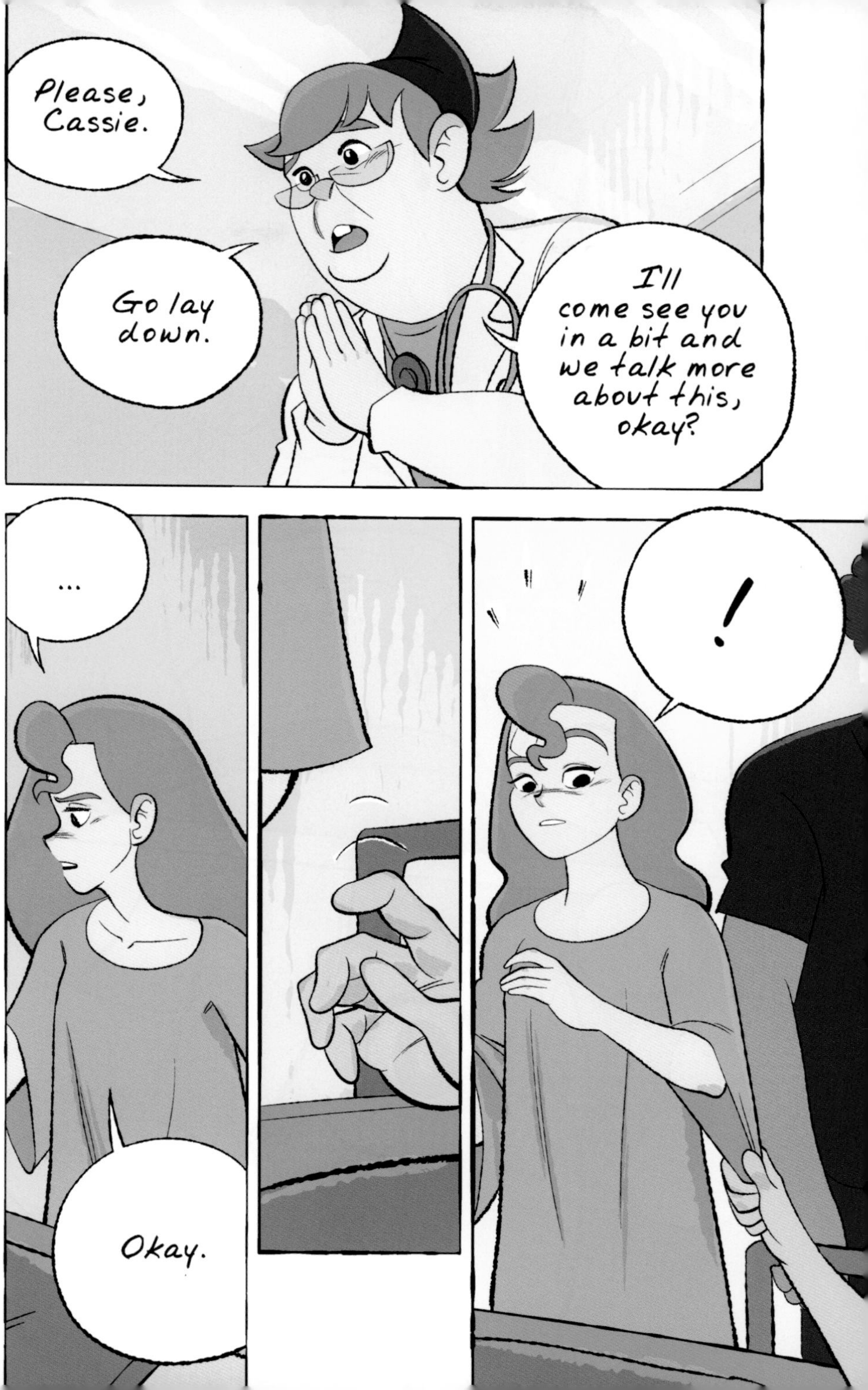
Please, Cassie.
Go lay down.
I'll come see you in a bit and we talk more about this, okay?
...
Okay.
!

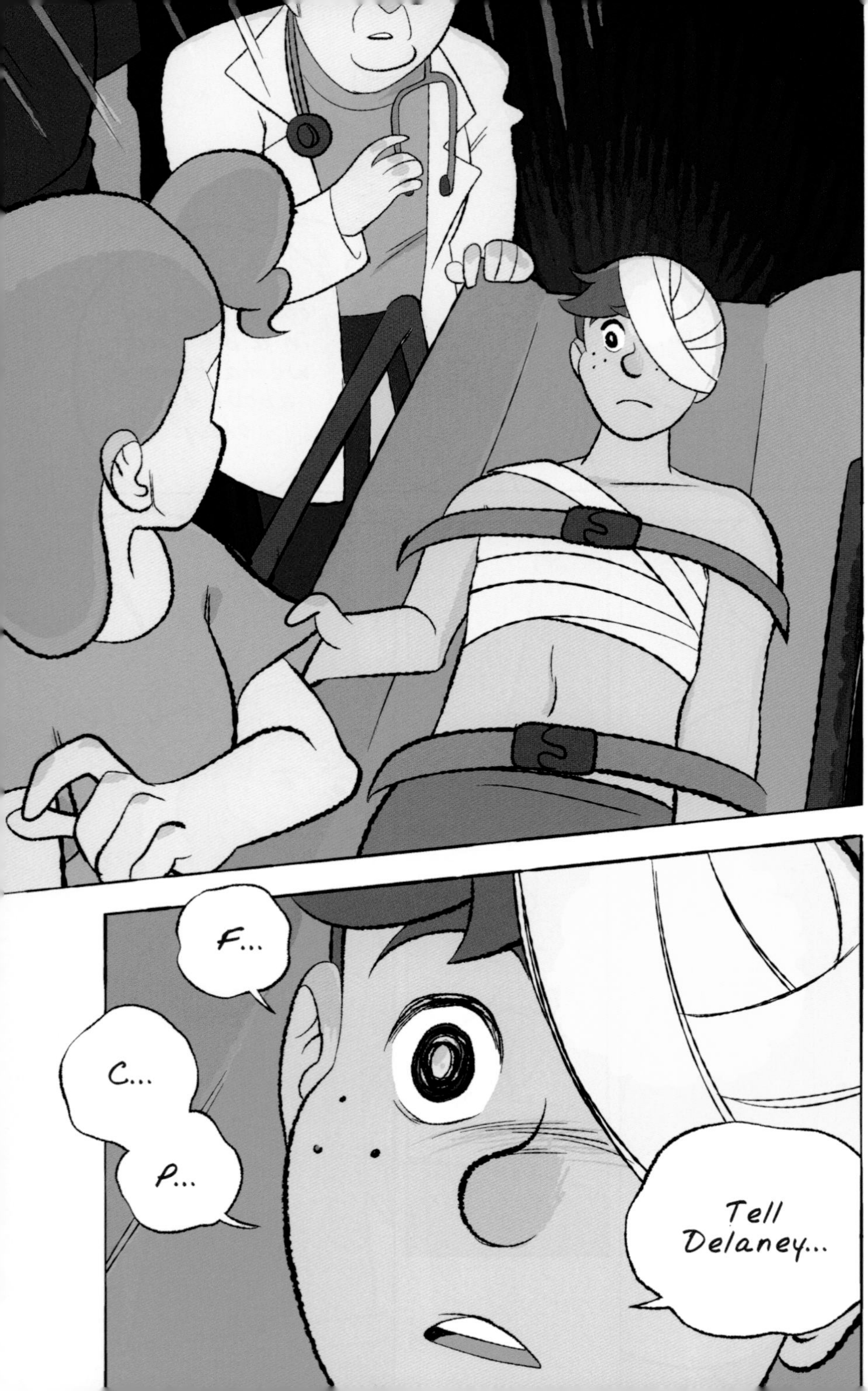
F...
C...
P...
Tell Delaney...

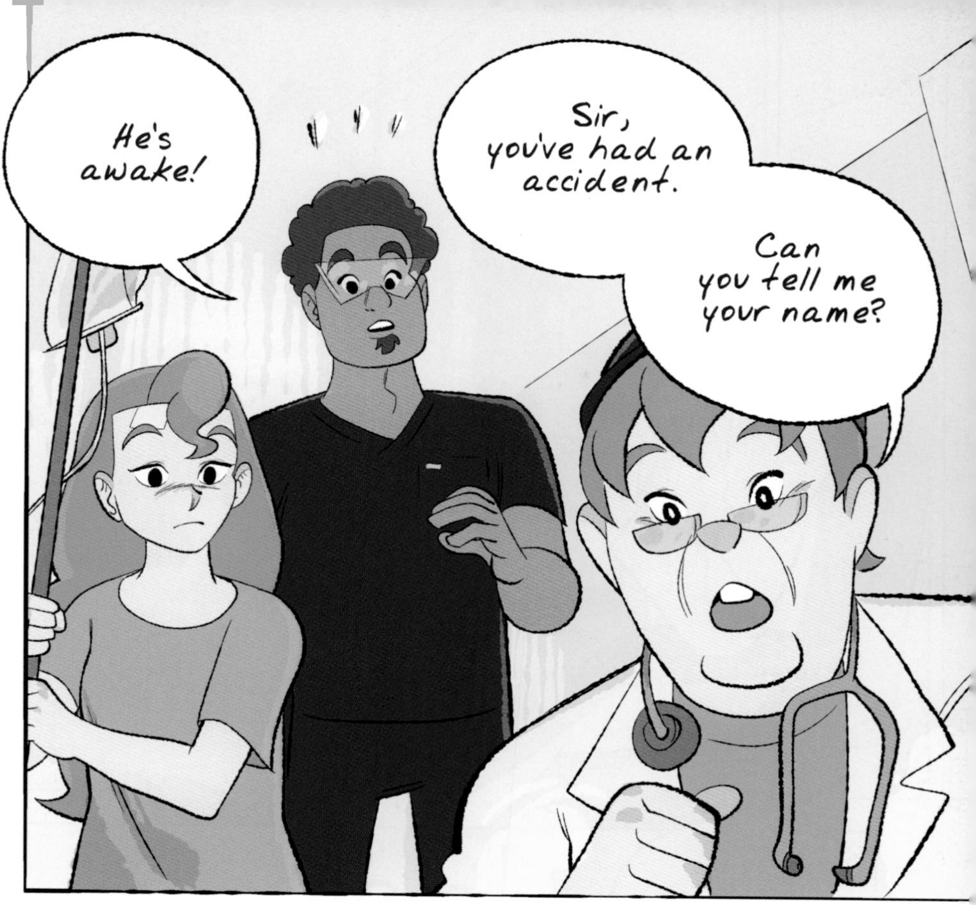
He's awake!
Sir, you've had an accident.
Can you tell me your name?

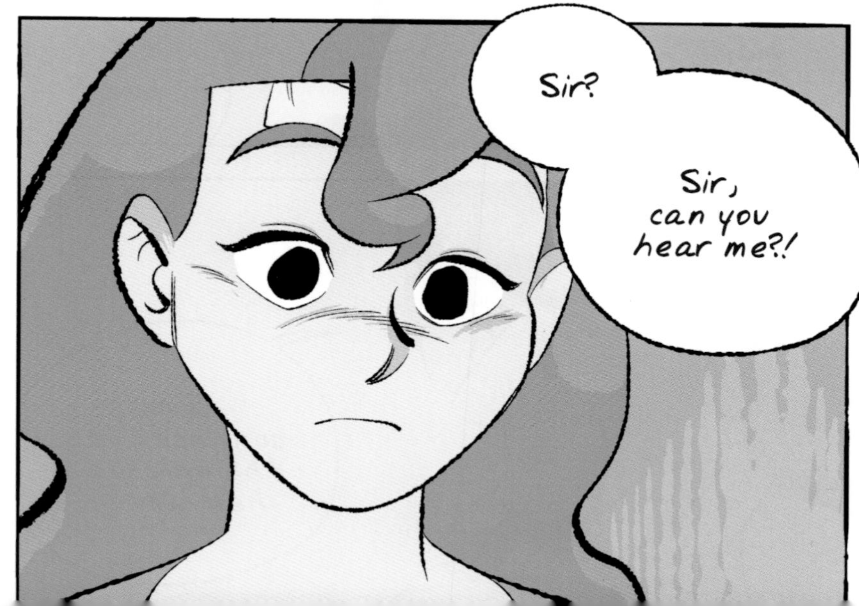
Sir?
Sir, can you hear me?!

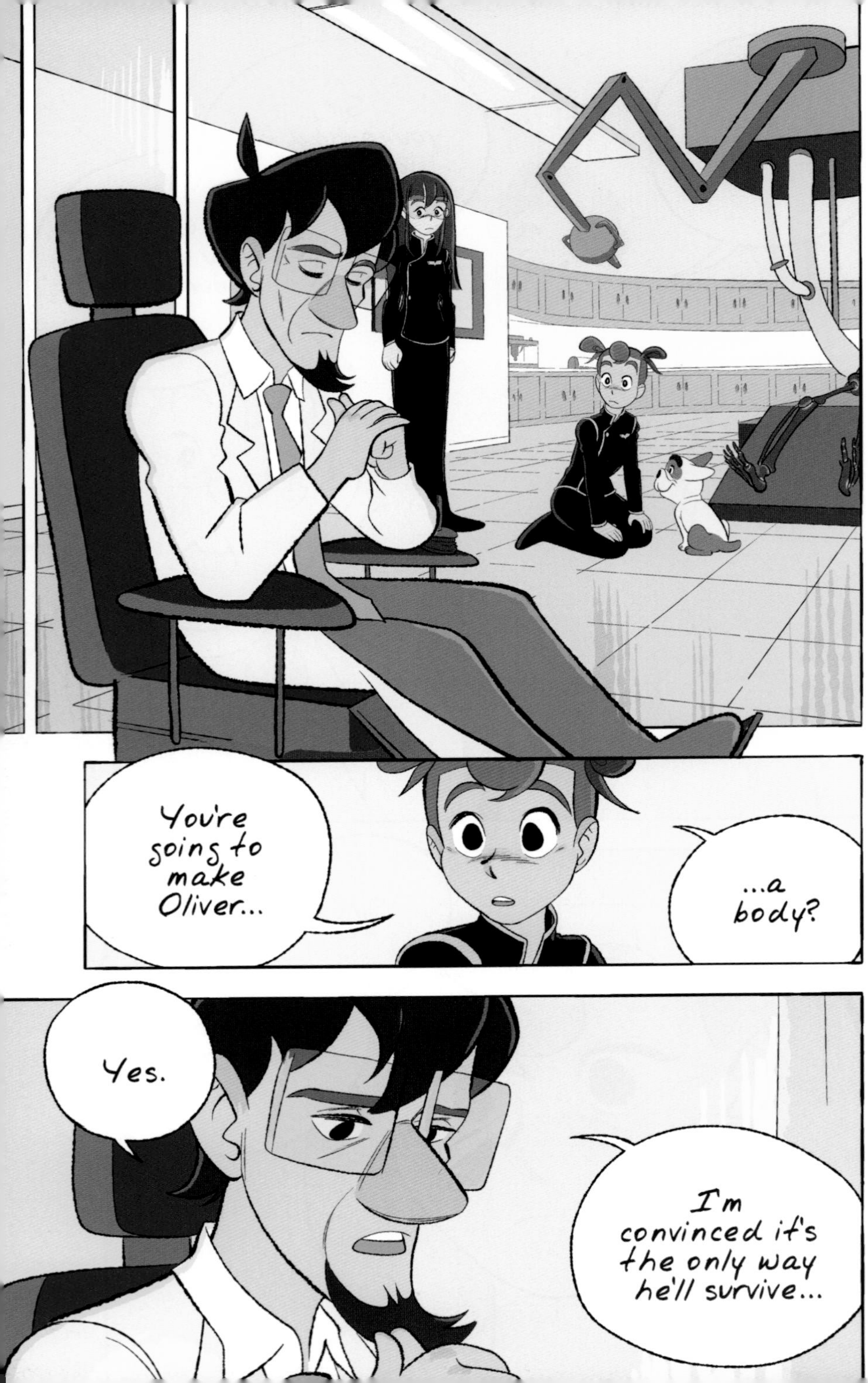
You're going to make Oliver...
...a body?
Yes.
I'm convinced it's the only way he'll survive...

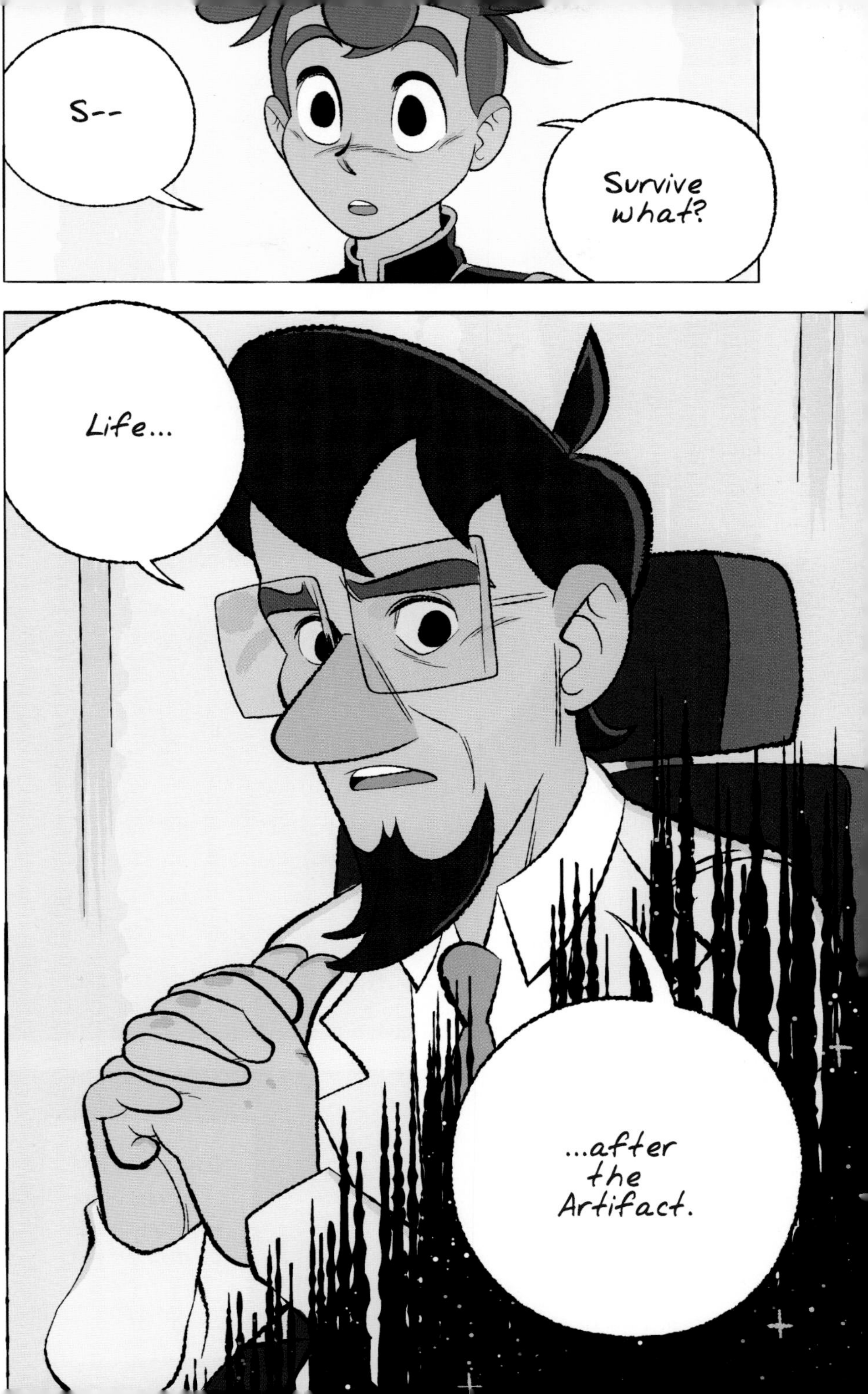
S--
Survive what?
Life...
...after the Artifact.

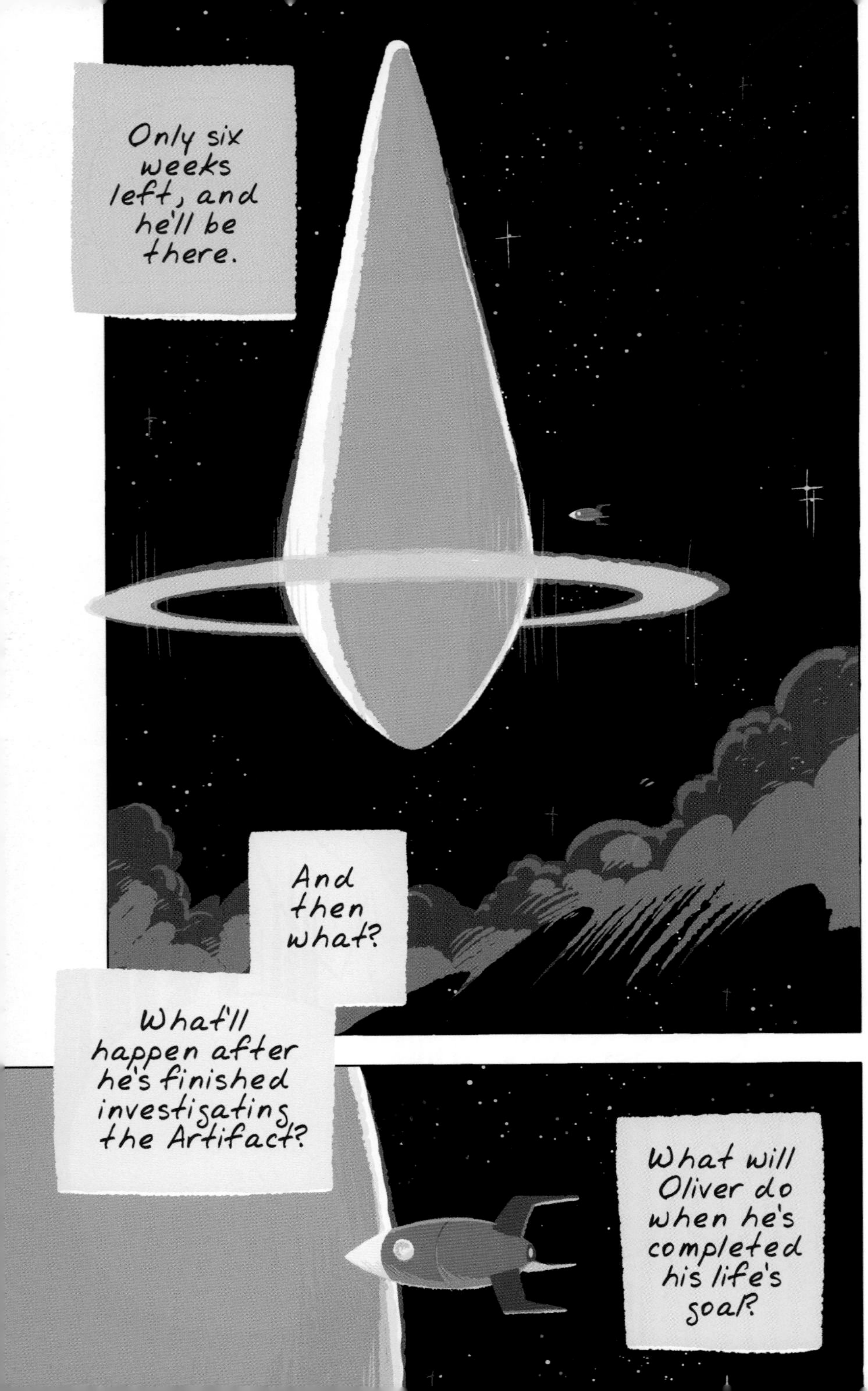
Only six weeks left, and he'll be there.
And then what?
What'll happen after he's finished investigating the Artifact?
What will Oliver do when he's completed his life's goal?

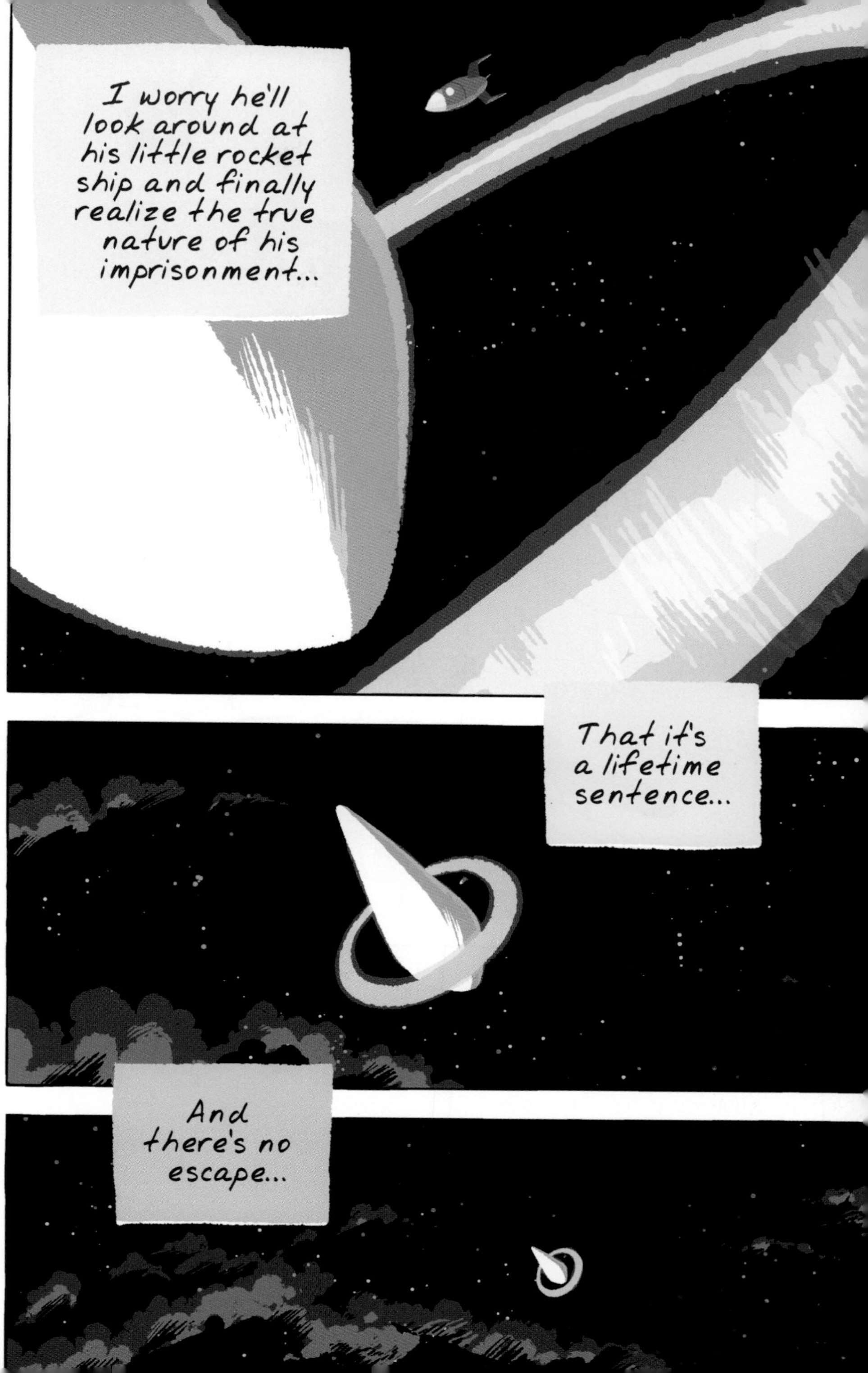
I worry he'll look around at his little rocket ship and finally realize the true nature of his imprisonment...
That it's a lifetime sentence...
And there's no escape...

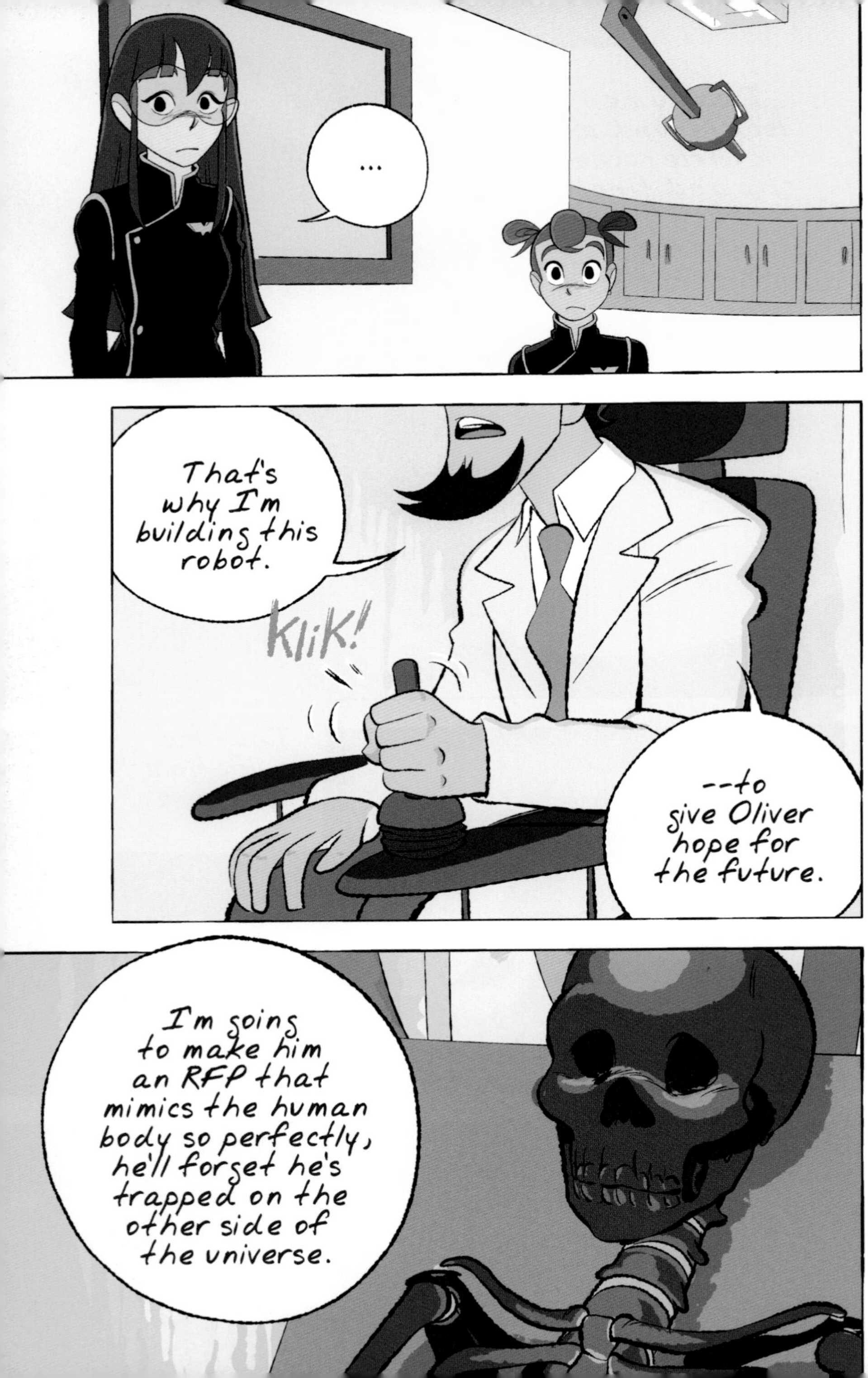
...
That's why I'm building this robot.
KliK!
--to give Oliver hope for the future.
I'm going to make him an RFP that mimics the human body so perfectly, he'll forget he's trapped on the other side of the universe.

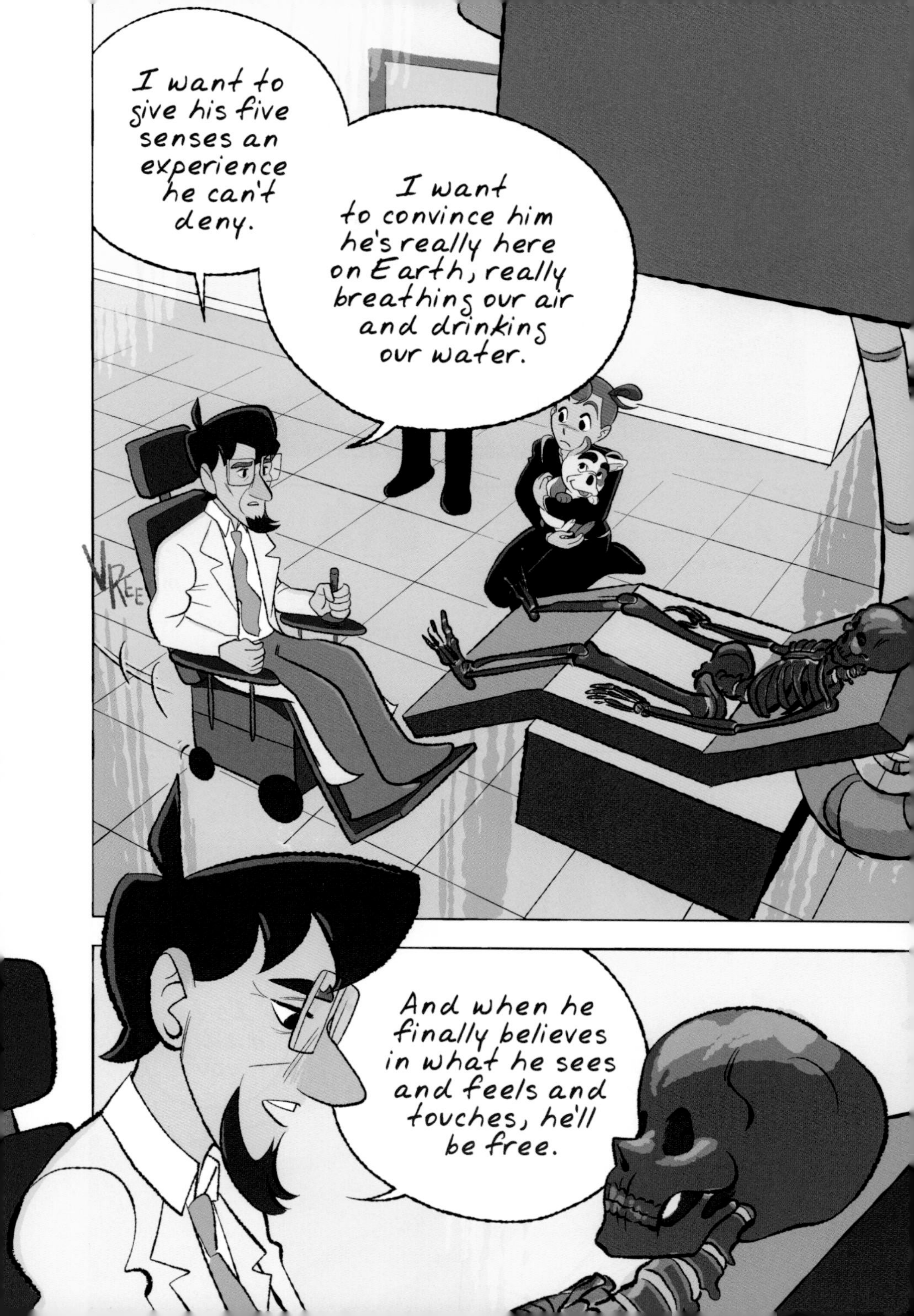
I want to give his five senses an experience he can't deny.
I want to convince him he's really here on Earth, really breathing our air and drinking our water.
VREE
And when he finally believes in what he sees and feels and touches, he'll be free.

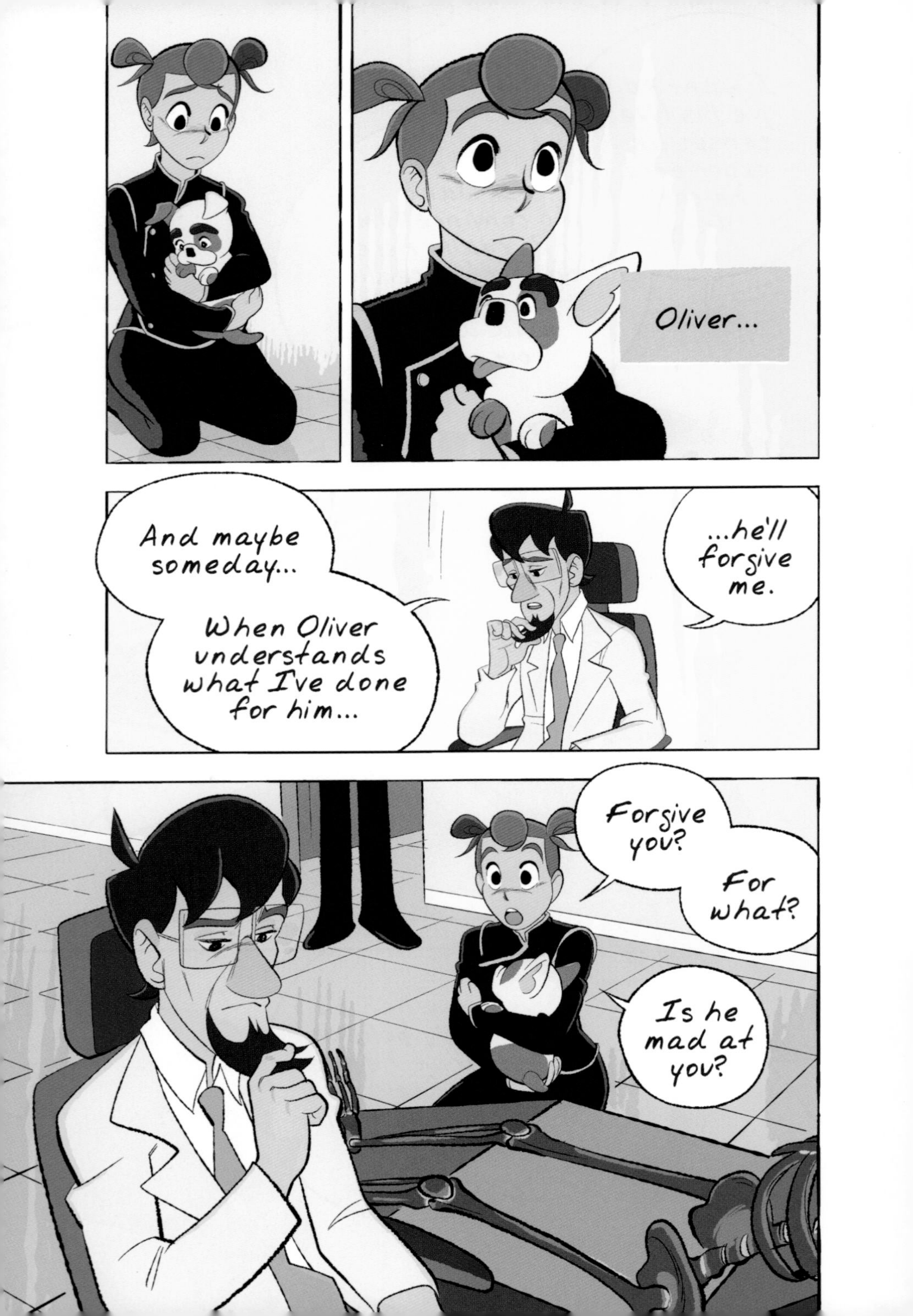
Oliver...
And maybe someday...
When Oliver understands what I've done for him...
...he'll forgive me.
Forgive you?
For what?
Is he mad at you?

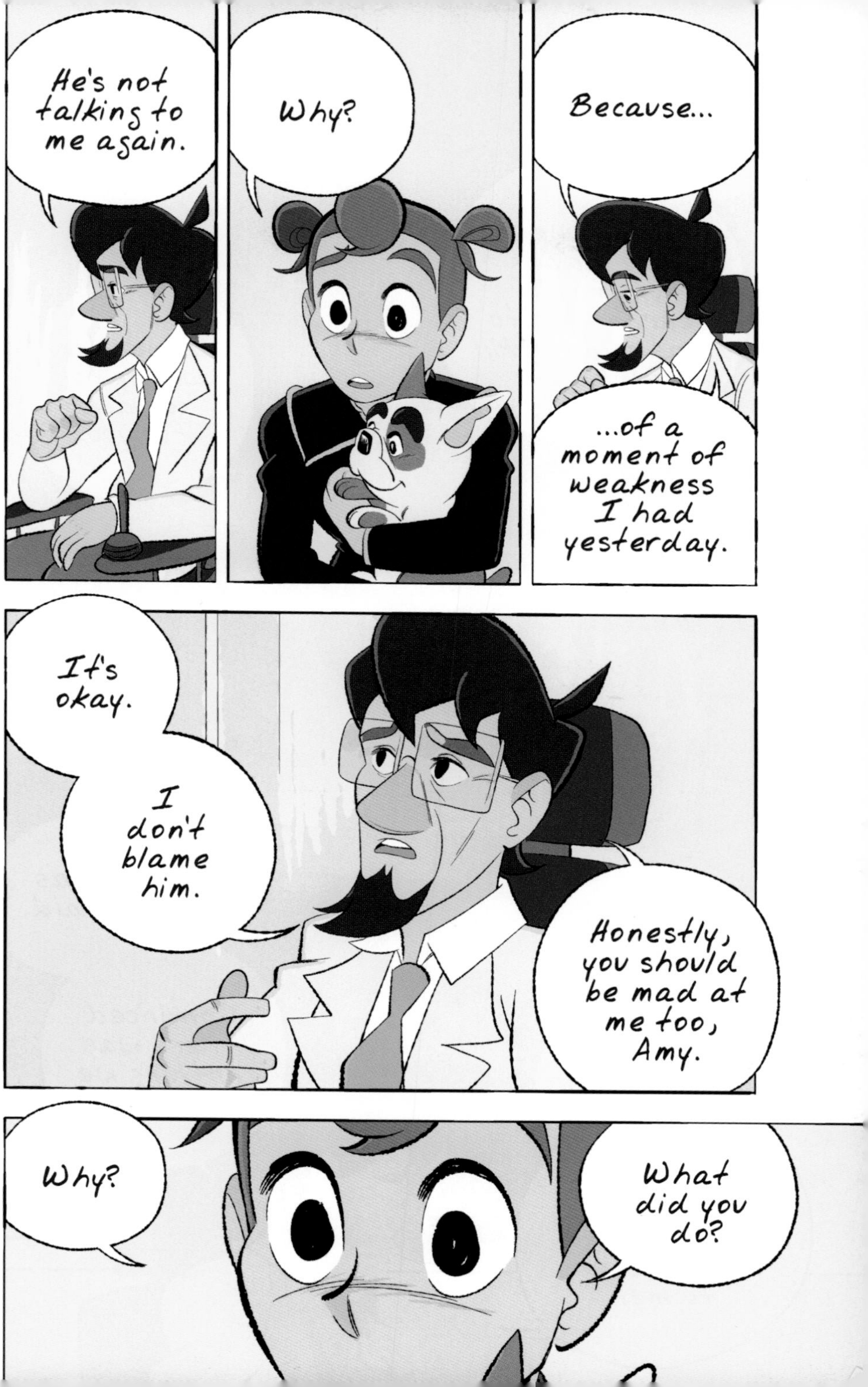
He's not talking to me again.
Why?
Because...
...of a moment of weakness I had yesterday.
It's okay.
I don't blame him.
Honestly, you should be mad at me too, Amy.
Why?
What did you do?

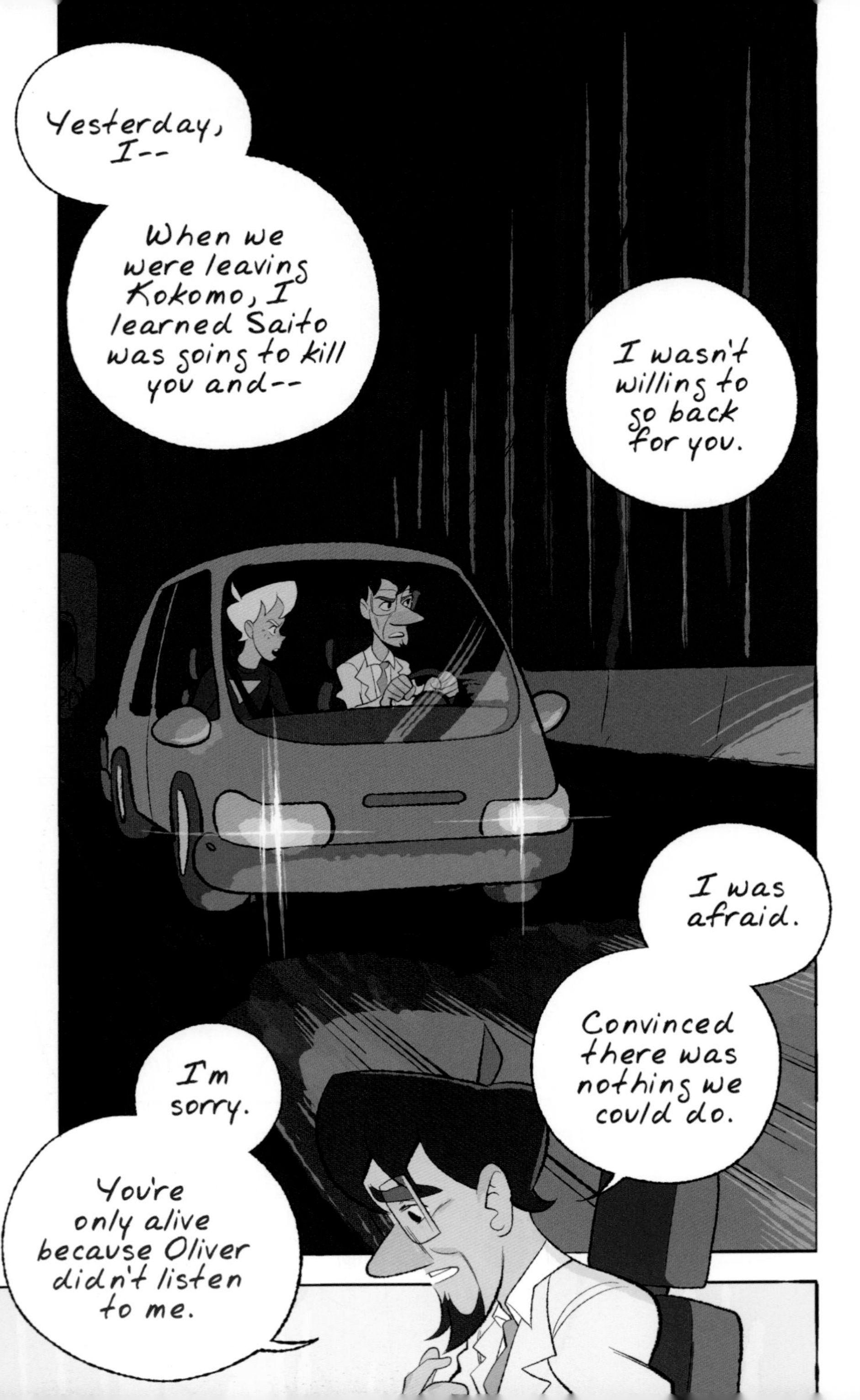
Yesterday, I--
When we were leaving Kokomo, I learned Saito was going to kill you and--
I wasn't willing to go back for you.
I was afraid.
Convinced there was nothing we could do.
I'm sorry.
You're only alive because Oliver didn't listen to me.

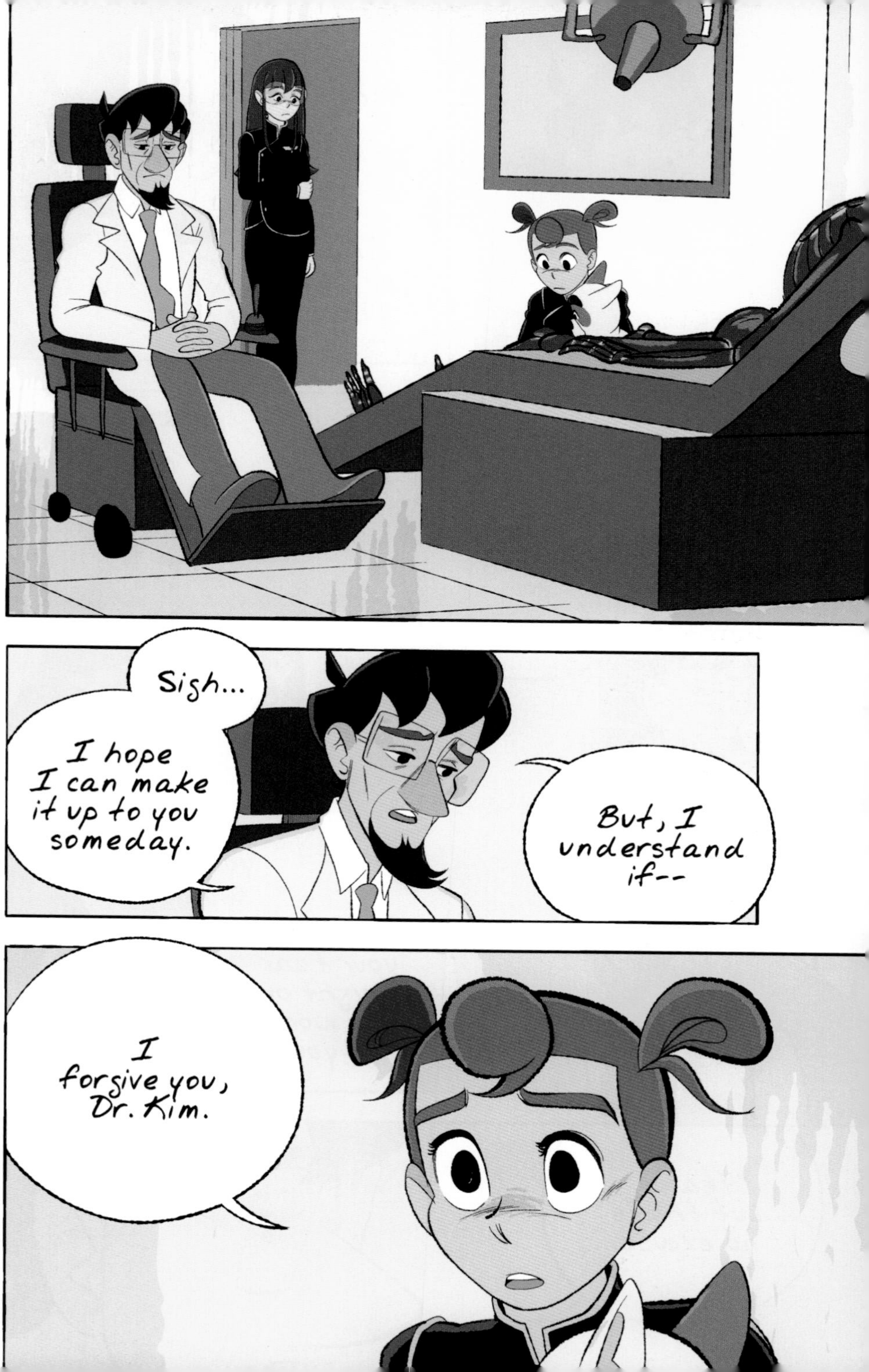
Sigh...
I hope I can make it up to you someday.
But, I understand if--
I forgive you, Dr. Kim.

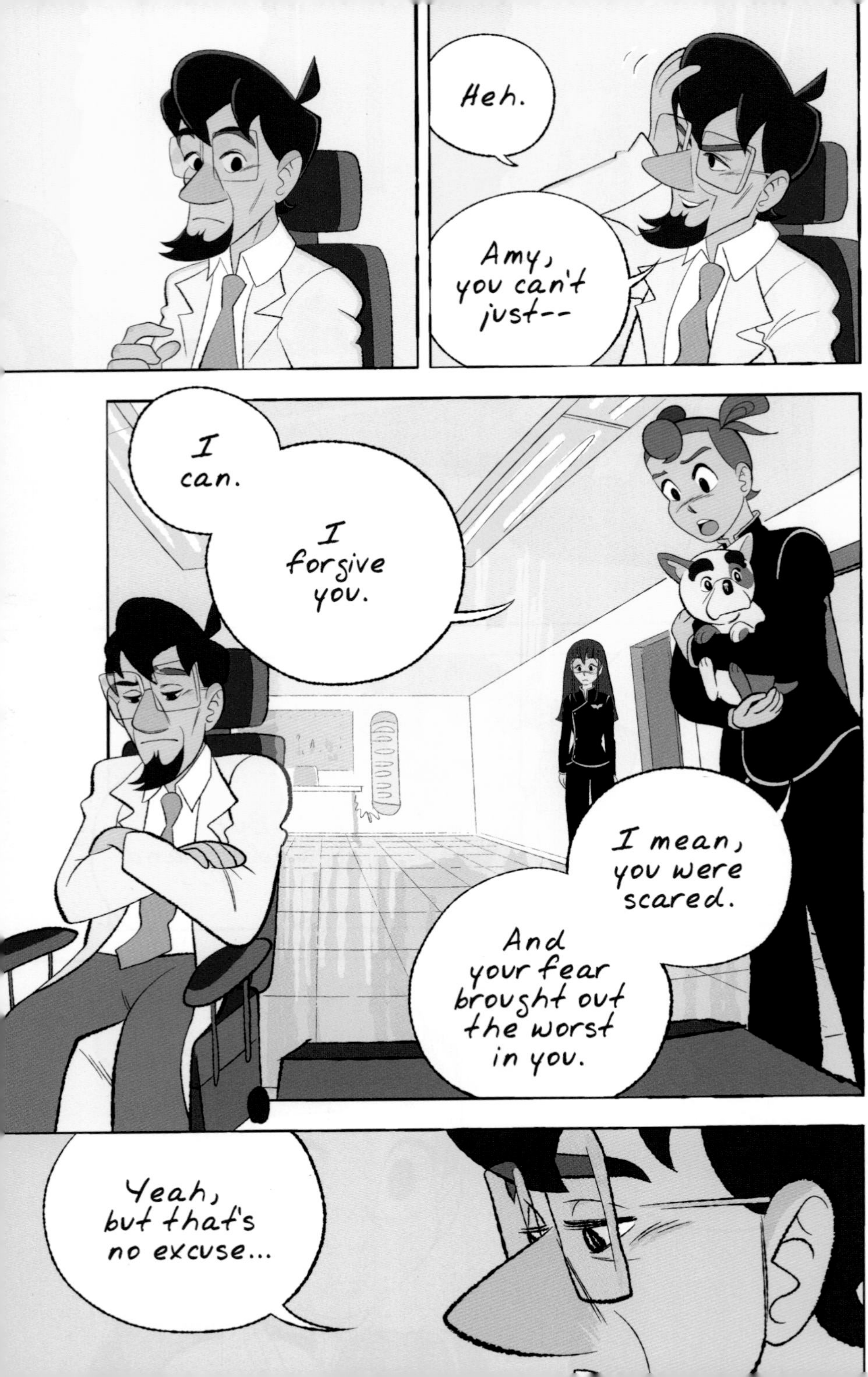
Heh.
Amy, you can't just--
I can.
I forgive you.
I mean, you were scared.
And your fear brought out the worst in you.
Yeah, but that's no excuse...

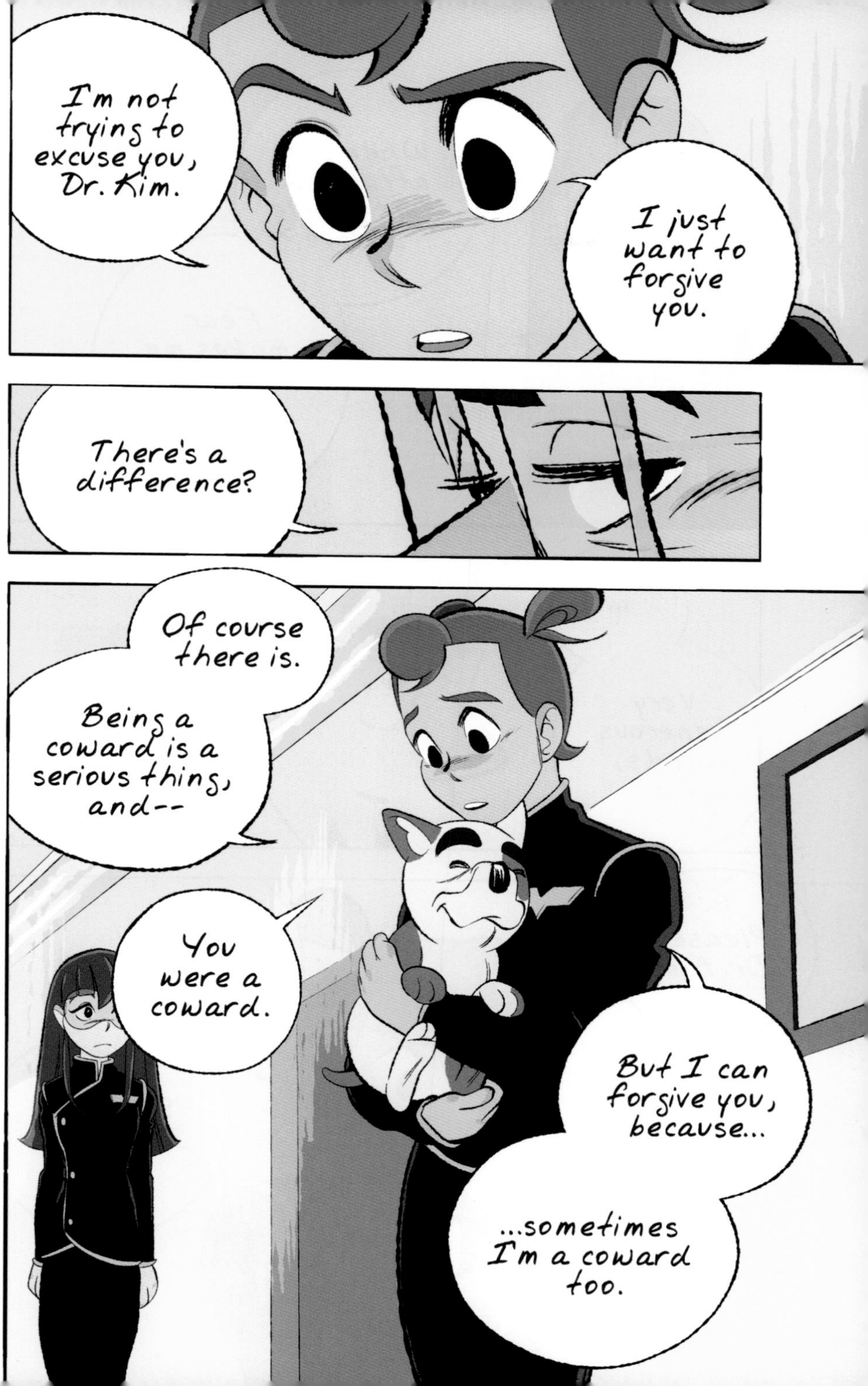
I'm not trying to excuse you, Dr. Kim.
I just want to forgive you.
There's a difference?
Of course there is.
Being a coward is a serious thing, and--
You were a coward.
But I can forgive you, because...
...sometimes I'm a coward too.

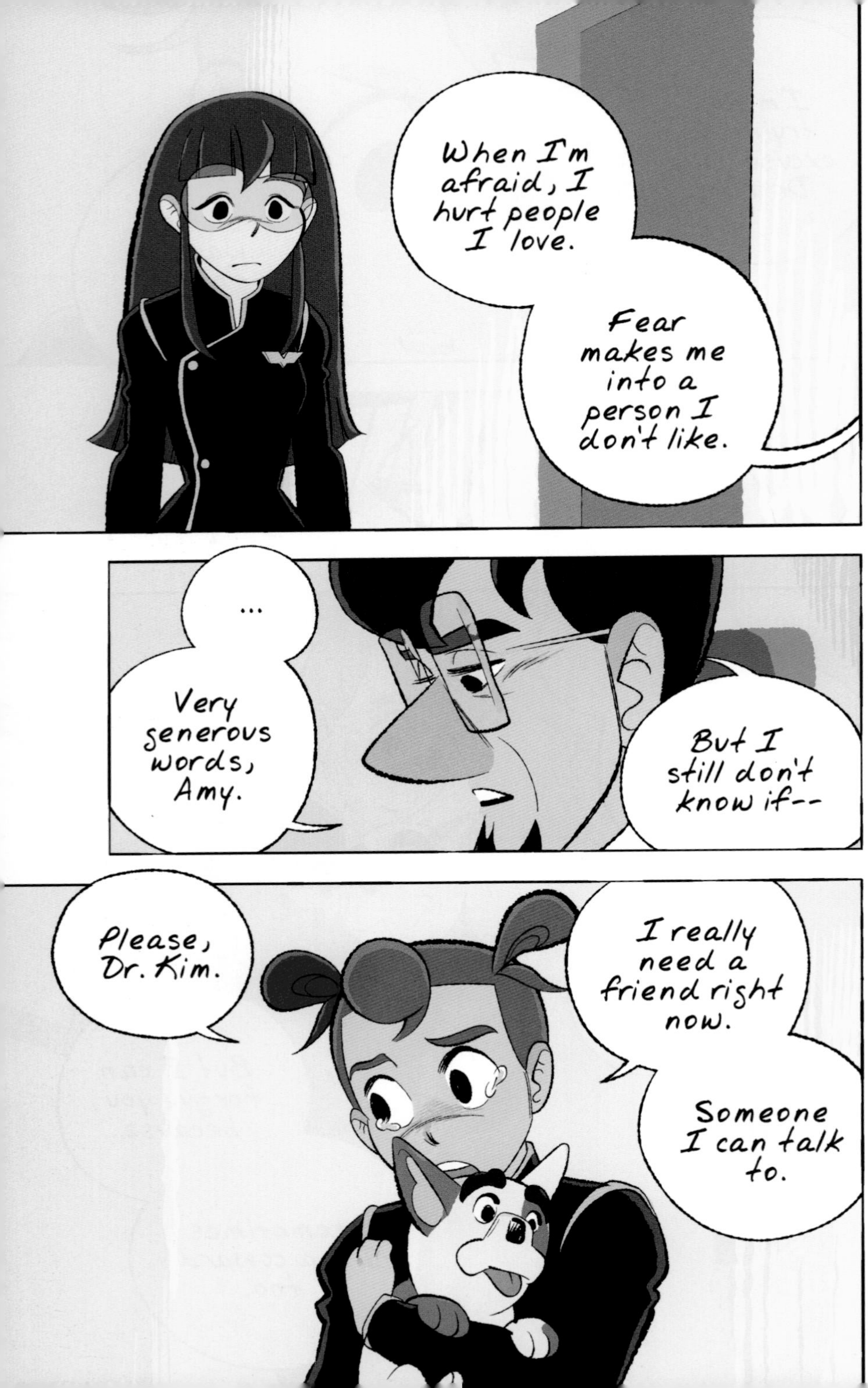
When I'm afraid, I hurt people I love.
Fear makes me into a person I don't like.
...
Very generous words, Amy.
But I still don't know if--
Please, Dr. Kim.
I really need a friend right now.
Someone I can talk to.

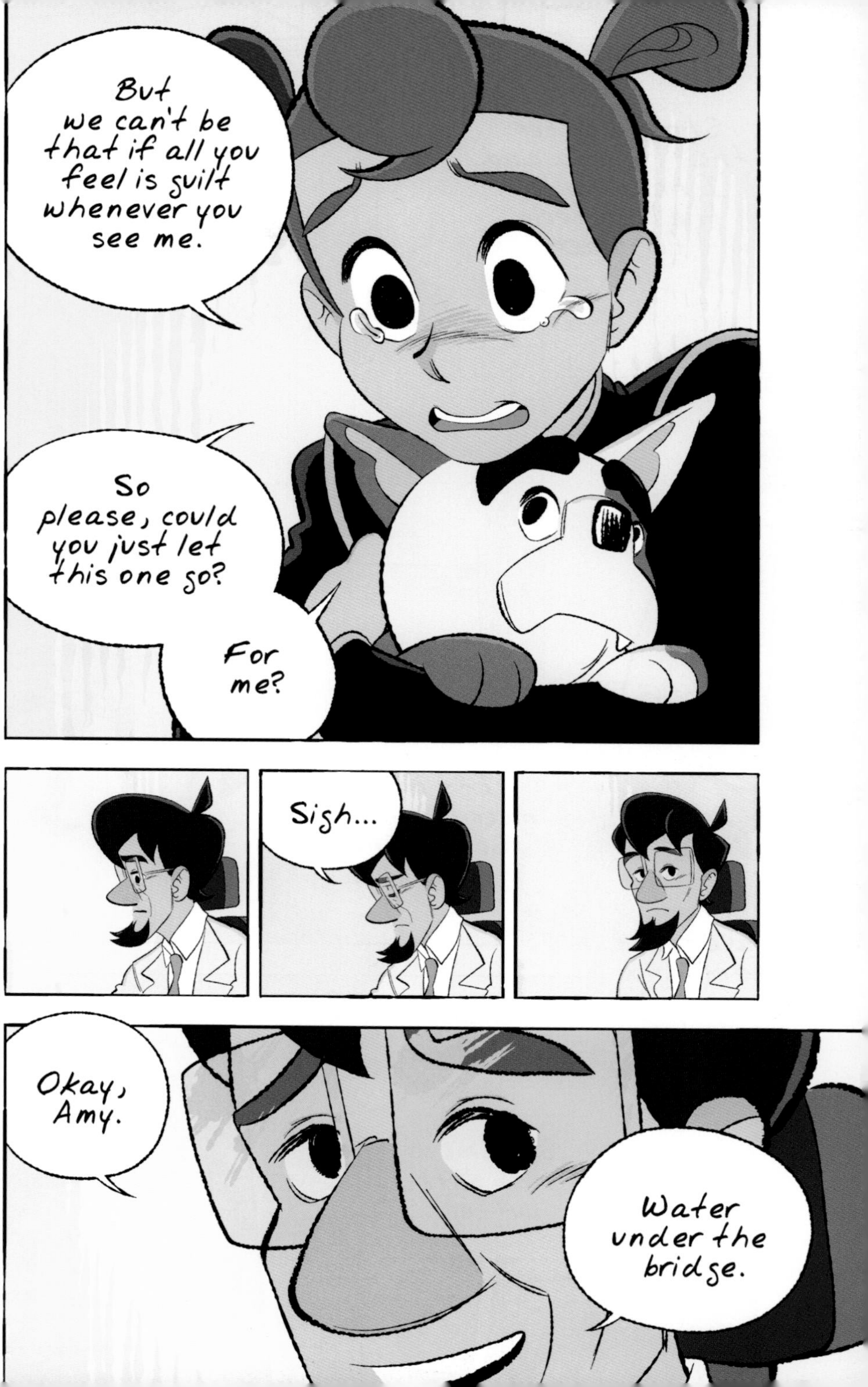
But we can't be that if all you feel is guilt whenever you see me.
So please, could you just let this one go?
For me?
Sigh...
Okay, Amy.
Water under the bridge.

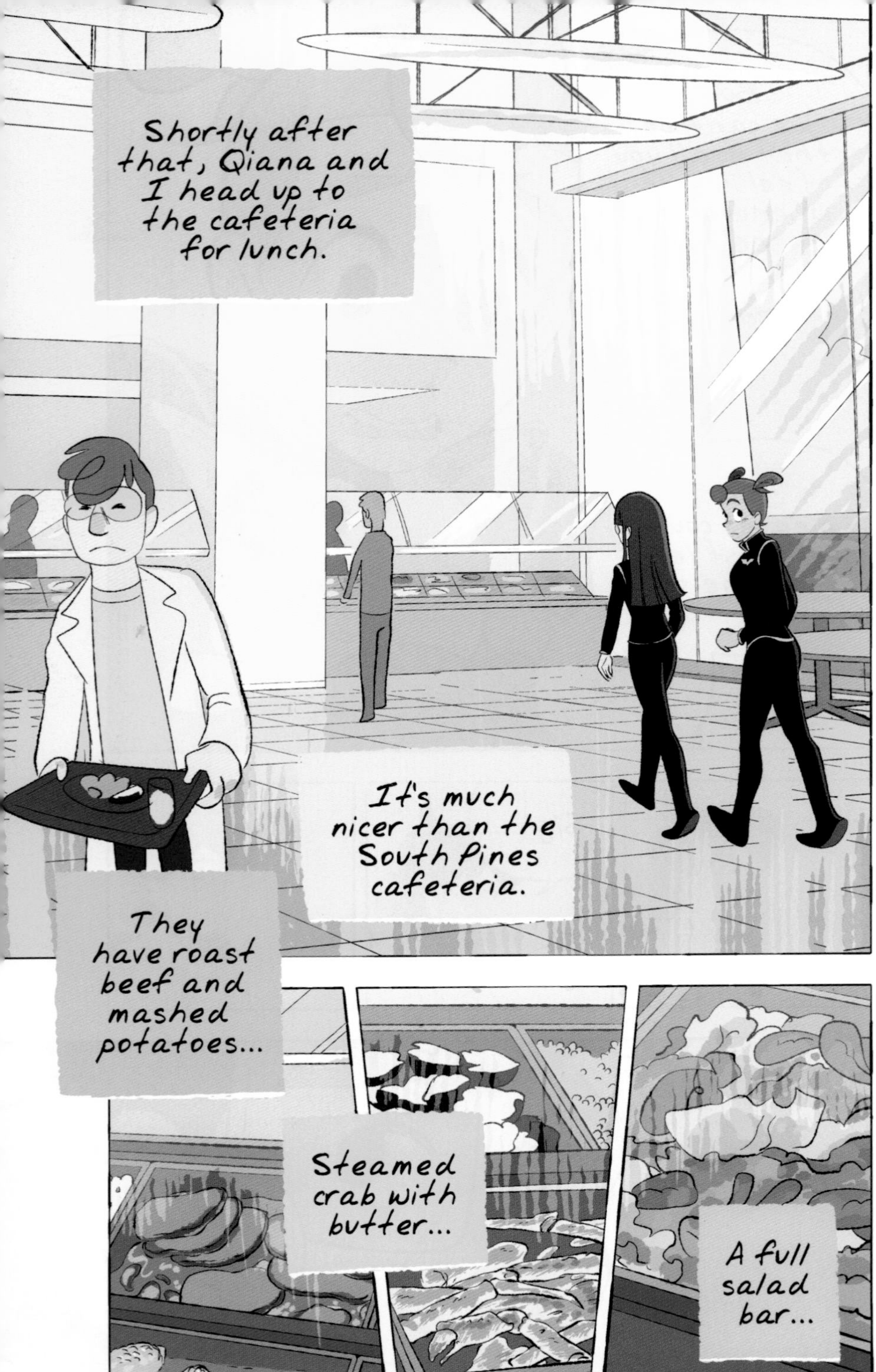
Shortly after that, Qiana and I head up to the cafeteria for lunch.
It's much nicer than the South Pines cafeteria.
They have roast beef and mashed potatoes...
Steamed crab with butter...
A full salad bar...

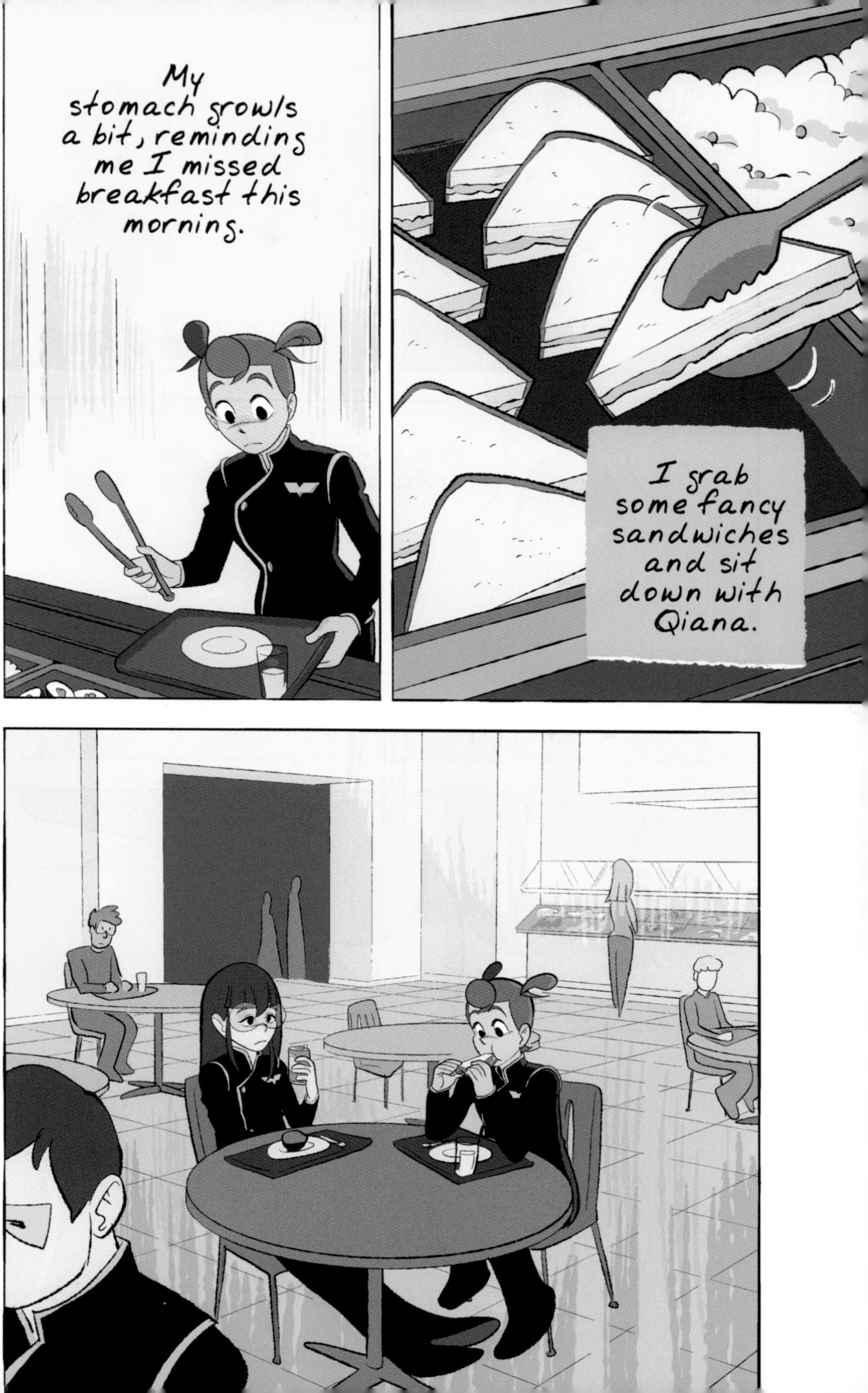
My stomach growls a bit, reminding me I missed breakfast this morning.
I grab some fancy sandwiches and sit down with Qiana.

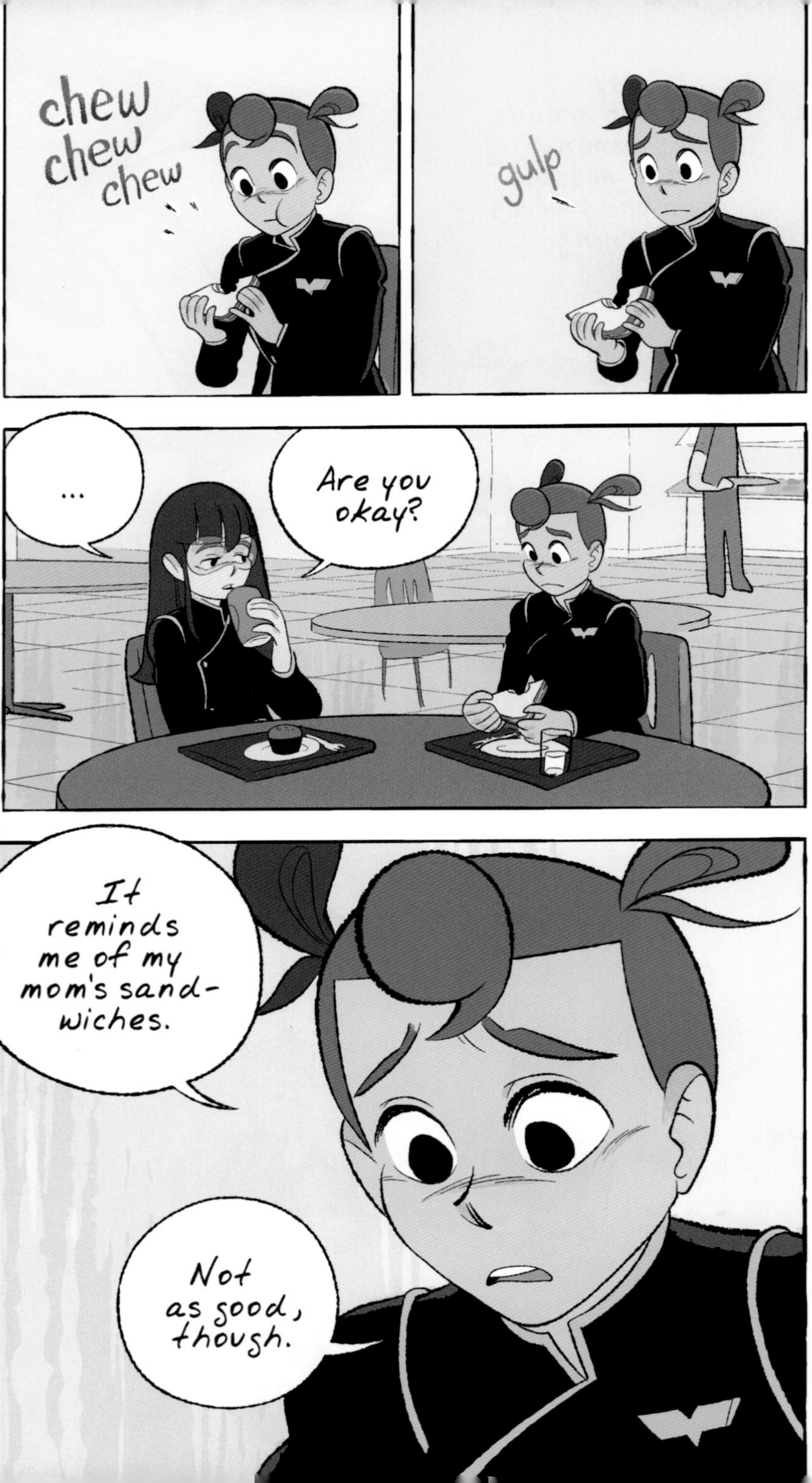
chew
chew
chew
gulp
...
Are you okay?
It reminds me of my mom's sand-wiches.
Not as good, though.

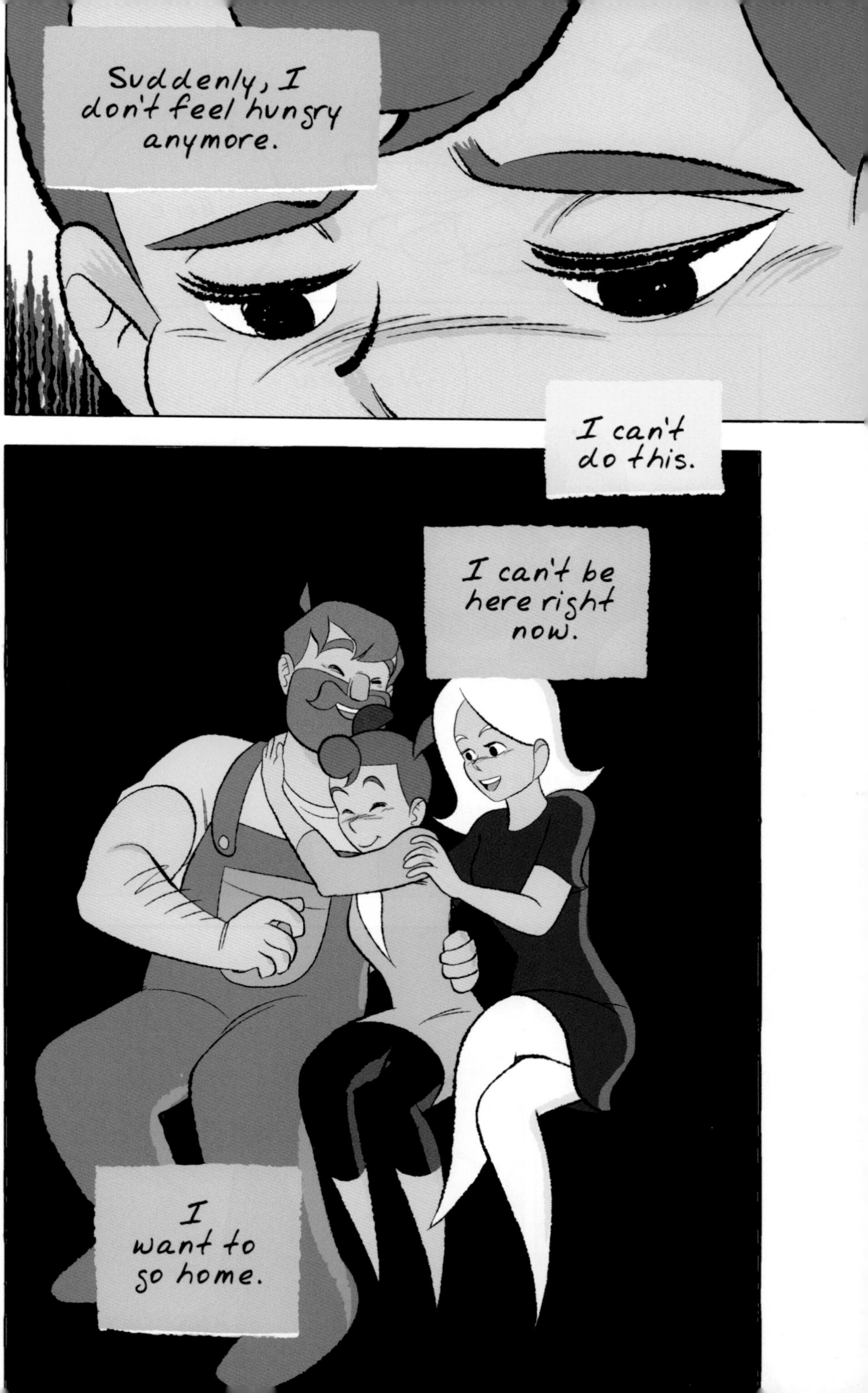
Suddenly, I don't feel hungry anymore.
I can't do this.
I can't be here right now.
I want to go home.

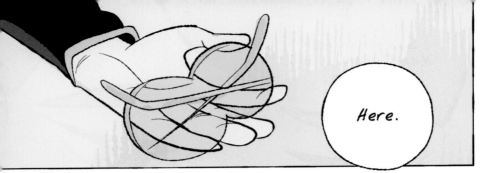

Here.

Net gear glasses?

sniff

A gift from Dr. Kim.

He wanted me to give them to you.

When did he--

Right before we left his lab...

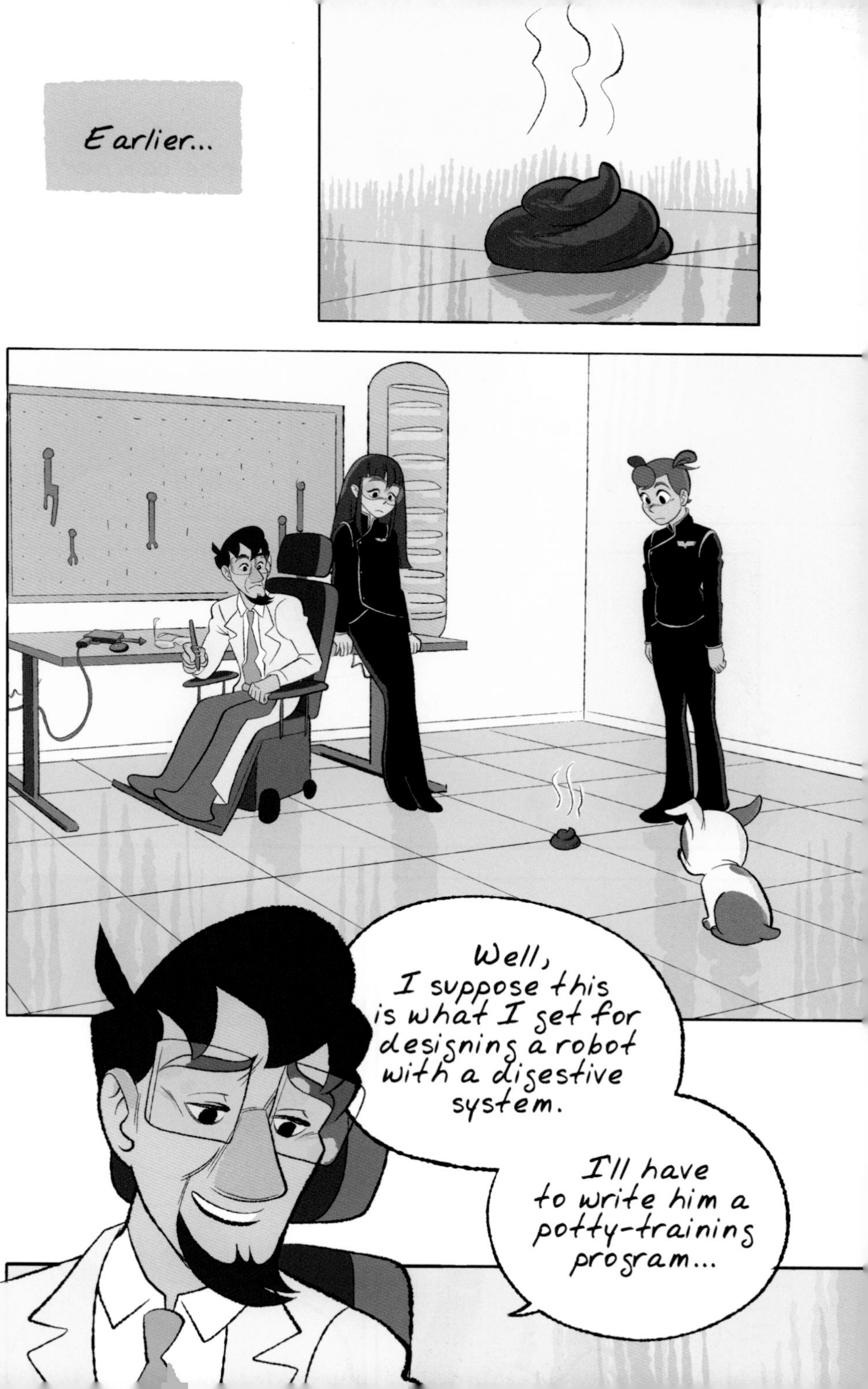
Earlier...
Well, I suppose this is what I get for designing a robot with a digestive system.
I'll have to write him a potty-training program...

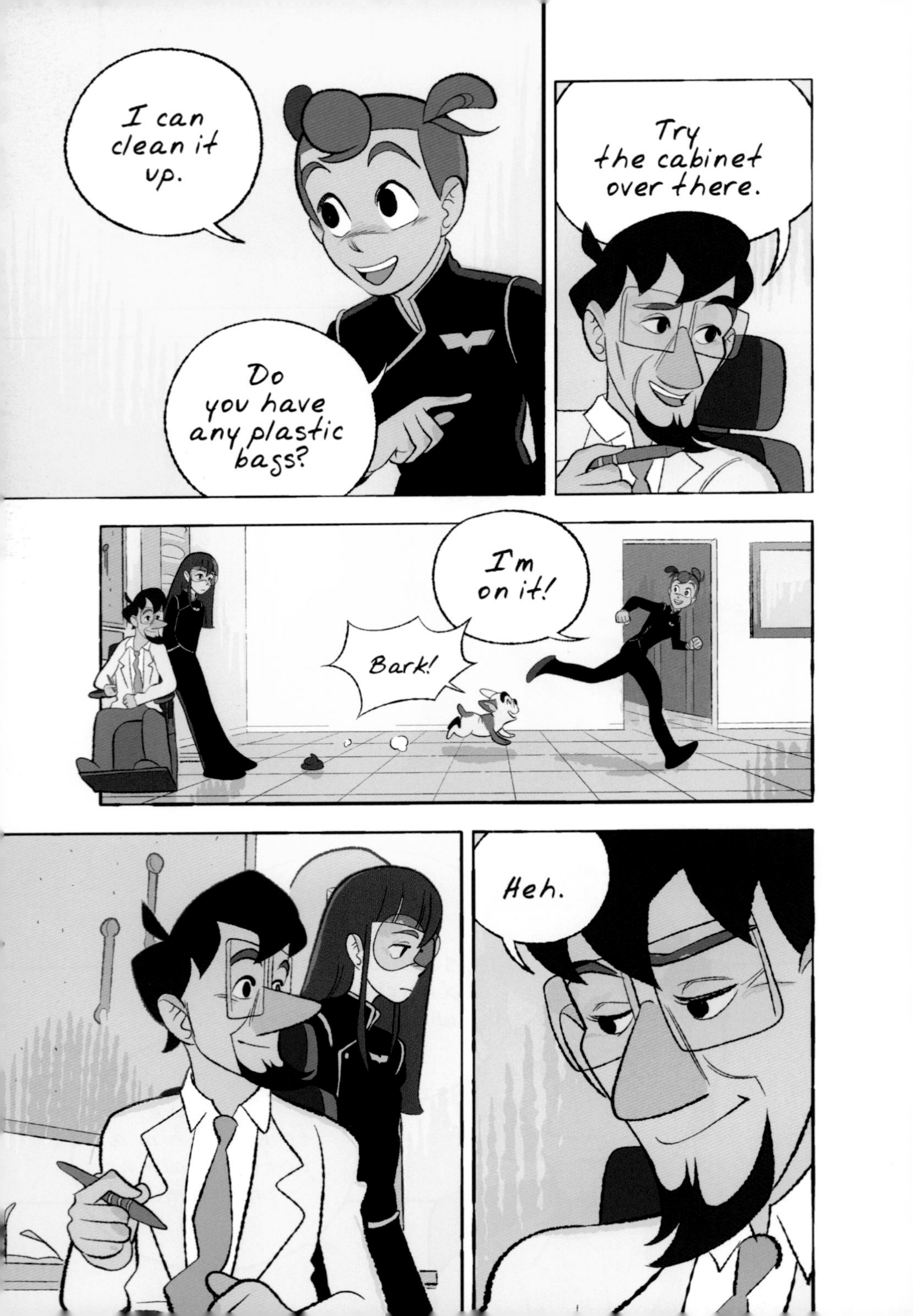
I can clean it up.
Do you have any plastic bags?
Try the cabinet over there.
I'm on it!
Bark!
Heh.

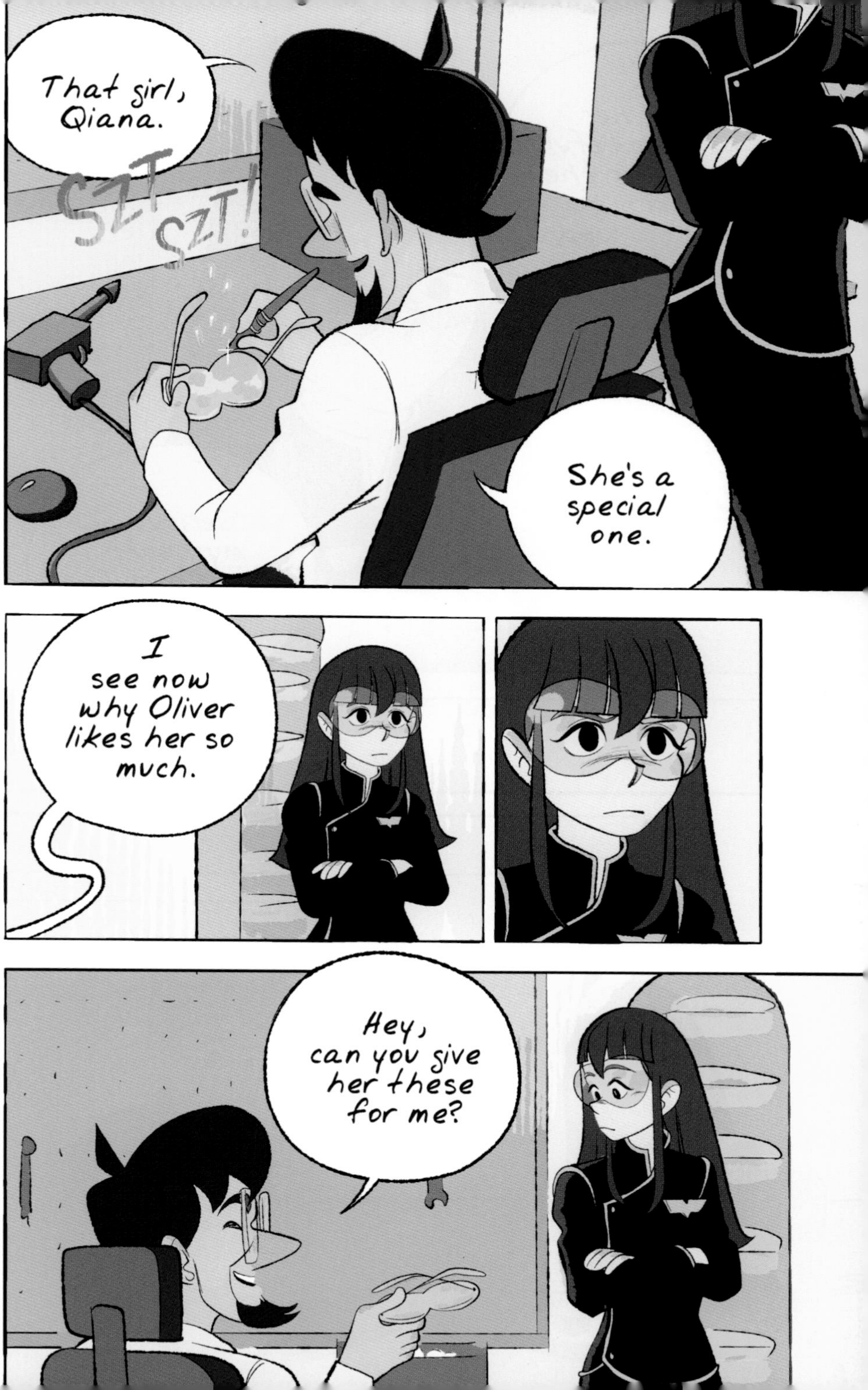
That girl, Qiana.
SZT SZT!
She's a special one.
I see now why Oliver likes her so much.
Hey, can you give her these for me?

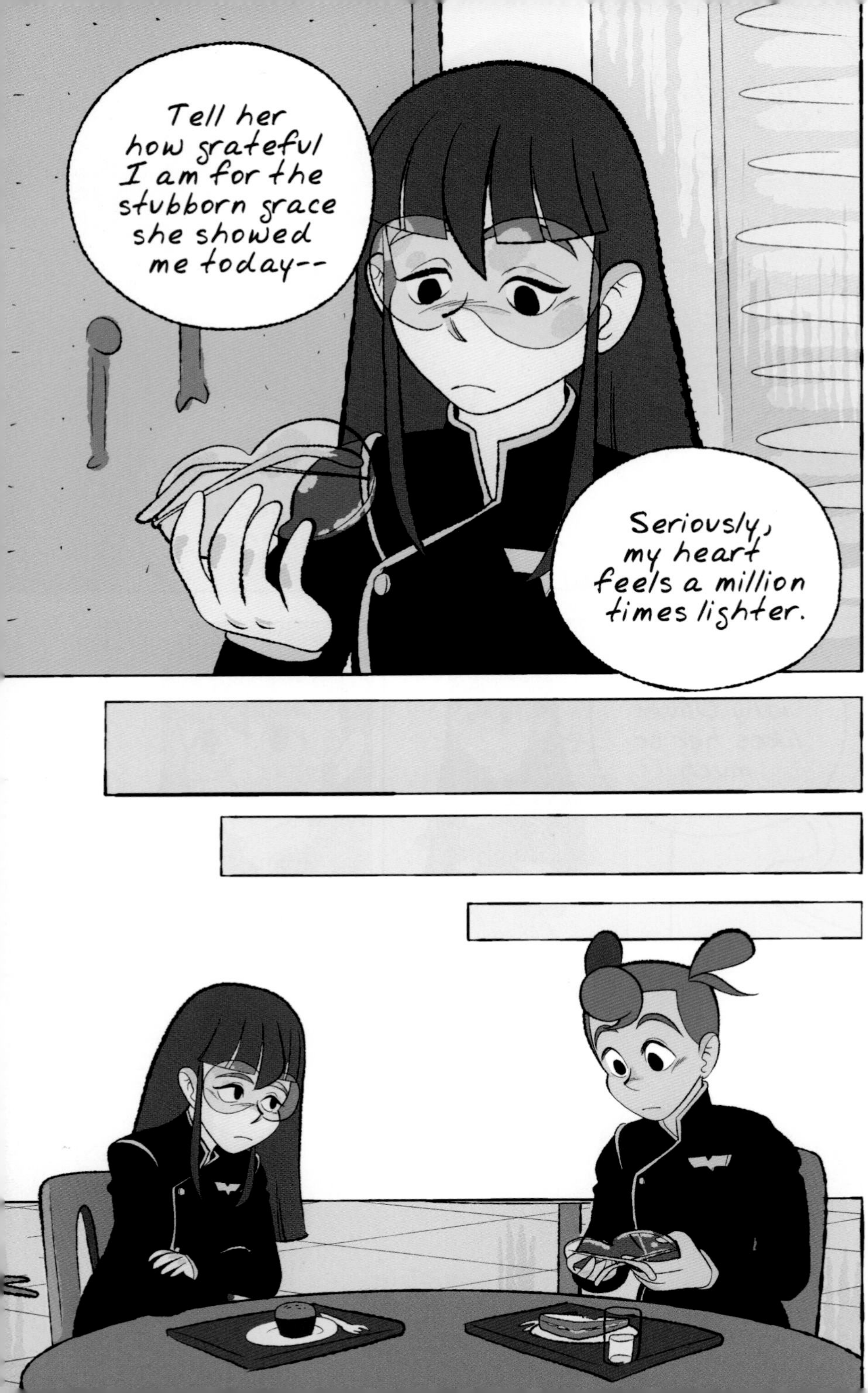
Tell her how grateful I am for the stubborn grace she showed me today--
Seriously, my heart feels a million times lighter.

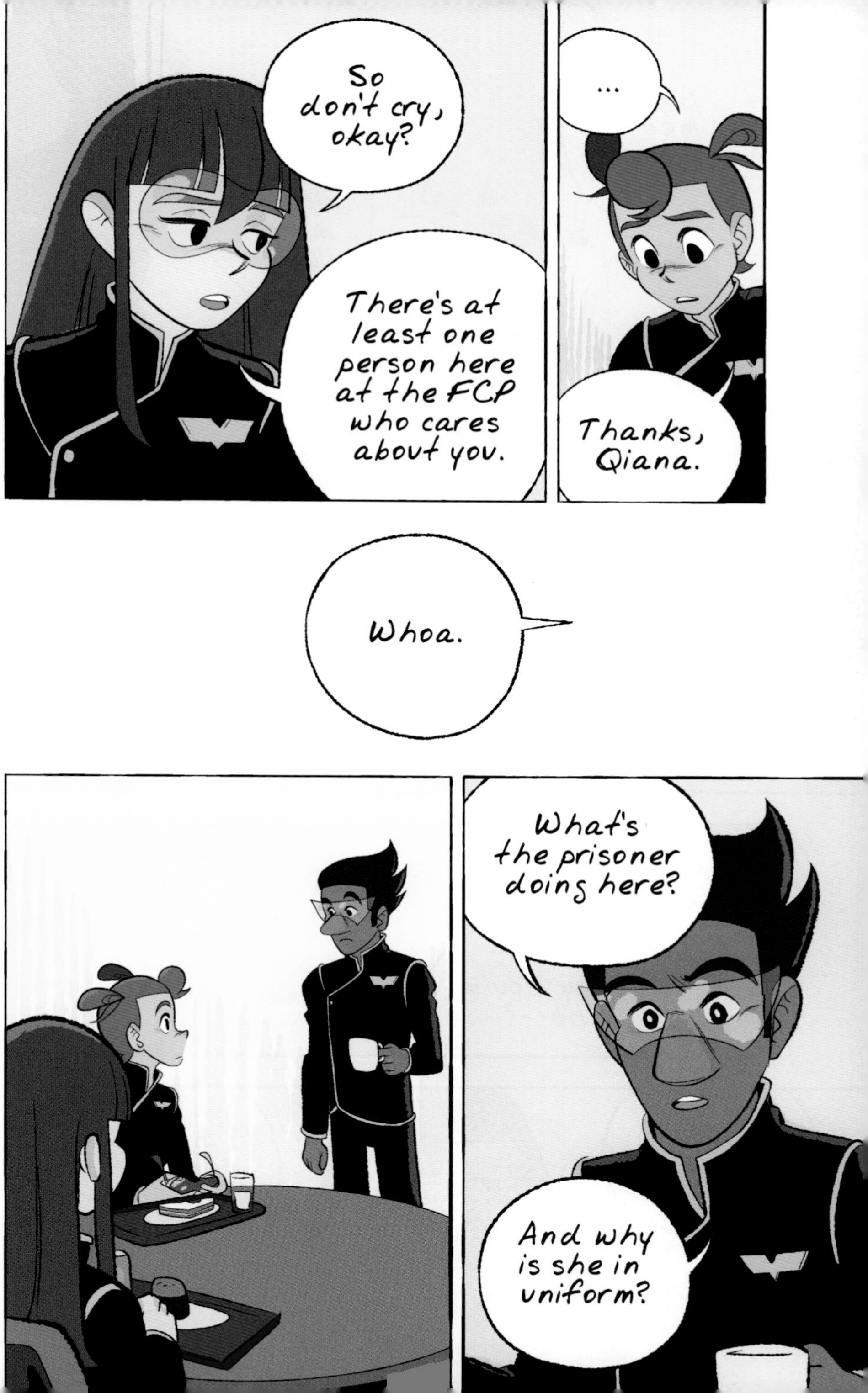
So don't cry, okay?
There's at least one person here at the FCP who cares about you.
...
Thanks, Qiana.
Whoa.
What's the prisoner doing here?
And why is she in uniform?

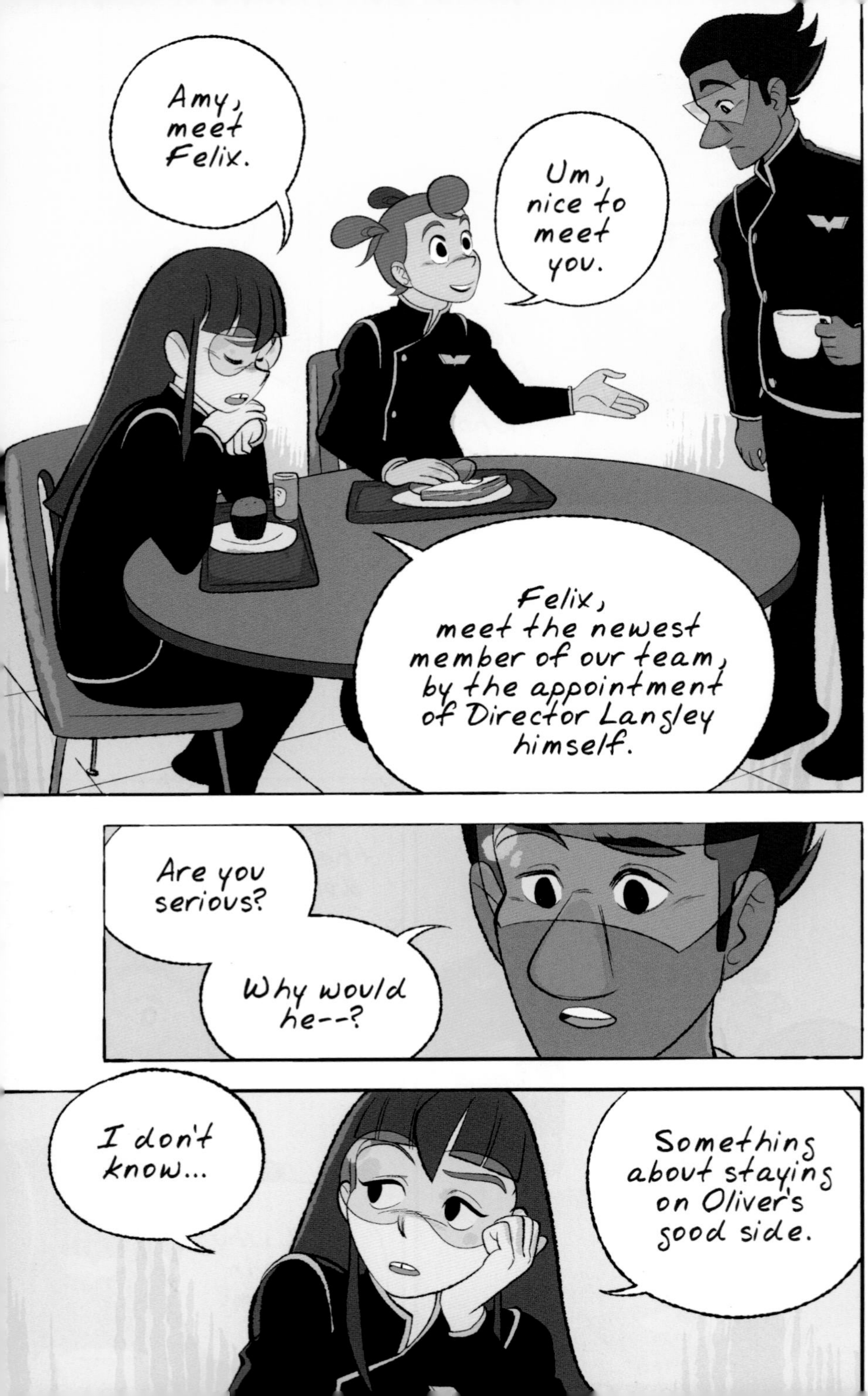
Amy, meet Felix.
Um, nice to meet you.
Felix, meet the newest member of our team, by the appointment of Director Langley himself.
Are you serious?
Why would he--?
I don't know...
Something about staying on Oliver's good side.

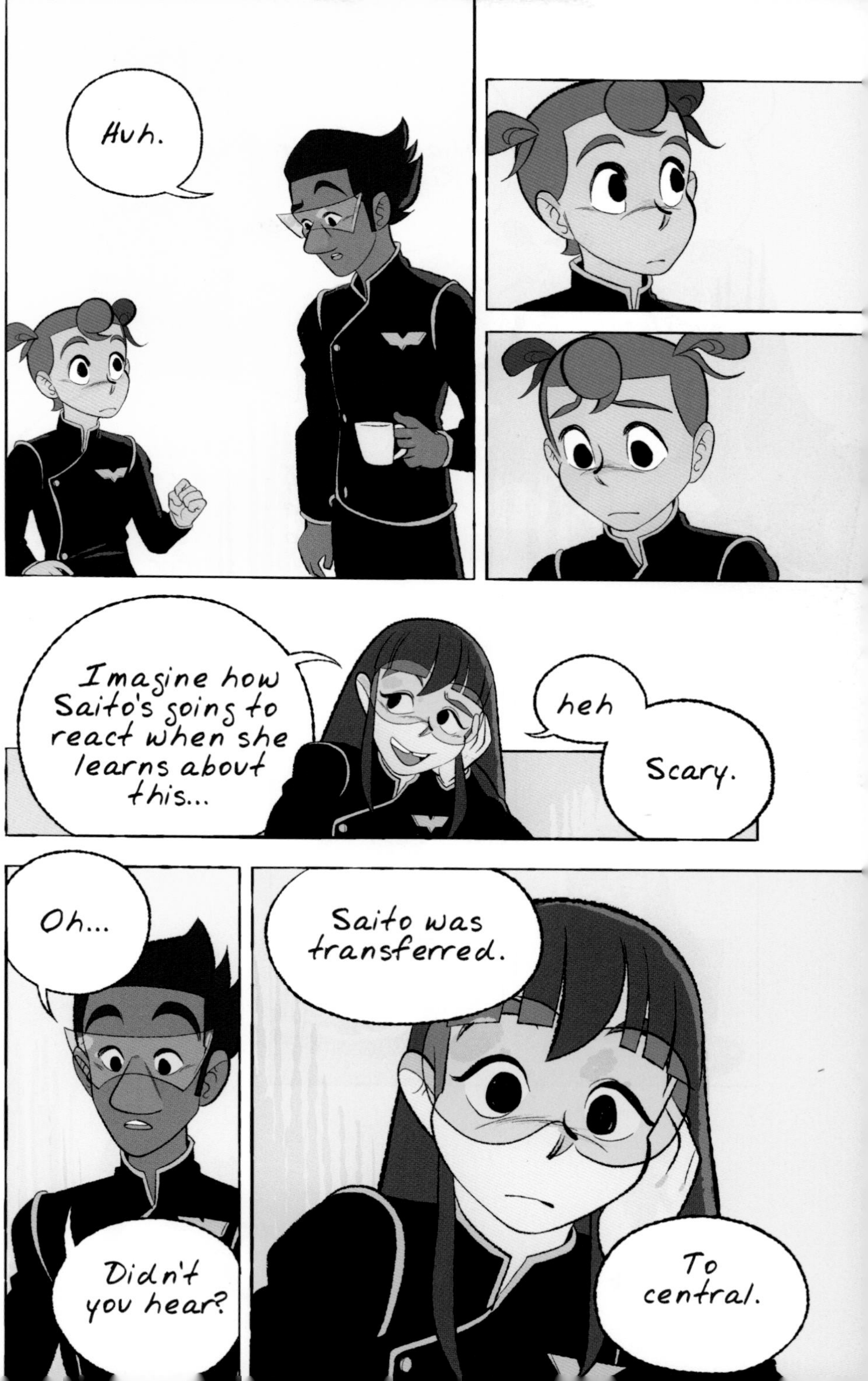
Huh.
Imagine how Saito's going to react when she learns about this...
heh
Scary.
Oh...
Didn't you hear?
Saito was transferred.
To central.

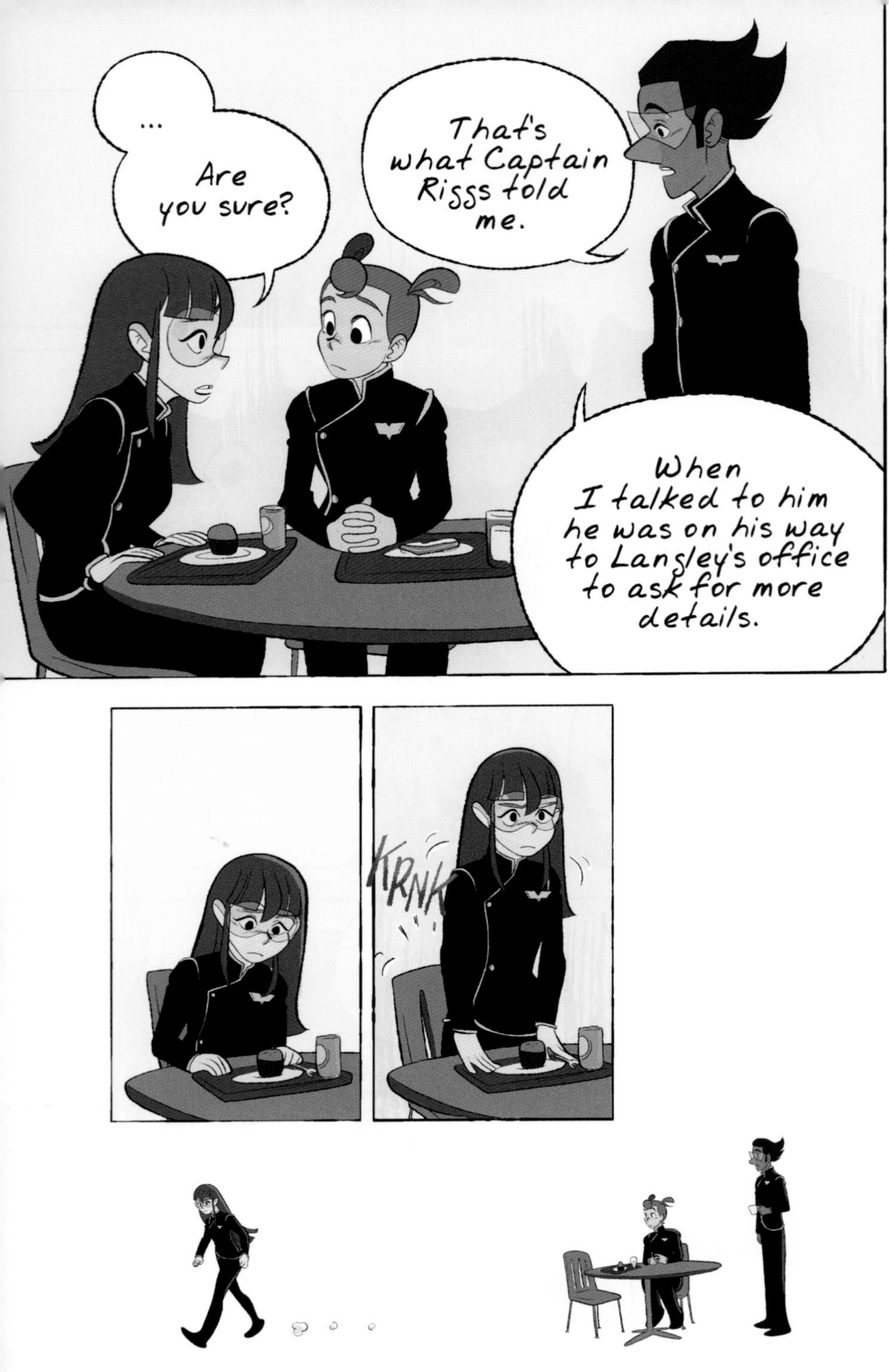
...
Are you sure?
That's what Captain Risss told me.
When I talked to him he was on his way to Langley's office to ask for more details.
KRNK

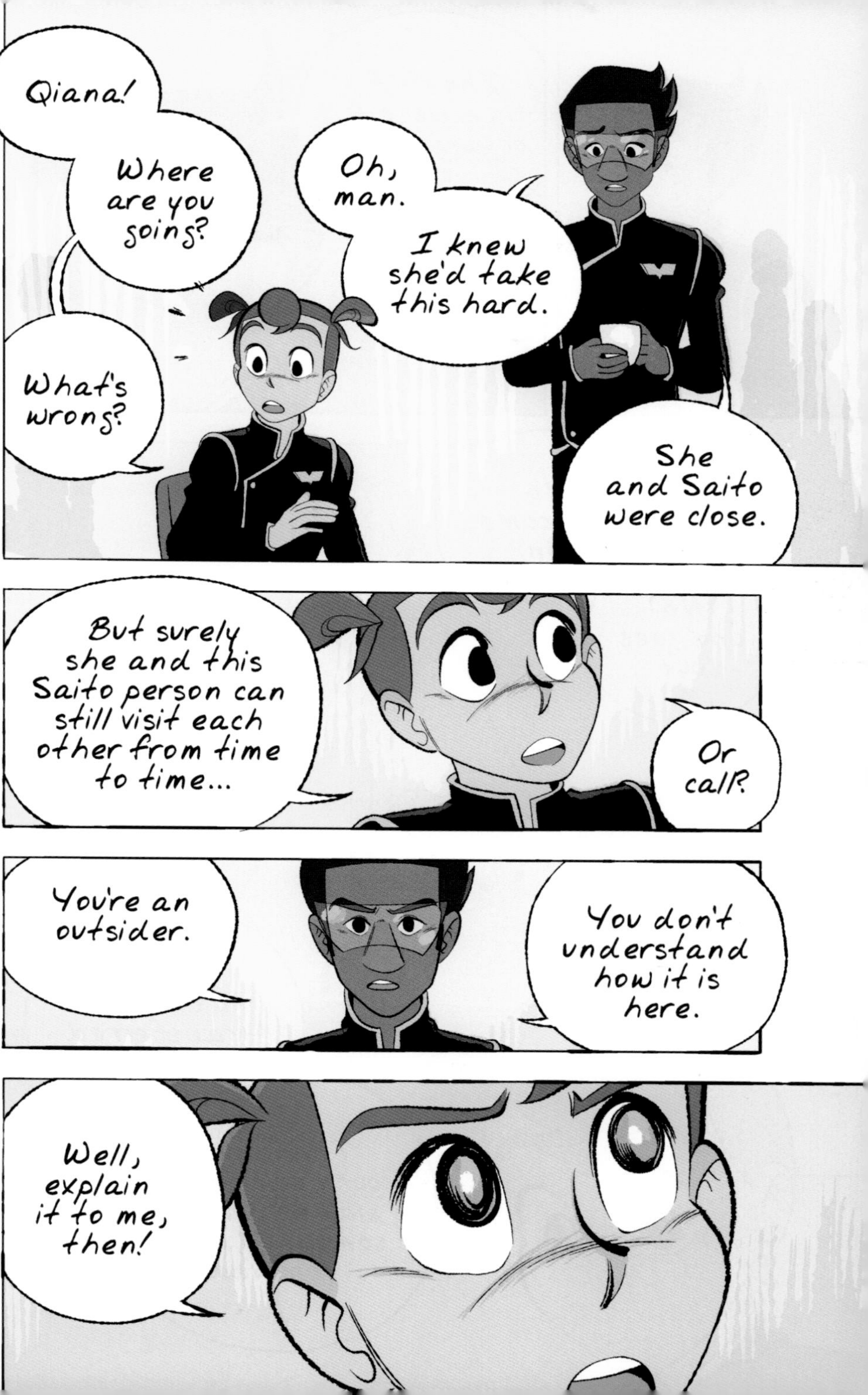
Qiana!
Where are you going?
What's wrong?
Oh, man.
I knew she'd take this hard.
She and Saito were close.
But surely she and this Saito person can still visit each other from time to time...
Or call?
You're an outsider.
You don't understand how it is here.
Well, explain it to me, then!

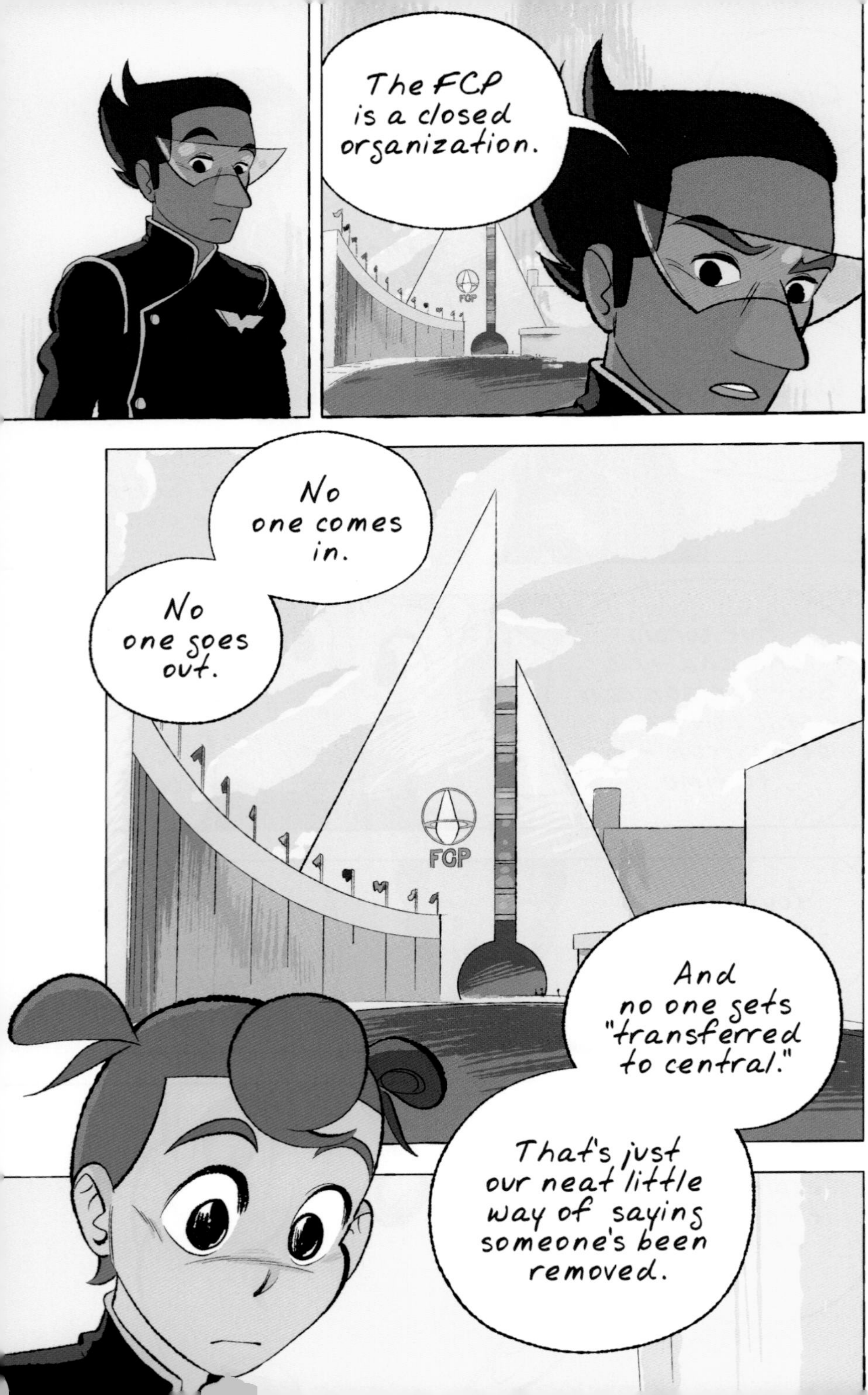
The FCP is a closed organization.
FCP
No one comes in.
No one goes out.
FCP
And no one gets "transferred to central."
That's just our neat little way of saying someone's been removed.

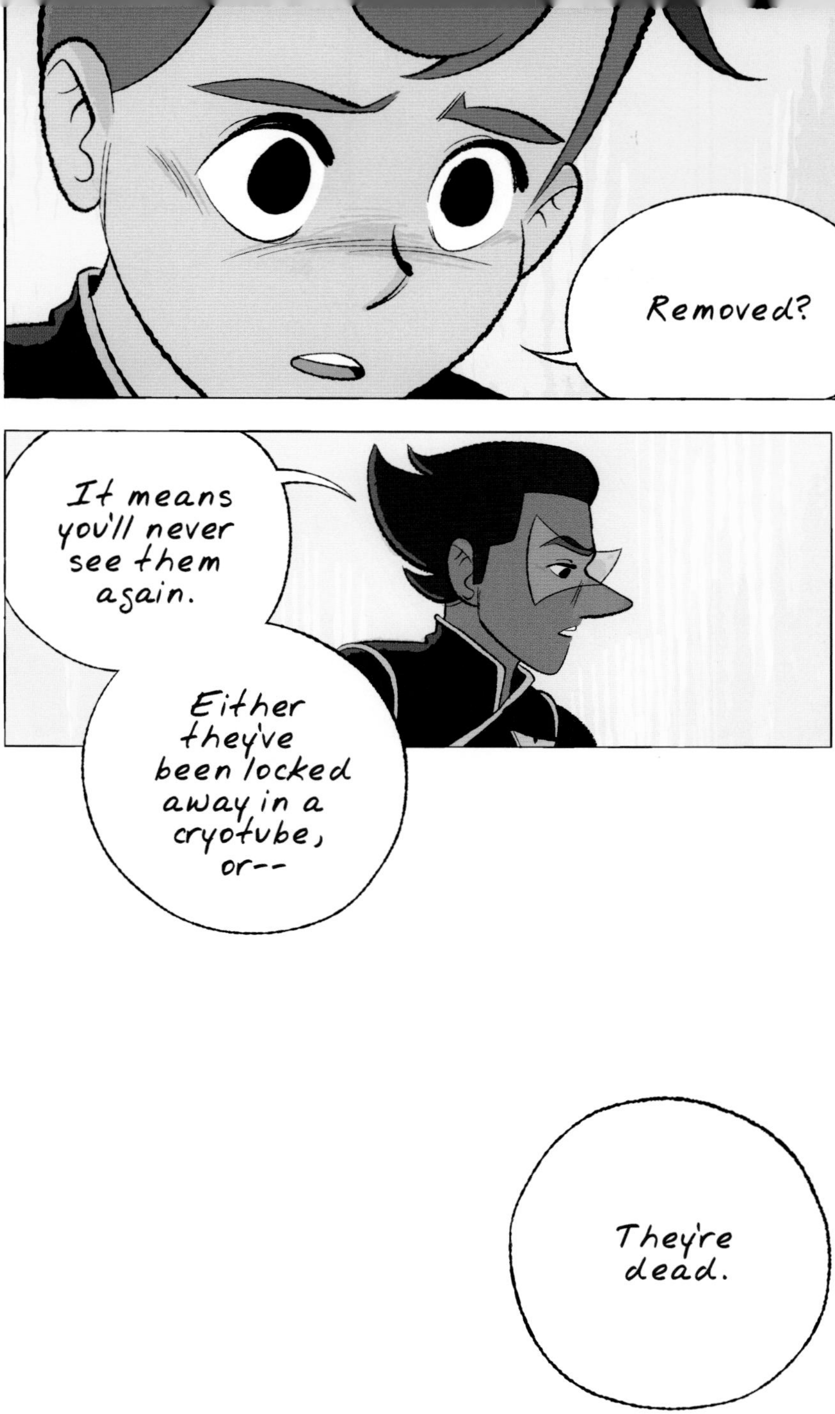
Removed?
It means you'll never see them again.
Either they've been locked away in a cryotube, or--
They're dead.

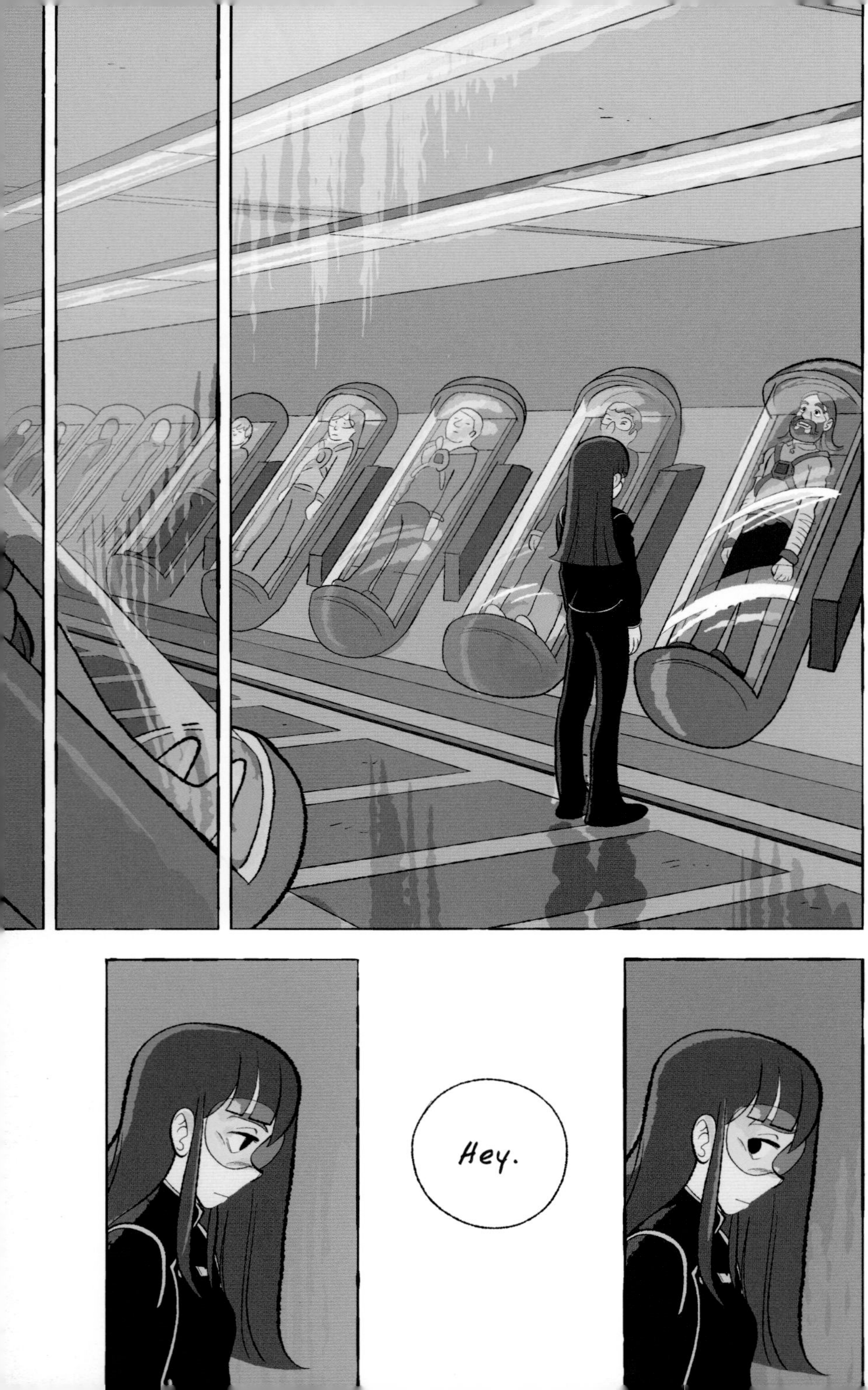
Hey.

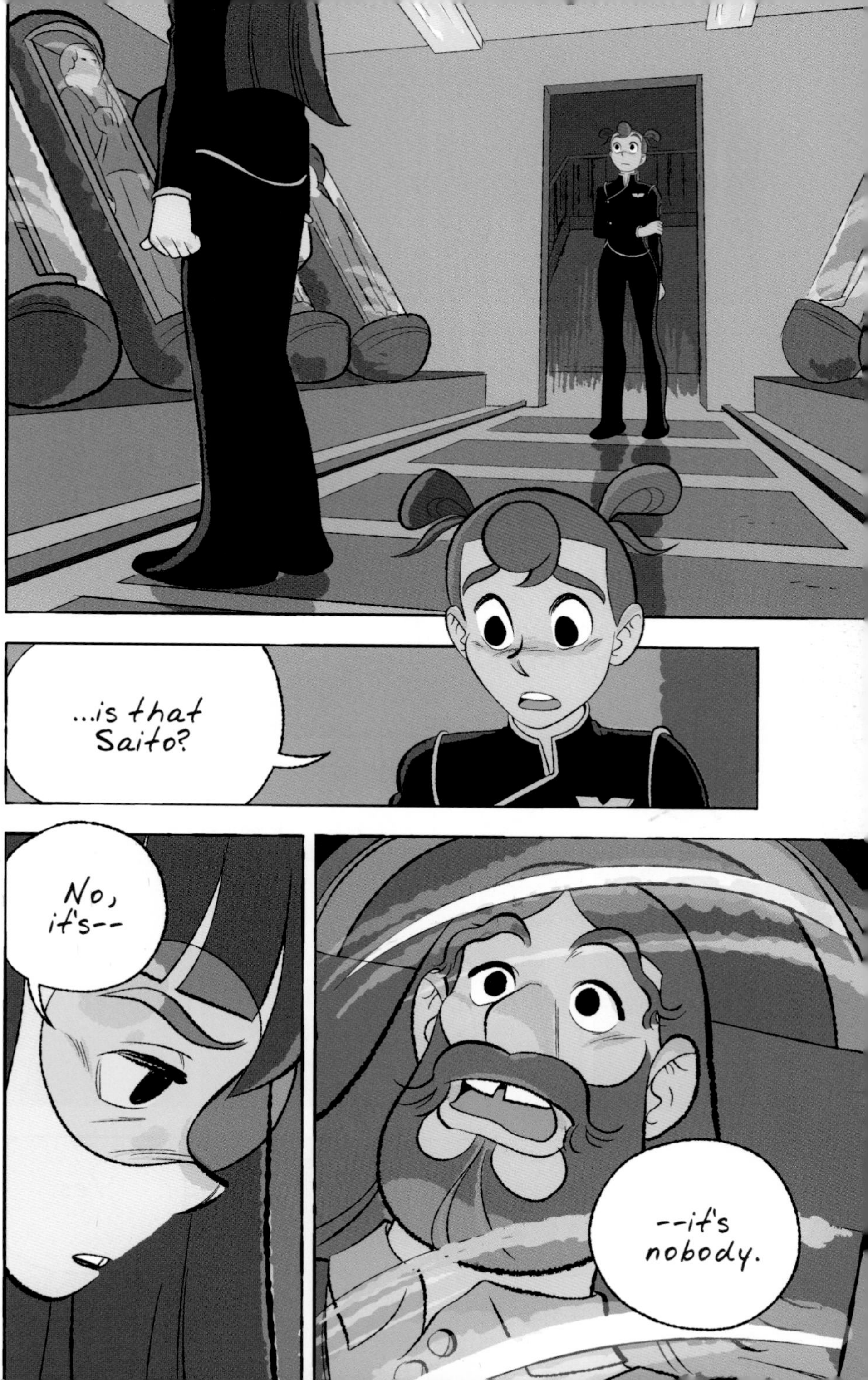
...is that Saito?
No, it's--
--it's nobody.

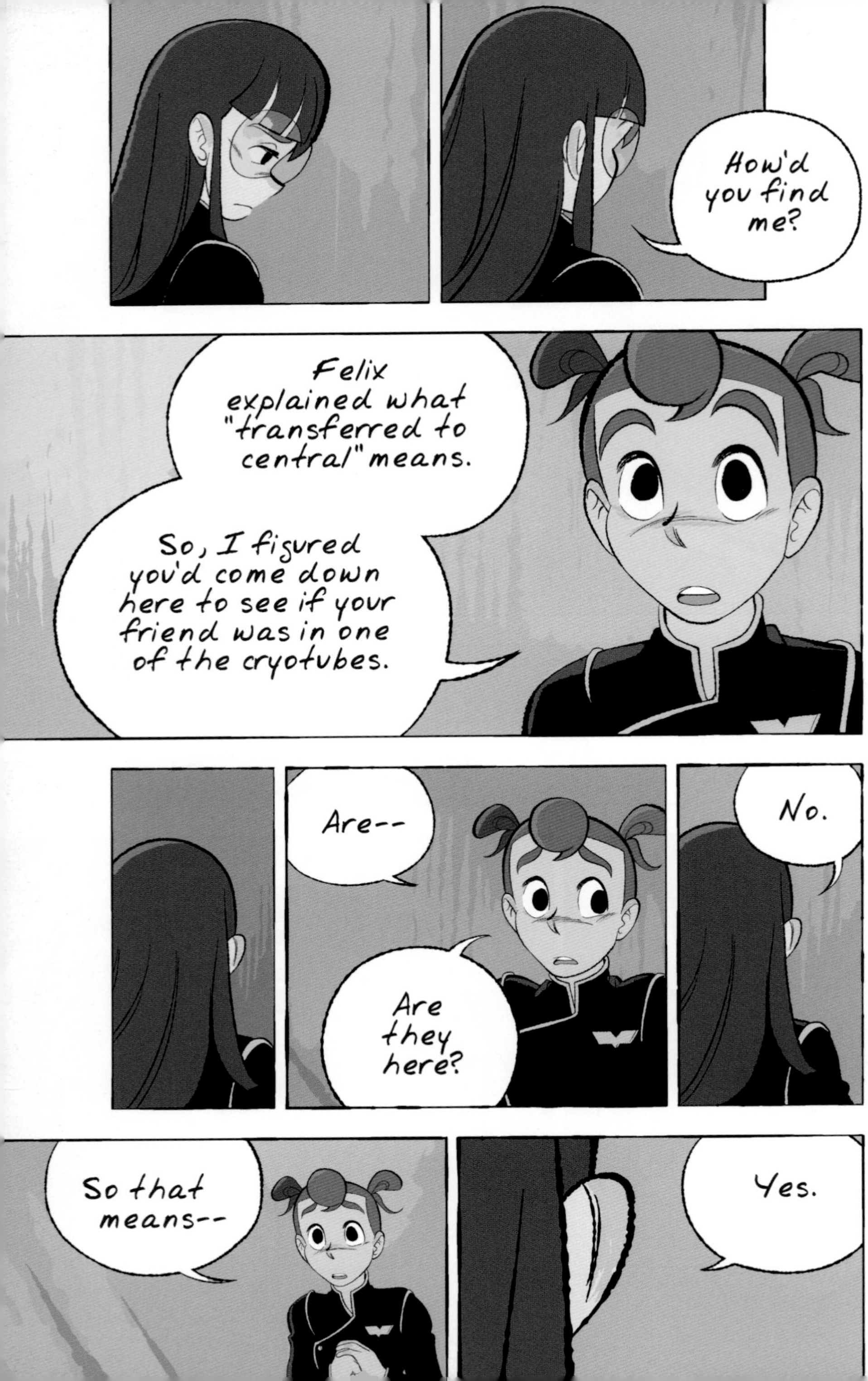
How'd you find me?
Felix explained what "transferred to central" means.
So, I figured you'd come down here to see if your friend was in one of the cryotubes.
Are--
Are they here?
No.
So that means--
Yes.

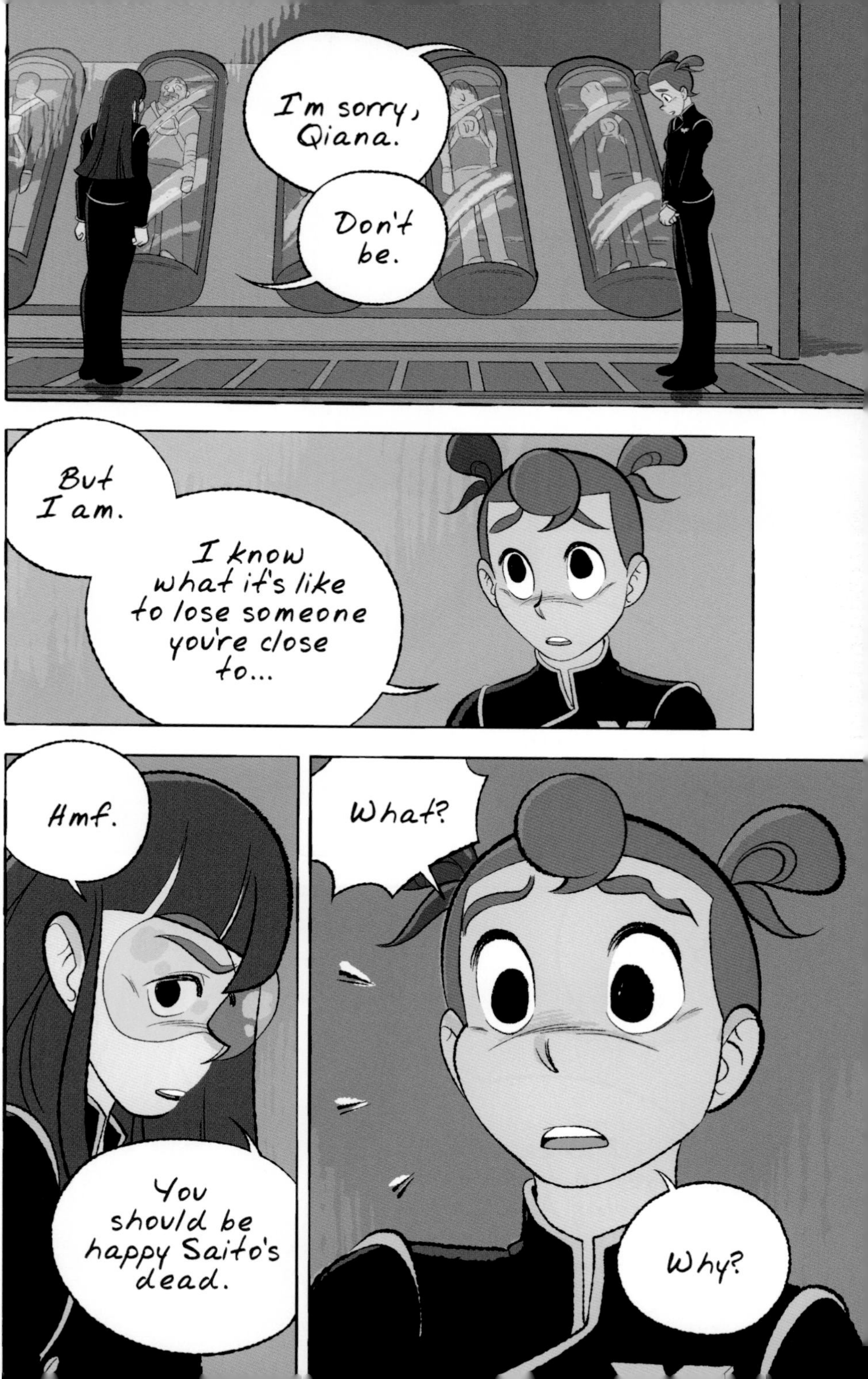
I'm sorry, Qiana.
Don't be.
But I am.
I know what it's like to lose someone you're close to...
Hmf.
What?
You should be happy Saito's dead.
Why?

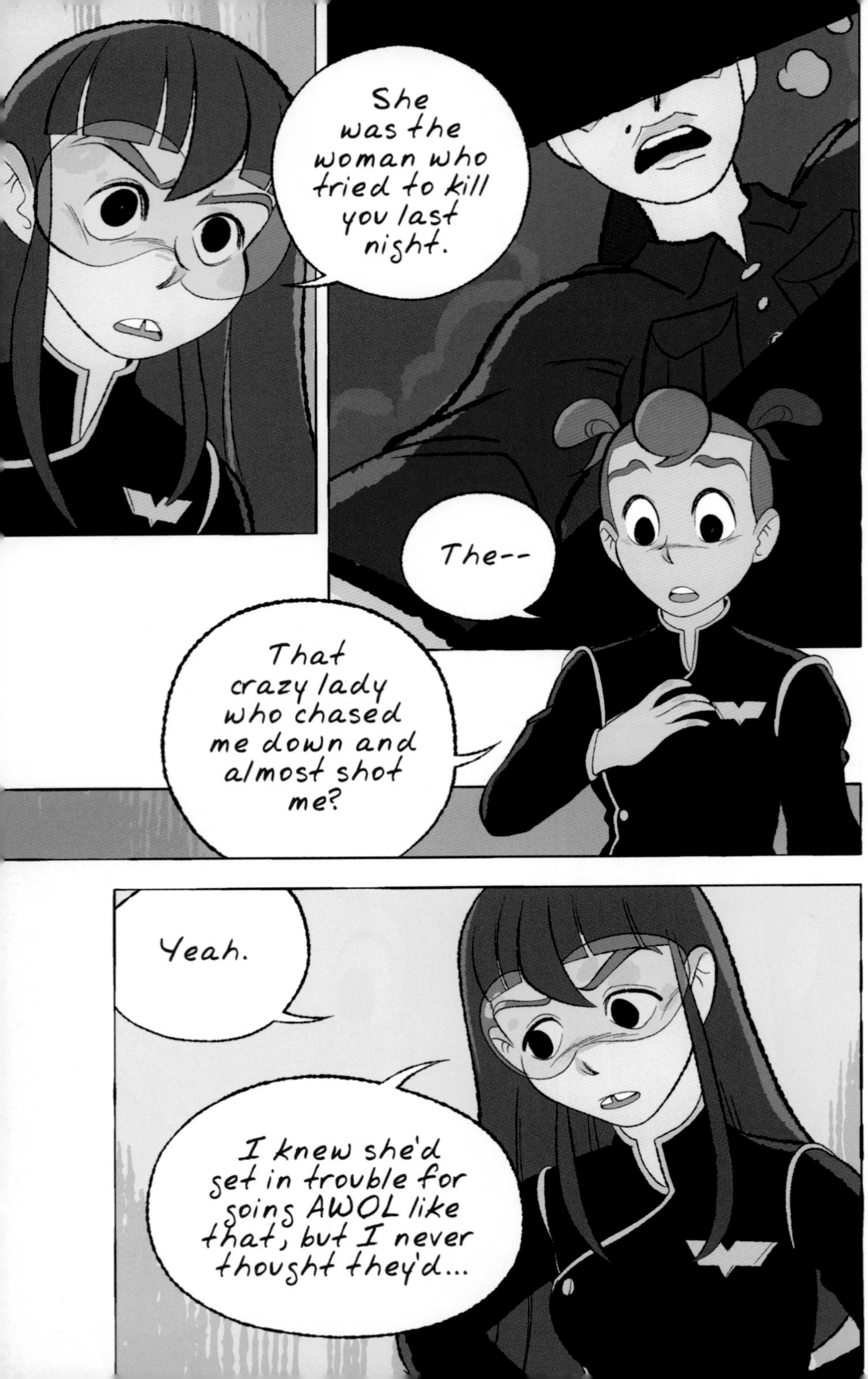
She was the woman who tried to kill you last night.
The--
That crazy lady who chased me down and almost shot me?
Yeah.
I knew she'd get in trouble for going AWOL like that, but I never thought they'd...

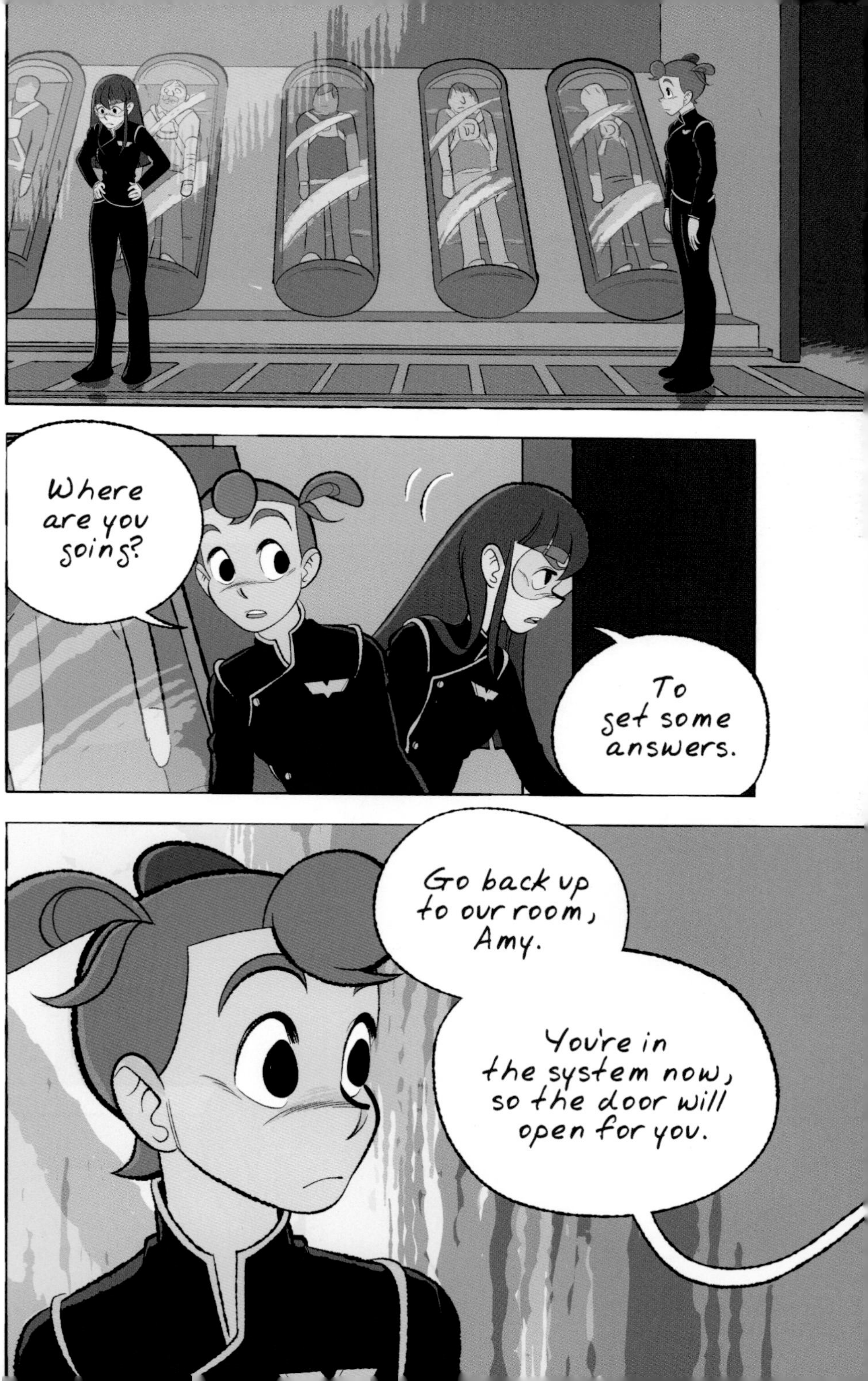
Where are you going?
To get some answers.
Go back up to our room, Amy.
You're in the system now, so the door will open for you.

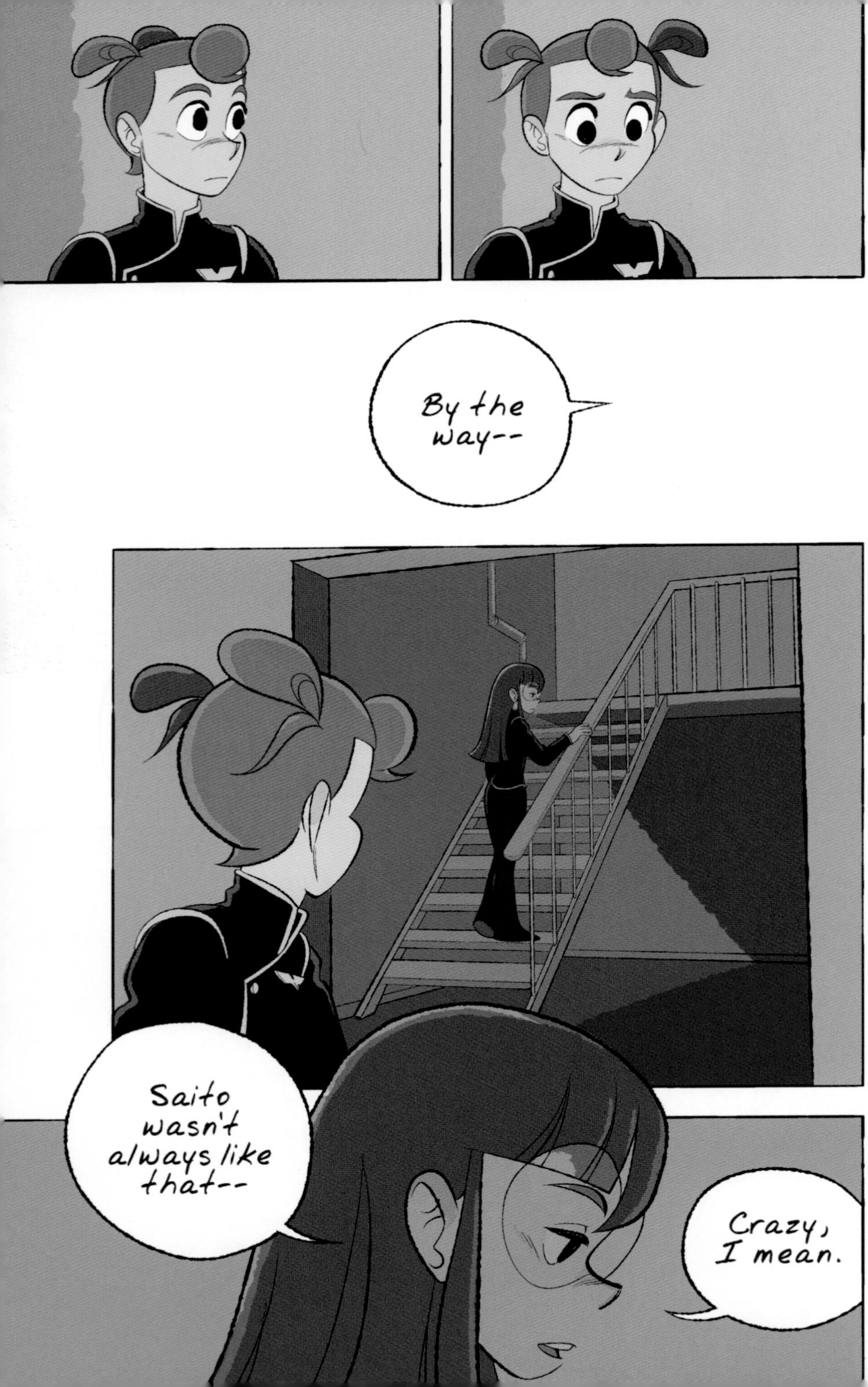
By the way--
Saito wasn't always like that--
Crazy, I mean.

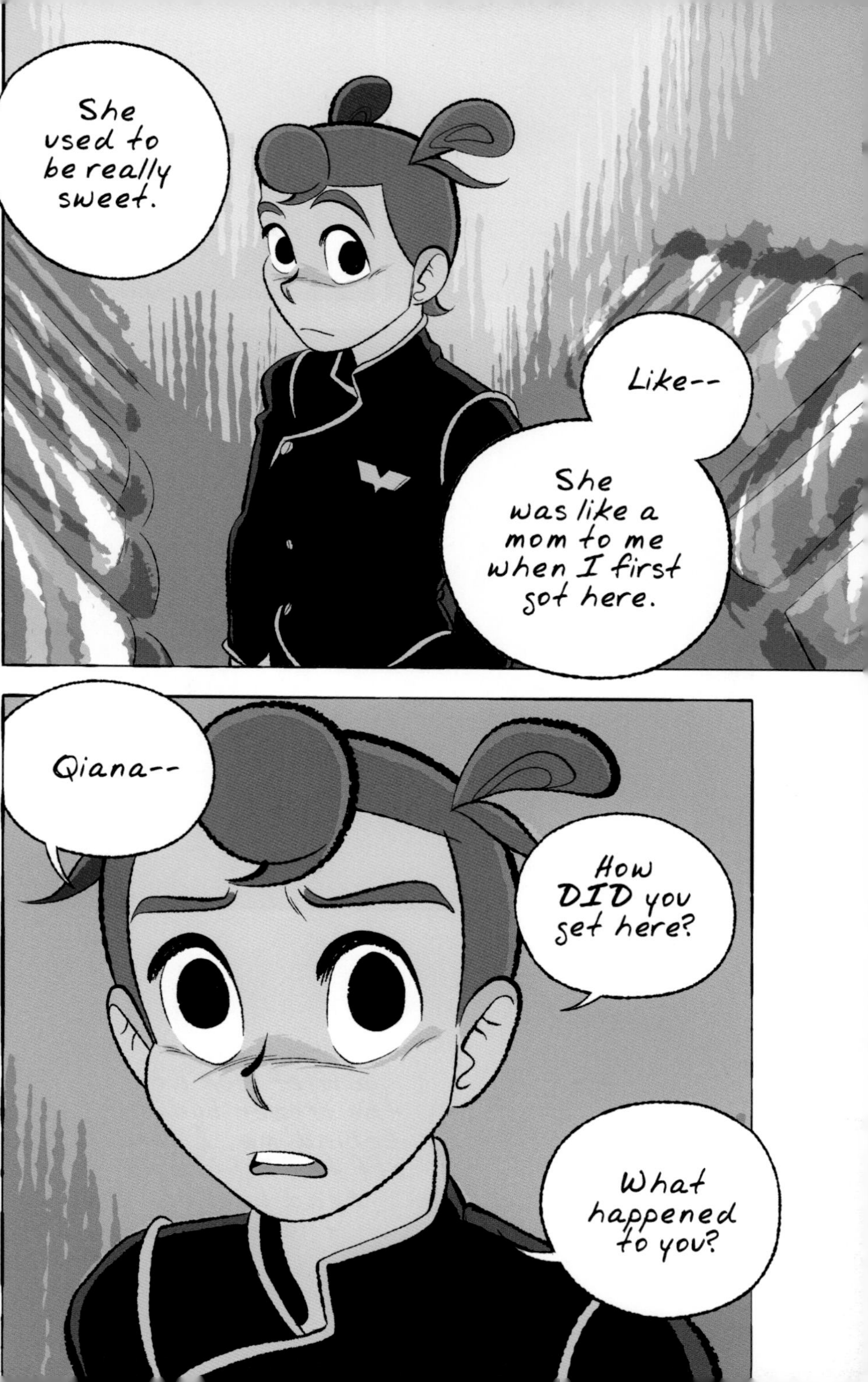
She used to be really sweet.
Like--
She was like a mom to me when I first got here.
Qiana--
How **DID** you get here?
What happened to you?

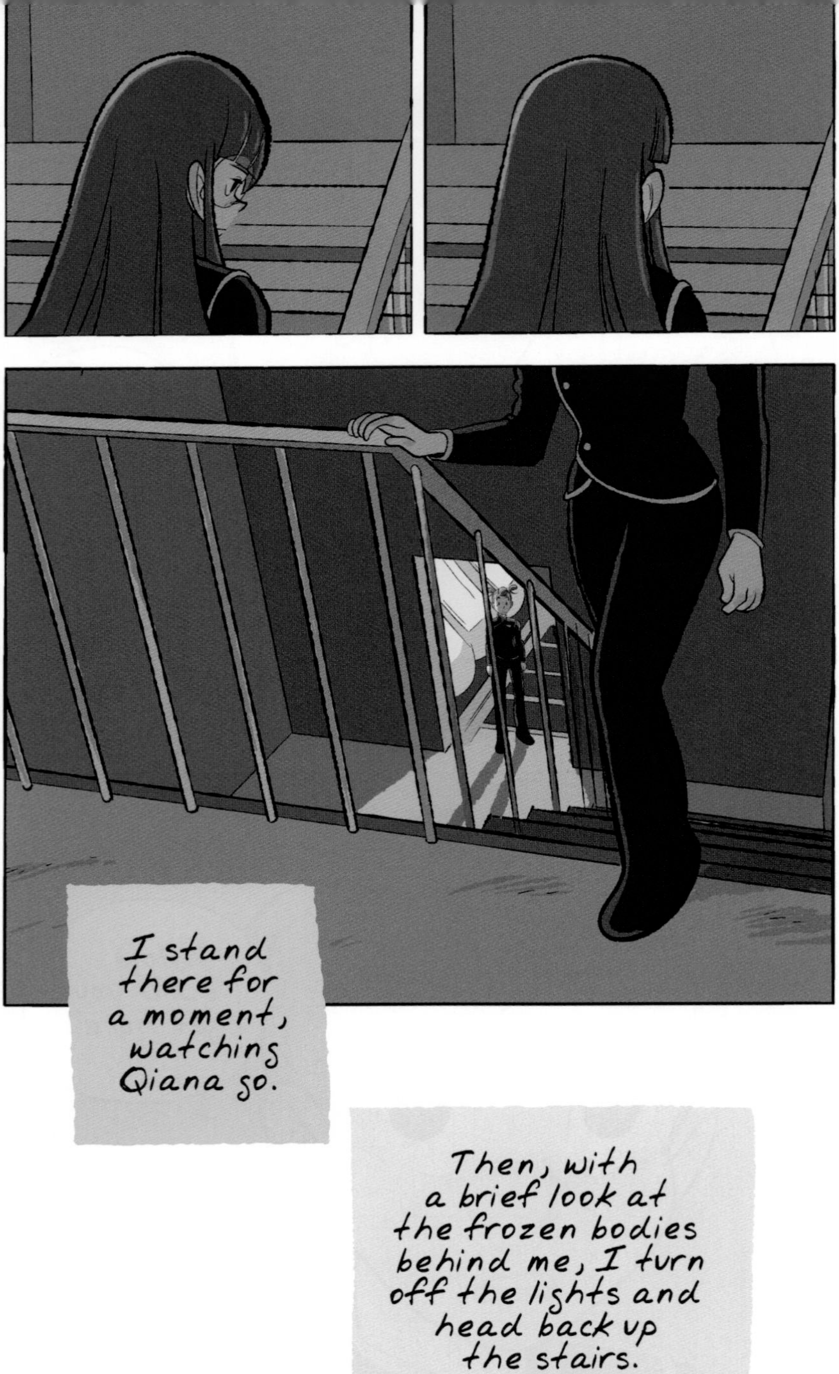
I stand there for a moment, watching Qiana go.
Then, with a brief look at the frozen bodies behind me, I turn off the lights and head back up the stairs.

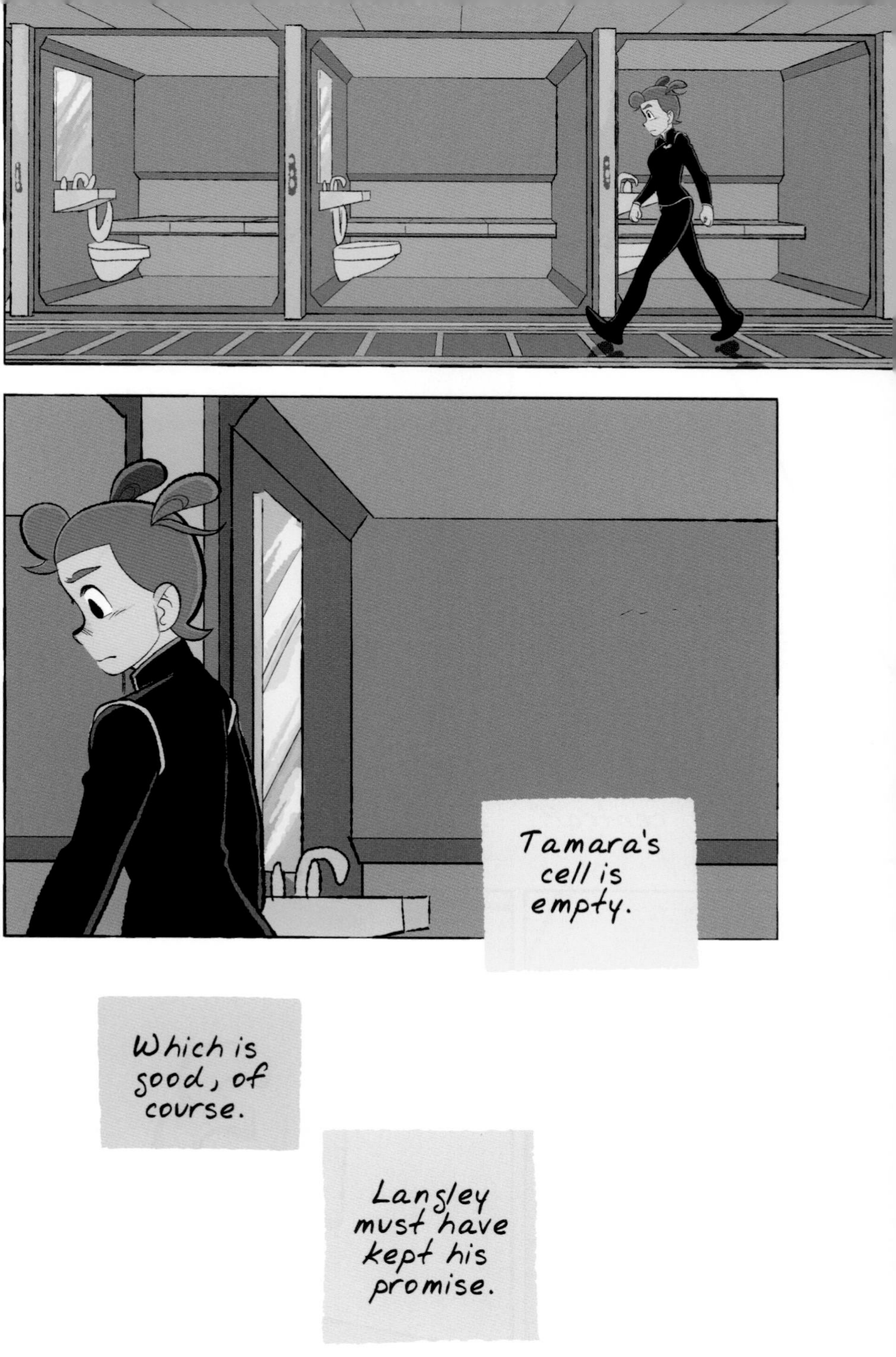
Tamara's cell is empty.
Which is good, of course.
Langley must have kept his promise.

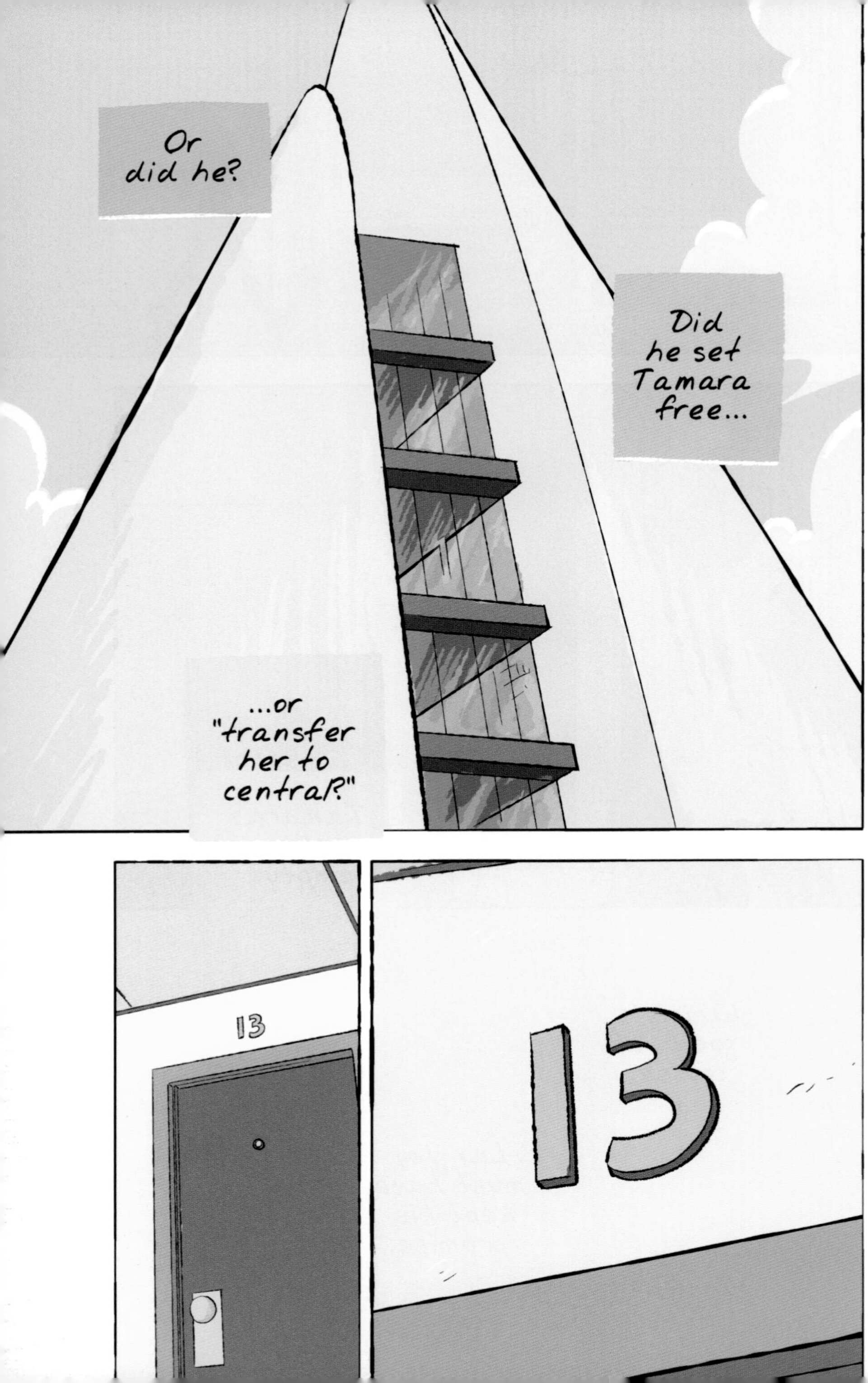
Or did he?
Did he set Tamara free...
...or "transfer her to central?"
13
13

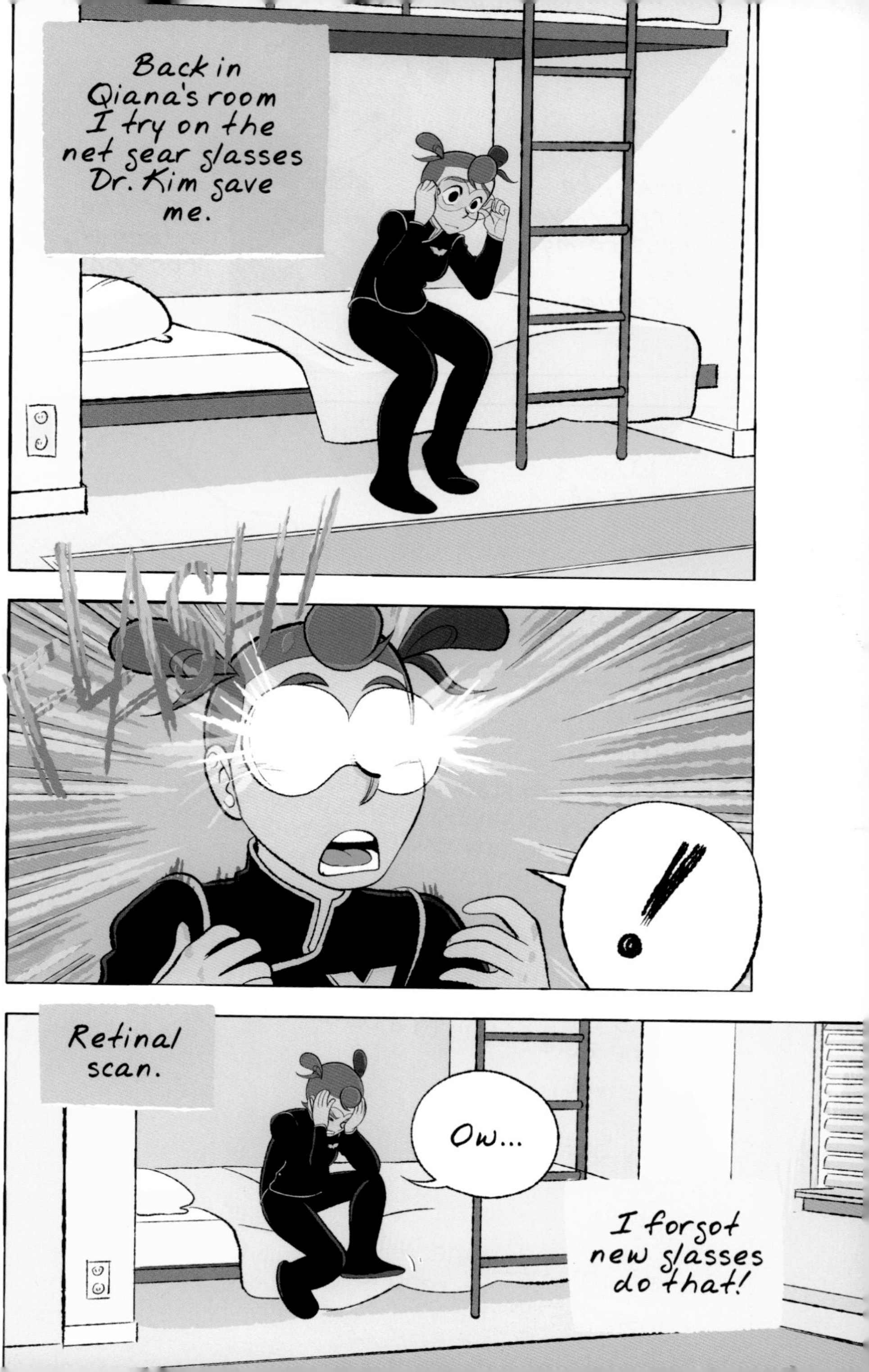
Back in Qiana's room I try on the net gear glasses Dr. Kim gave me.
!
Retinal scan.
Ow...
I forgot new glasses do that!

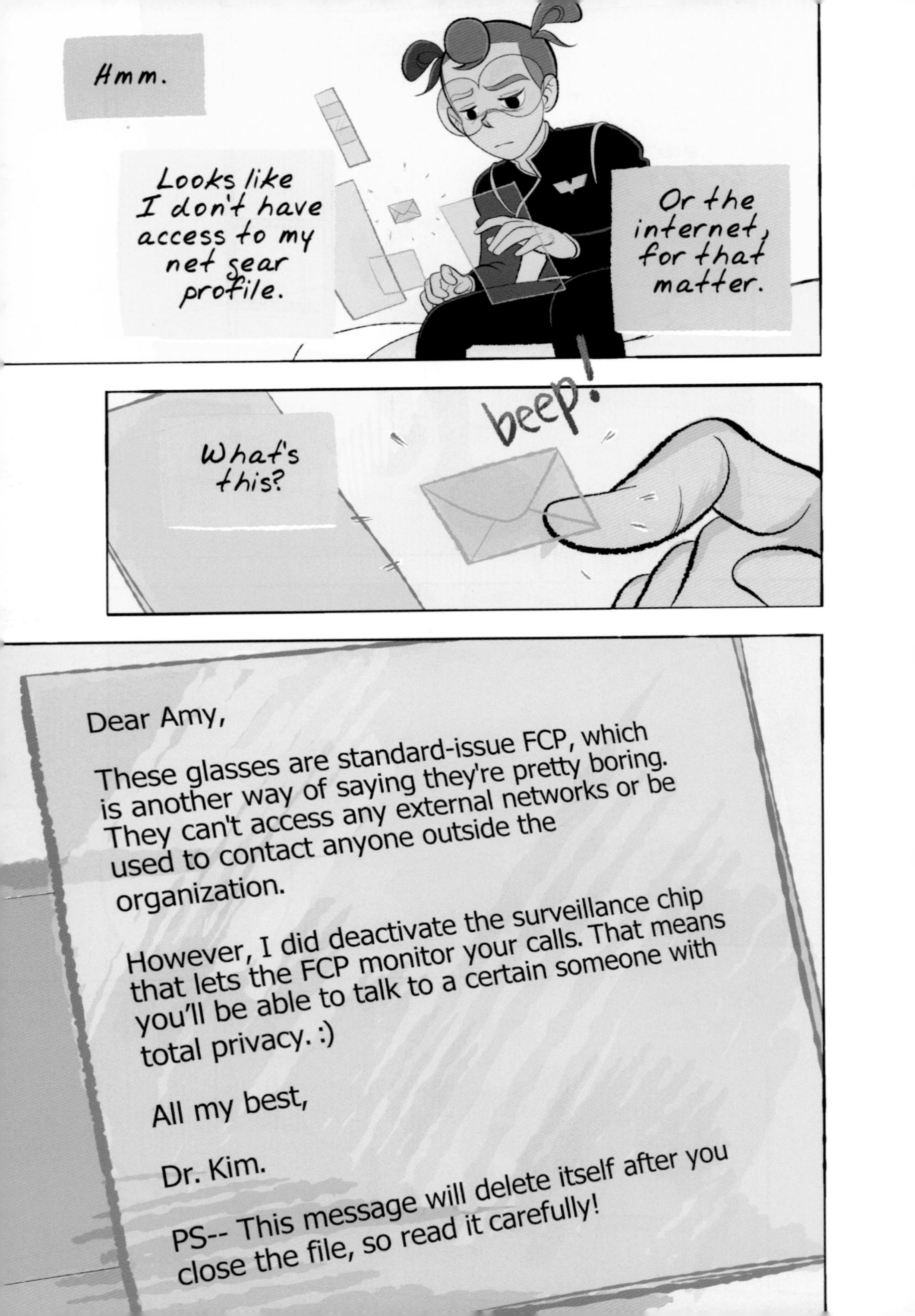
Hmm.
Looks like I don't have access to my net gear profile.
Or the internet, for that matter.
beep!
What's this?
Dear Amy,
These glasses are standard-issue FCP, which is another way of saying they're pretty boring. They can't access any external networks or be used to contact anyone outside the organization.
However, I did deactivate the surveillance chip that lets the FCP monitor your calls. That means you'll be able to talk to a certain someone with total privacy. :)
All my best,
Dr. Kim.
PS-- This message will delete itself after you close the file, so read it carefully!

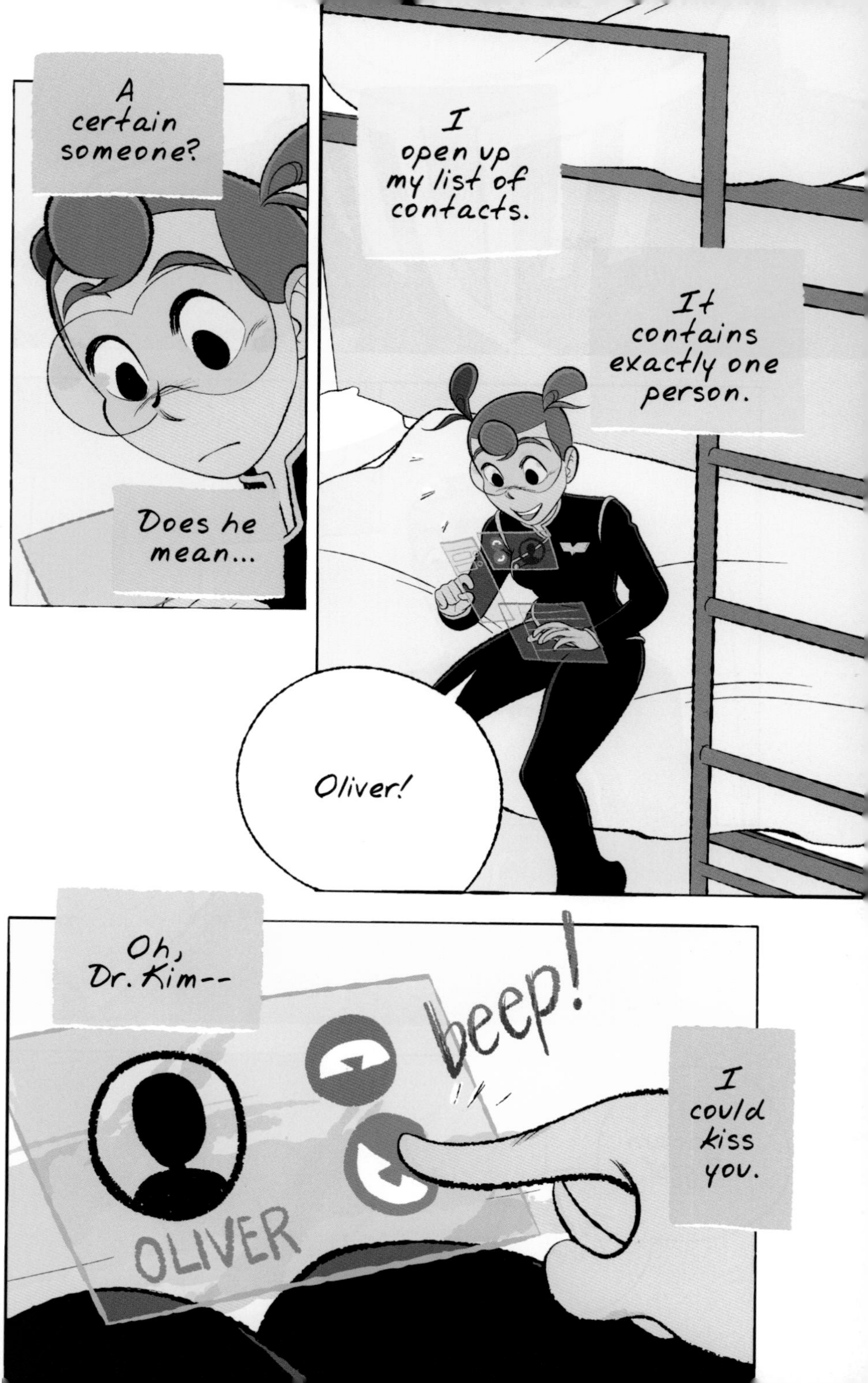
A certain someone?
Does he mean...
I open up my list of contacts.
It contains exactly one person.
Oliver!
Oh, Dr. Kim--
beep!
OLIVER
I could kiss you.

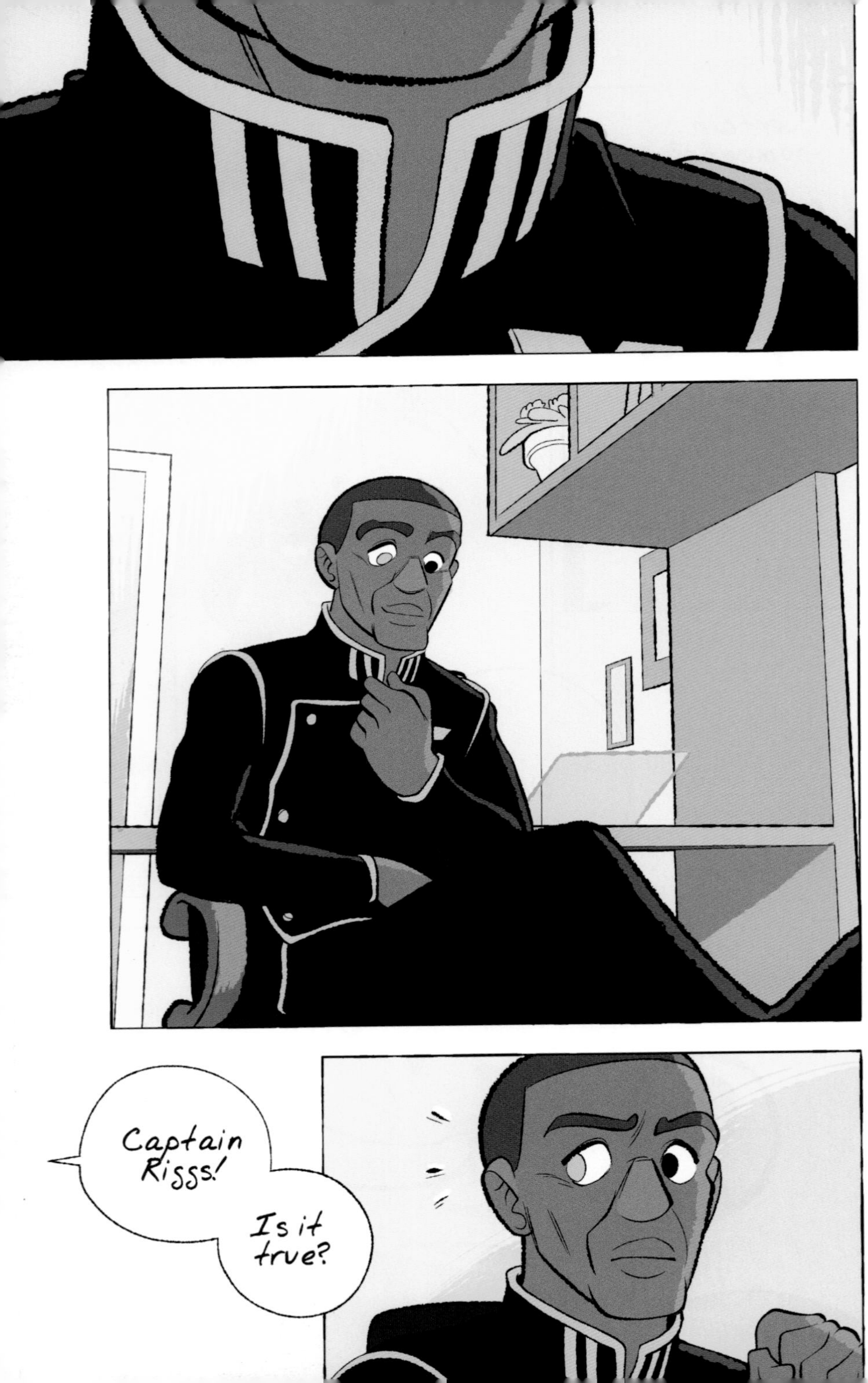
Captain Risss!
Is it true?

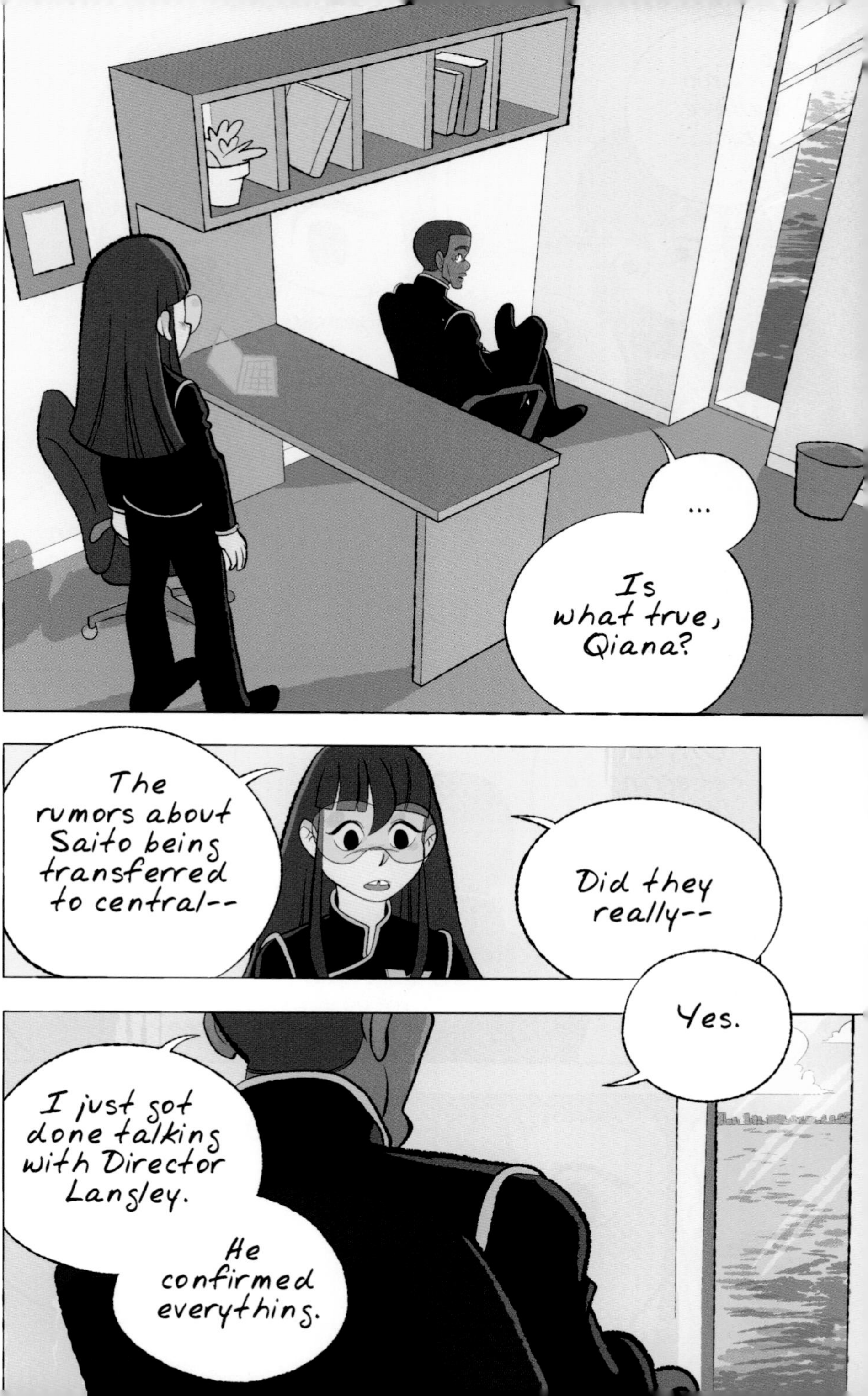
...
Is what true, Qiana?
The rumors about Saito being transferred to central--
Did they really--
Yes.
I just got done talking with Director Langley.
He confirmed everything.

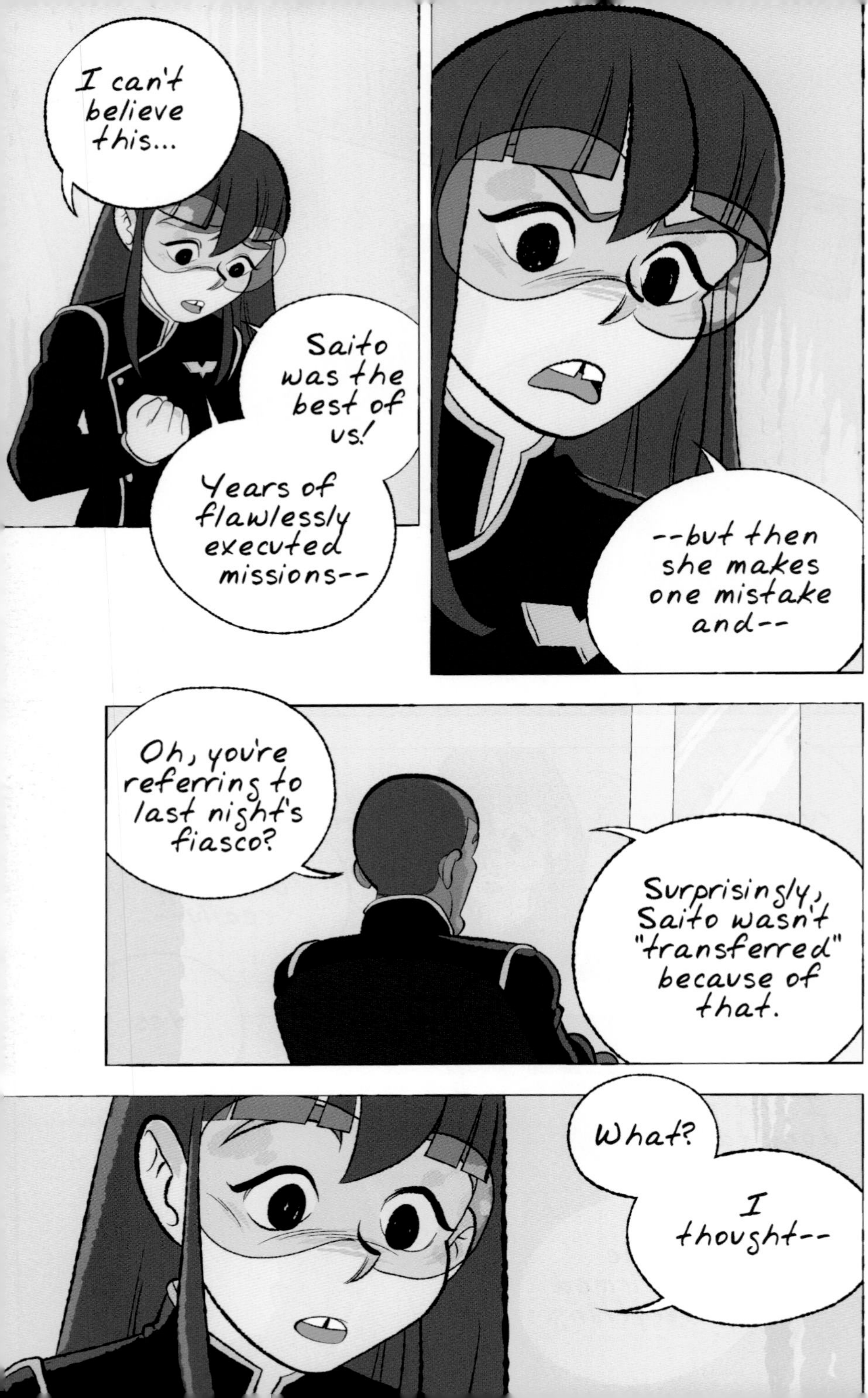
I can't believe this...
Saito was the best of us!
Years of flawlessly executed missions--
--but then she makes one mistake and--
Oh, you're referring to last night's fiasco?
Surprisingly, Saito wasn't "transferred" because of that.
What?
I thought--

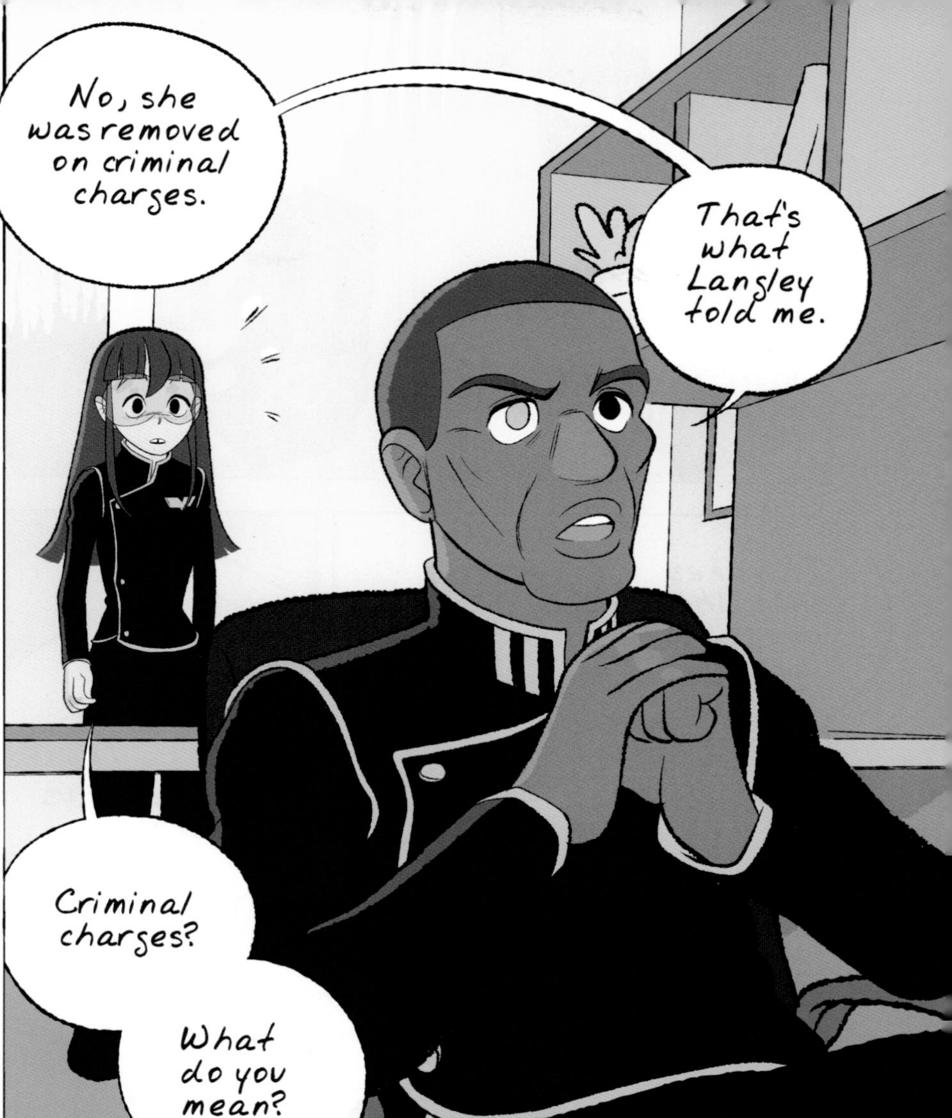
No, she was removed on criminal charges.
That's what Langley told me.
Criminal charges?
What do you mean?

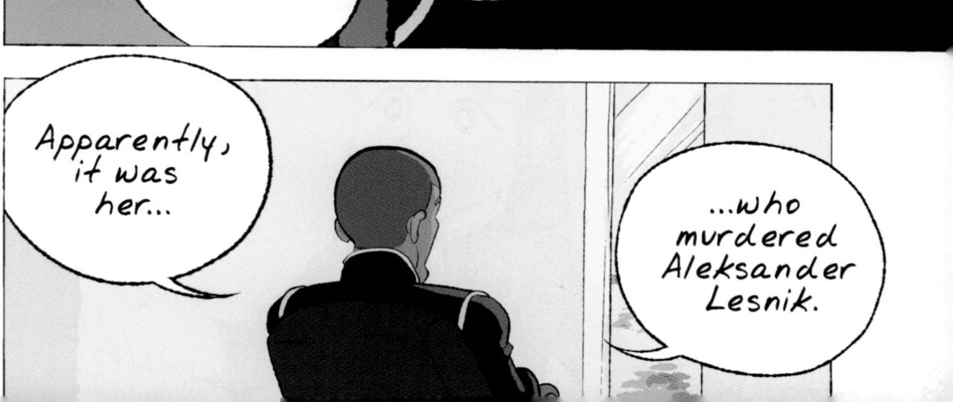
Apparently, it was her...
...who murdered Aleksander Lesnik.

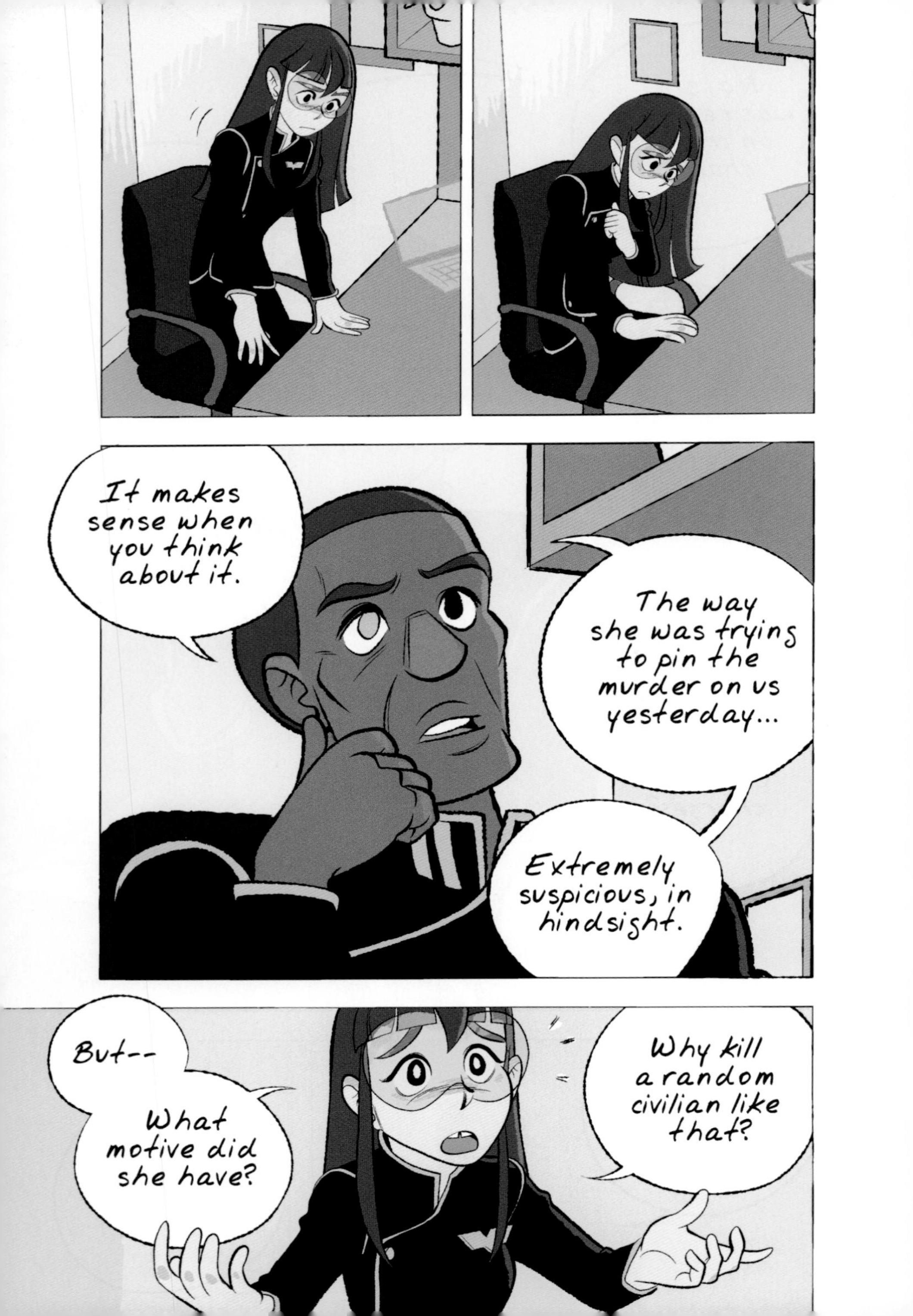
It makes sense when you think about it.
The way she was trying to pin the murder on us yesterday...
Extremely suspicious, in hindsight.
But--
What motive did she have?
Why kill a random civilian like that?

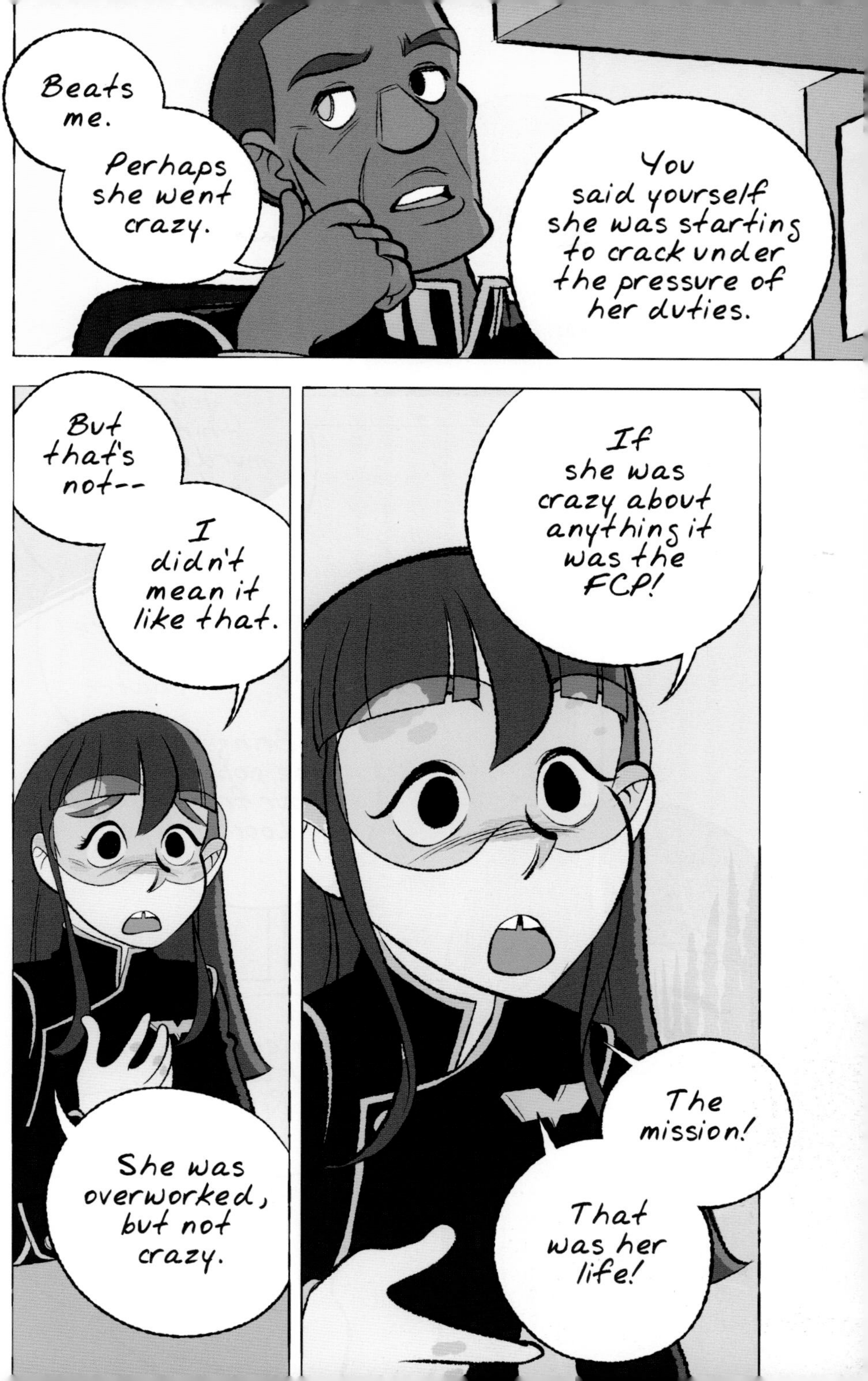
Beats me.
Perhaps she went crazy.
You said yourself she was starting to crack under the pressure of her duties.
But that's not--
I didn't mean it like that.
She was overworked, but not crazy.
If she was crazy about anything it was the FCP!
The mission!
That was her life!

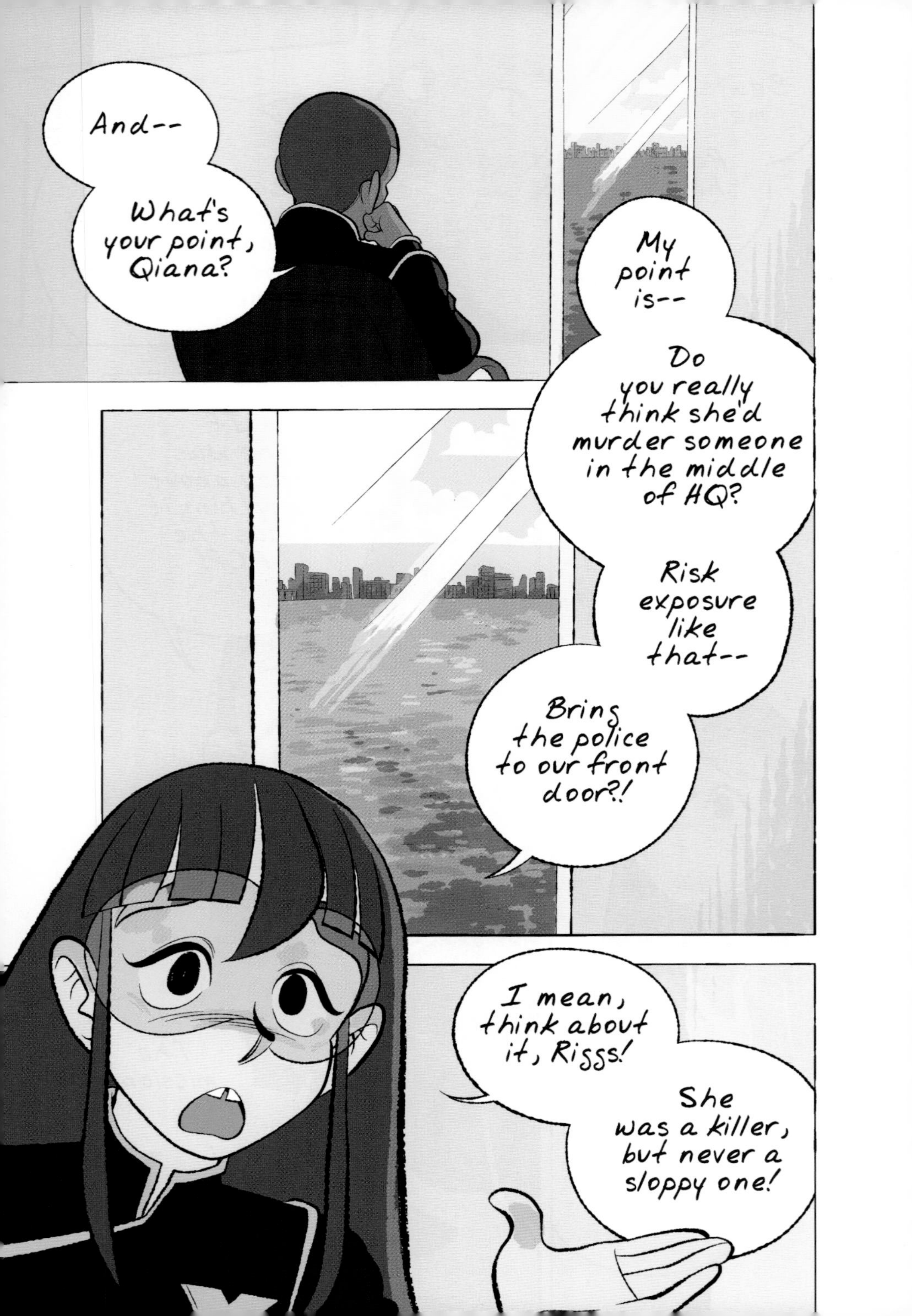
And--
What's your point, Qiana?
My point is--
Do you really think she'd murder someone in the middle of HQ?
Risk exposure like that--
Bring the police to our front door?!
I mean, think about it, Risss!
She was a killer, but never a sloppy one!

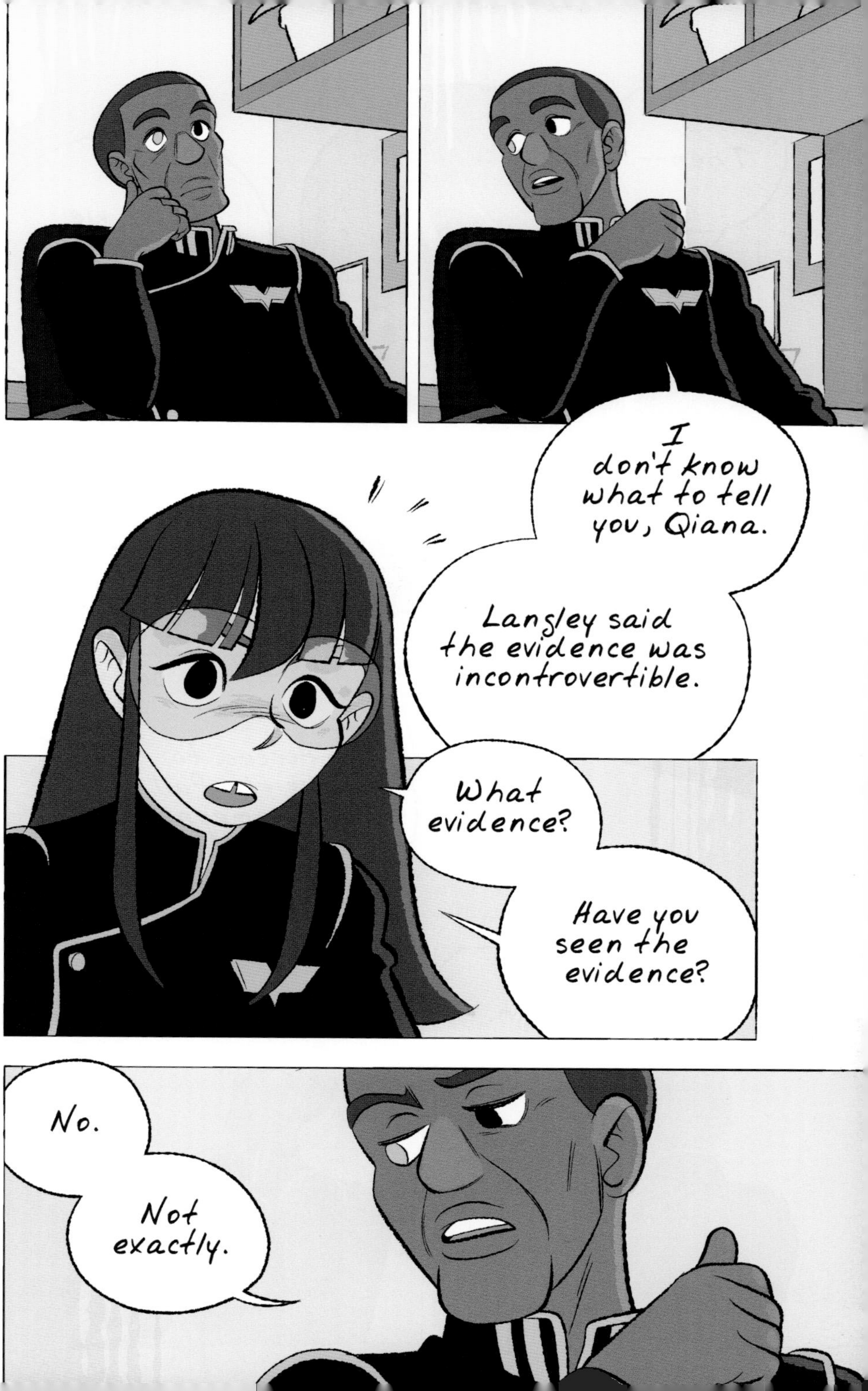
I don't know what to tell you, Qiana.
Langley said the evidence was incontrovertible.
What evidence?
Have you seen the evidence?
No.
Not exactly.

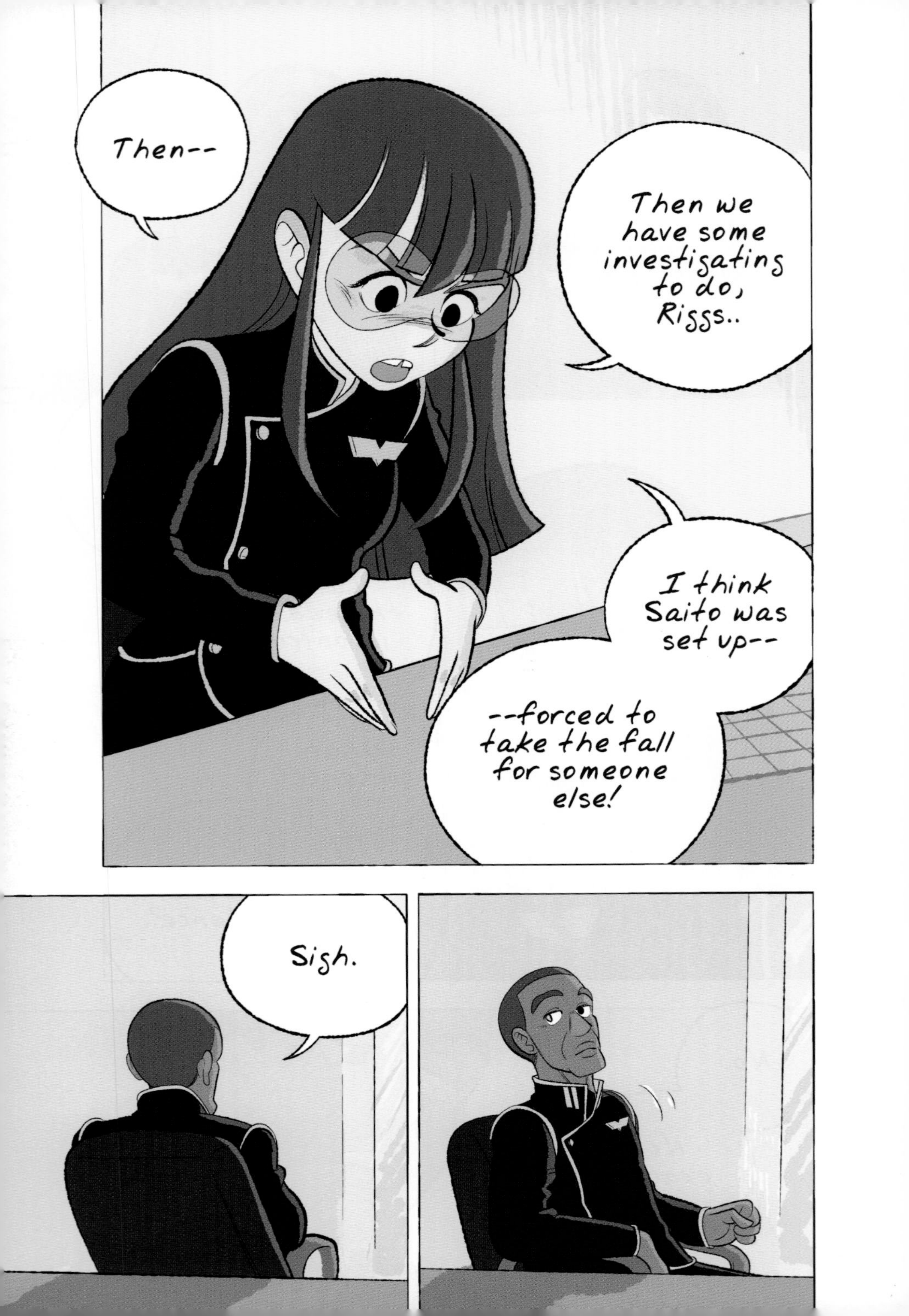
Then--
Then we have some investigating to do, Riggs..
I think Saito was set up--
--forced to take the fall for someone else!
Sigh.

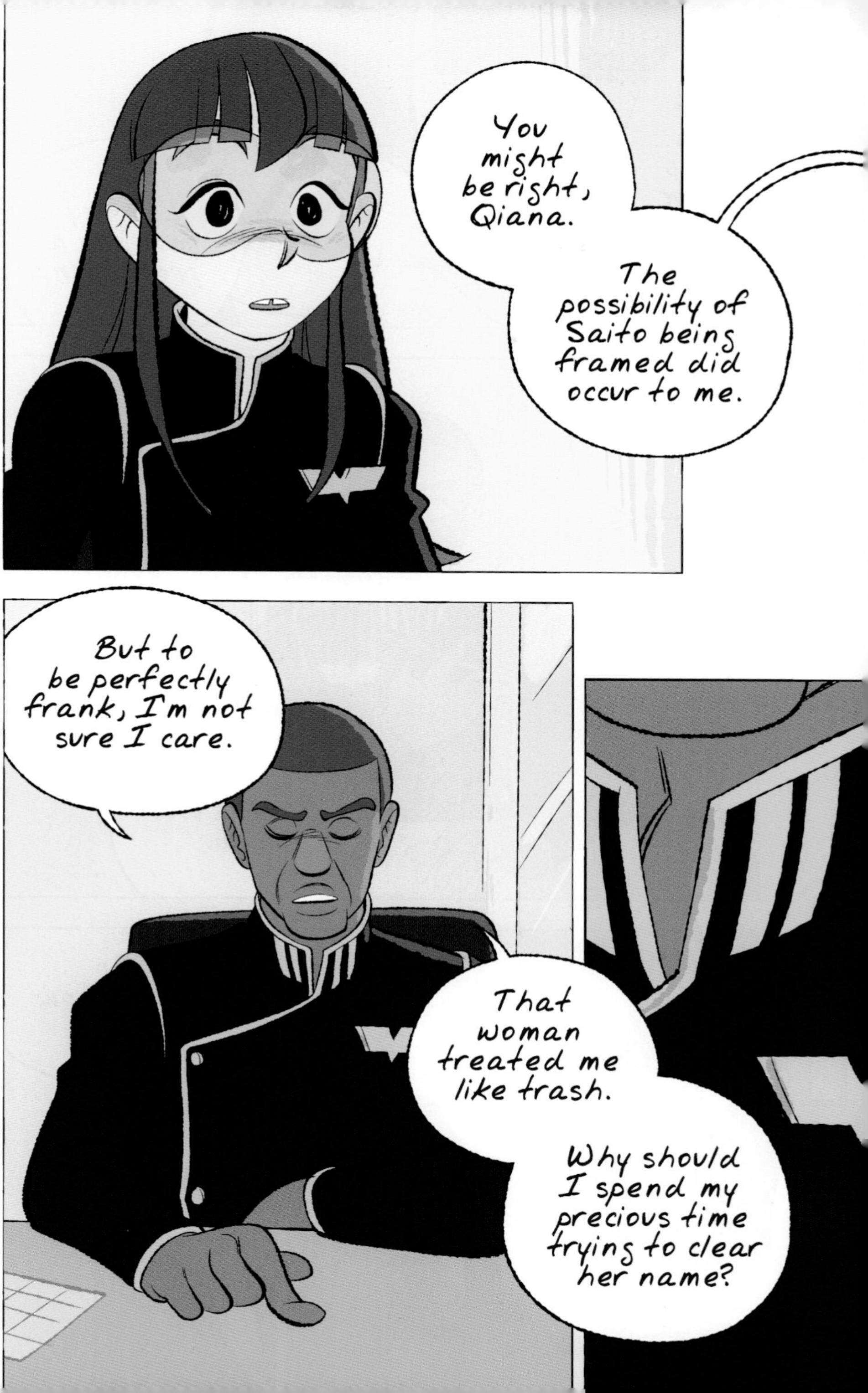
You might be right, Qiana.
The possibility of Saito being framed did occur to me.
But to be perfectly frank, I'm not sure I care.
That woman treated me like trash.
Why should I spend my precious time trying to clear her name?

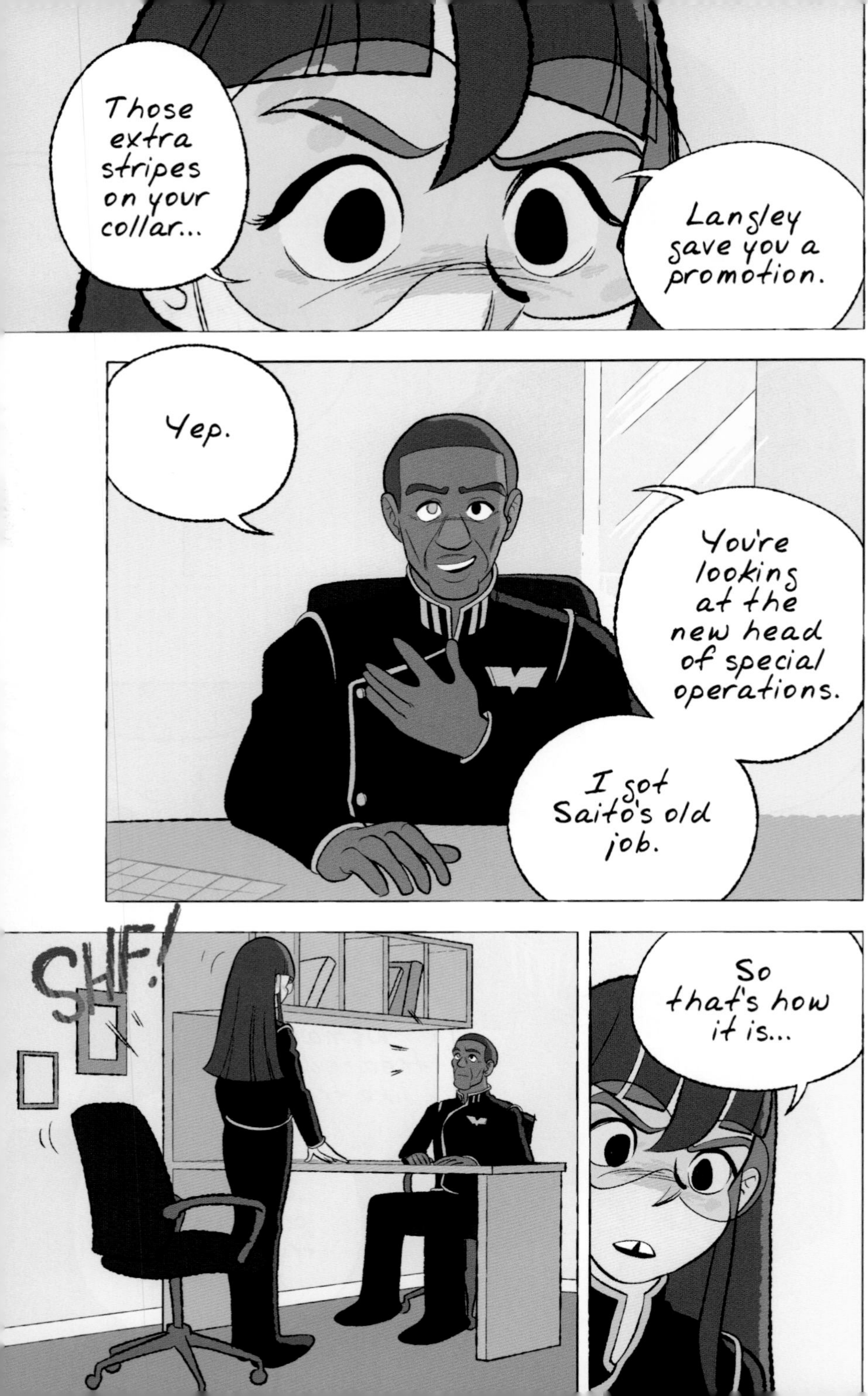
Those extra stripes on your collar...
Langley save you a promotion.
Yep.
You're lookings at the new head of special operations.
I got Saito's old job.
SHF!
So that's how it is...

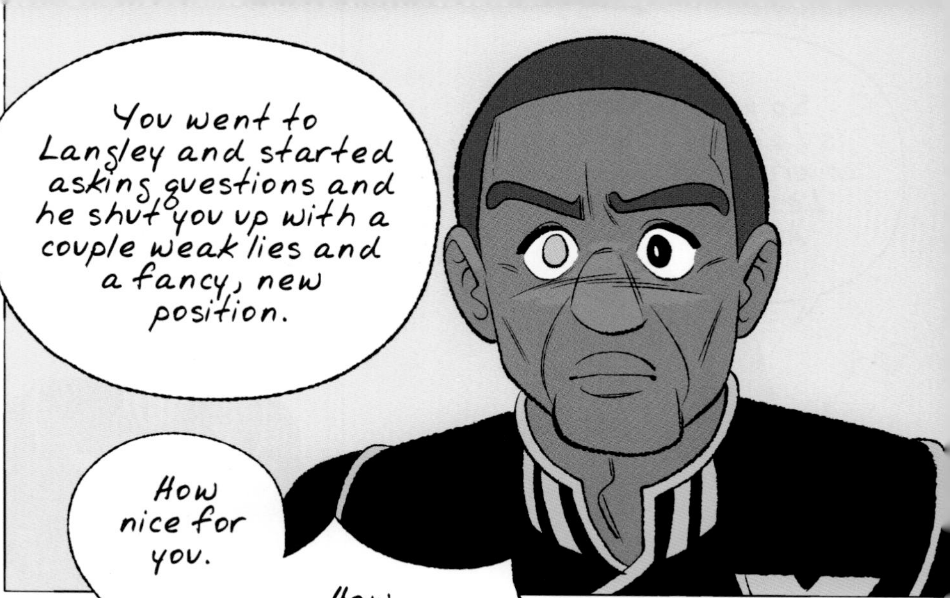
You went to Langley and started asking questions and he shut you up with a couple weak lies and a fancy, new position.
How nice for you.
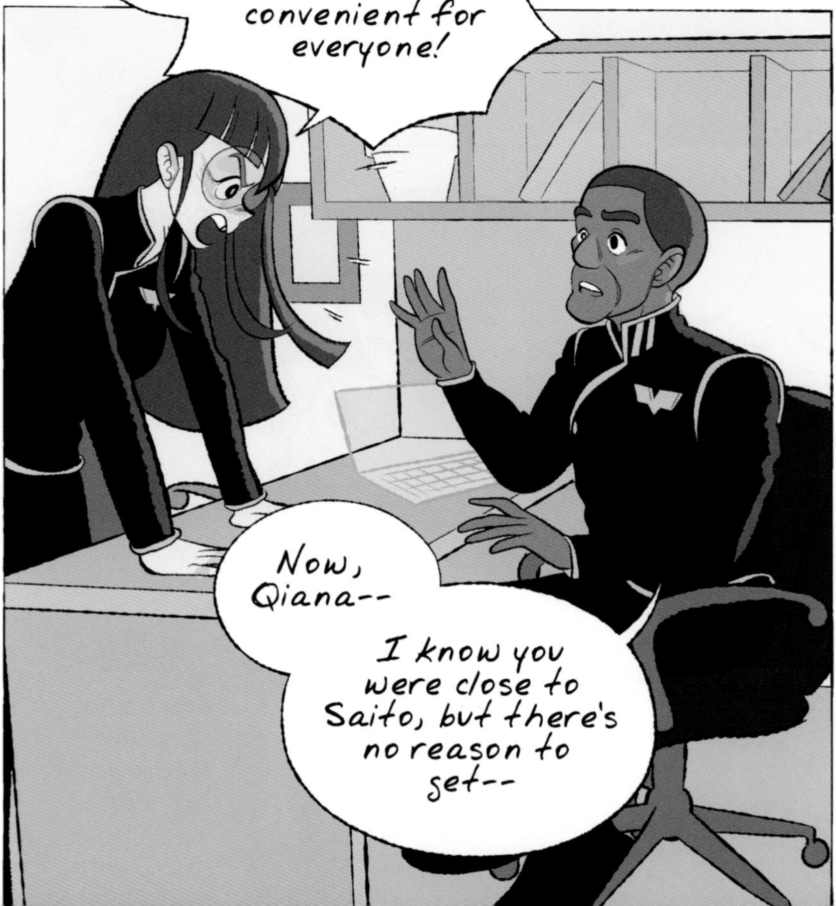
How convenient for everyone!
Now, Qiana--
I know you were close to Saito, but there's no reason to get--

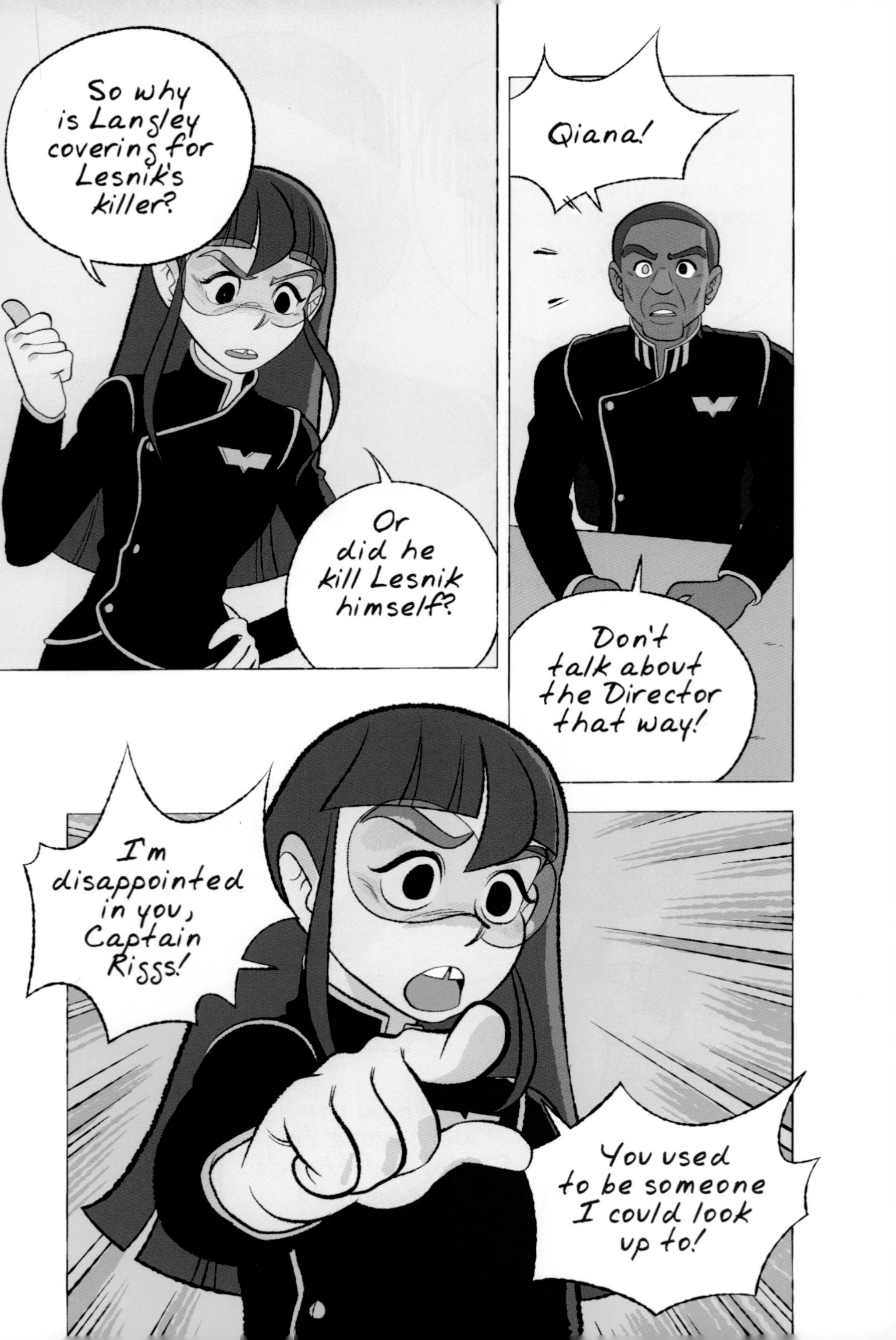
So why is Langley covering for Lesnik's killer?
Or did he kill Lesnik himself?
Qiana!
Don't talk about the Director that way!
I'm disappointed in you, Captain Riggs!
You used to be someone I could look up to!

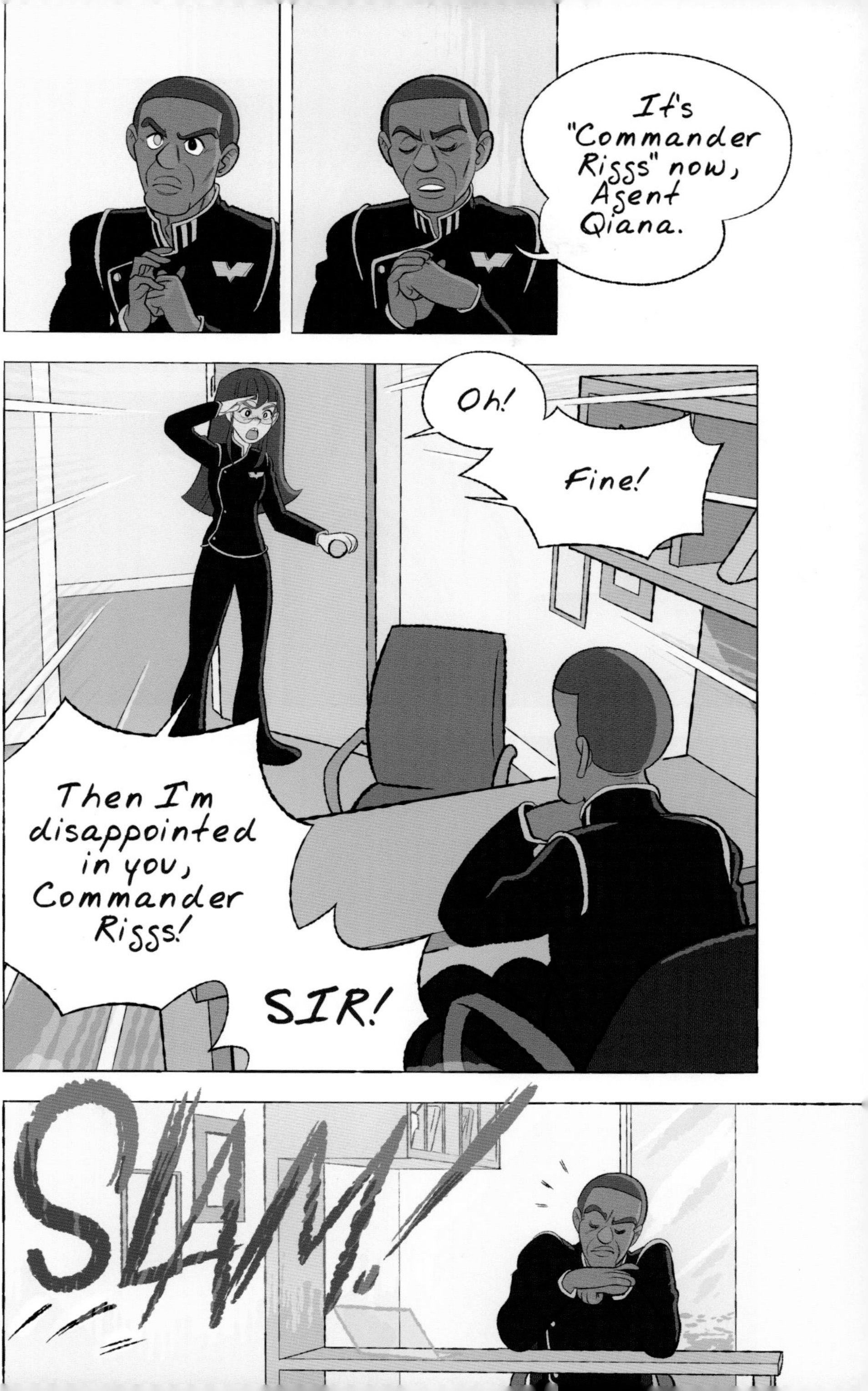
It's "Commander Risss" now, Agent Qiana.
Oh!
Fine!
Then I'm disappointed in you, Commander Risss!
SIR!
SLAM!

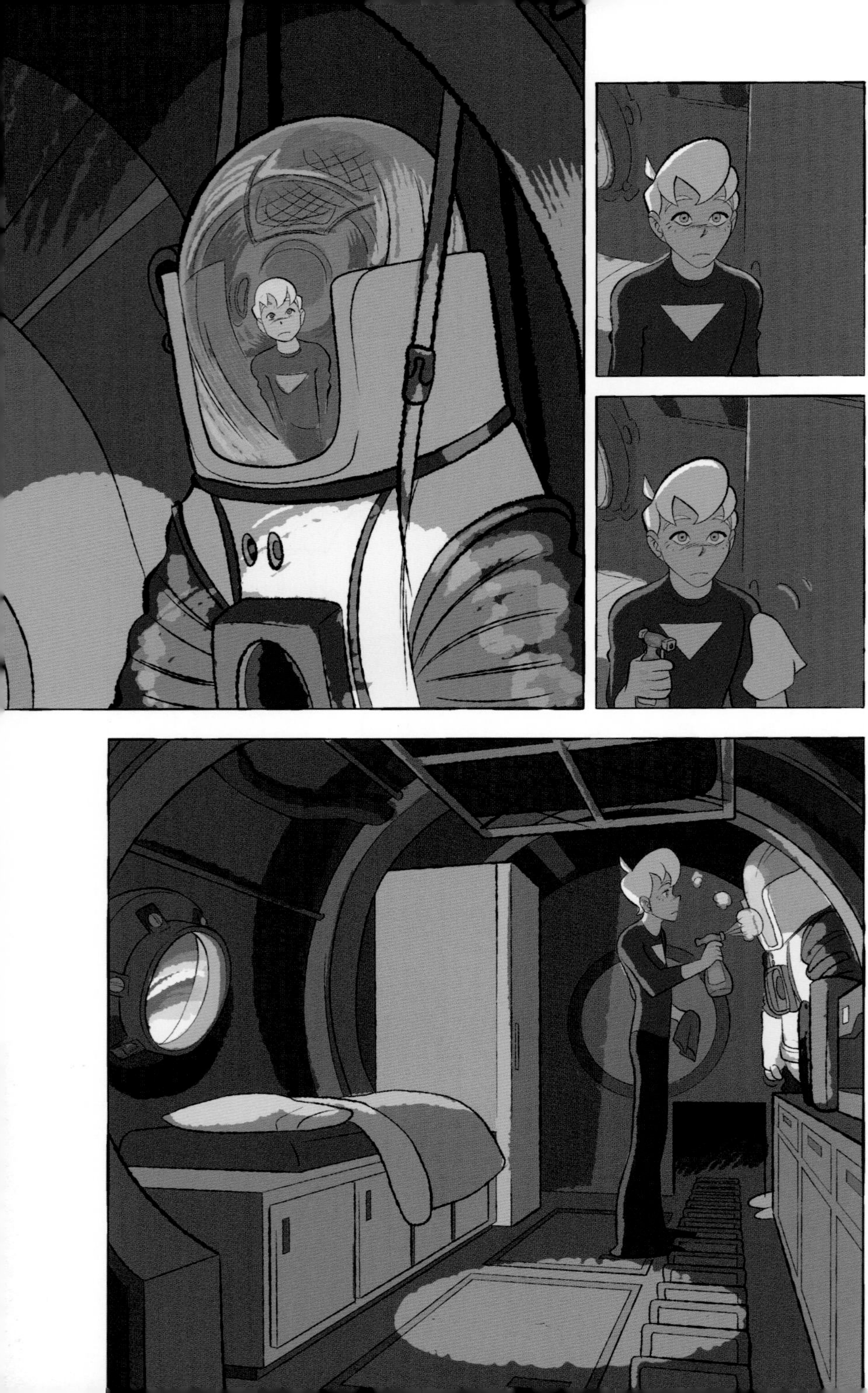

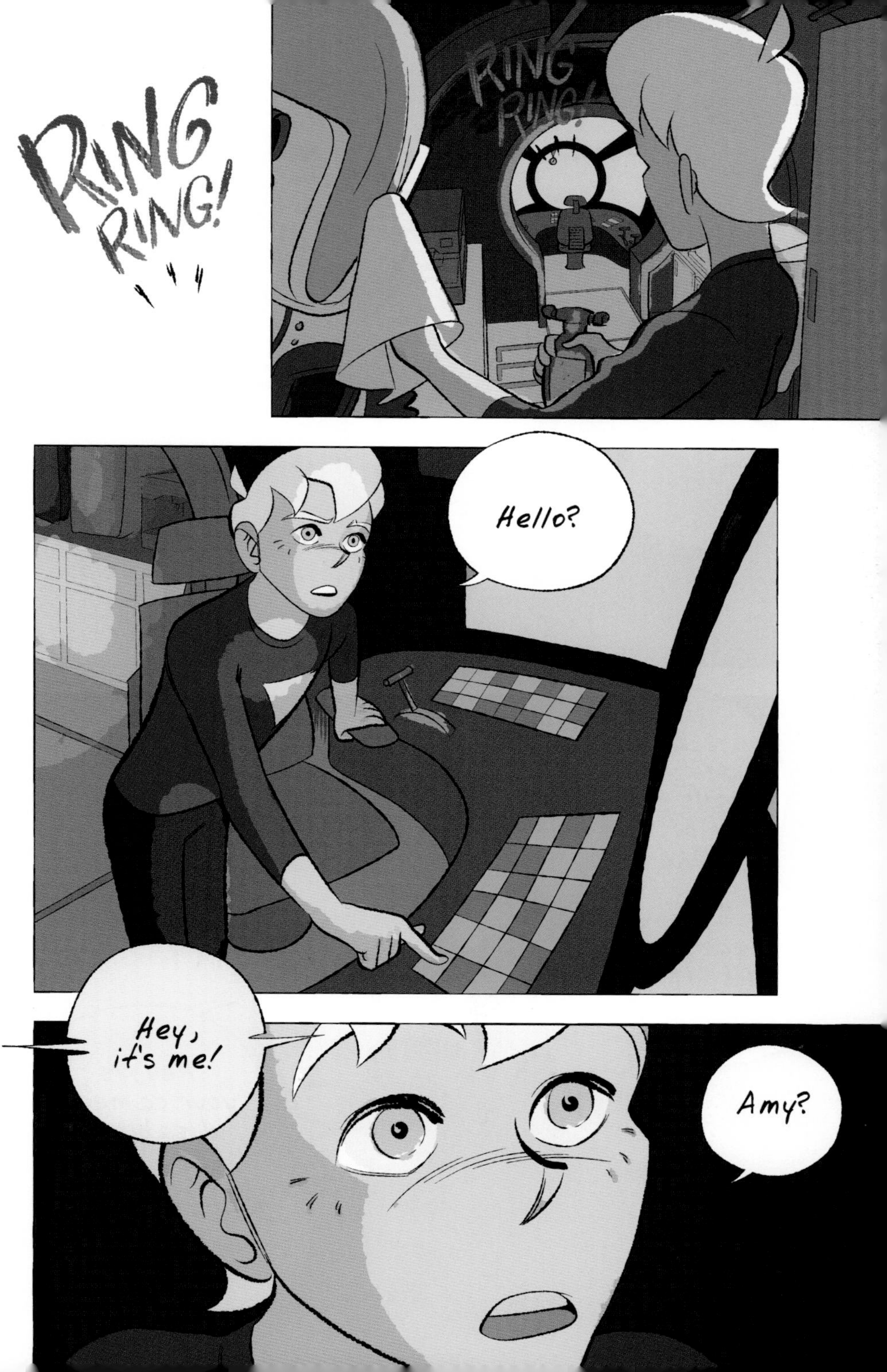
RING RING!
RING RING!
Hello?
Hey, it's me!
Amy?

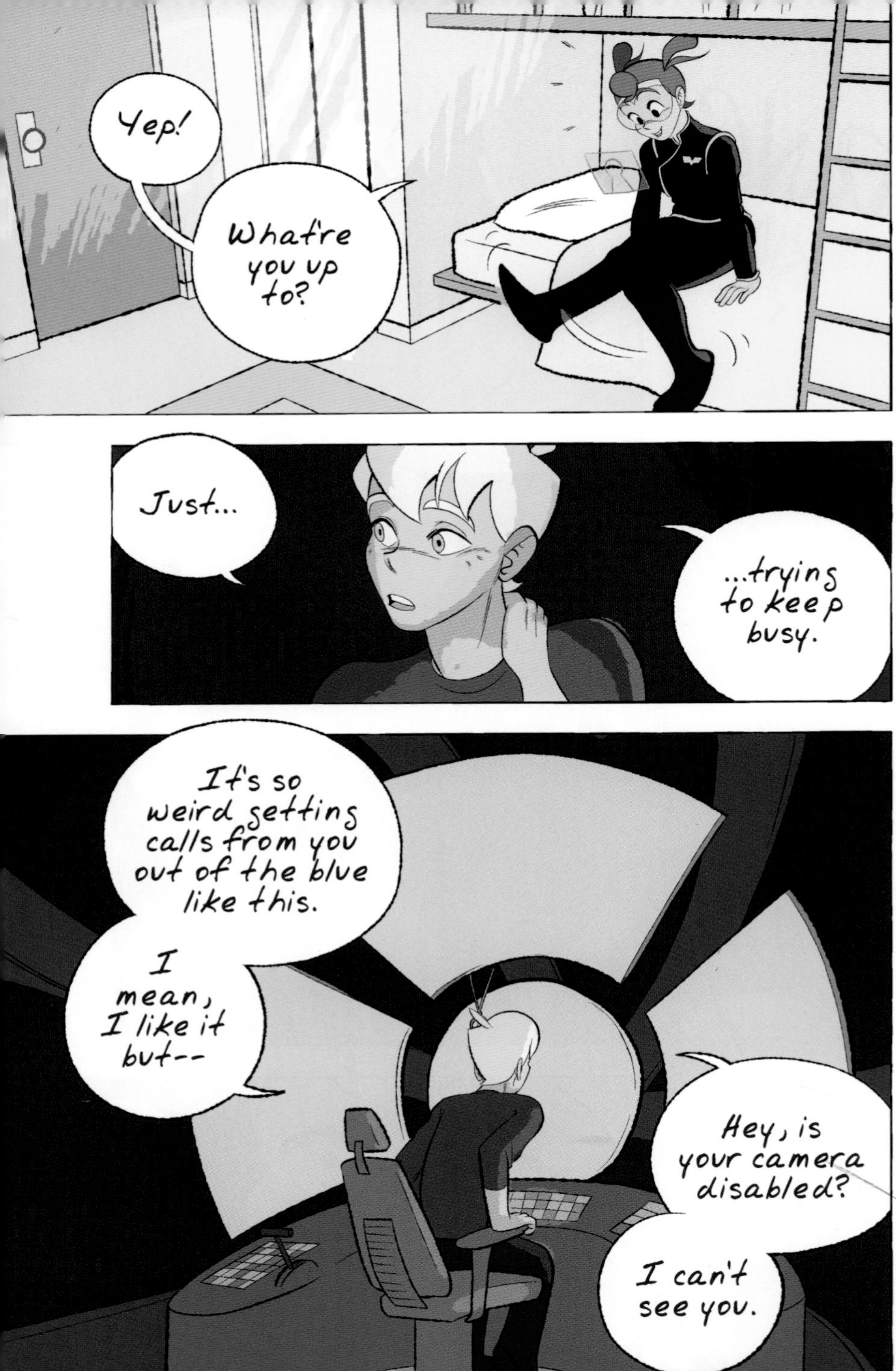
Yep!
Whatre you up to?
Just...
...trying to keep busy.
It's so weird getting calls from you out of the blue like this.
I mean, I like it but--
Hey, is your camera disabled?
I can't see you.

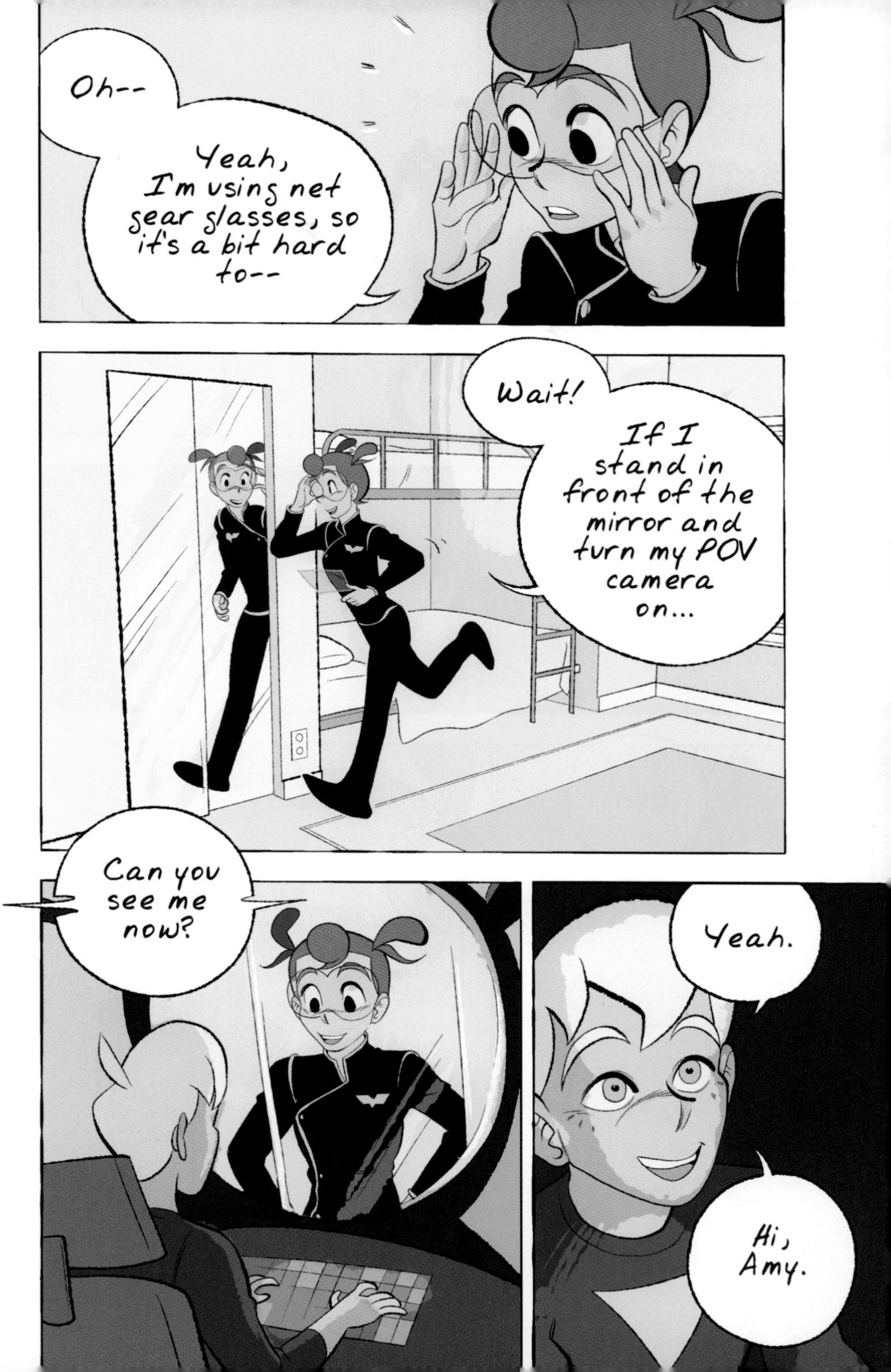

Oh--
Yeah, I'm using net gear glasses, so it's a bit hard to--
Wait!
If I stand in front of the mirror and turn my POV camera on...
Can you see me now?
Yeah.
Hi, Amy.

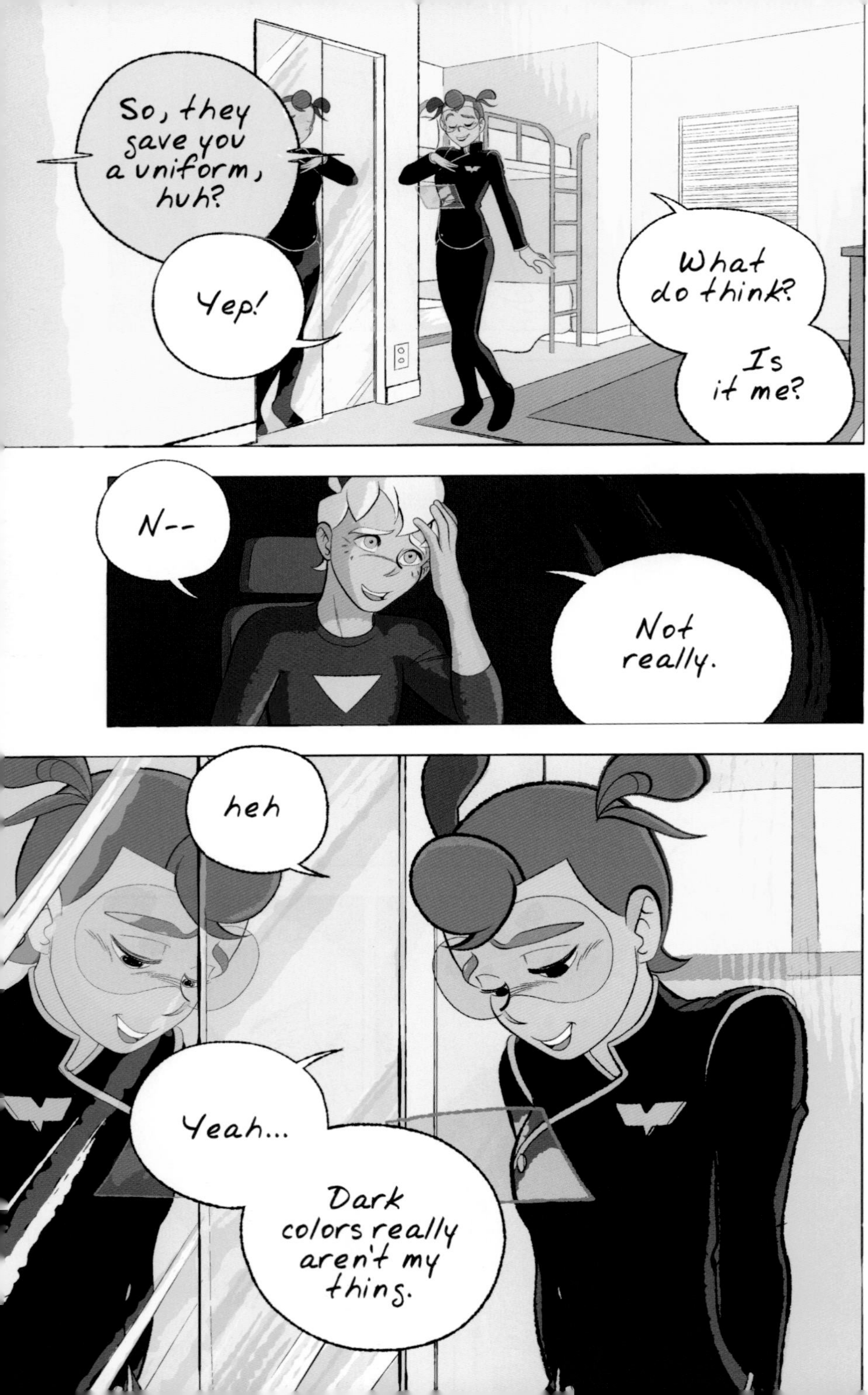
So, they gave you a uniform, huh?
Yep!
What do think?
Is it me?
N--
Not really.
heh
Yeah...
Dark colors really aren't my thing.

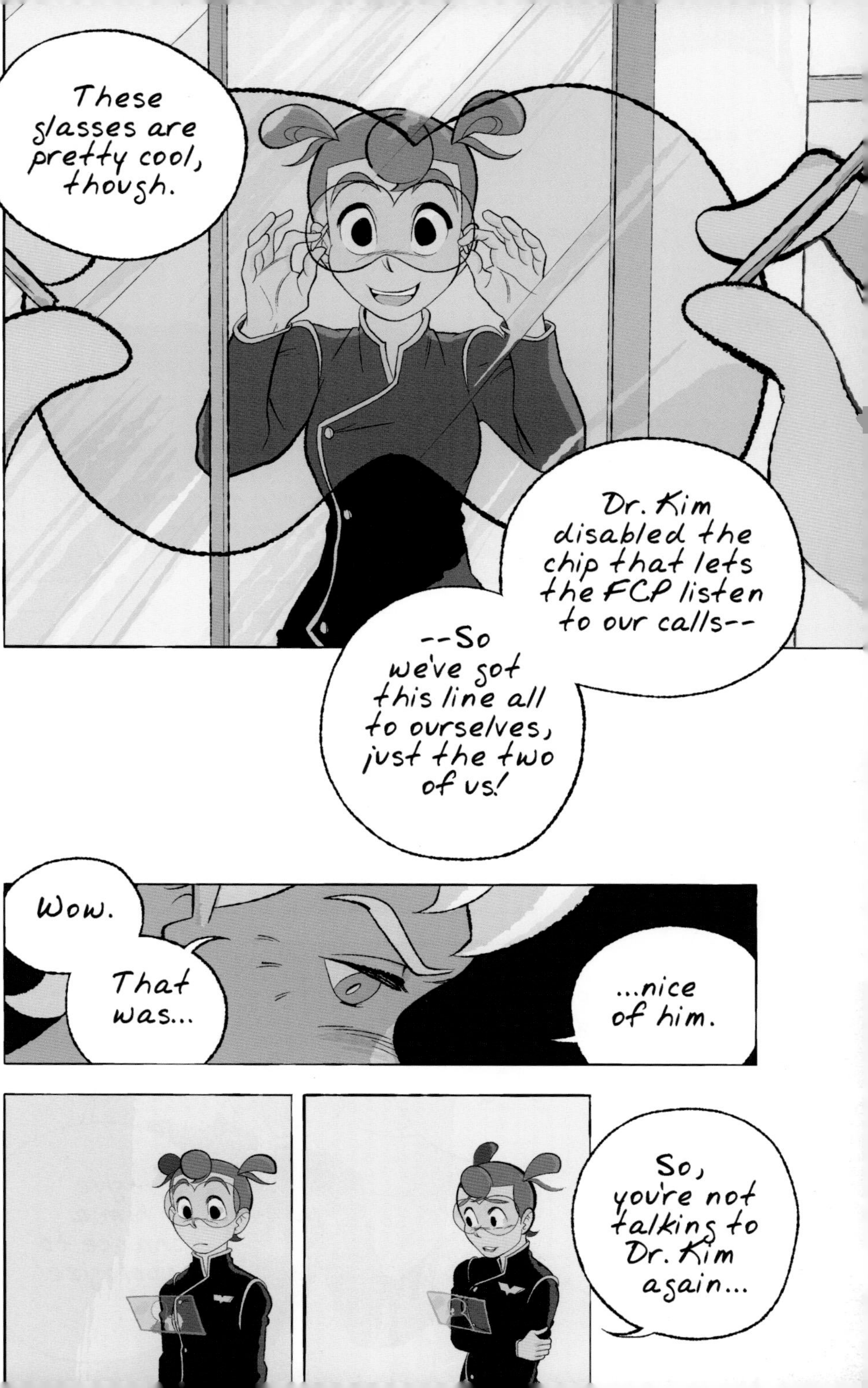
These glasses are pretty cool, though.
Dr. Kim disabled the chip that lets the FCP listen to our calls--
--So we've got this line all to ourselves, just the two of us!
Wow.
That was...
...nice of him.
So, you're not talking to Dr. Kim again...

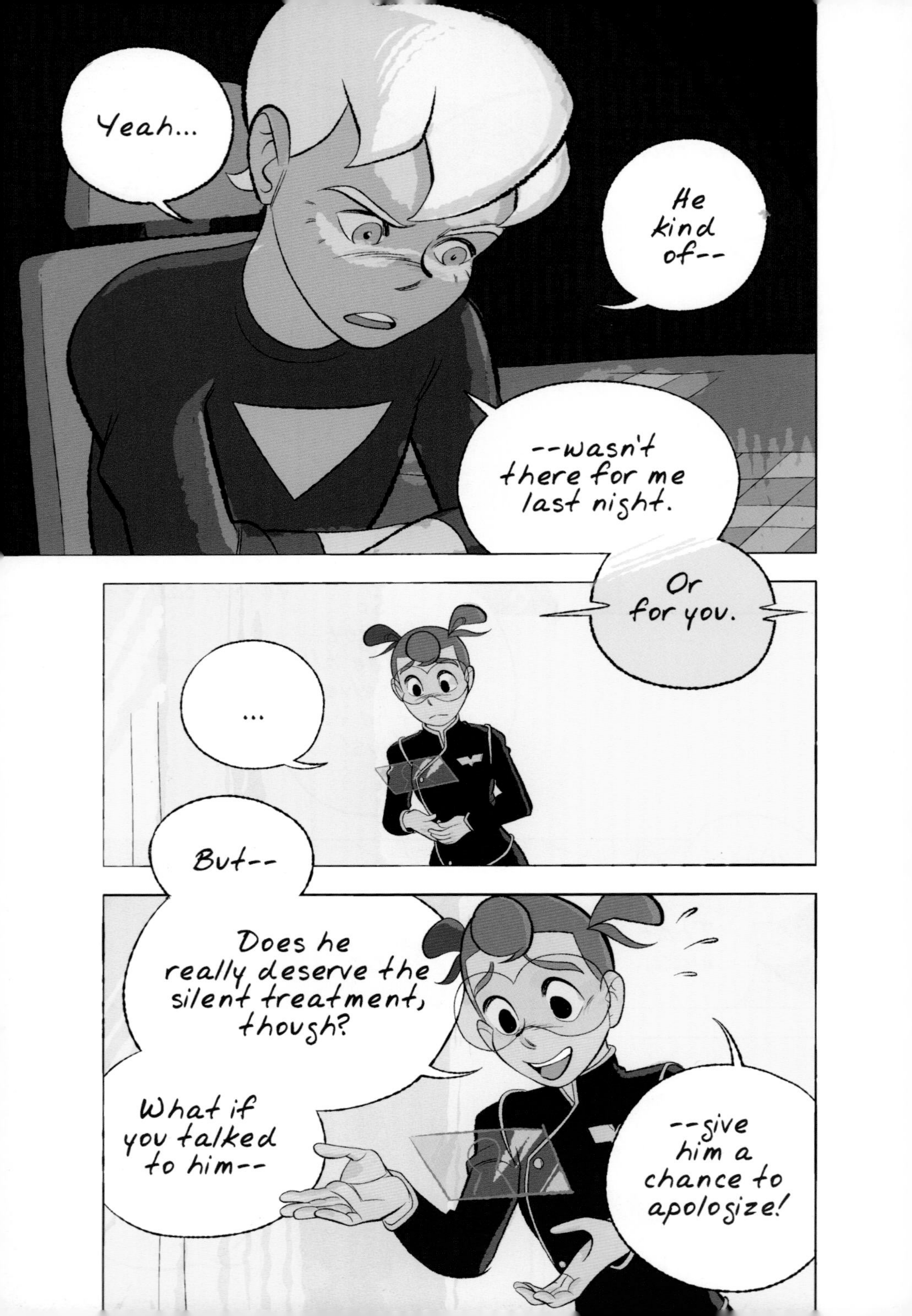
Yeah...
He kind of--
--wasn't there for me last night.
Or for you.
...
But--
Does he really deserve the silent treatment, though?
What if you talked to him--
--give him a chance to apologize!

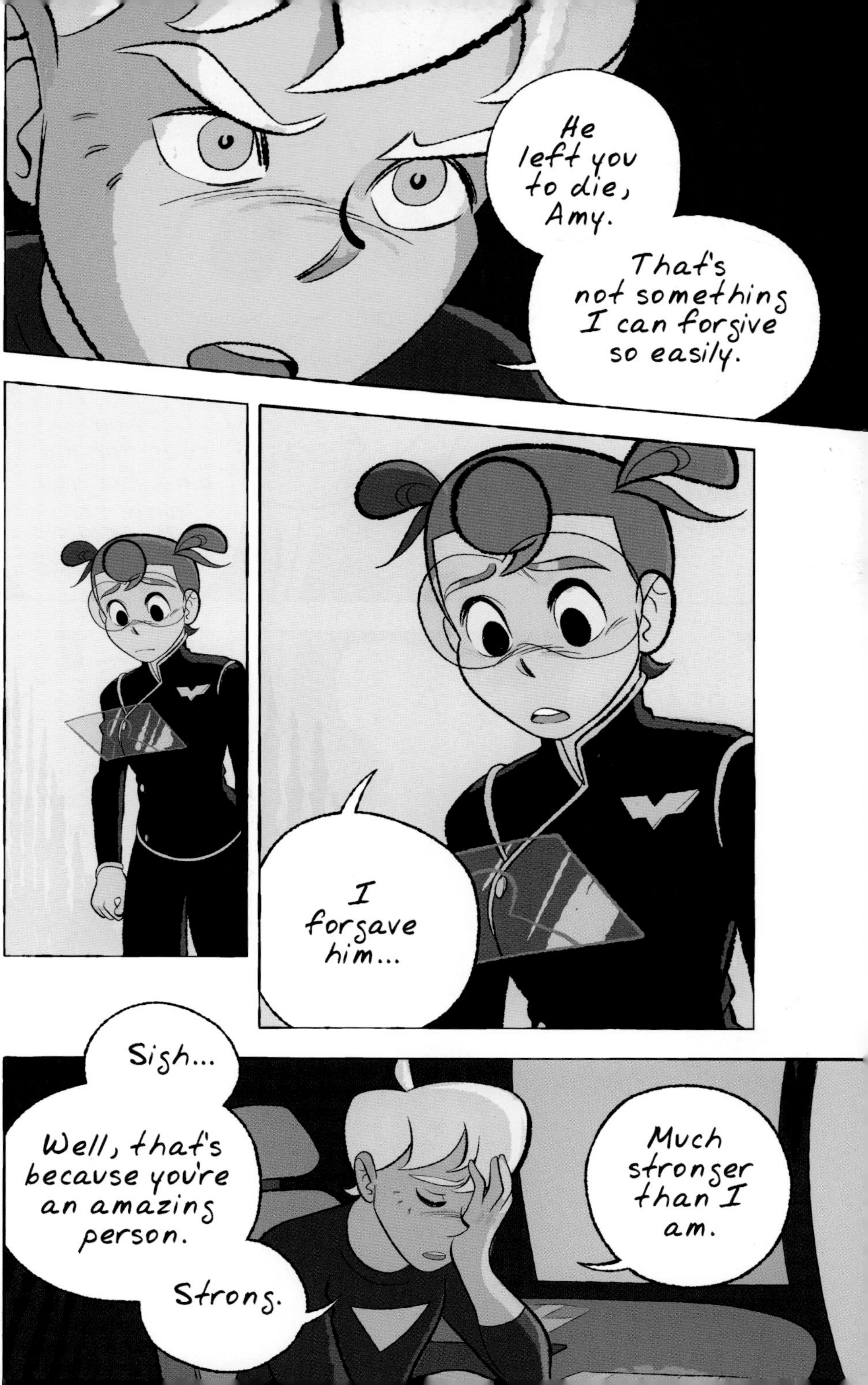
He left you to die, Amy.
That's not something I can forgive so easily.
I forgave him...
Sigh...
Well, that's because you're an amazing person.
Strong.
Much stronger than I am.

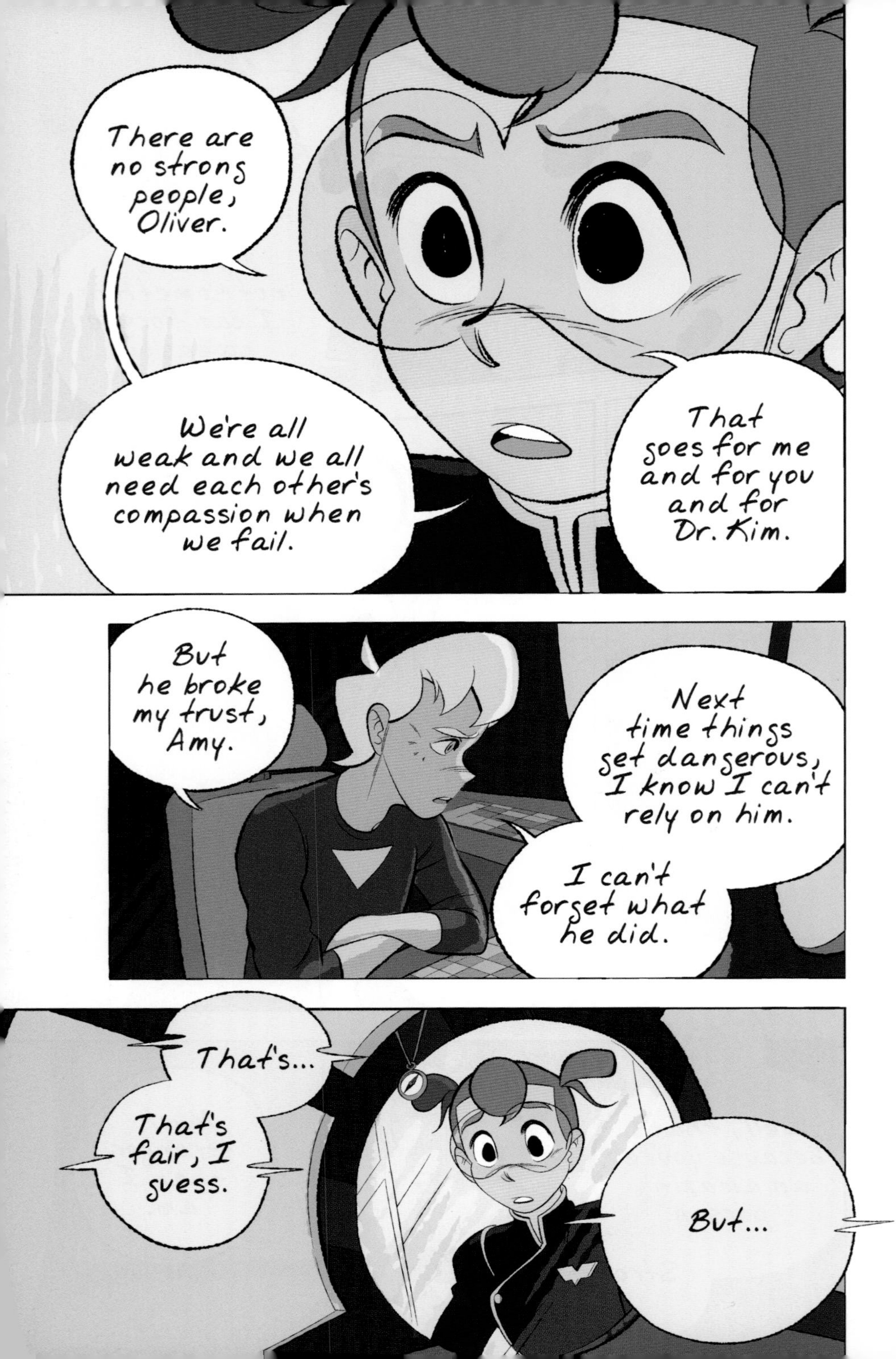
There are no strong people, Oliver.
We're all weak and we all need each other's compassion when we fail.
That goes for me and for you and for Dr. Kim.
But he broke my trust, Amy.
Next time things get dangerous, I know I can't rely on him.
I can't forget what he did.
That's...
That's fair, I guess.
But...

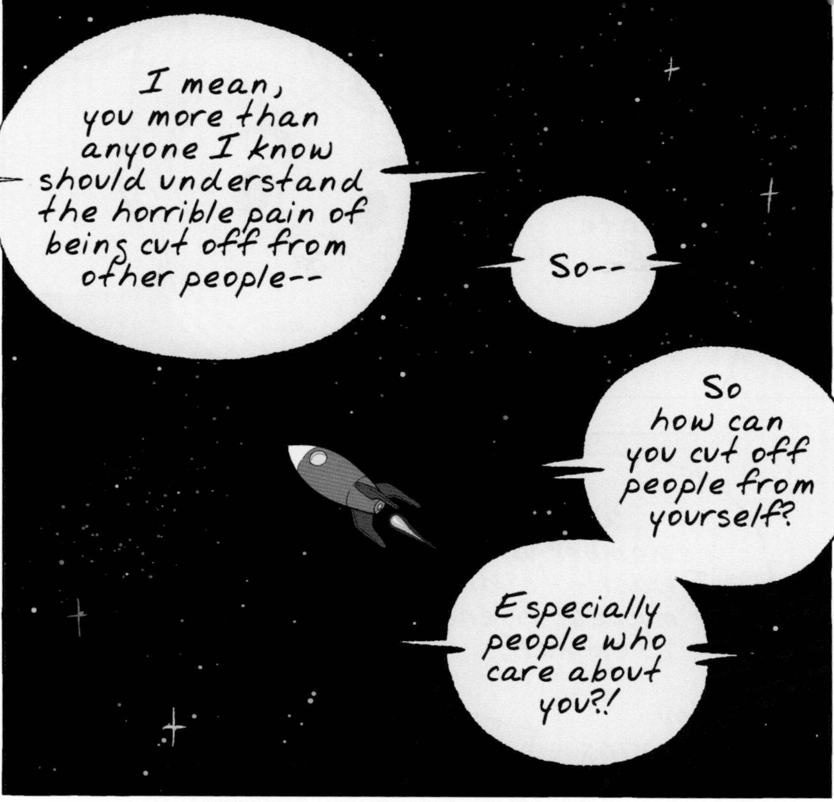
I mean, you more than anyone I know should understand the horrible pain of being cut off from other people--
So--
So how can you cut off people from yourself?
Especially people who care about you?!

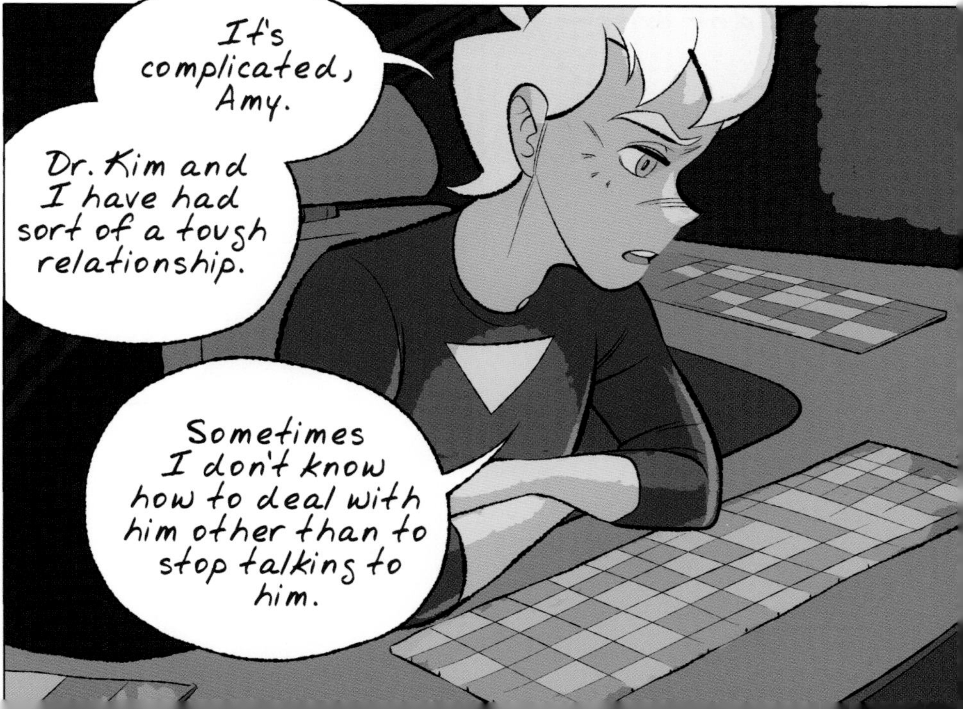
It's complicated, Amy.
Dr. Kim and I have had sort of a tough relationship.
Sometimes I don't know how to deal with him other than to stop talking to him.

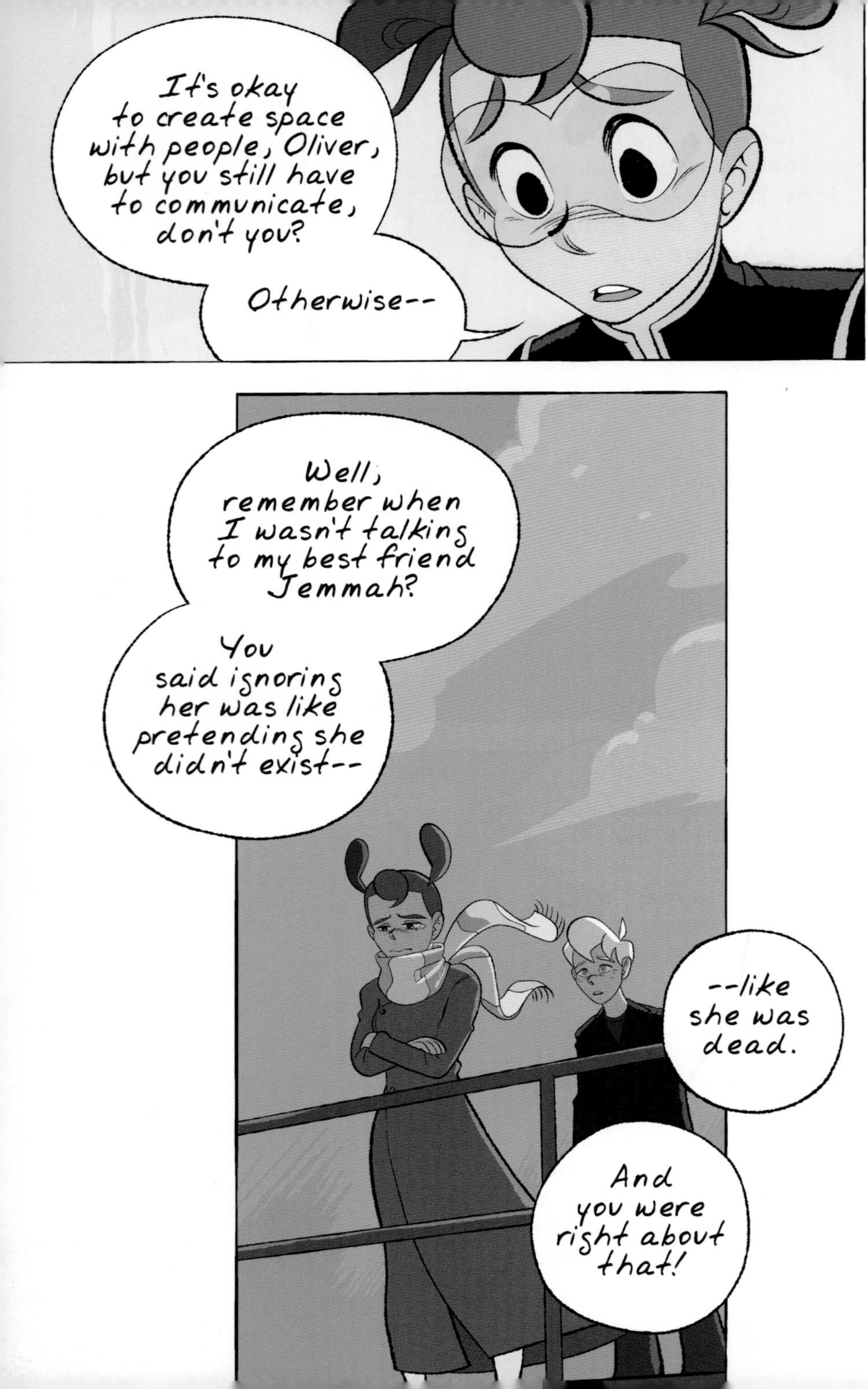
It's okay to create space with people, Oliver, but you still have to communicate, don't you?
Otherwise--
Well, remember when I wasn't talking to my best friend Jemmah?
You said ignoring her was like pretending she didn't exist--
--like she was dead.
And you were right about that!

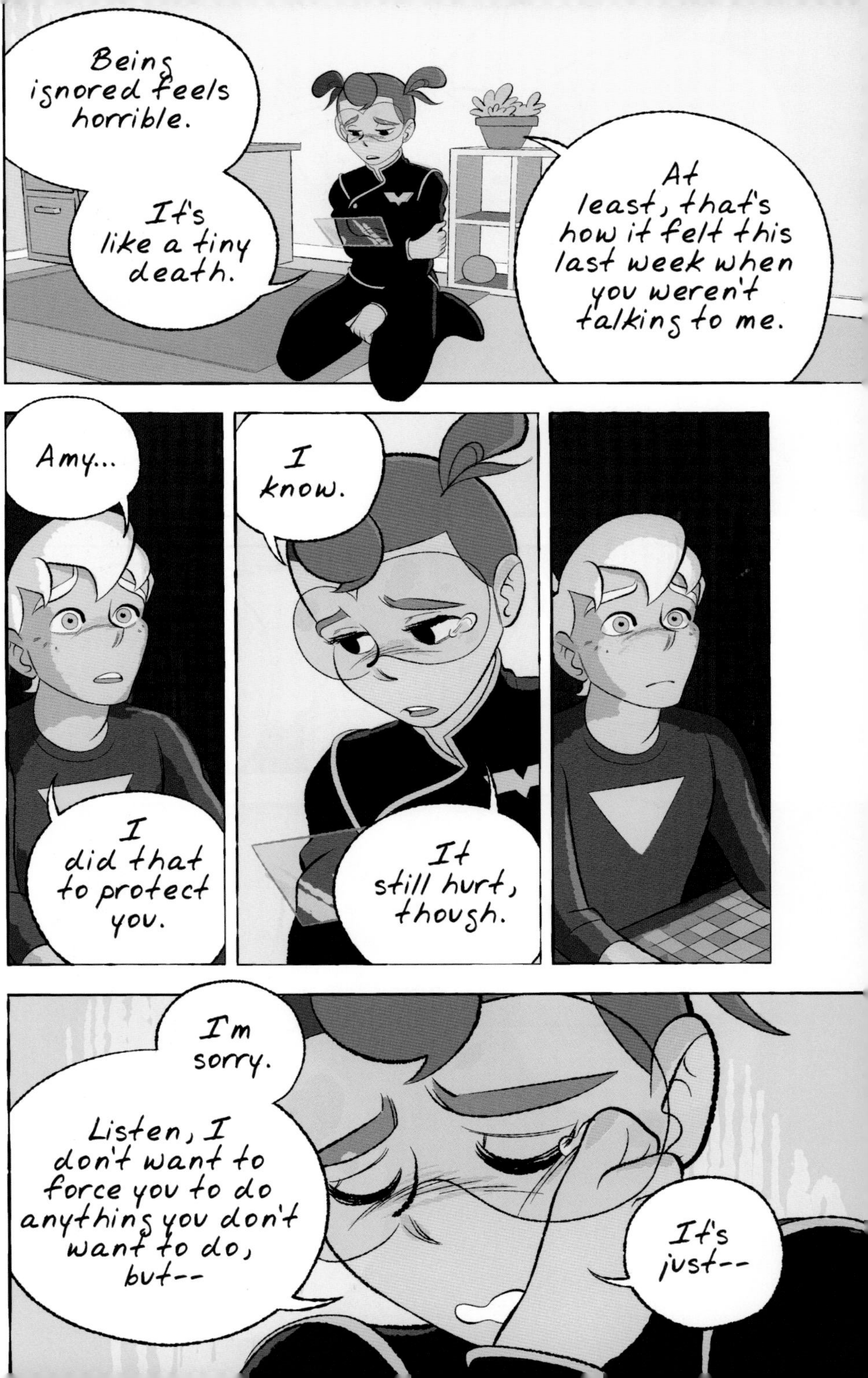

Being ignored feels horrible.
It's like a tiny death.
At least, that's how it felt this last week when you weren't talking to me.
Amy...
I did that to protect you.
I know.
It still hurt, though.
I'm sorry.
Listen, I don't want to force you to do anything you don't want to do, but--
It's just--

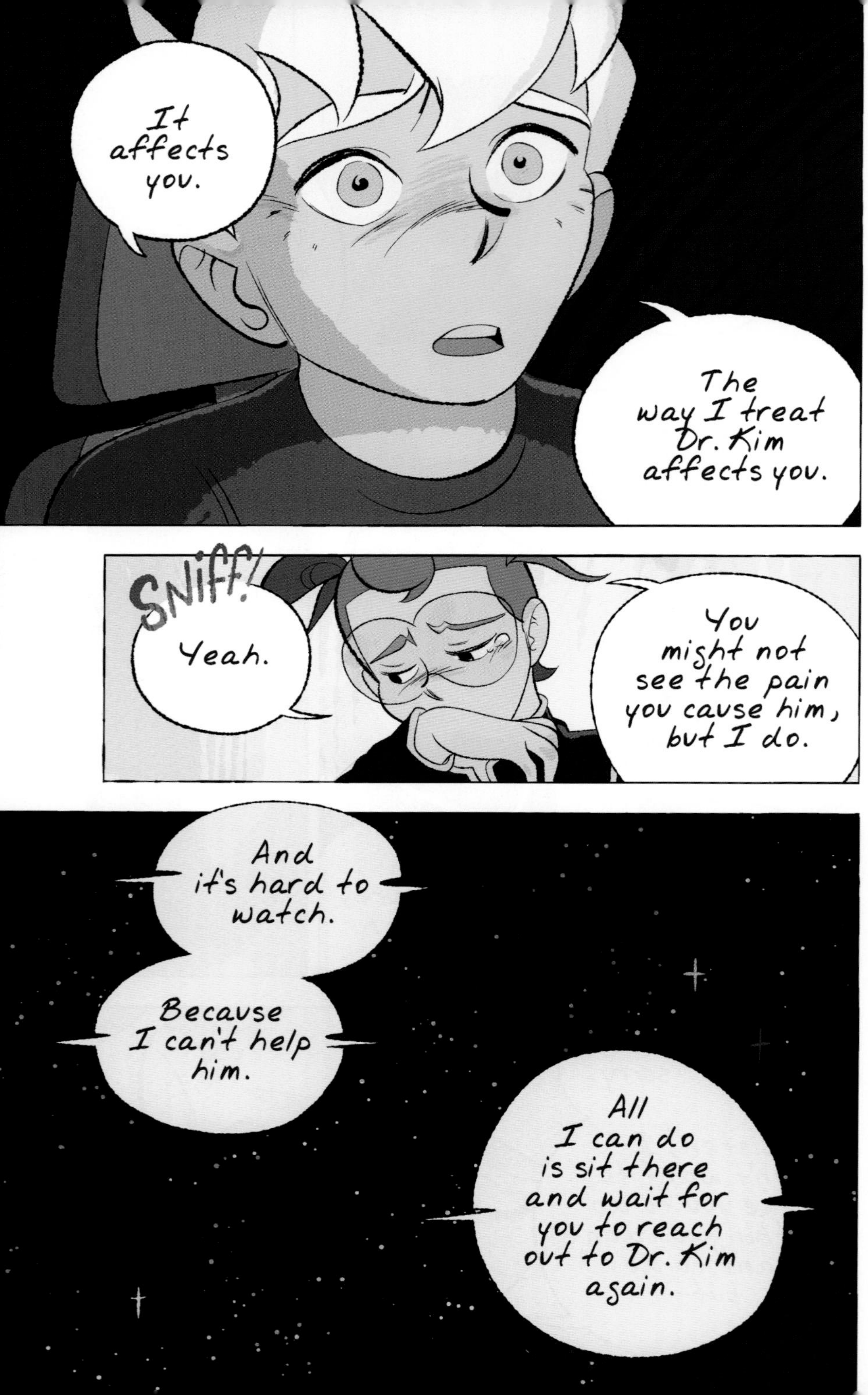
It affects you.
The way I treat Dr. Kim affects you.
SNIFF!
Yeah.
You might not see the pain you cause him, but I do.
And it's hard to watch.
Because I can't help him.
All I can do is sit there and wait for you to reach out to Dr. Kim again.

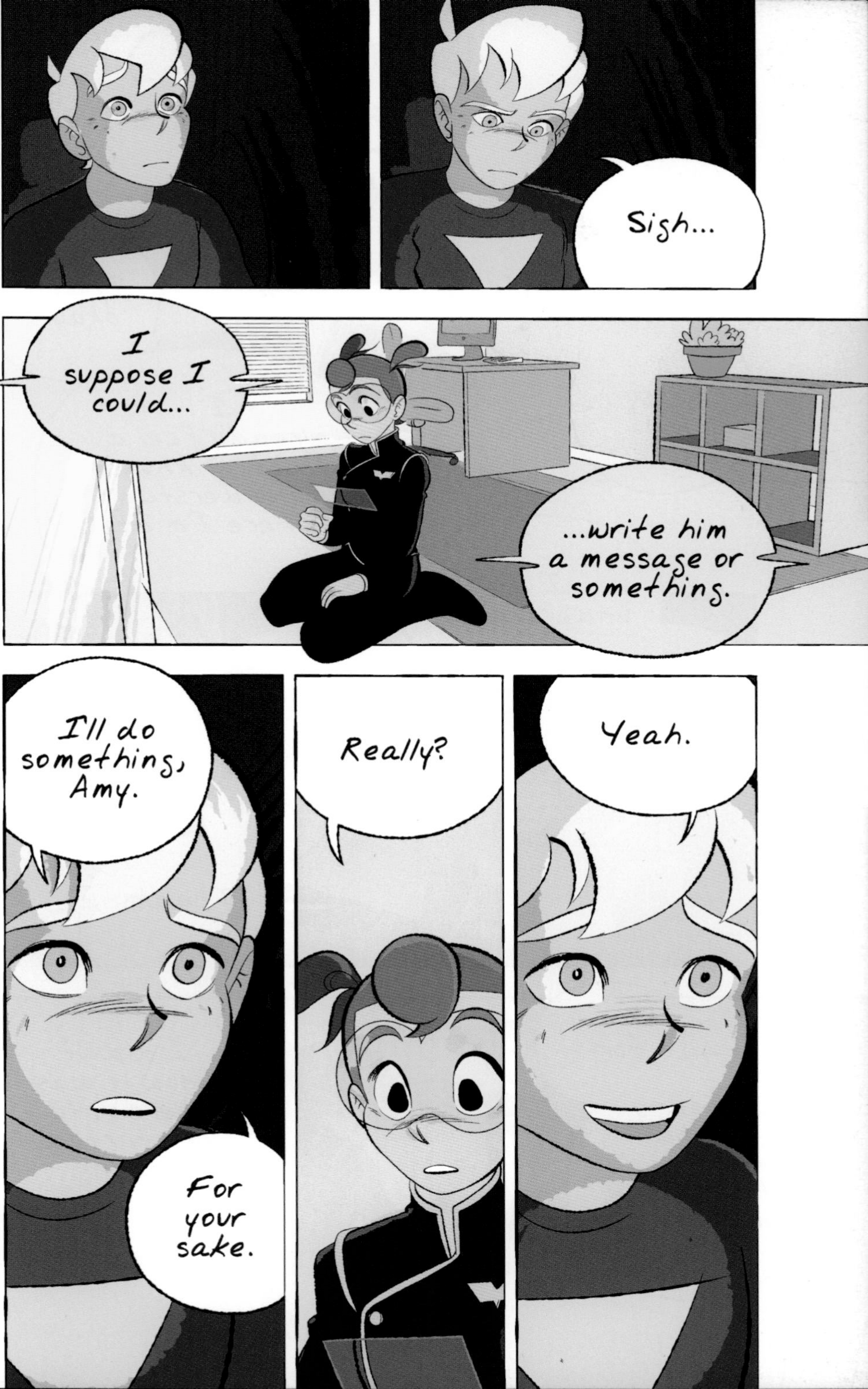
Sigh...
I suppose I could...
...write him a message or something.
I'll do something, Amy.
For your sake.
Really?
Yeah.

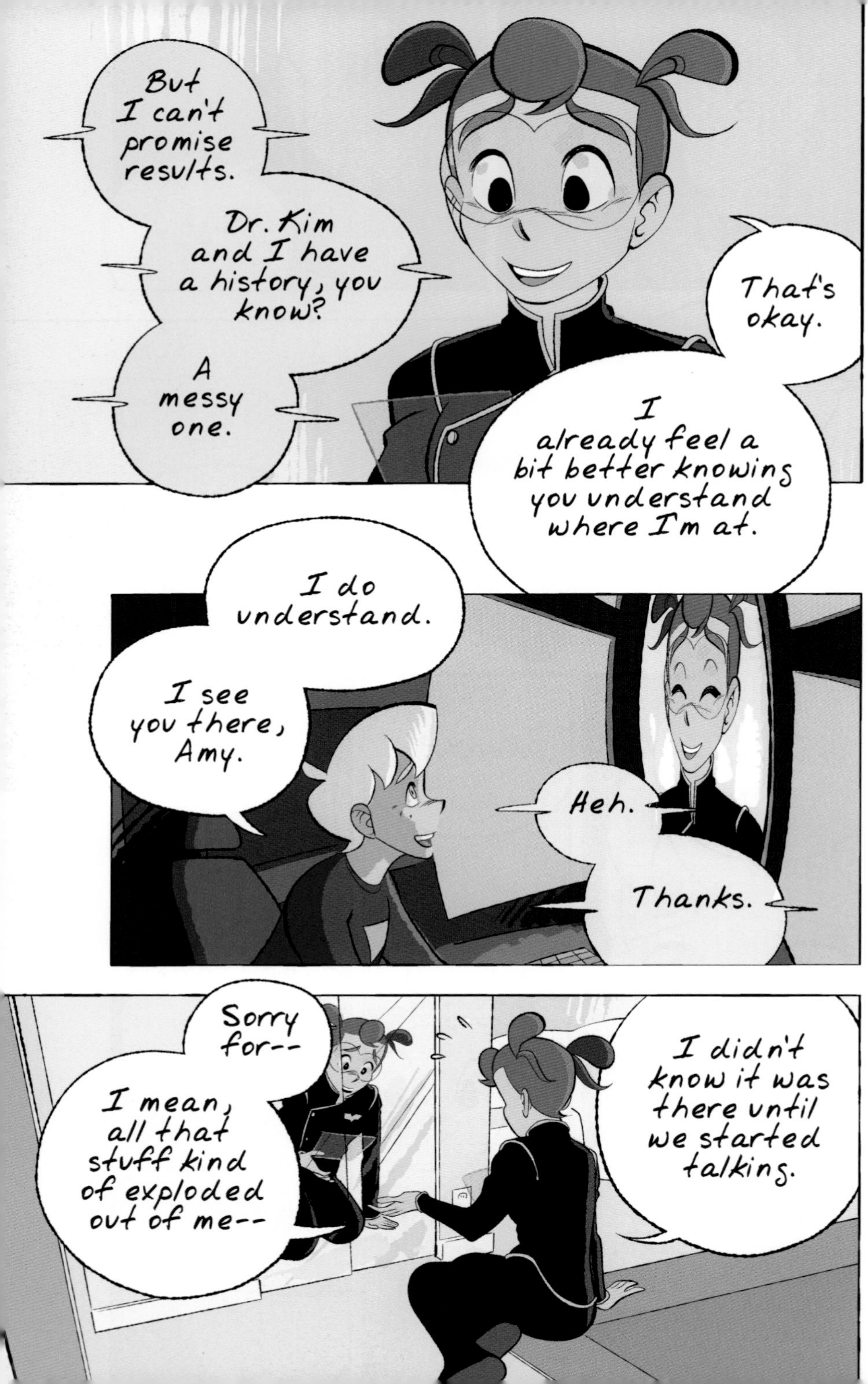
But I can't promise results.
Dr. Kim and I have a history, you know?
A messy one.
That's okay.
I already feel a bit better knowing you understand where I'm at.
I do understand.
I see you there, Amy.
Heh.
Thanks.
Sorry for--
I mean, all that stuff kind of exploded out of me--
I didn't know it was there until we started talking.

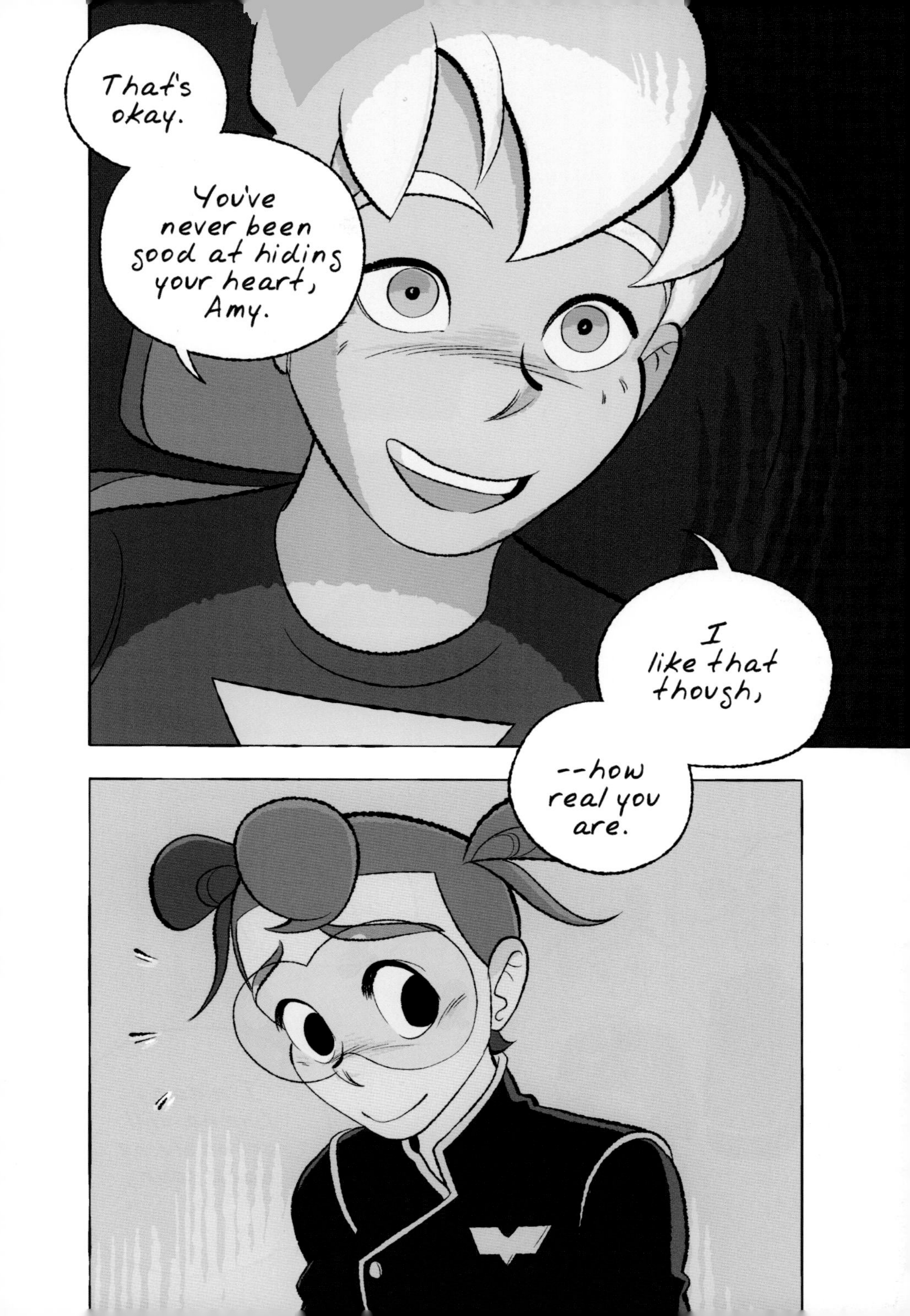
That's okay.
You've never been good at hiding your heart, Amy.
I like that though,
--how real you are.

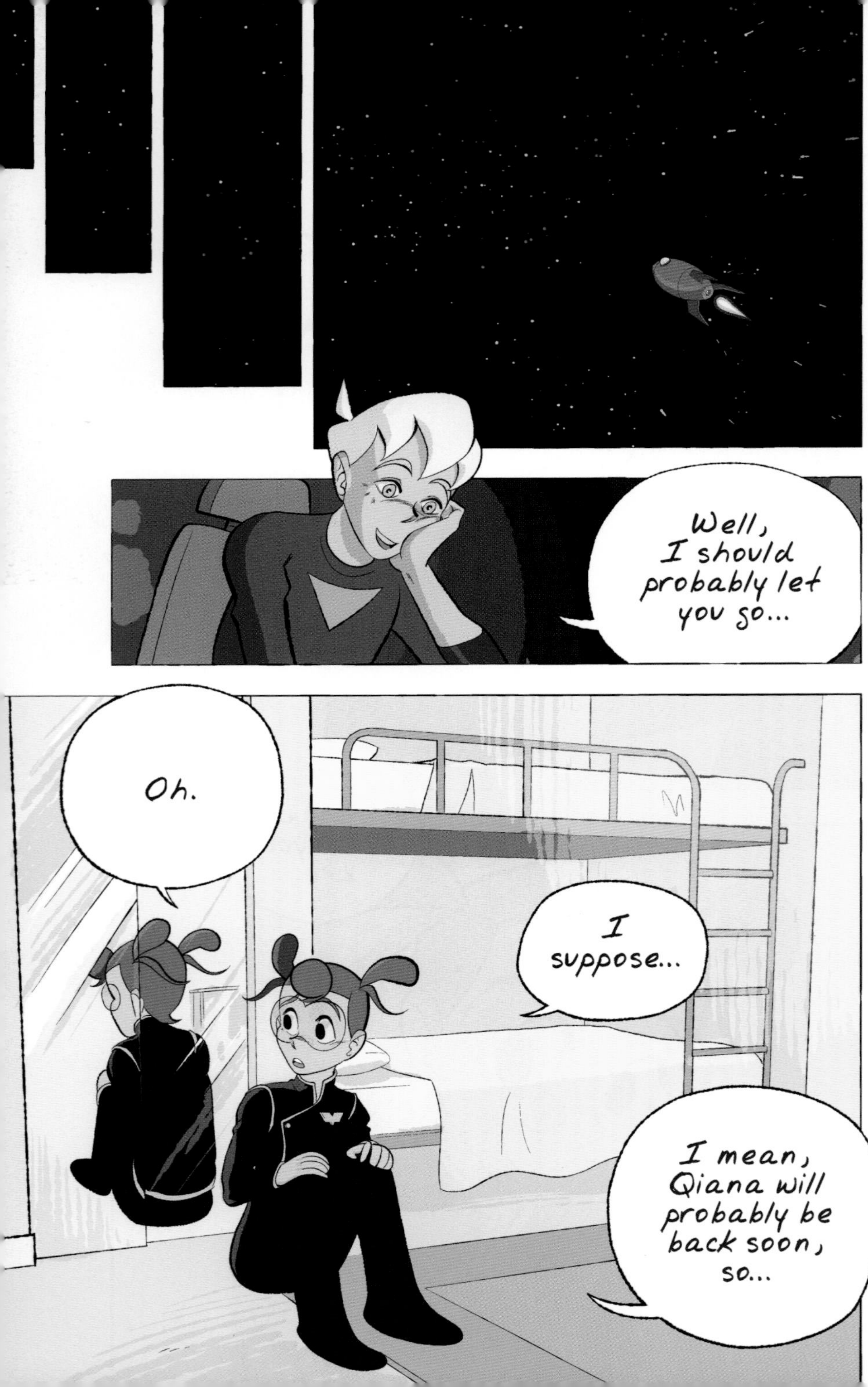
Well, I should probably let you go...
Oh.
I suppose...
I mean, Qiana will probably be back soon, so...

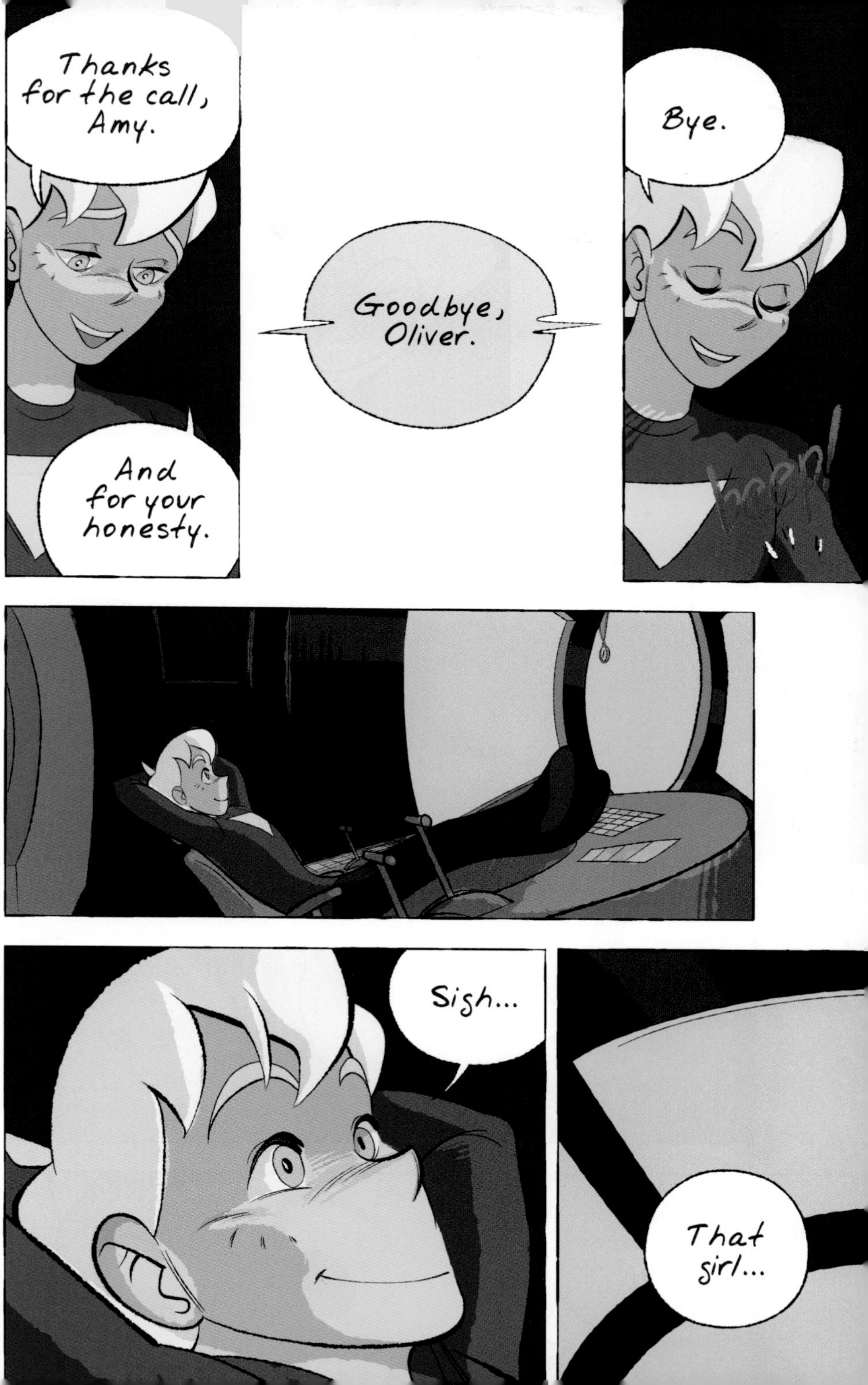
Thanks for the call, Amy.
And for your honesty.
Goodbye, Oliver.
Bye.
beep!
Sigh...
That girl...

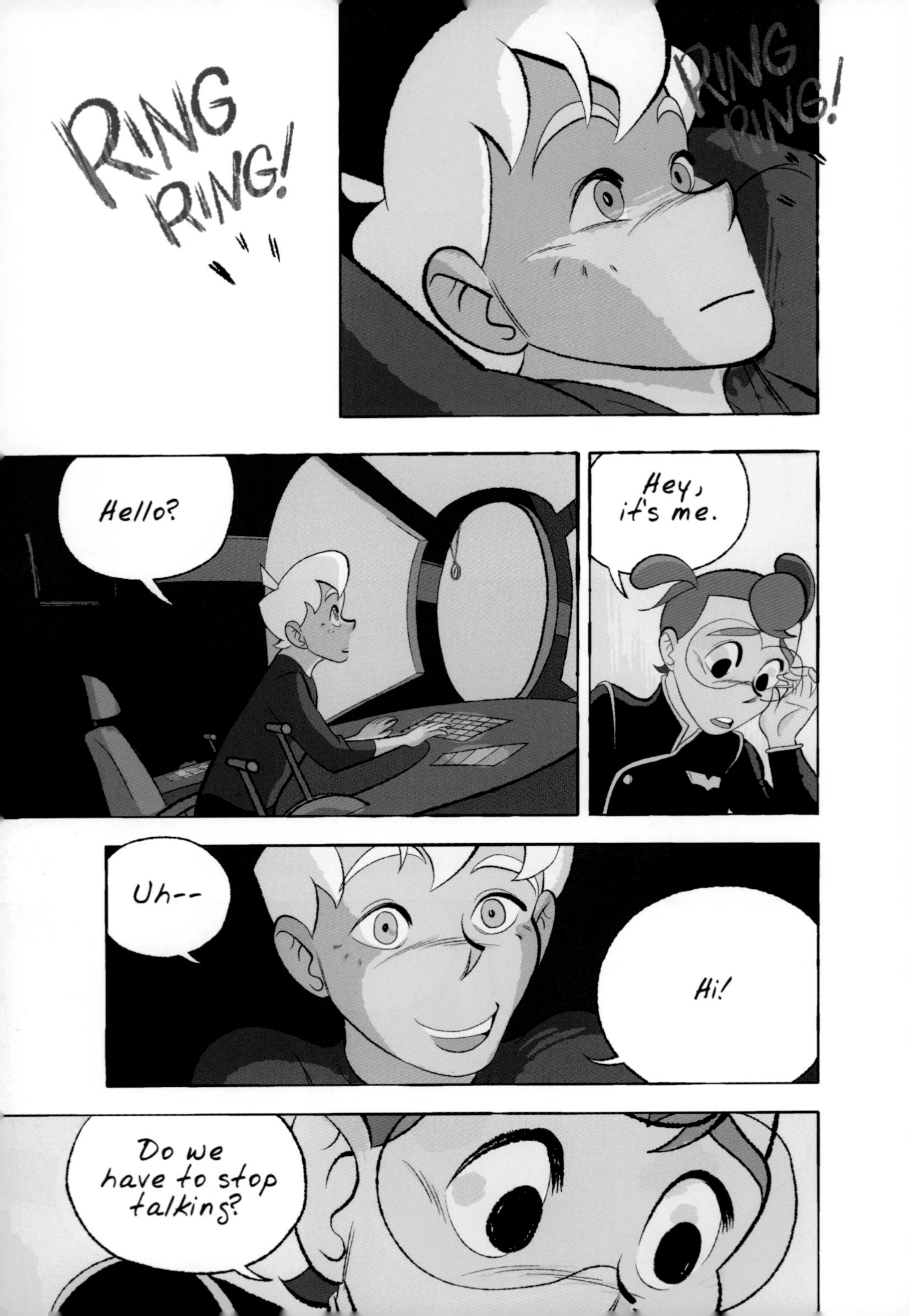
RING RING!
RING RING!
Hello?
Hey, it's me.
Uh--
Hi!
Do we have to stop talking?

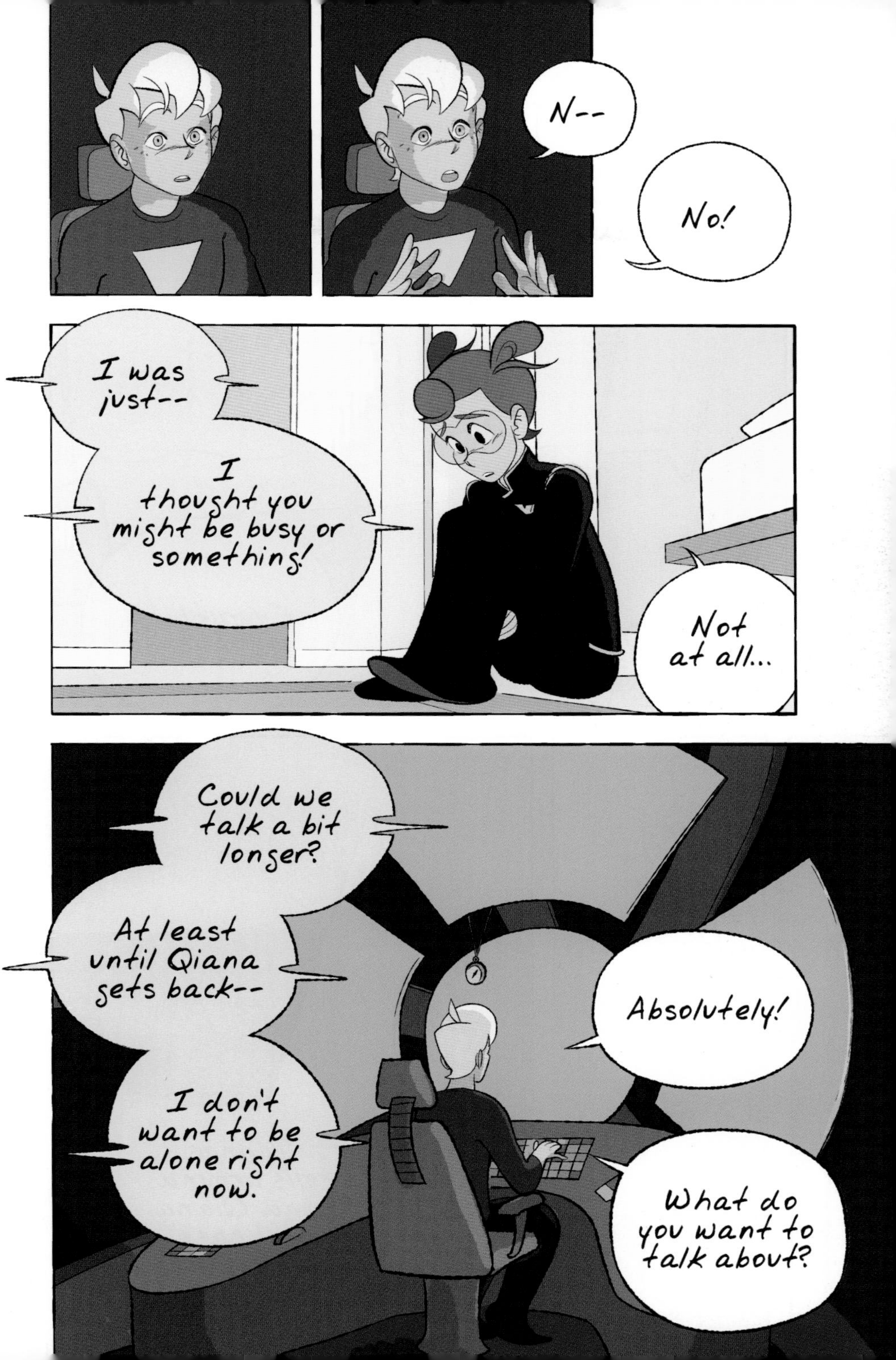
N--
No!
I was just--
I thought you might be busy or something!
Not at all...
Could we talk a bit longer?
At least until Qiana gets back--
I don't want to be alone right now.
Absolutely!
What do you want to talk about?

Anythin**g**.

Everythin**g**.

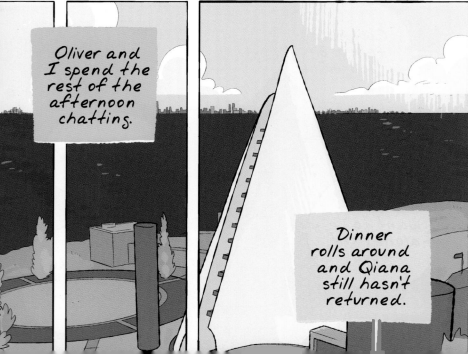

Oliver and I spend the rest of the afternoon chattin**g**.

Dinner rolls around and Qiana still hasn't returned.

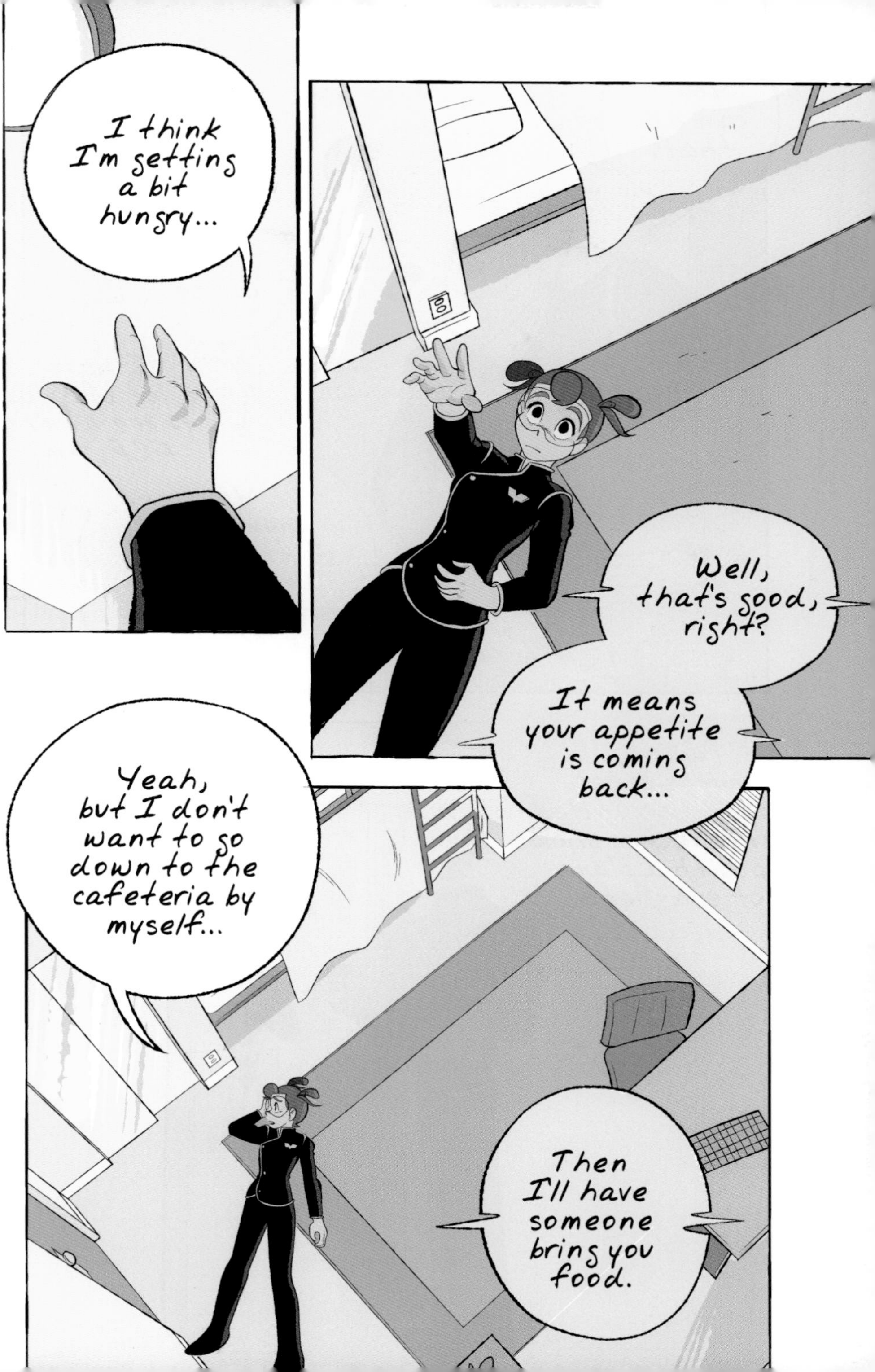
I think I'm getting a bit hungry...
Well, that's good, right?
It means your appetite is coming back...
Yeah, but I don't want to go down to the cafeteria by myself...
Then I'll have someone bring you food.

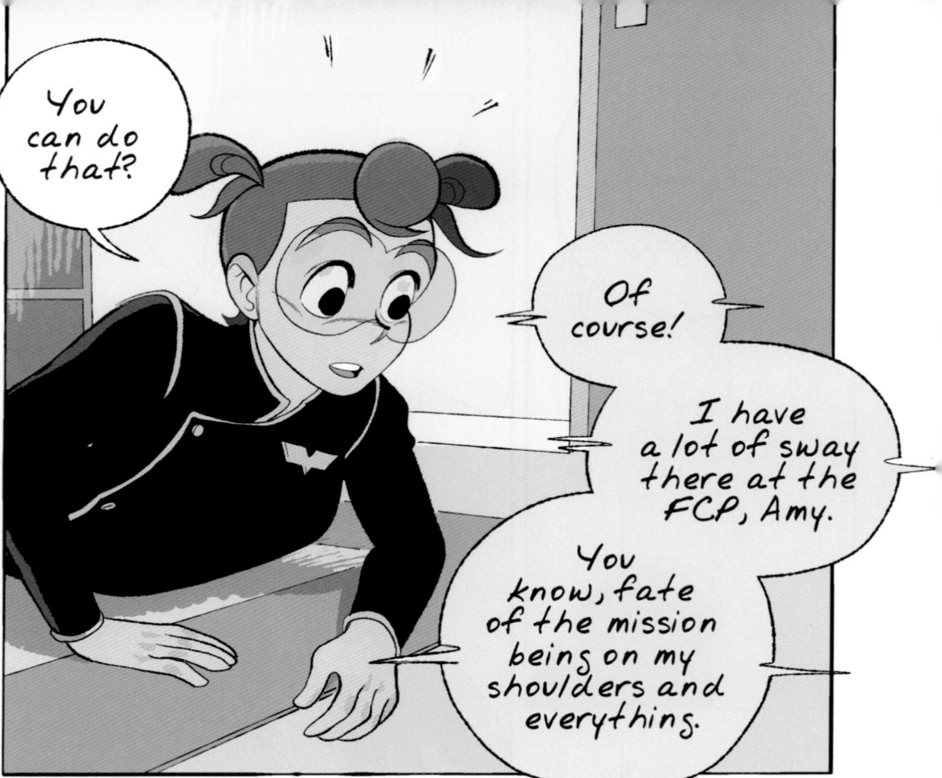
You can do that?
Of course!
I have a lot of sway there at the FCP, Amy.
You know, fate of the mission being on my shoulders and everything.

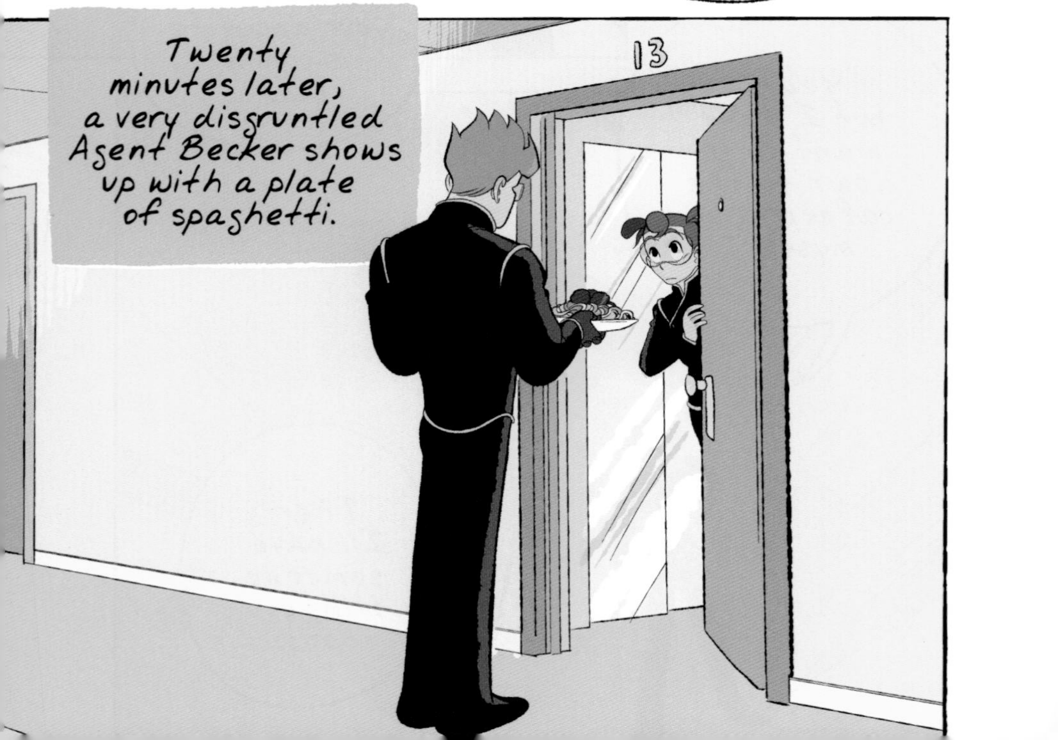
Twenty minutes later, a very disgruntled Agent Becker shows up with a plate of spaghetti.
13

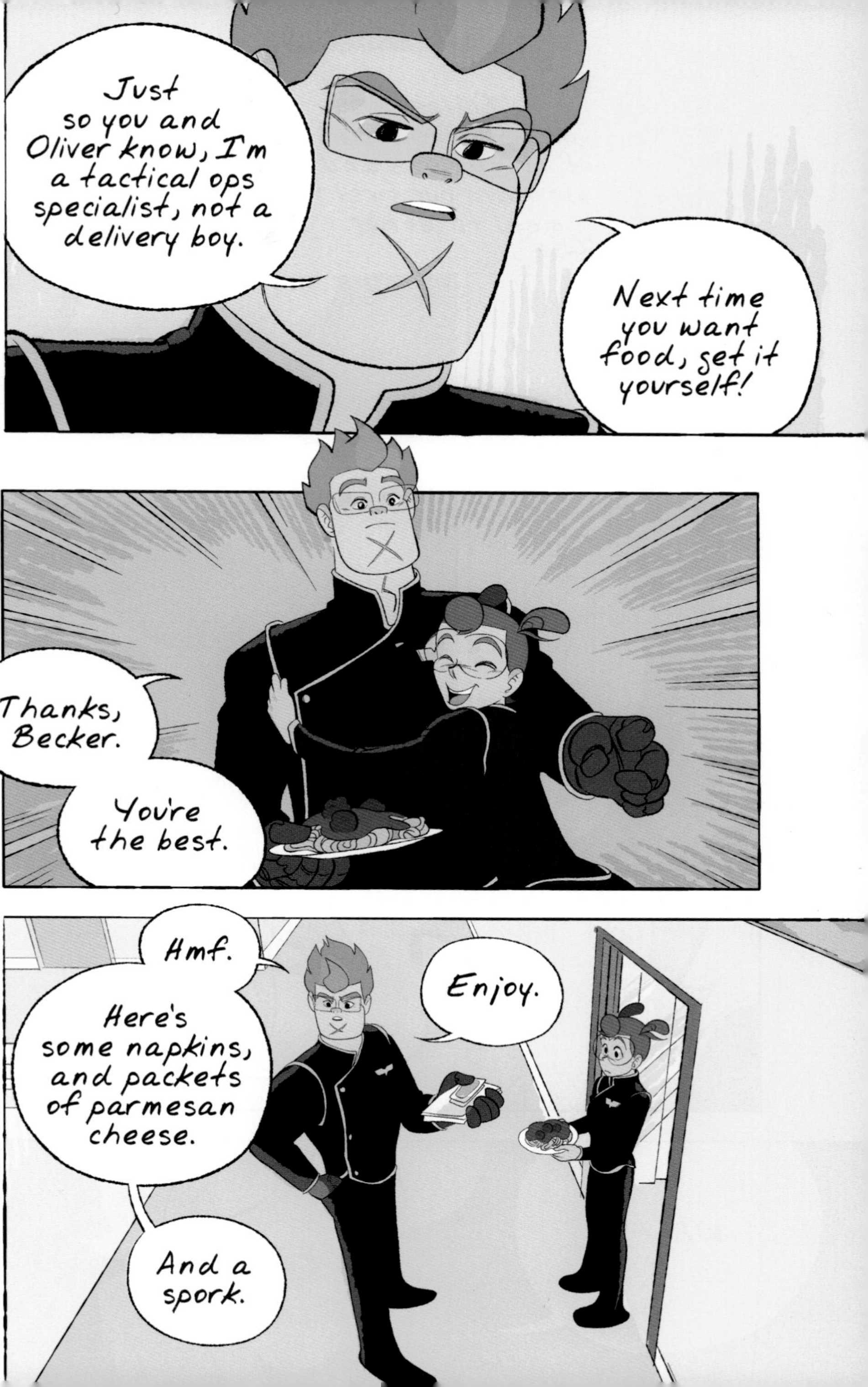

Just so you and Oliver know, I'm a tactical ops specialist, not a delivery boy.
Next time you want food, get it yourself!
Thanks, Becker.
You're the best.
Hmf.
Enjoy.
Here's some napkins, and packets of parmesan cheese.
And a spork.

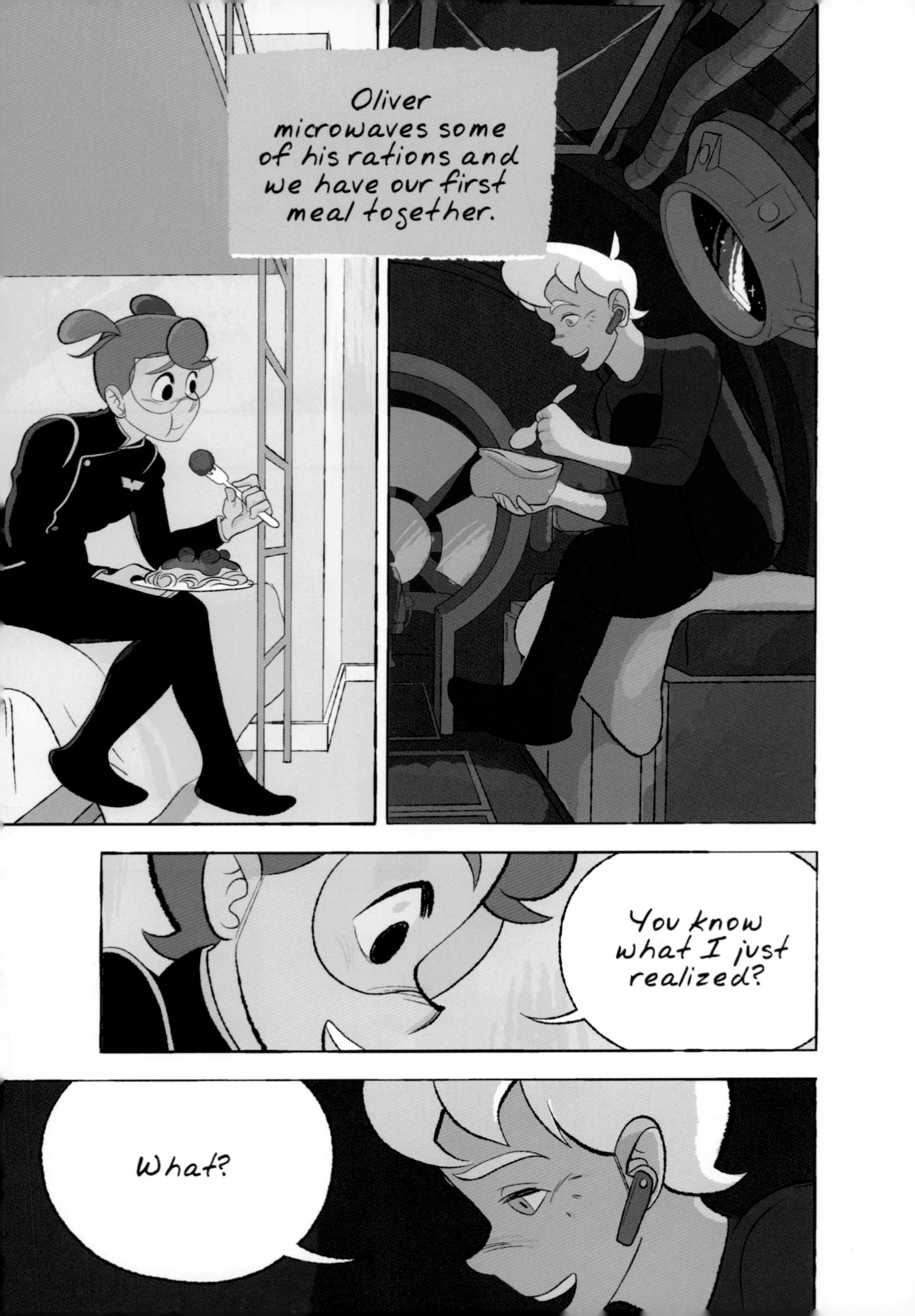
Oliver microwaves some of his rations and we have our first meal together.
You know what I just realized?
What?

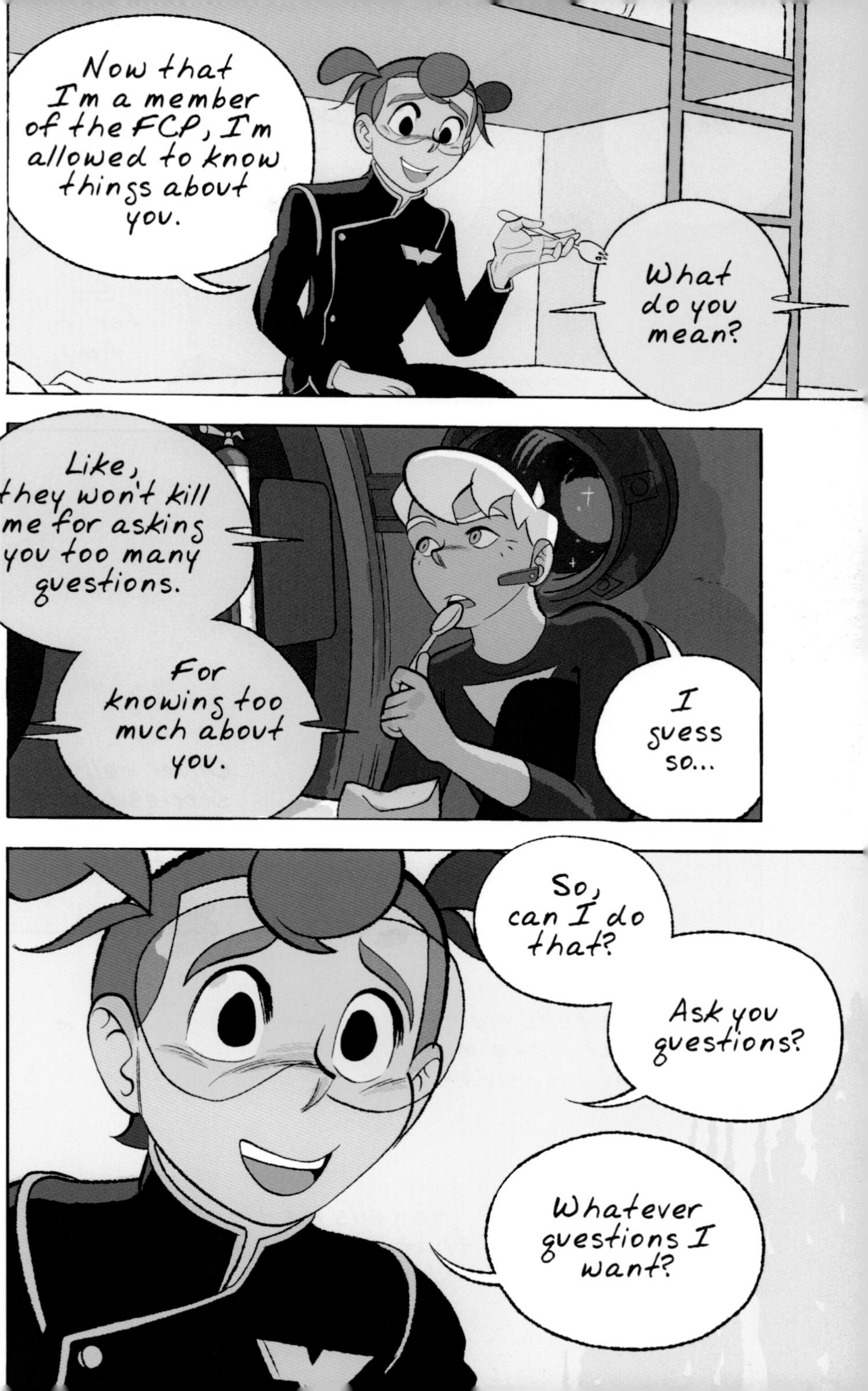
Now that I'm a member of the FCP, I'm allowed to know things about you.
What do you mean?
Like, they won't kill me for asking you too many questions.
For knowing too much about you.
I guess so...
So, can I do that?
Ask you questions?
Whatever questions I want?

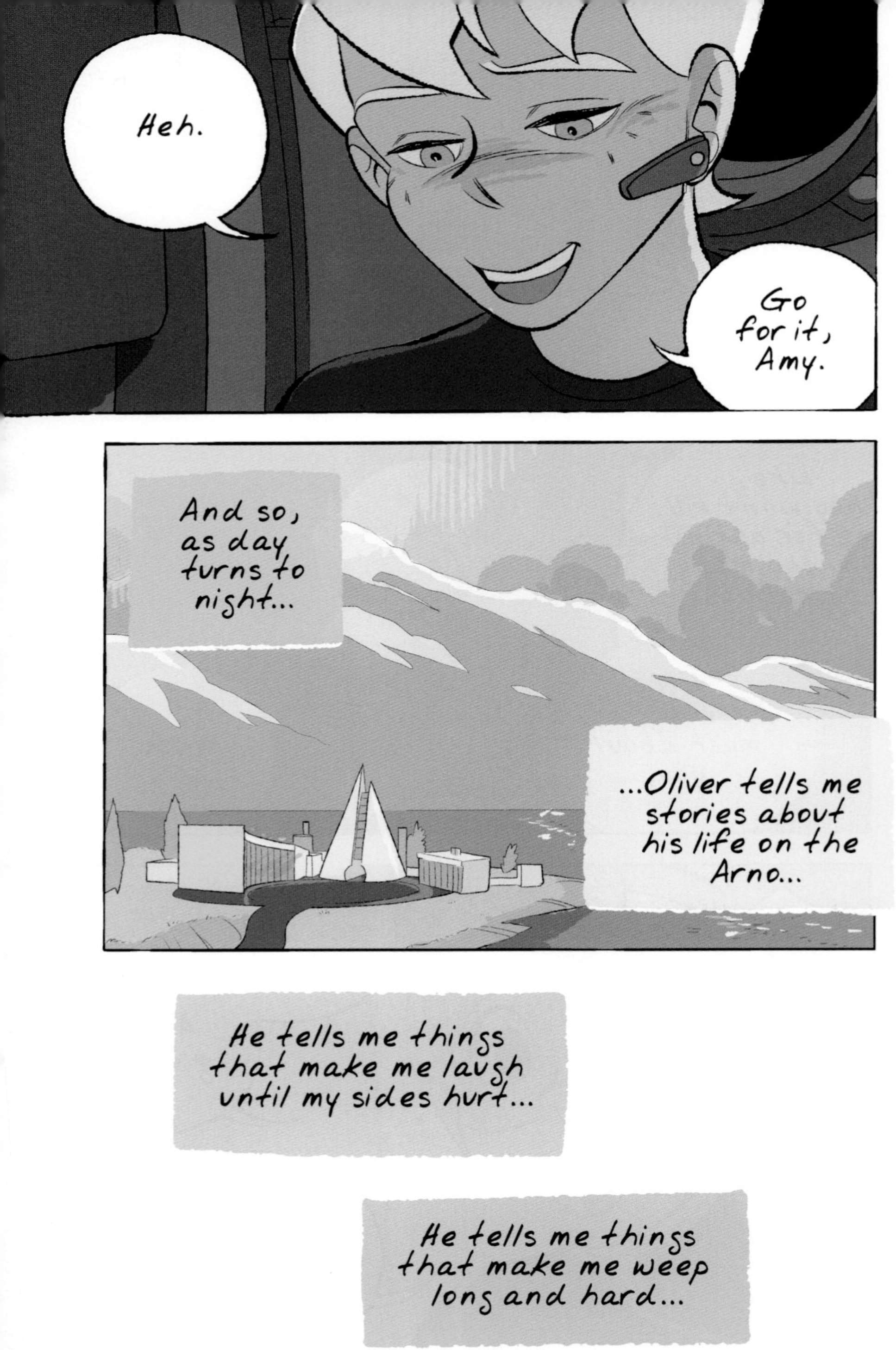
Heh.
Go for it, Amy.
And so, as day turns to night...
...Oliver tells me stories about his life on the Arno...
He tells me things that make me laugh until my sides hurt...
He tells me things that make me weep long and hard...

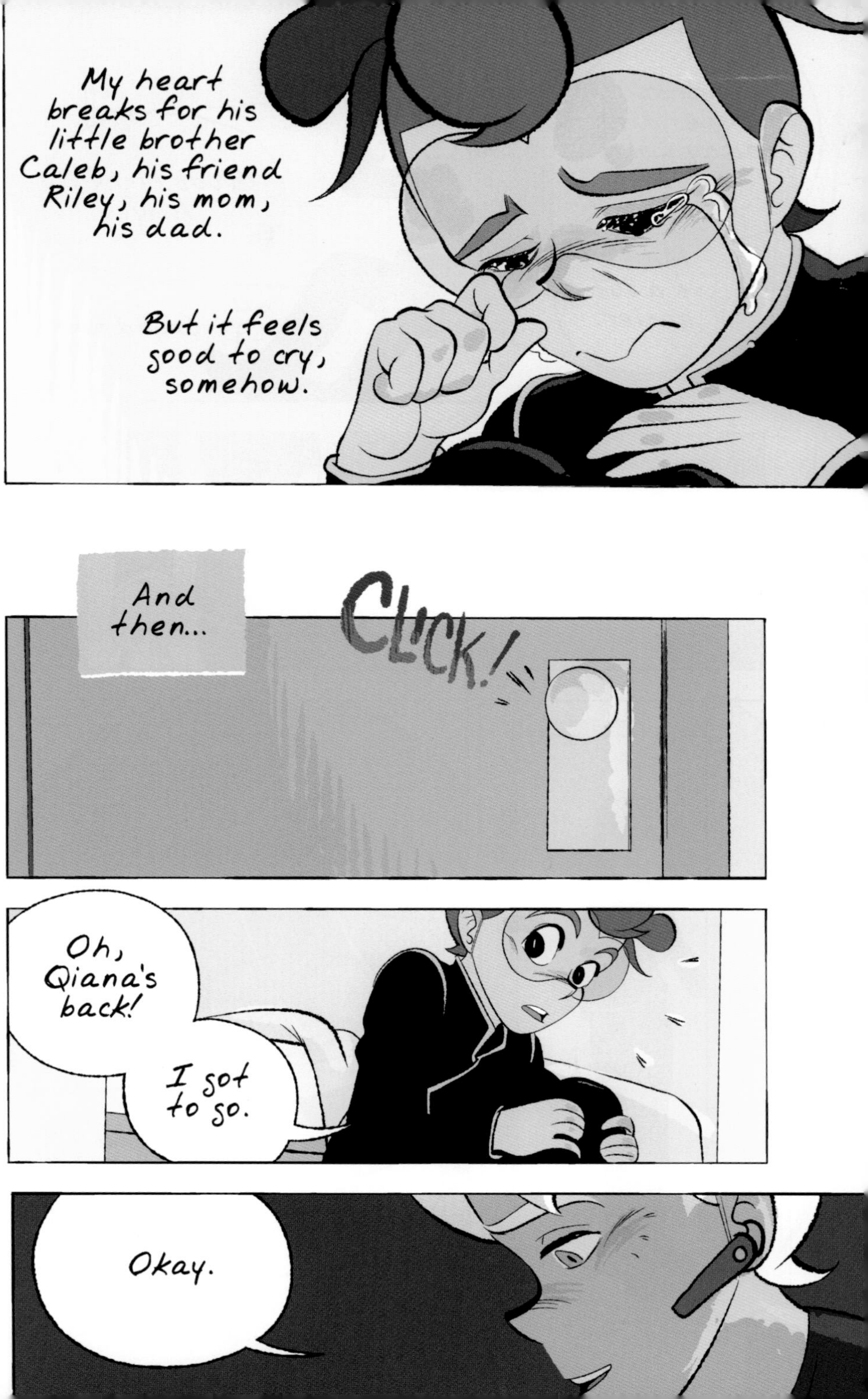
My heart breaks for his little brother Caleb, his friend Riley, his mom, his dad.
But it feels good to cry, somehow.
And then...
CLICK!
Oh, Qiana's back!
I got to go.
Okay.

Thanks for spending today with me--

Made it a lot easier.

Goodnight, Amy.

Goodnight!

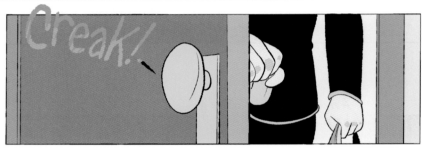

Creak!

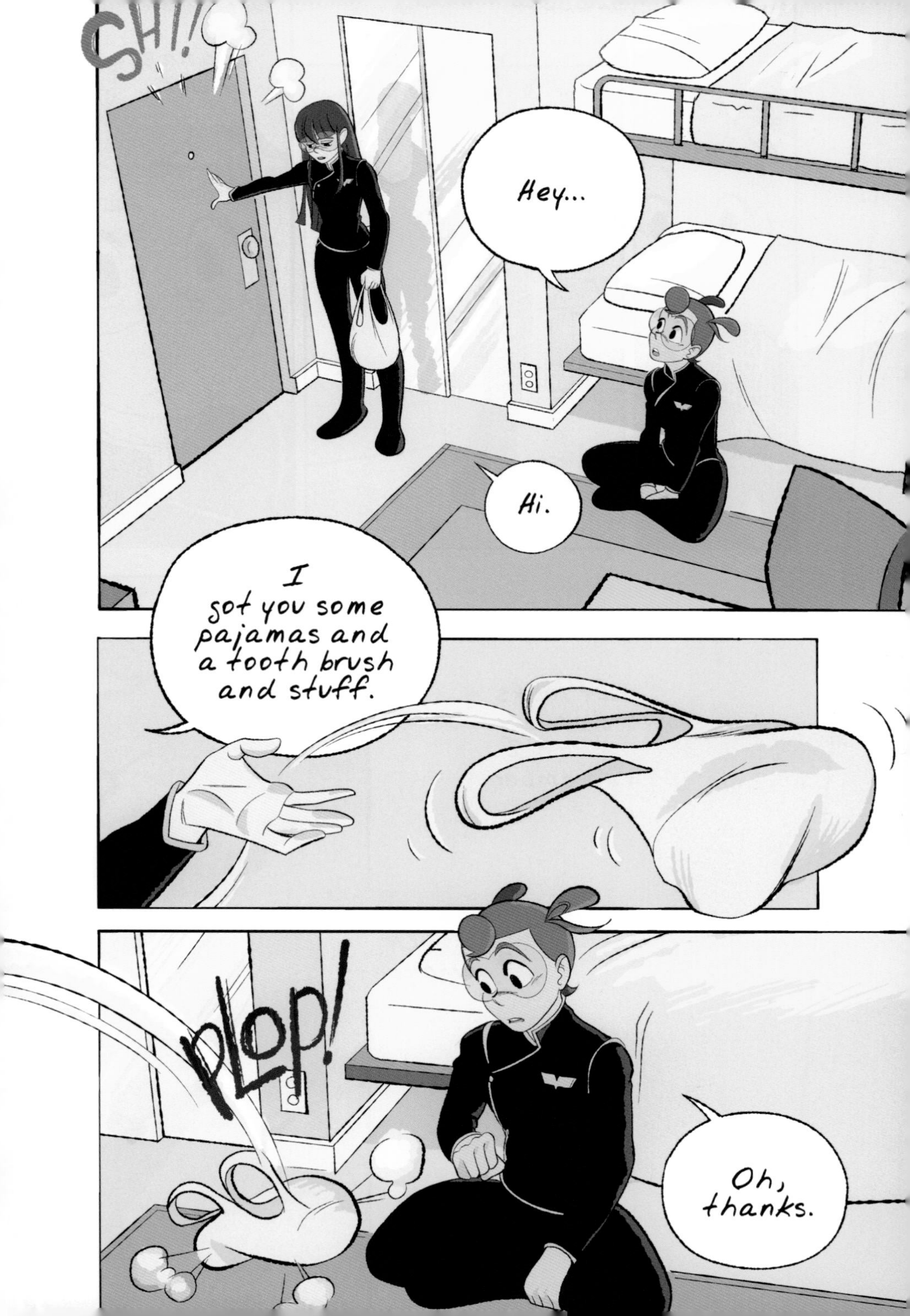
SHH!
Hey...
Hi.
I got you some pajamas and a tooth brush and stuff.
PLOP!
Oh, thanks.

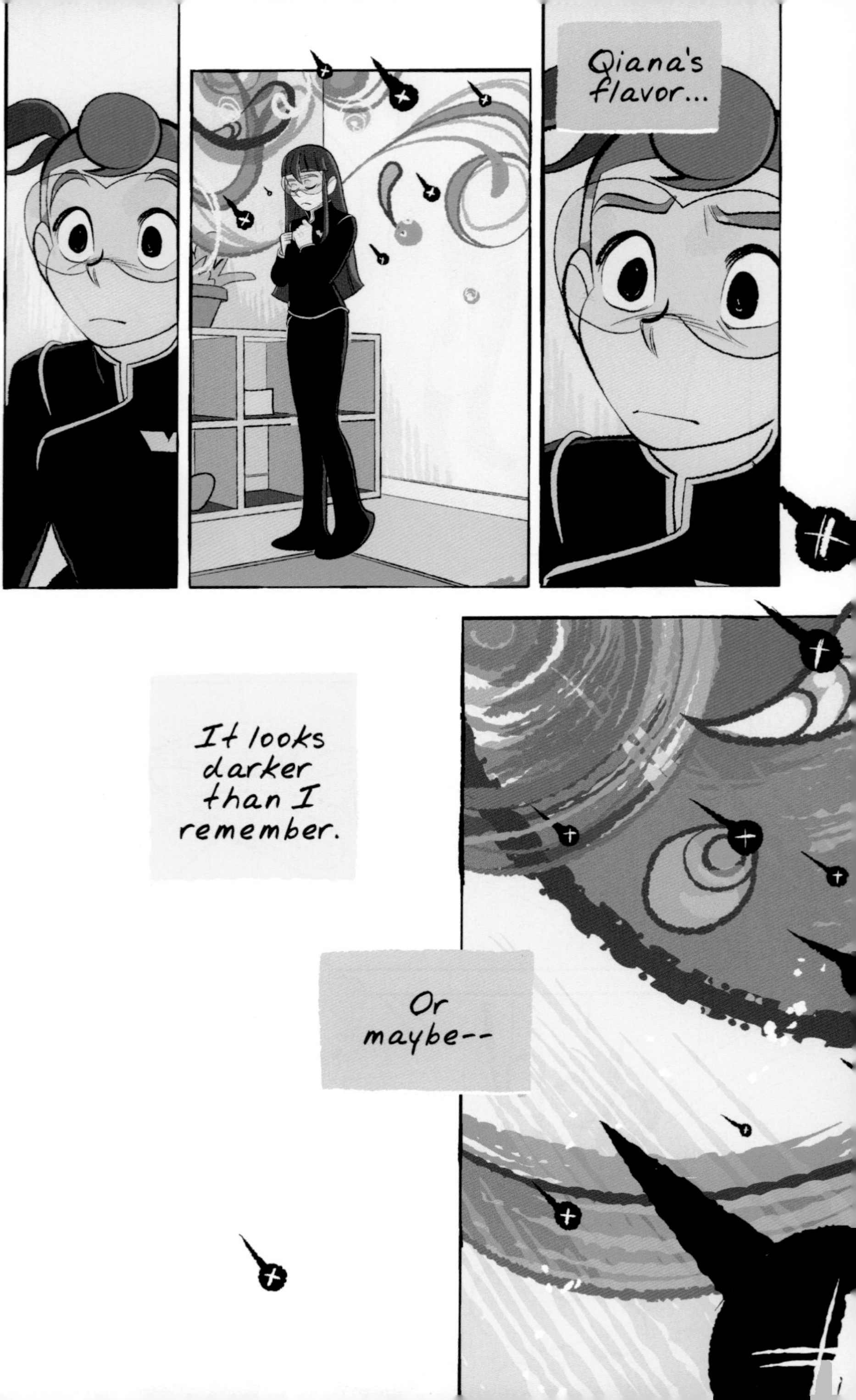
Qiana's flavor...
It looks darker than I remember.
Or maybe--

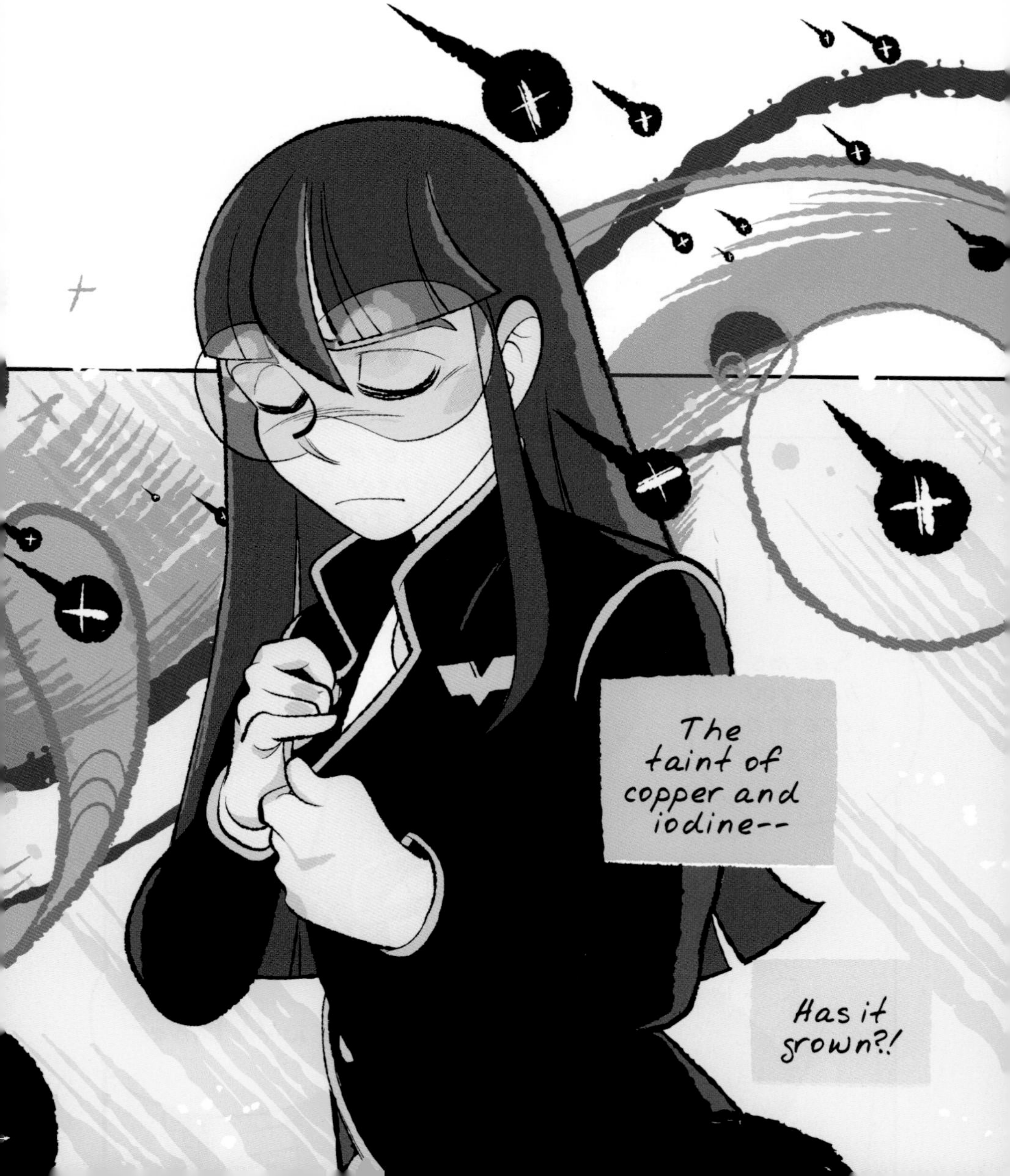
The taint of copper and iodine--
Has it grown?!

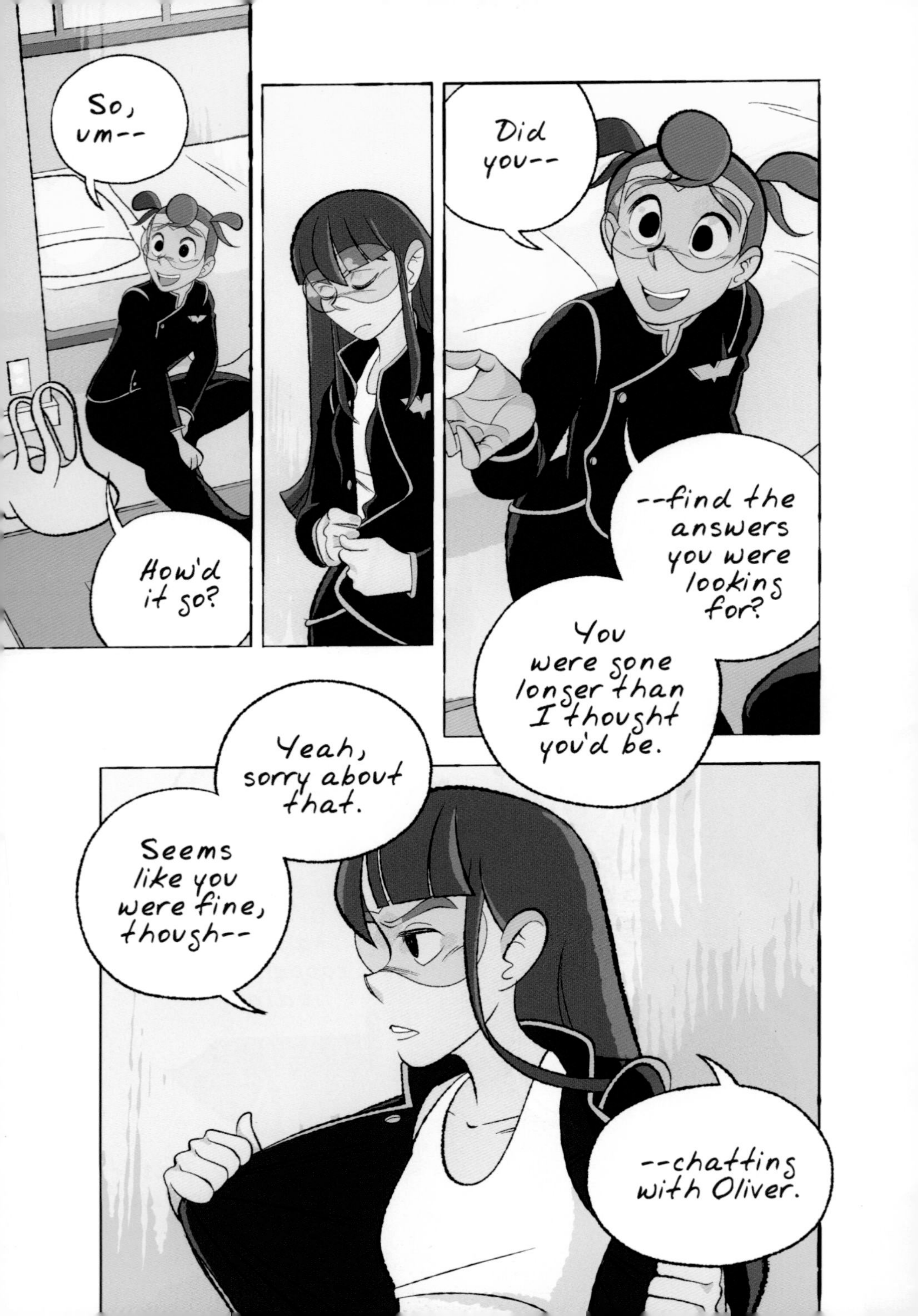
So, um--
How'd it go?
Did you--
--find the answers you were looking for?
You were gone longer than I thought you'd be.
Yeah, sorry about that.
Seems like you were fine, though--
--chatting with Oliver.

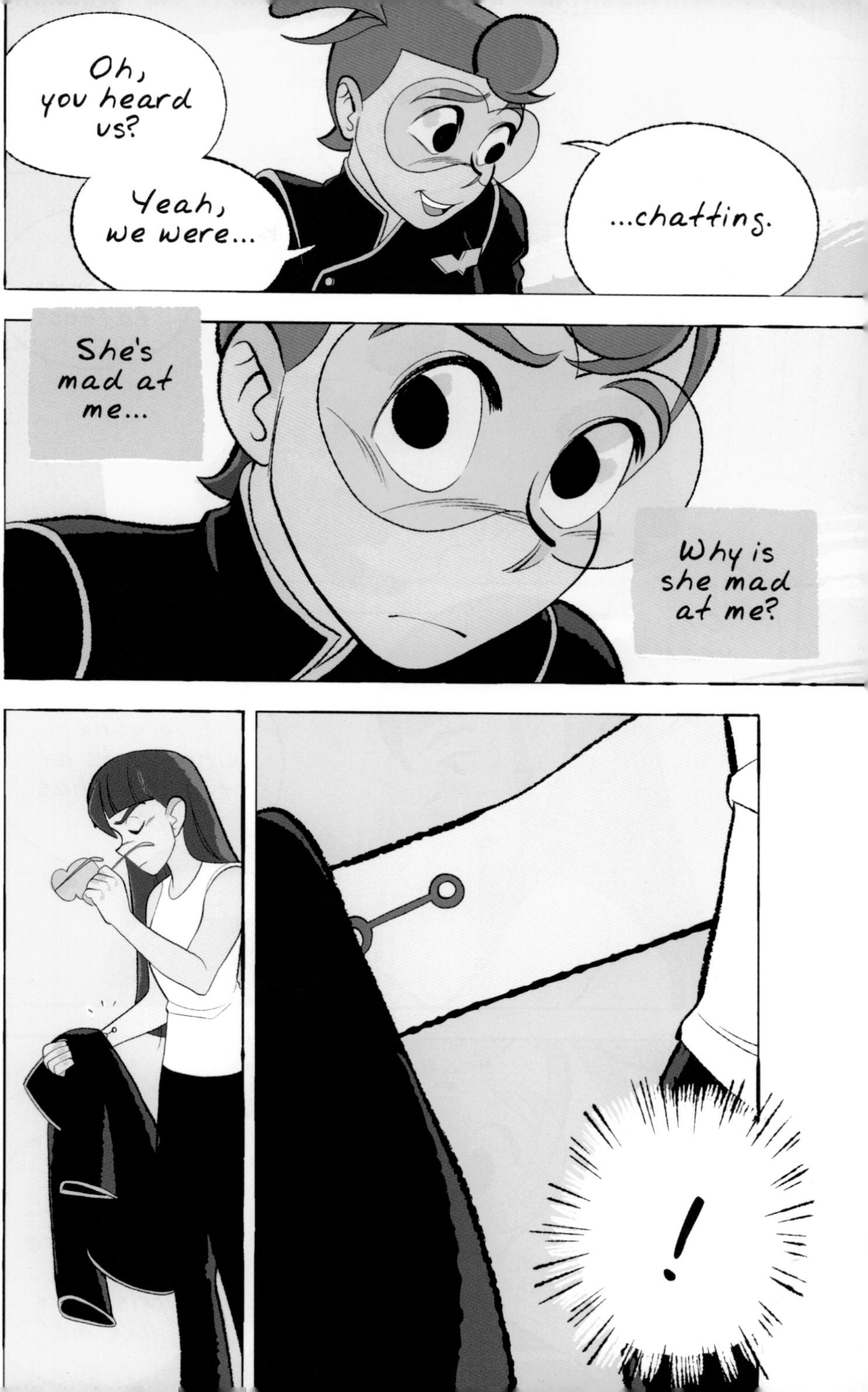
Oh, you heard us?
Yeah, we were...
...chatting.
She's mad at me...
Why is she mad at me?
!

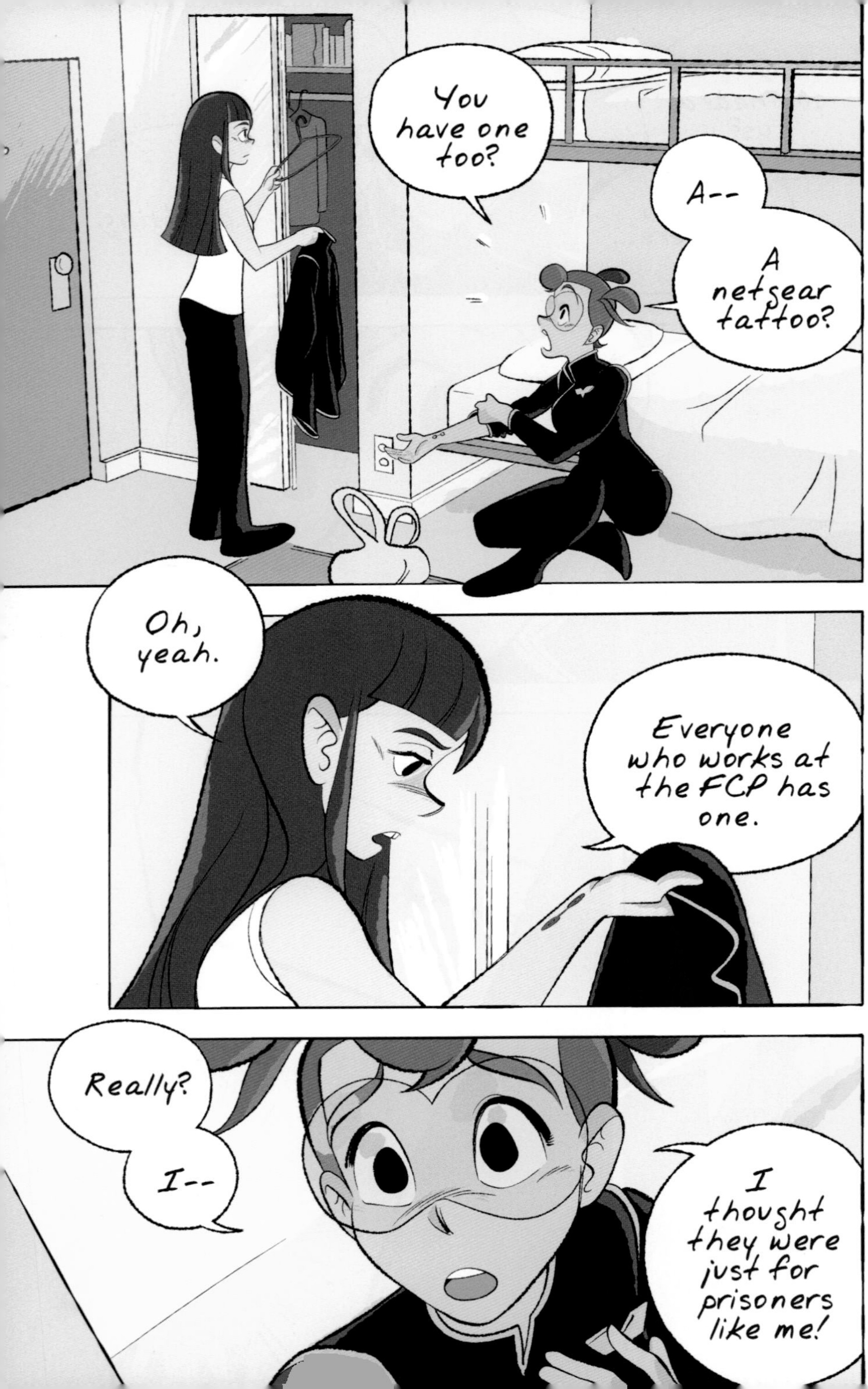
You have one too?
A--
A netgear tattoo?
Oh, yeah.
Everyone who works at the FCP has one.
Really?
I--
I thought they were just for prisoners like me!

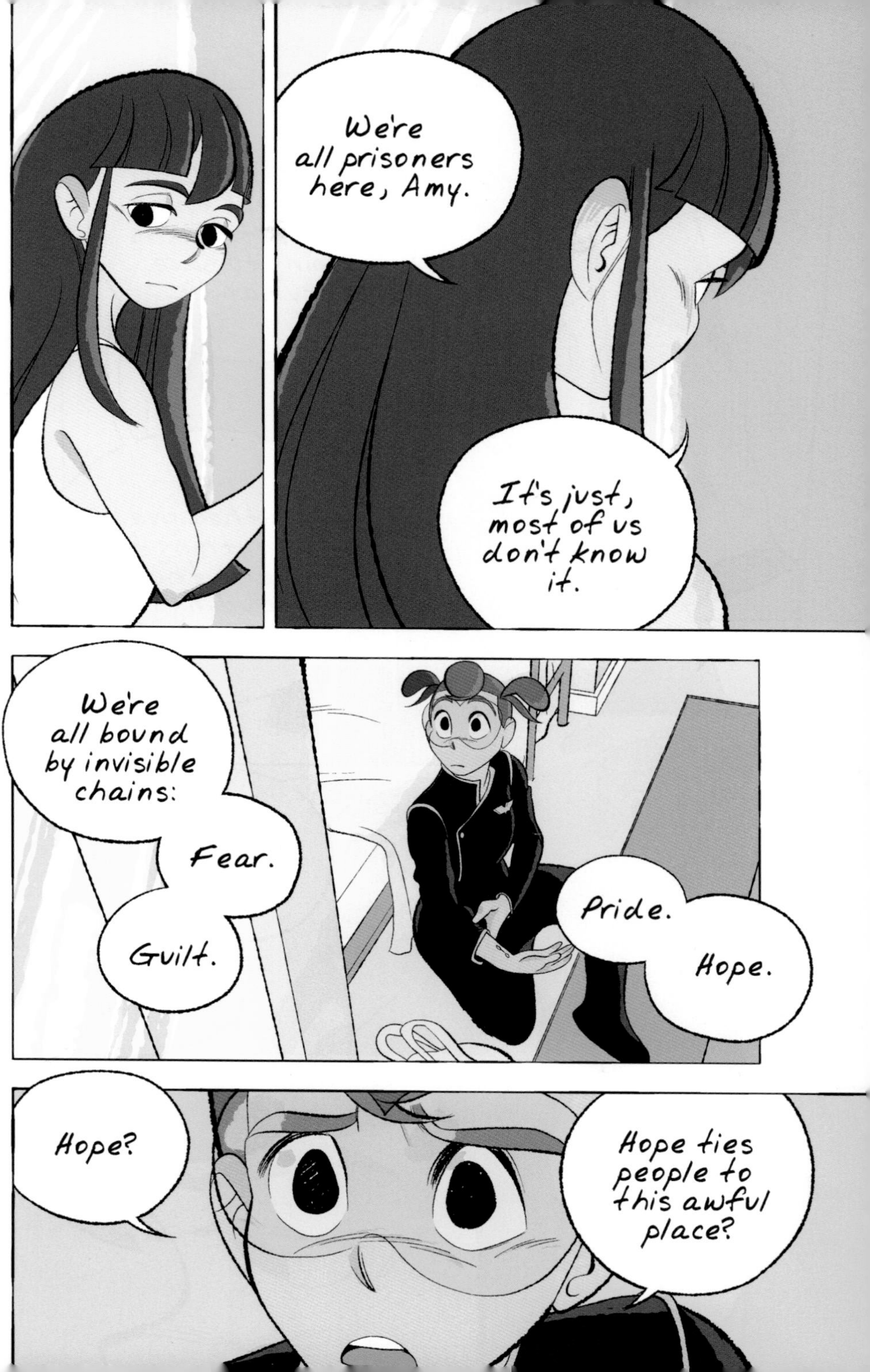
We're all prisoners here, Amy.
It's just, most of us don't know it.
We're all bound by invisible chains:
Fear.
Guilt.
Pride.
Hope.
Hope?
Hope ties people to this awful place?

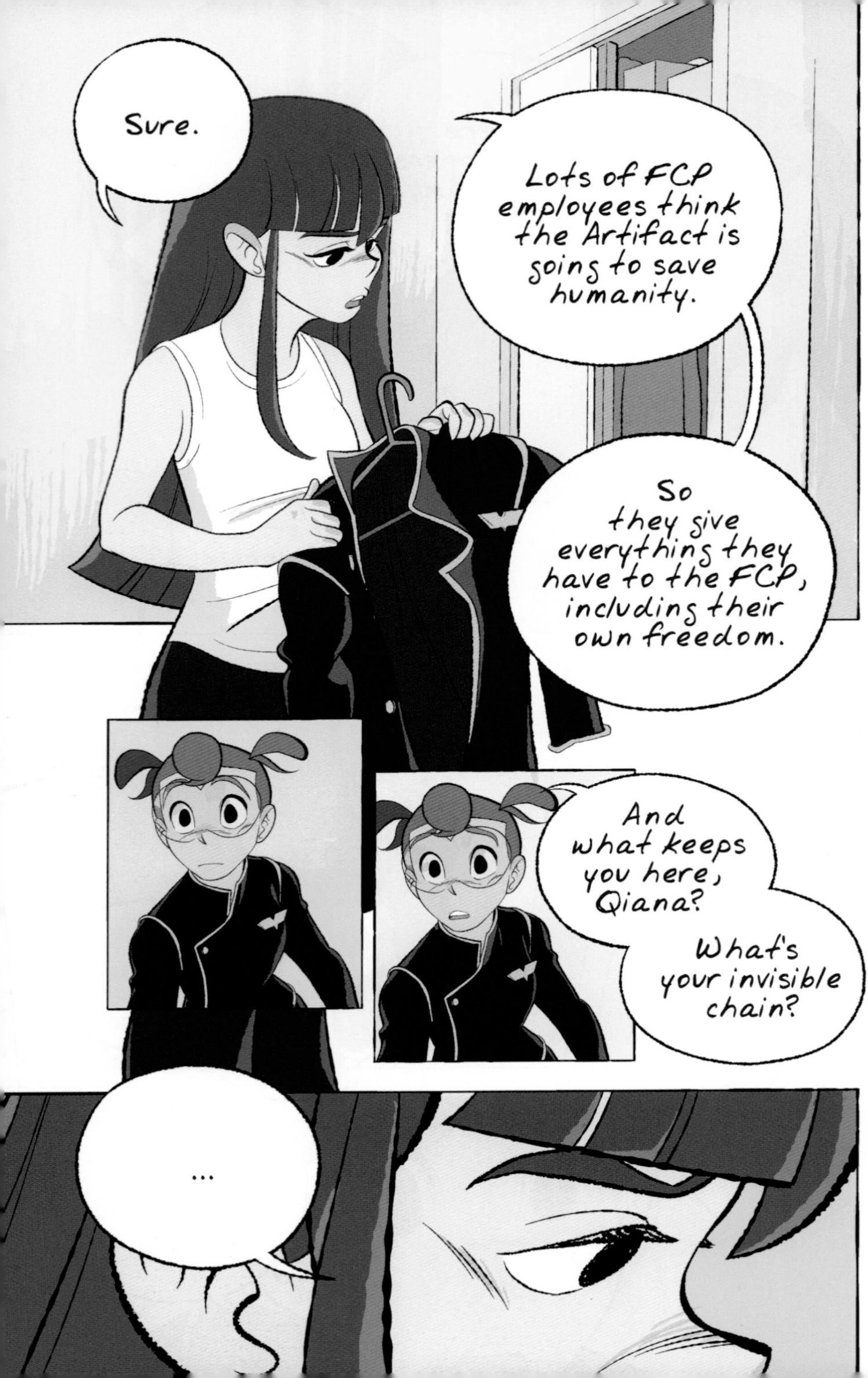
Sure.
Lots of FCP employees think the Artifact is going to save humanity.
So they give everything they have to the FCP, including their own freedom.
And what keeps you here, Qiana?
What's your invisible chain?
...

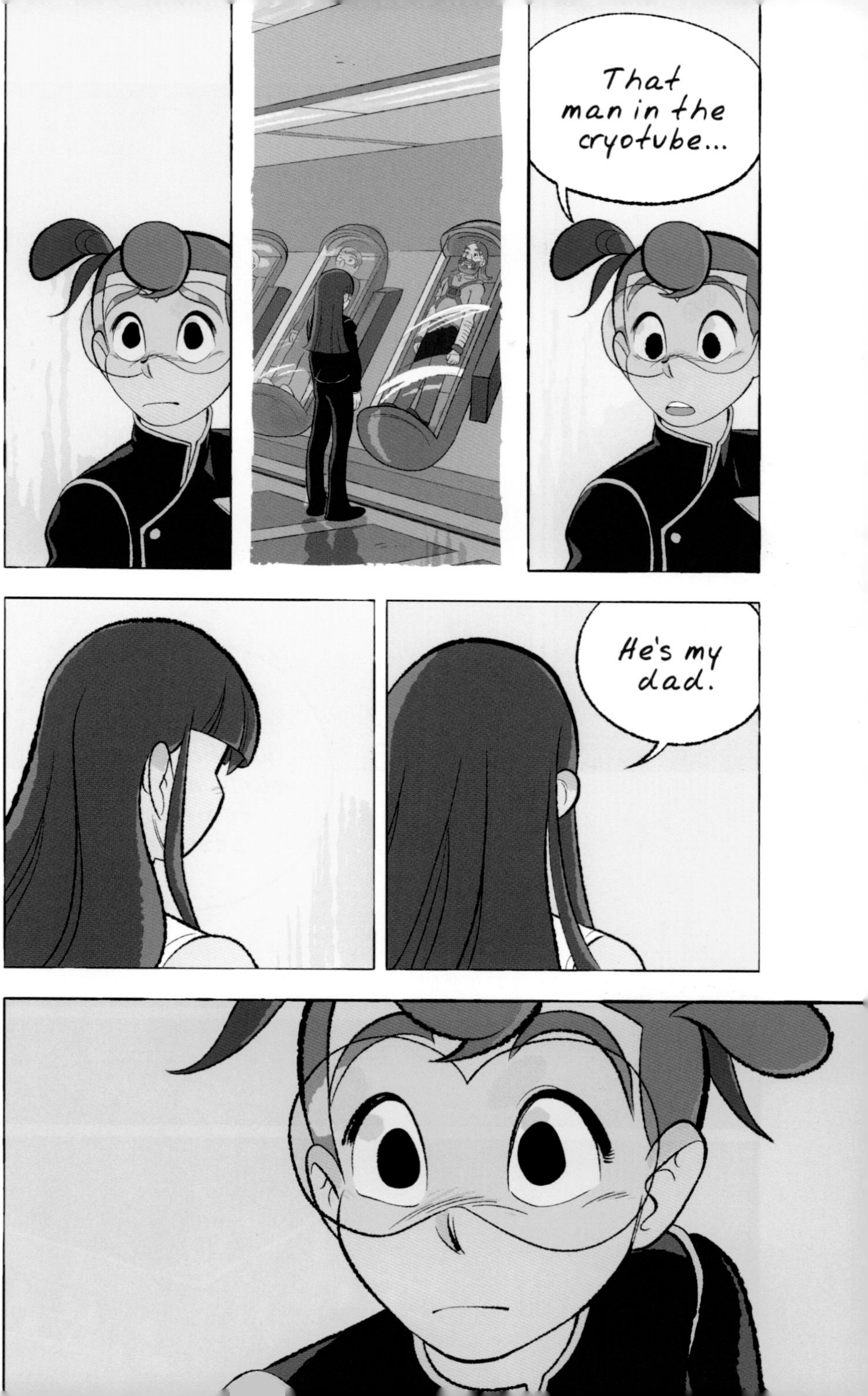
That man in the cryotube...
He's my dad.

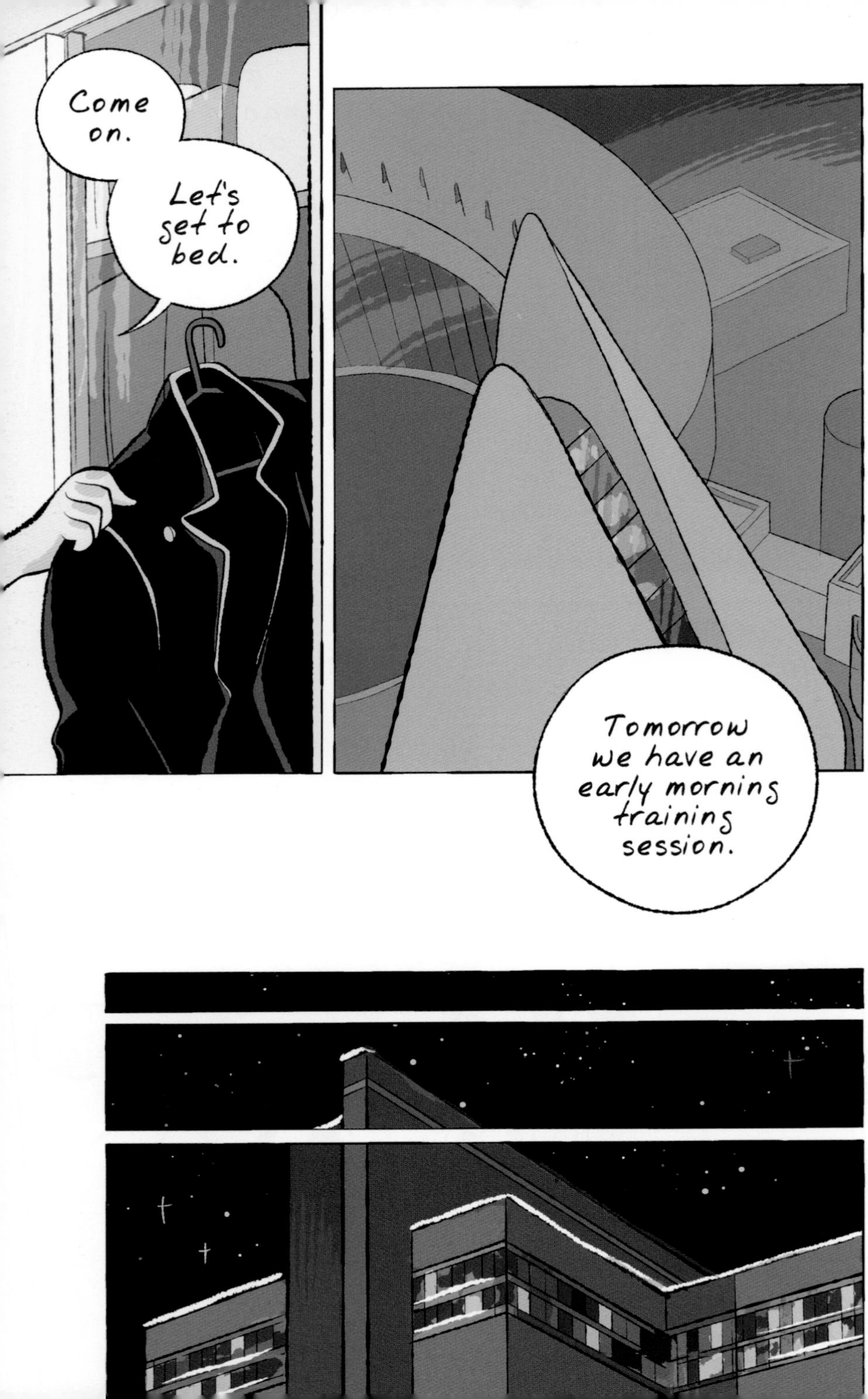
Come on.
Let's get to bed.
Tomorrow we have an early morning training session.

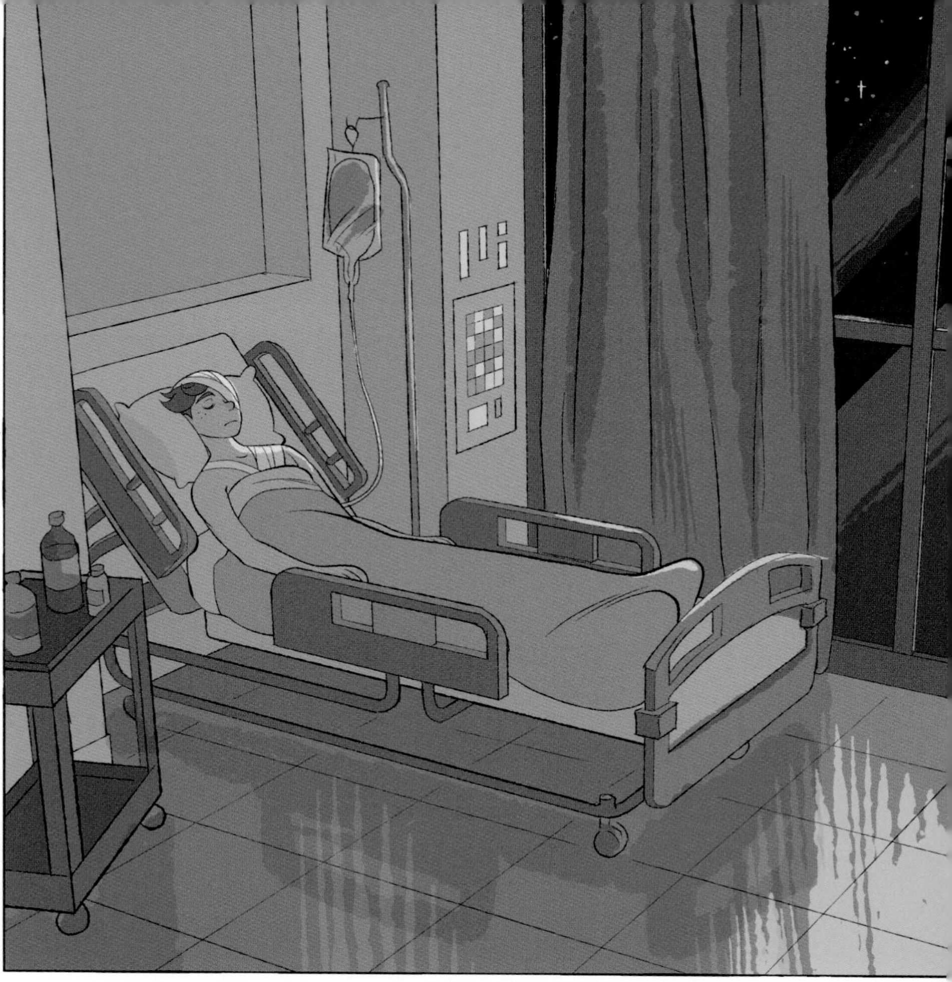

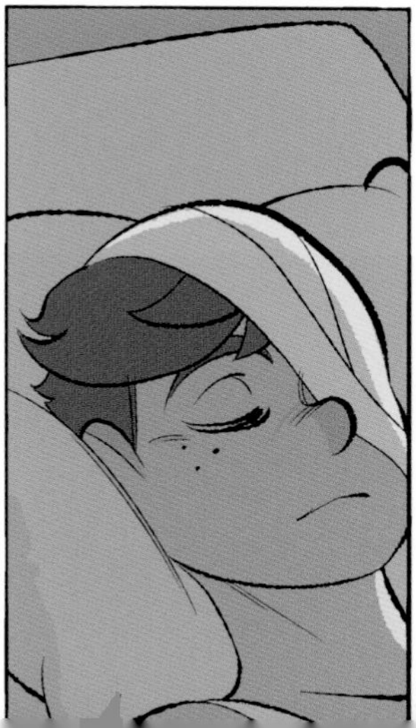

clack

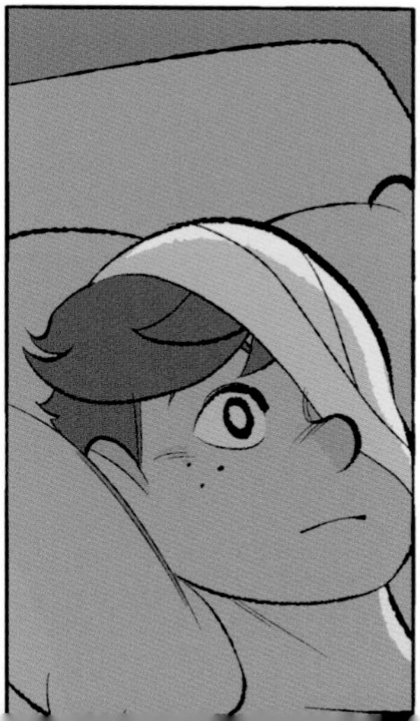

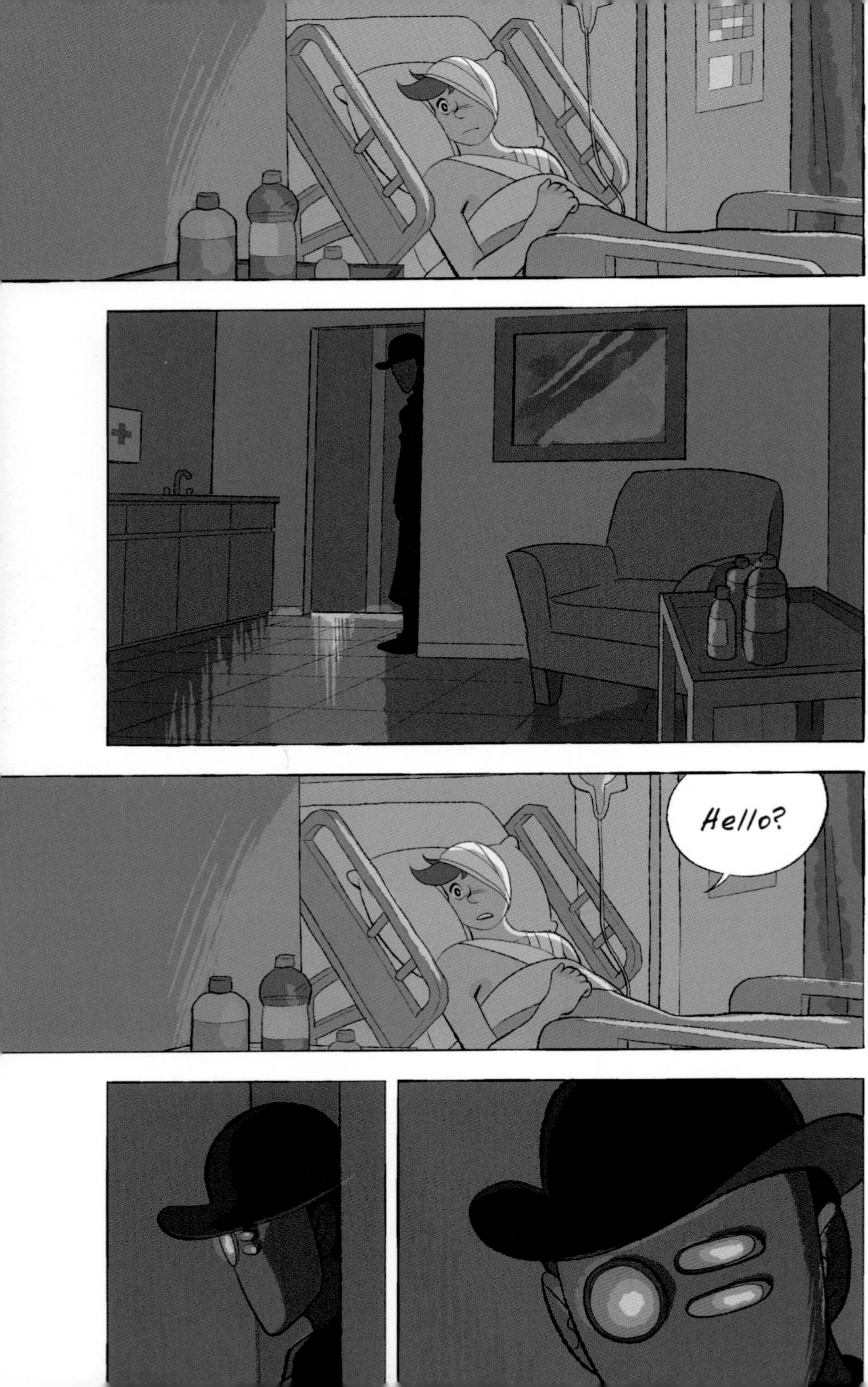
Hello?

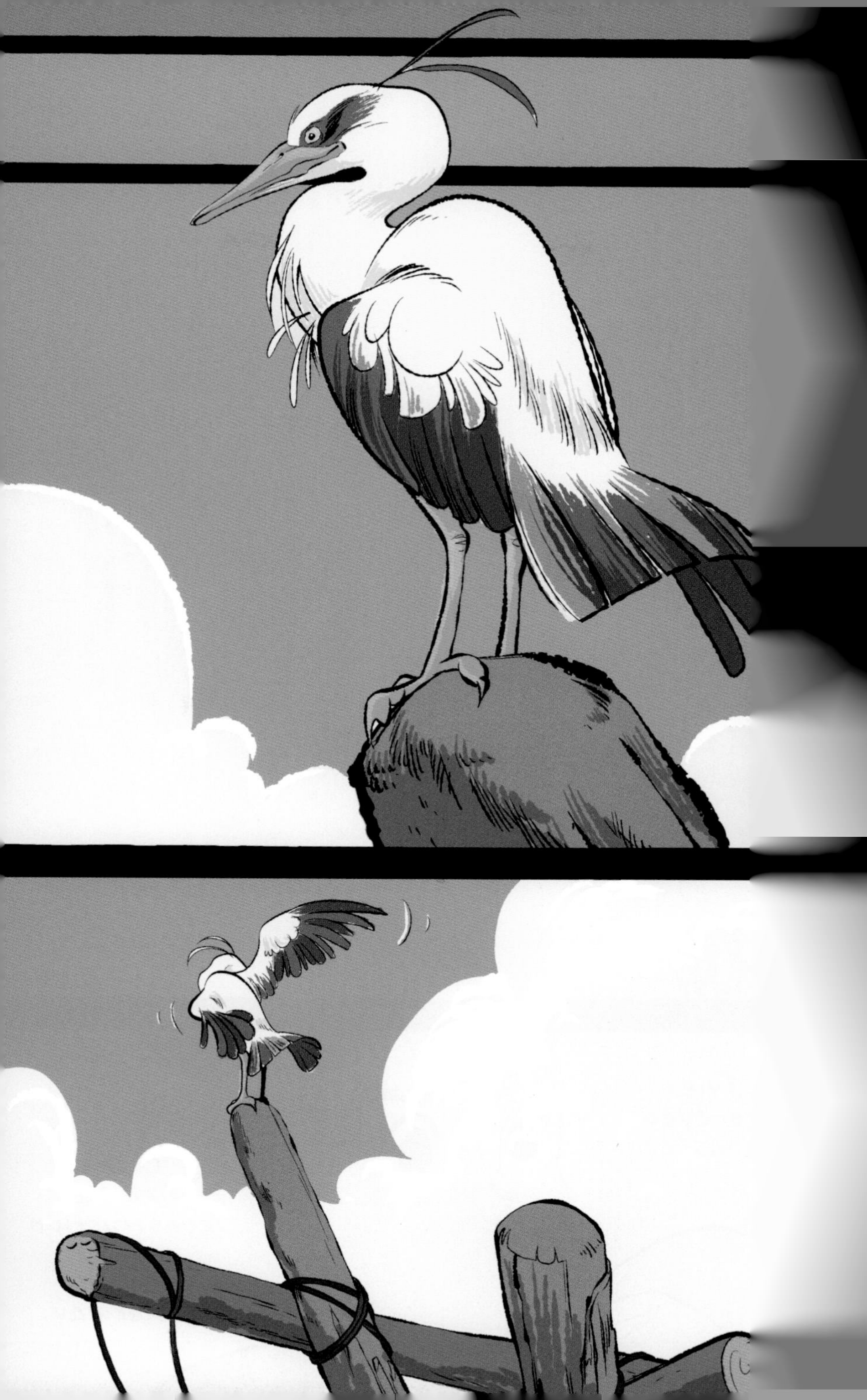

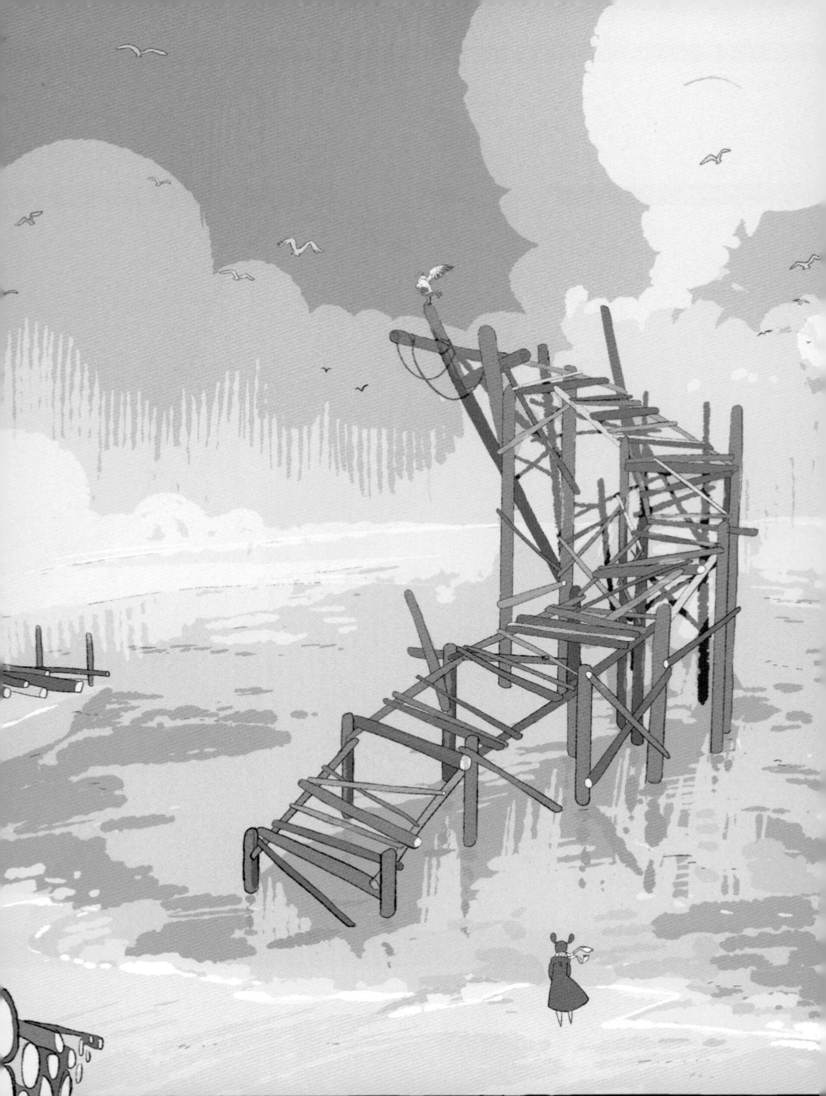

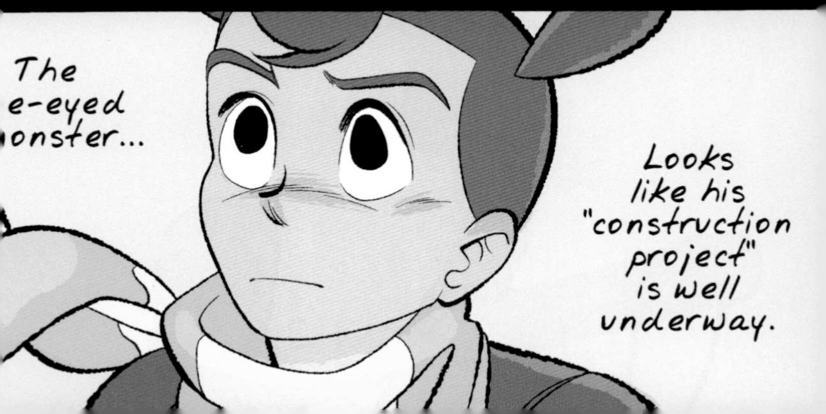
The
e-eyed
onster...
Looks like his "construction project" is well underway.

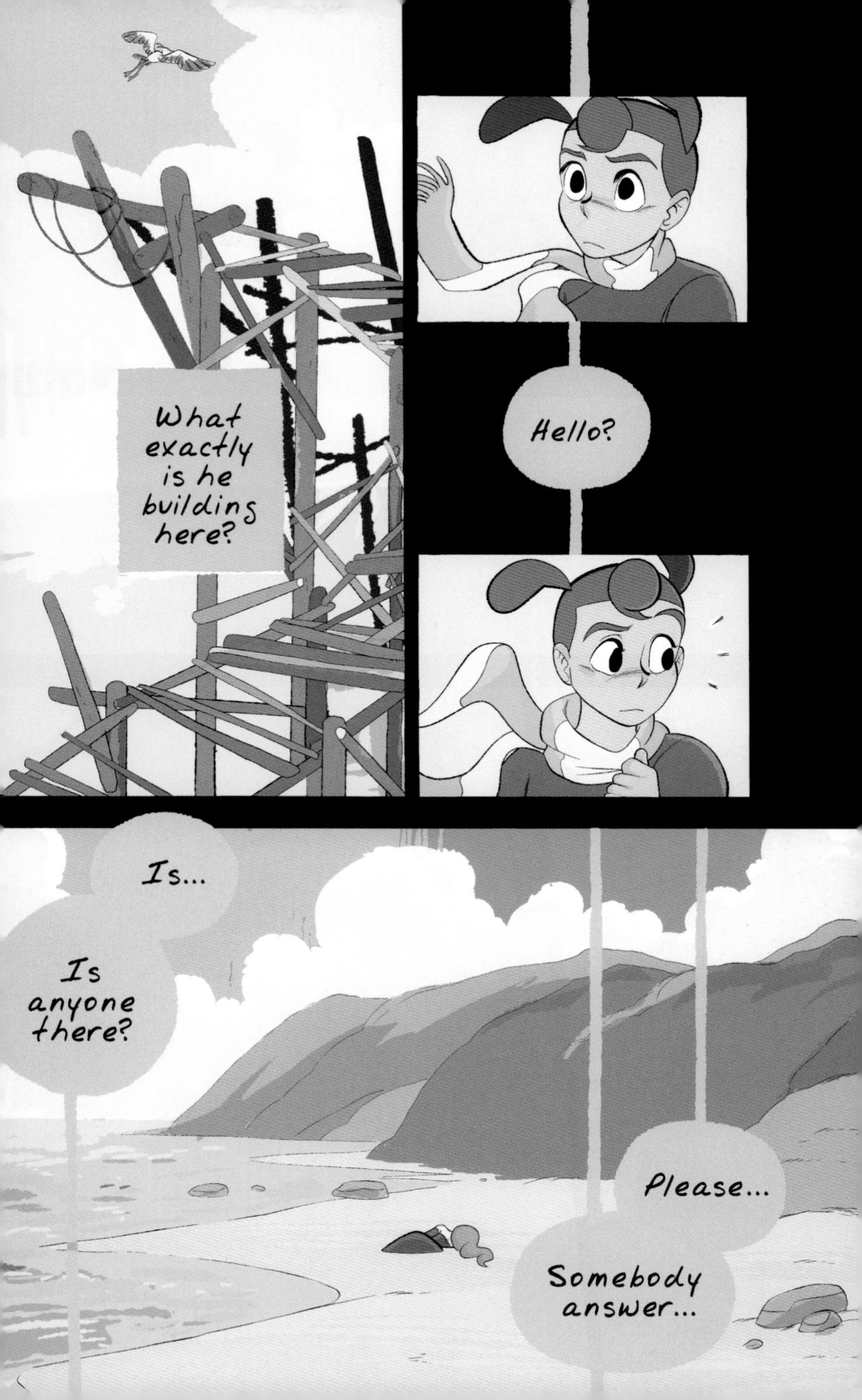
What exactly is he building here?
Hello?
Is...
Is anyone there?
Please...
Somebody answer...

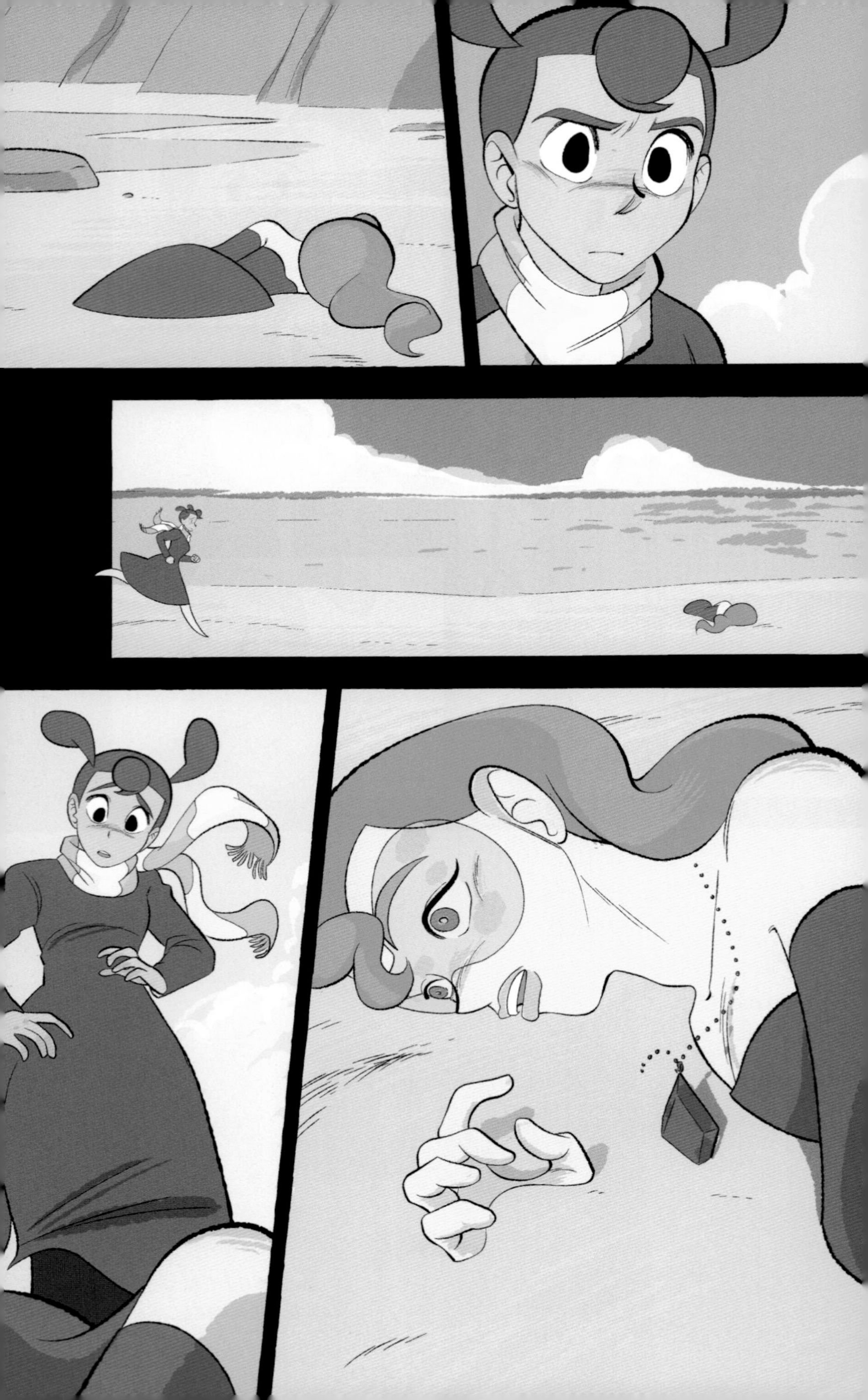

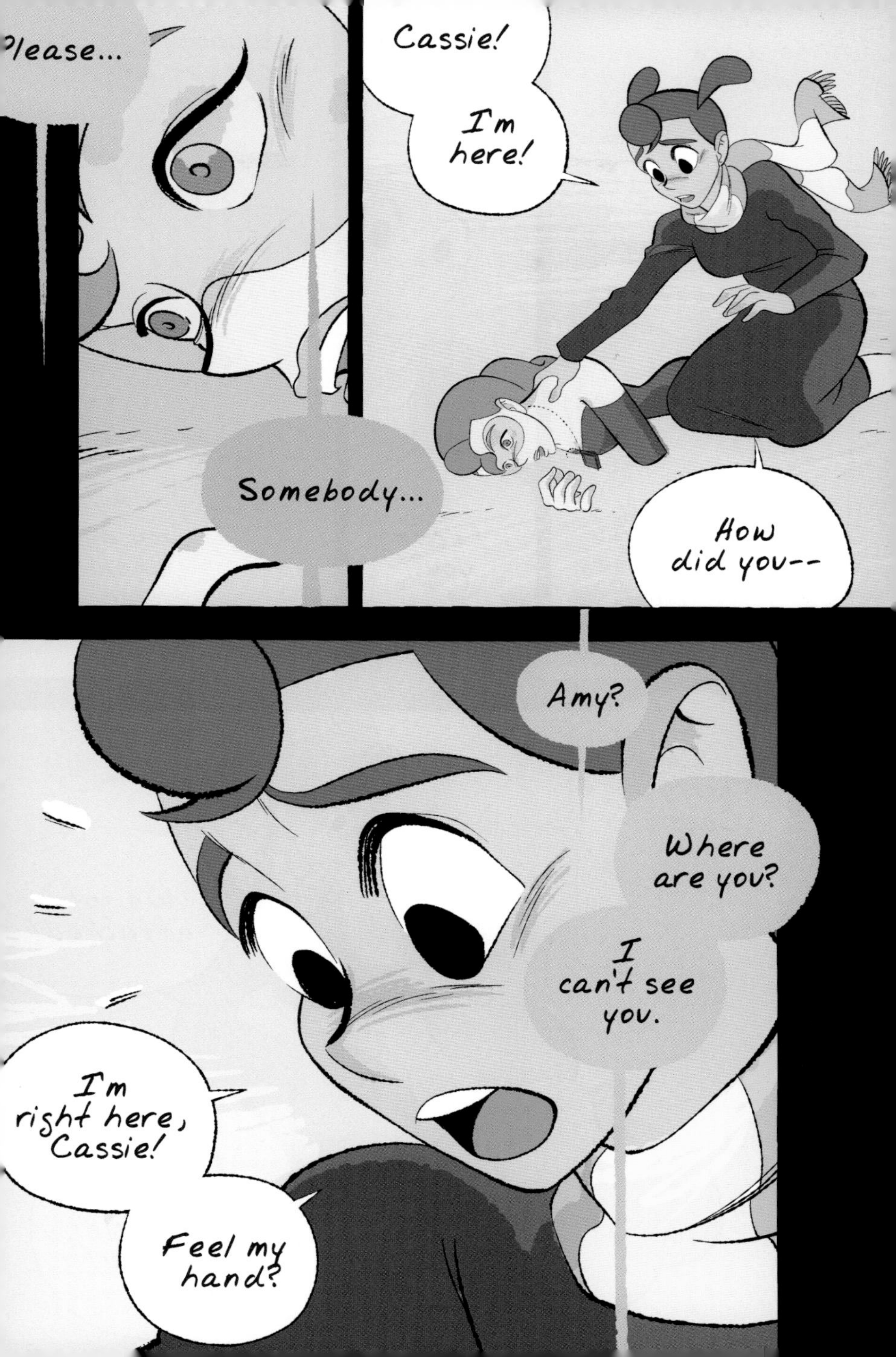
Please...
Somebody...
Cassie!
I'm here!
How did you--
Amy?
Where are you?
I can't see you.
I'm right here, Cassie!
Feel my hand?

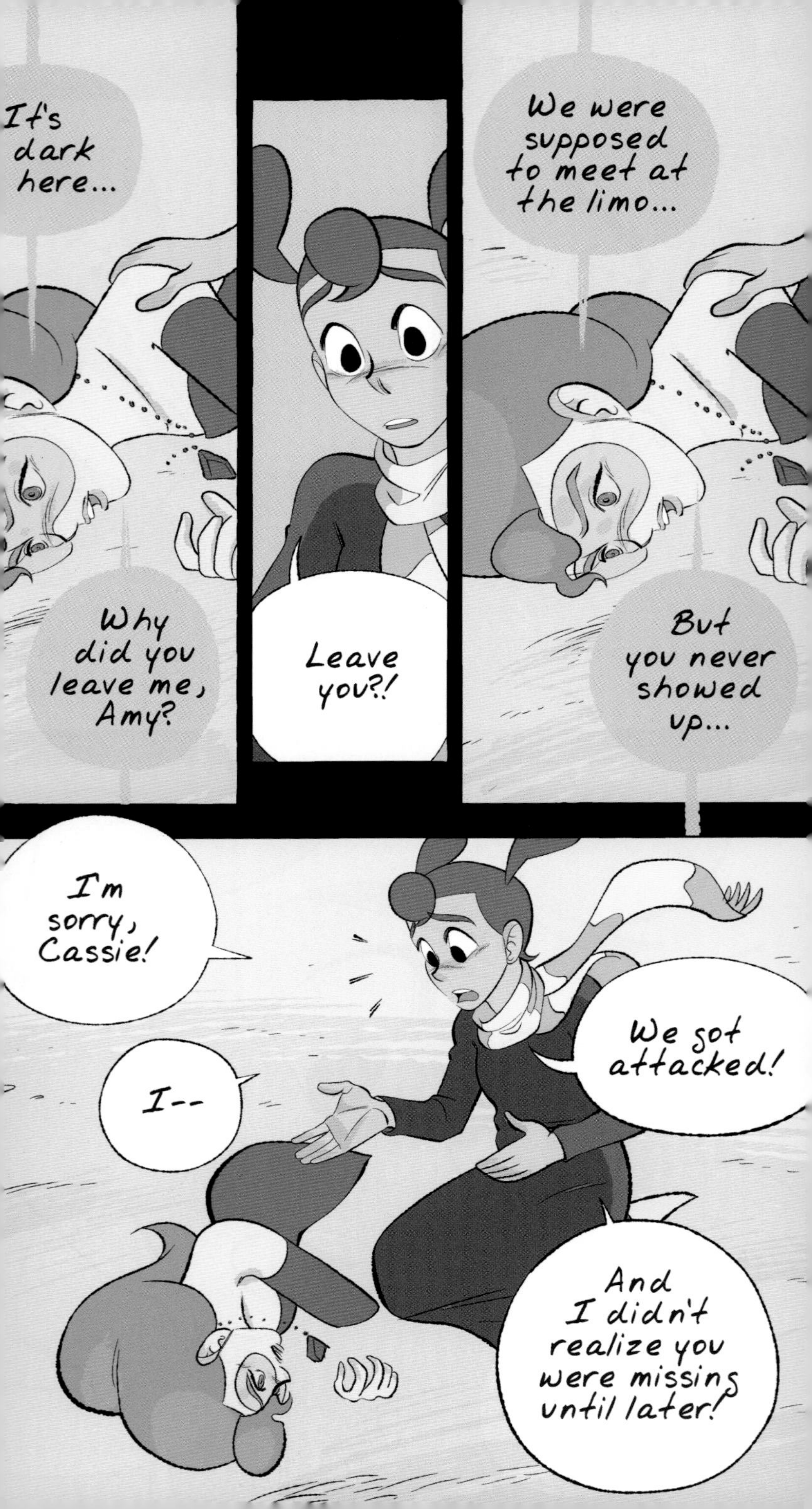
It's dark here...
Why did you leave me, Amy?
Leave you?!
We were supposed to meet at the limo...
But you never showed up...
I'm sorry, Cassie!
I--
We got attacked!
And I didn't realize you were missing until later!

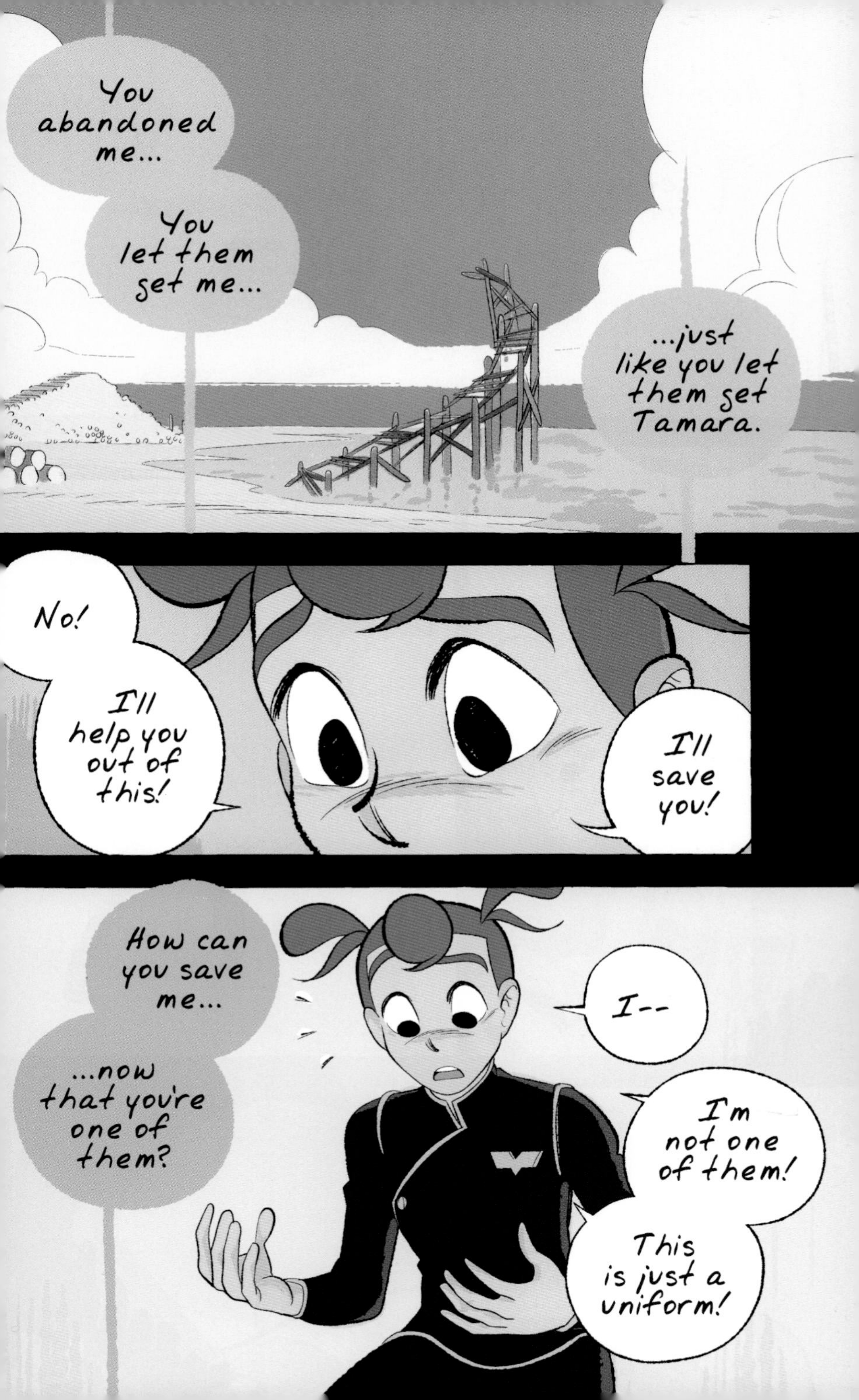

You abandoned me...
You let them get me...
...just like you let them get Tamara.
No!
I'll help you out of this!
I'll save you!
How can you save me...
...now that you're one of them?
I--
I'm not one of them!
This is just a uniform!

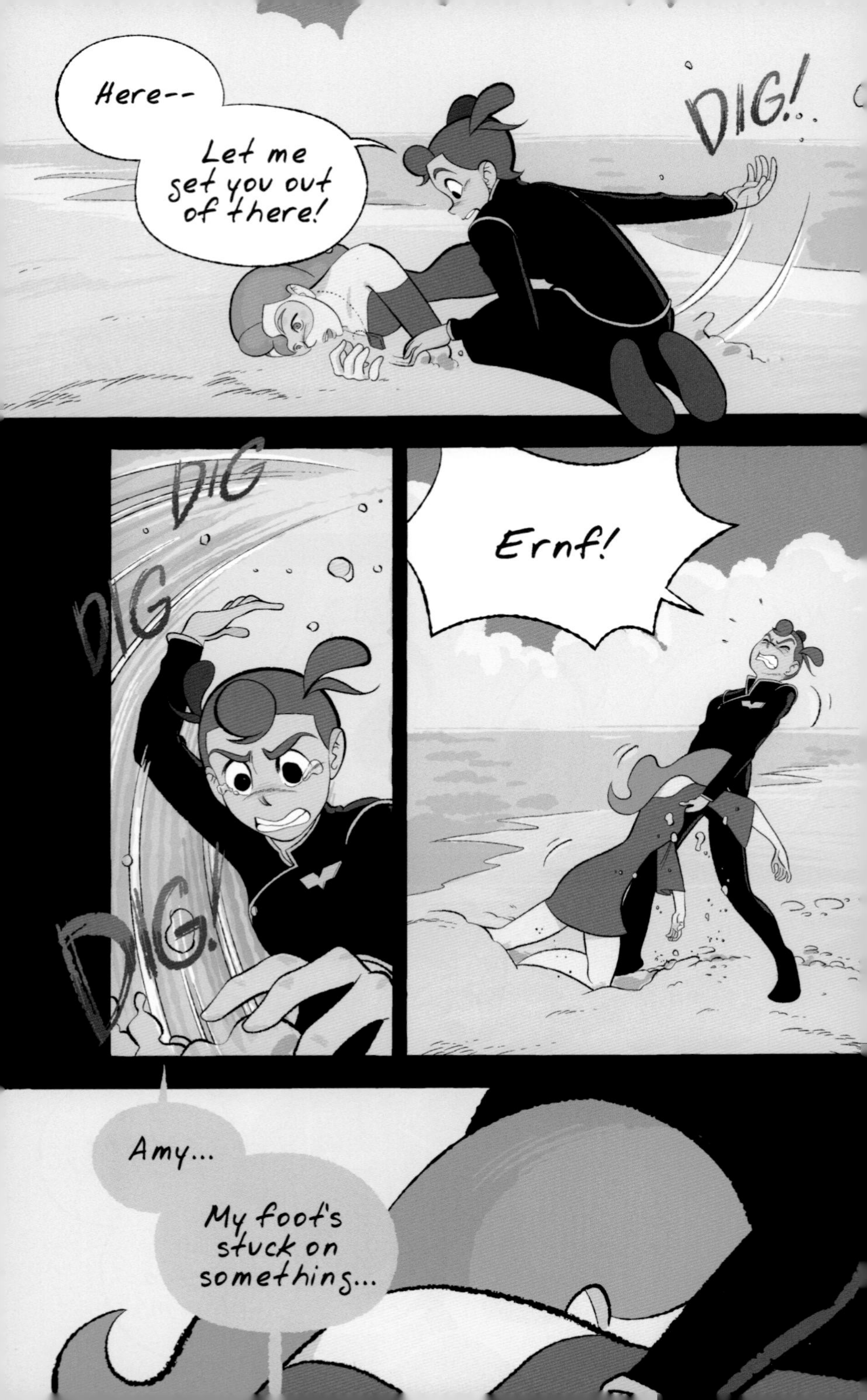
Here--
Let me get you out of there!
DIG!
DIG
DIG
DIG!
Ernf!
Amy...
My foot's stuck on somethin...

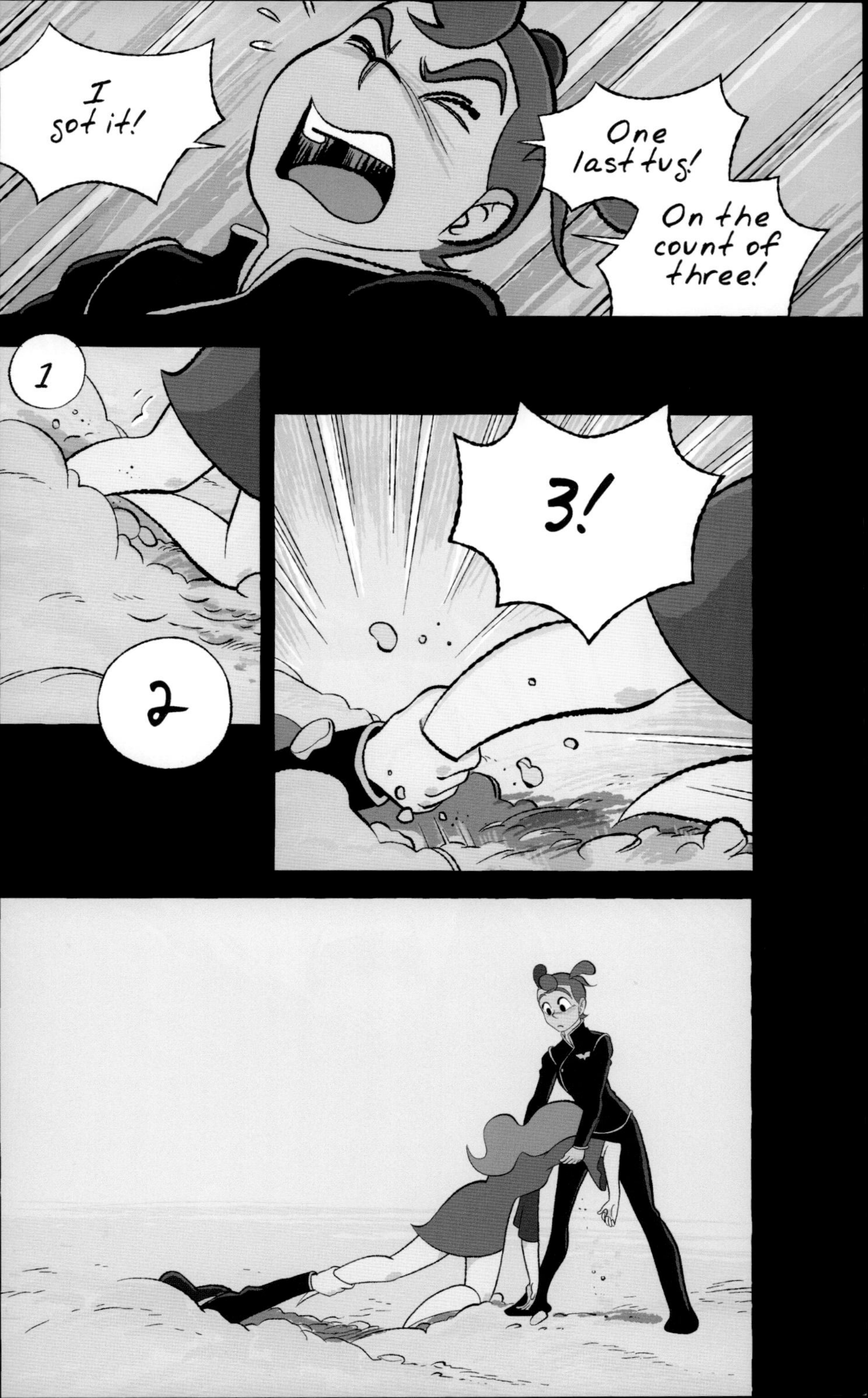
I got it!
One last tug!
On the count of three!
1
2
3!

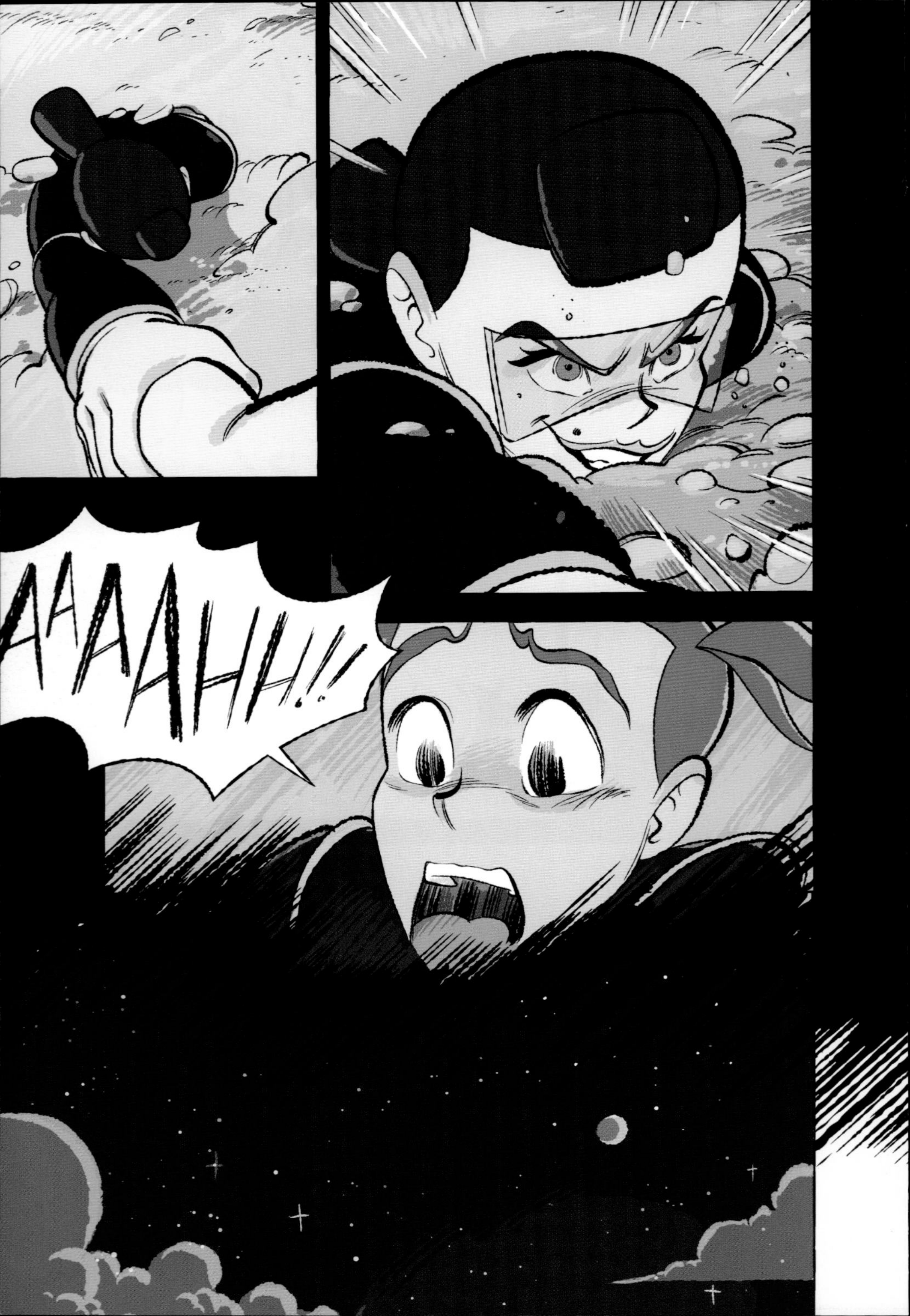
AAAAAHH!!

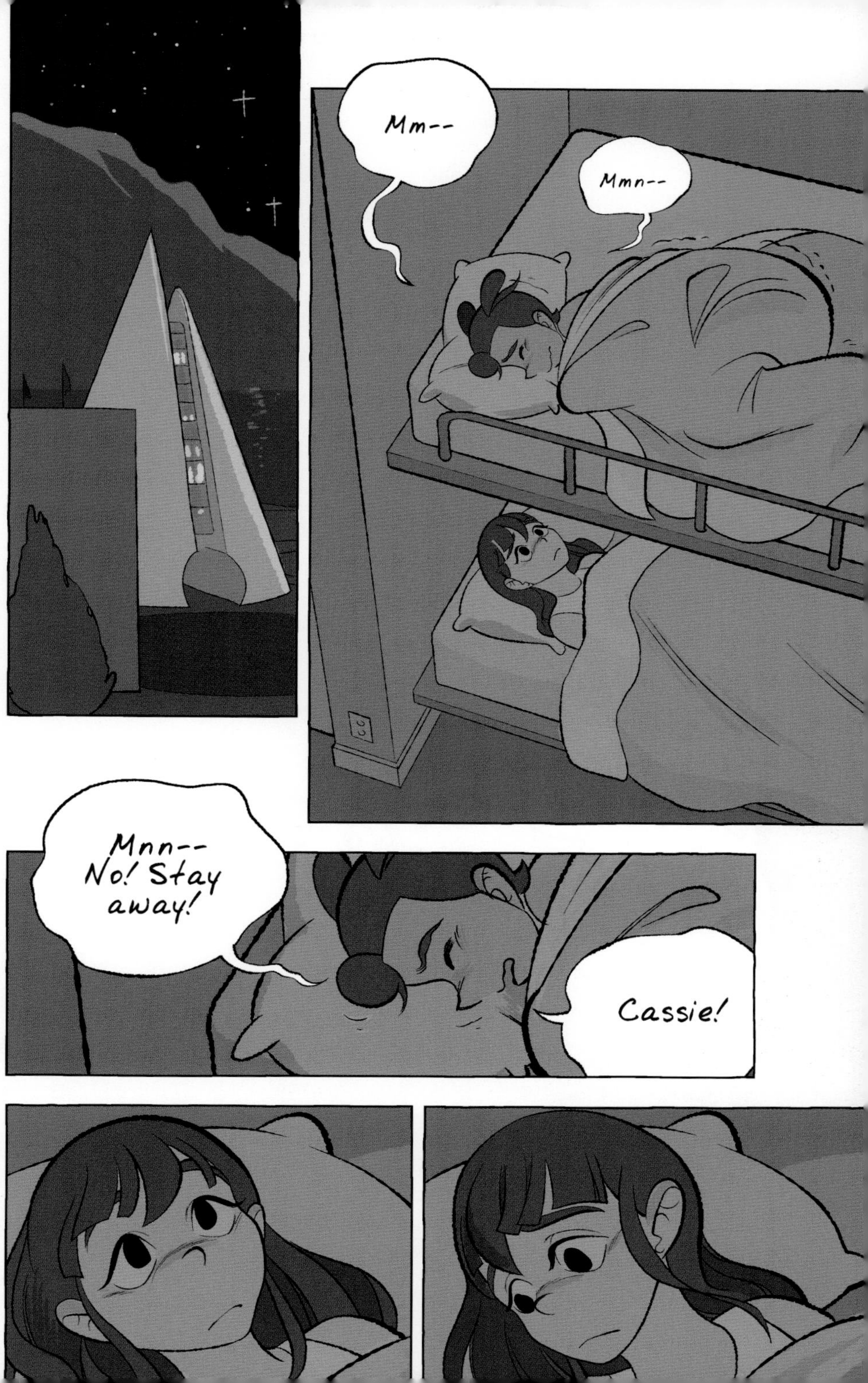
Mm--
Mmn--
Mnn-- No! Stay away!
Cassie!

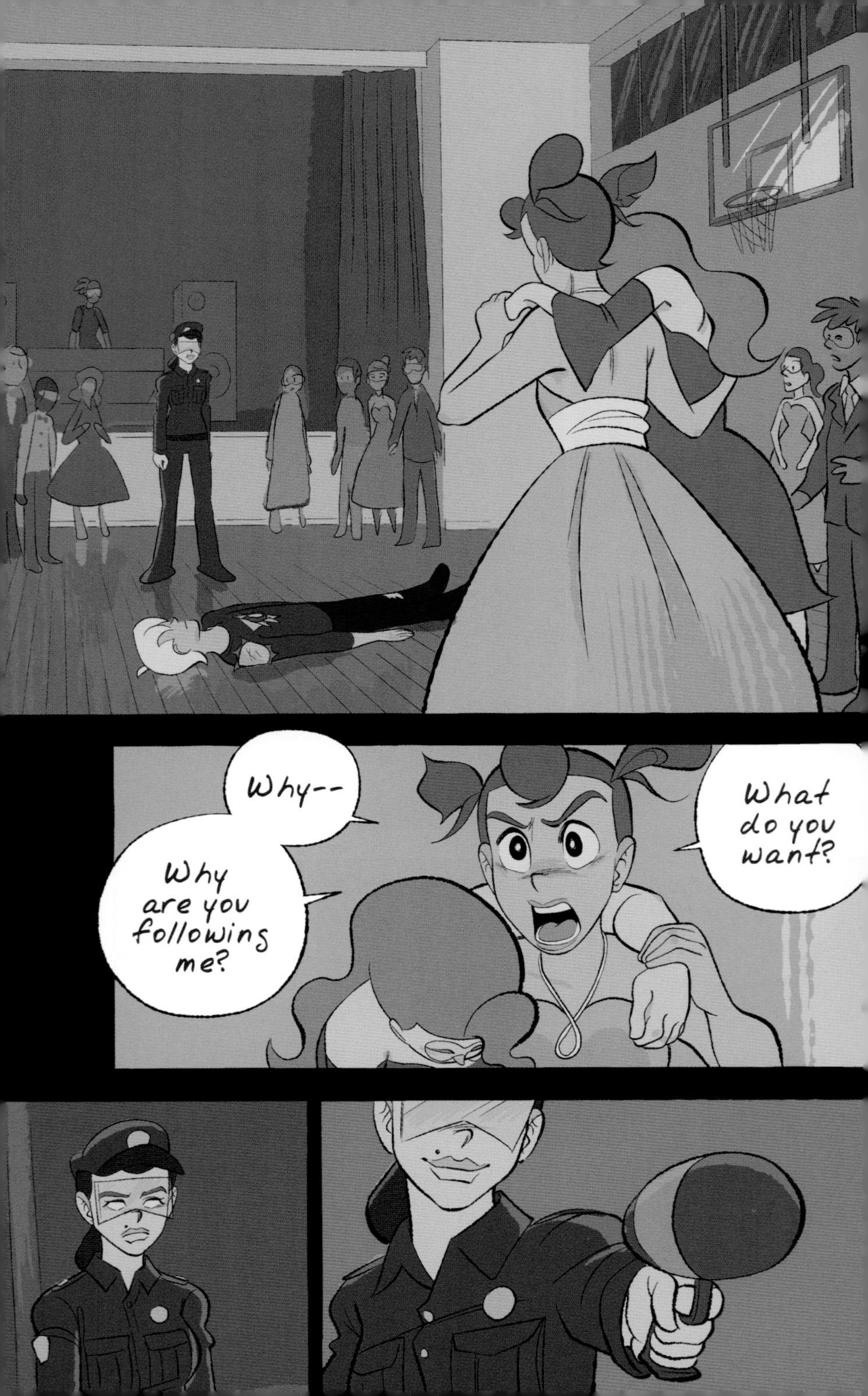

Why--
Why are you followings me?
What do you want?

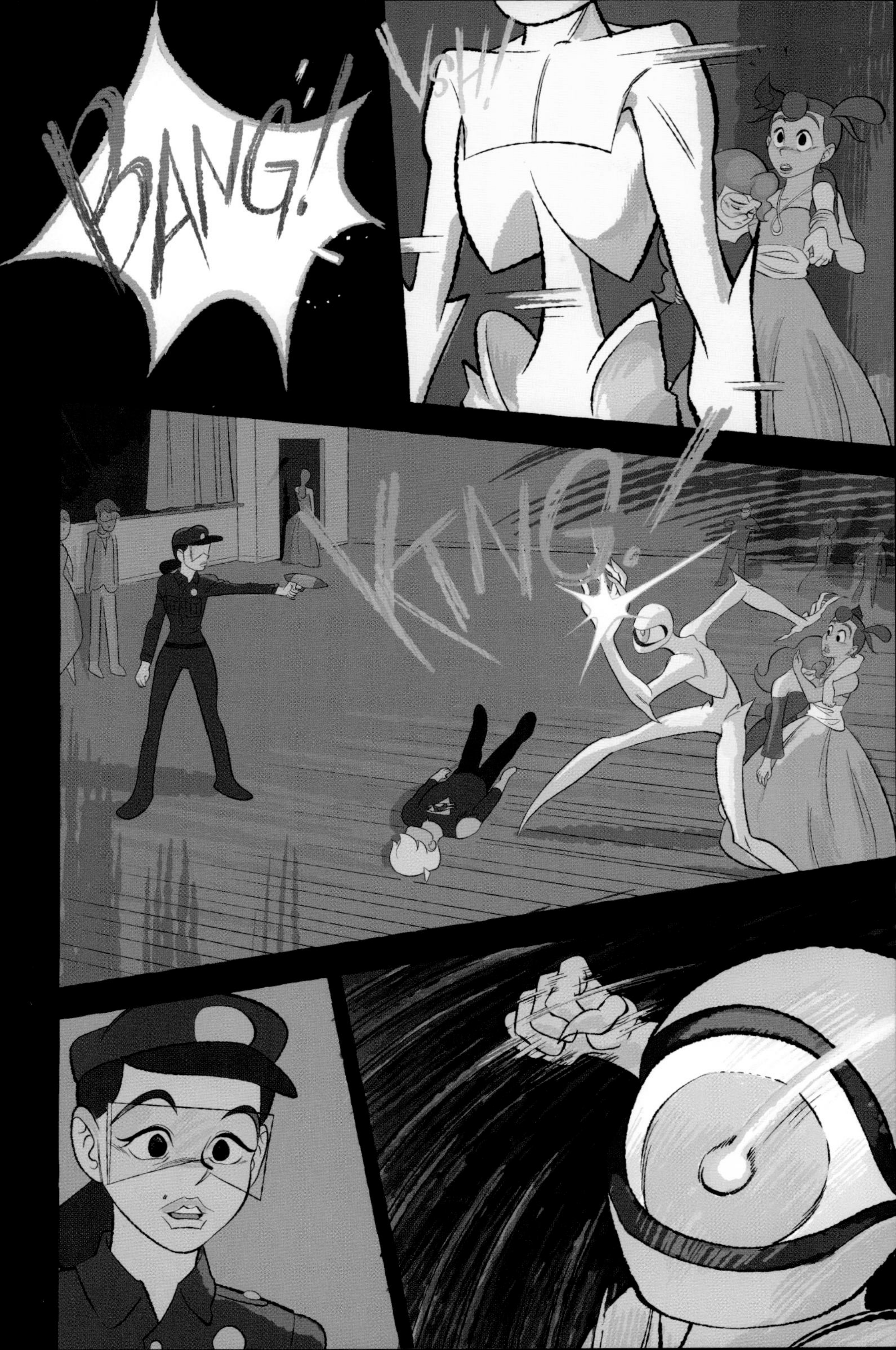
BANG!
VSH!
KTING!

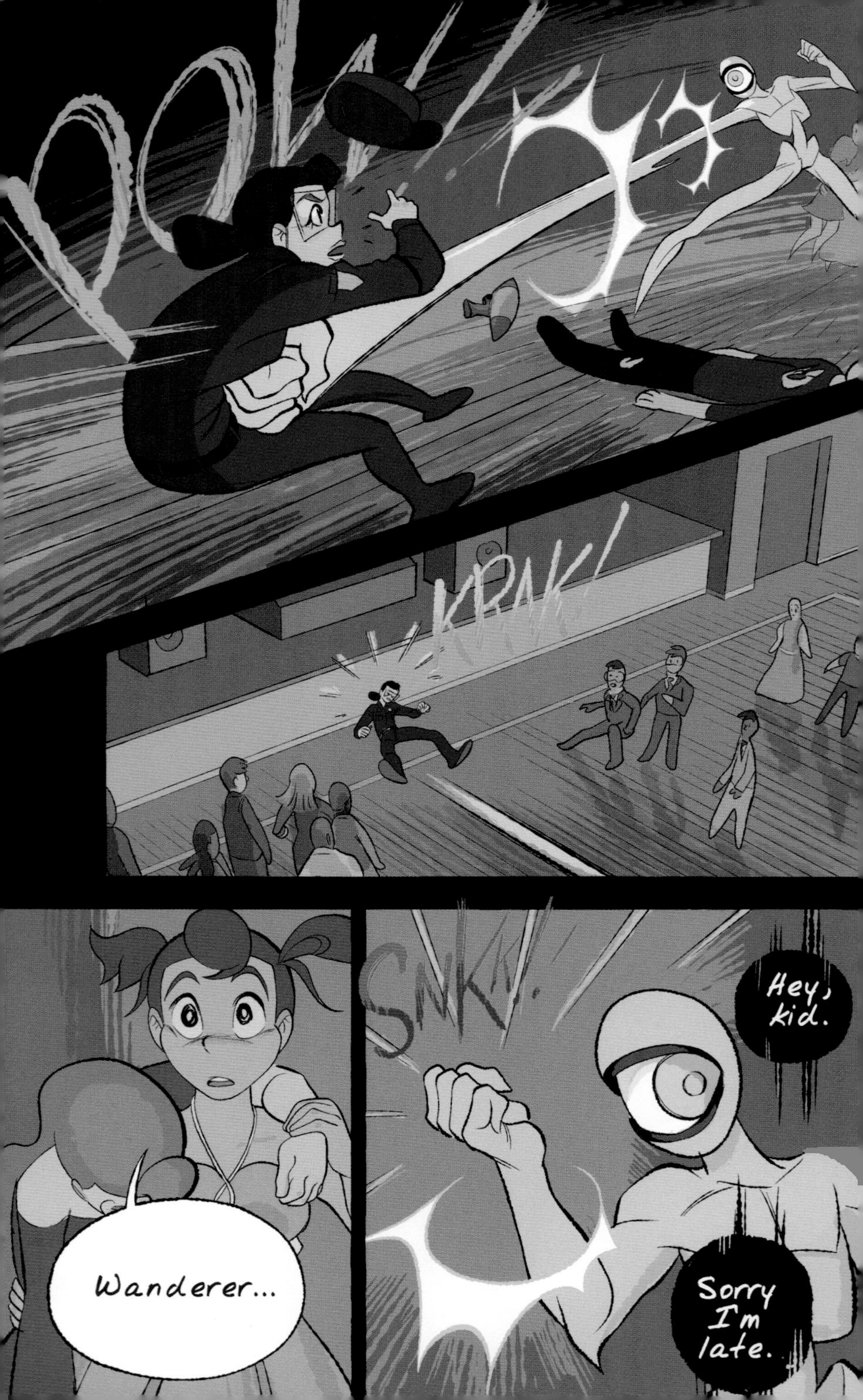

KRAK!
Wanderer...
SNK!
Hey, kid.
Sorry I'm late.

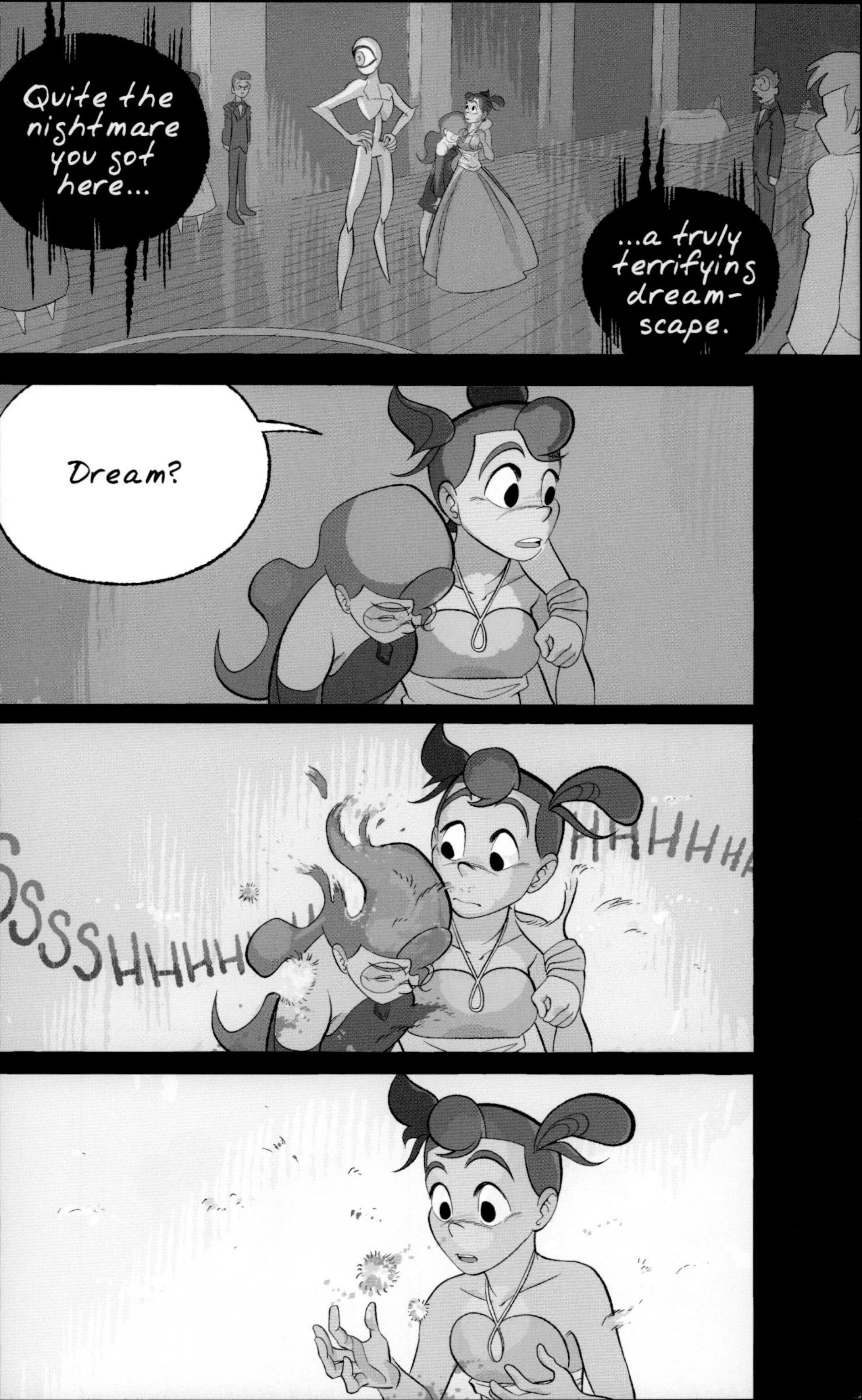
Quite the nightmare you got here...
...a truly terrifying dream-scape.
Dream?
SSSSHHHHH
HHHHHH

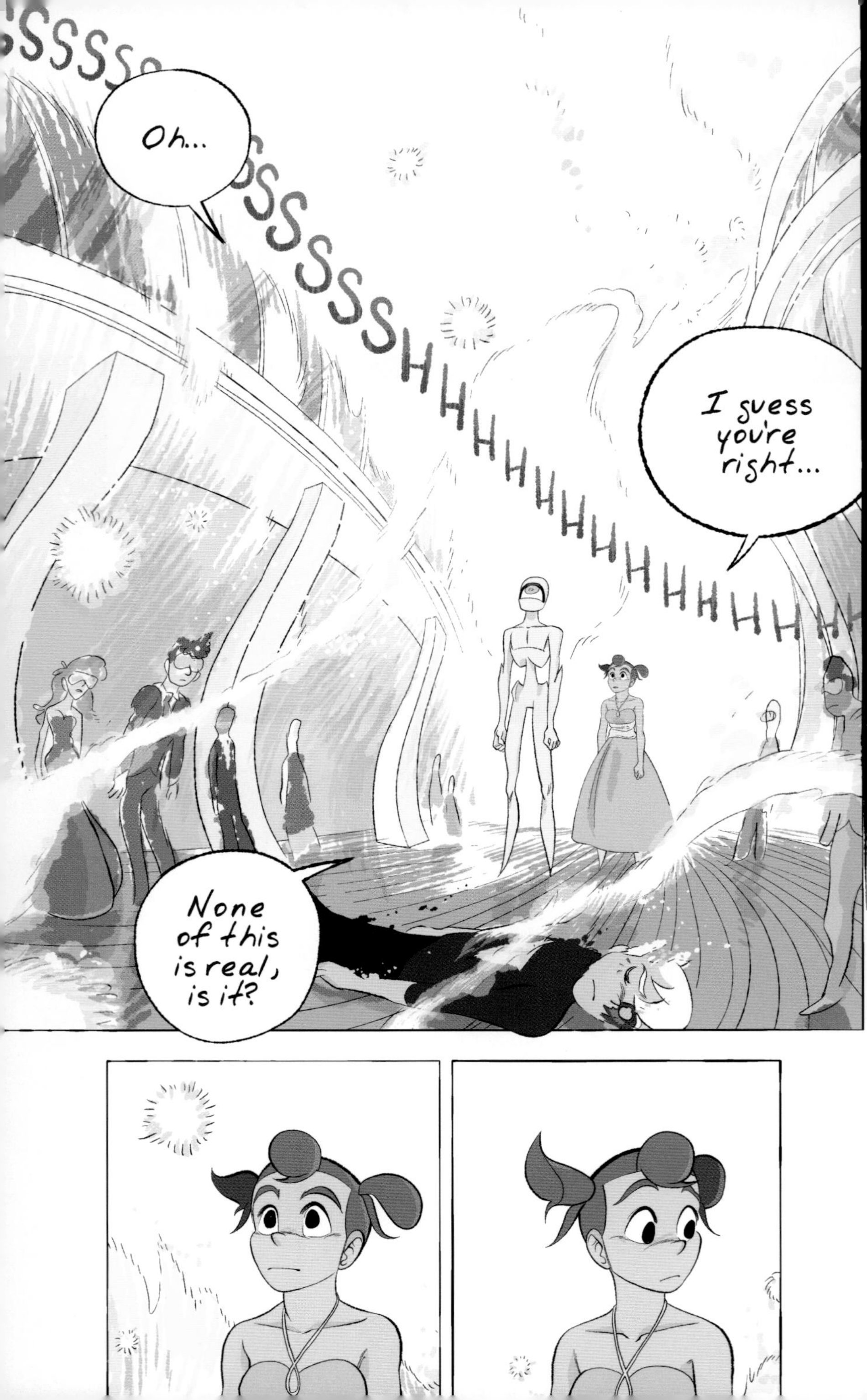

SSSSSSSSSSSHHHHHHHHHHHHH
Oh...
I guess you're right...
None of this is real, is it?

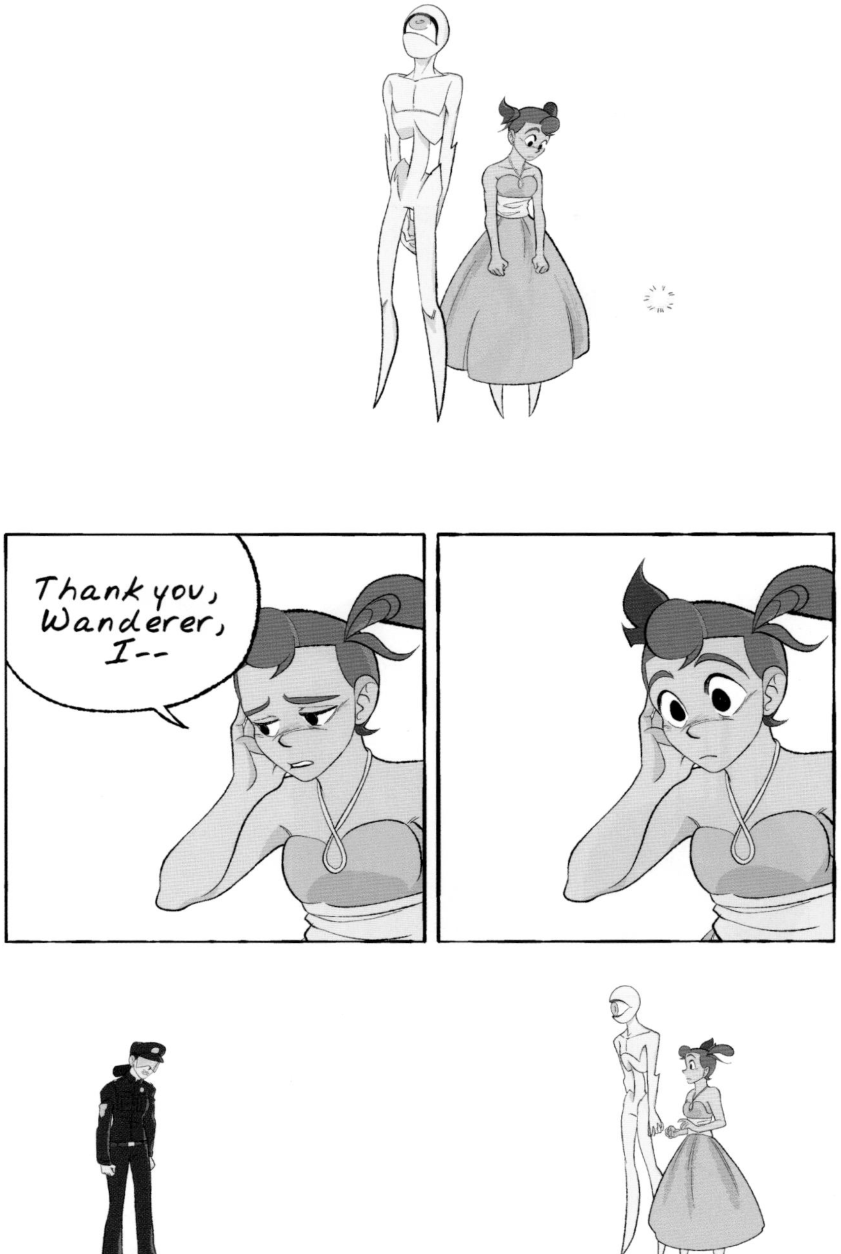
Thank you, Wanderer, I--

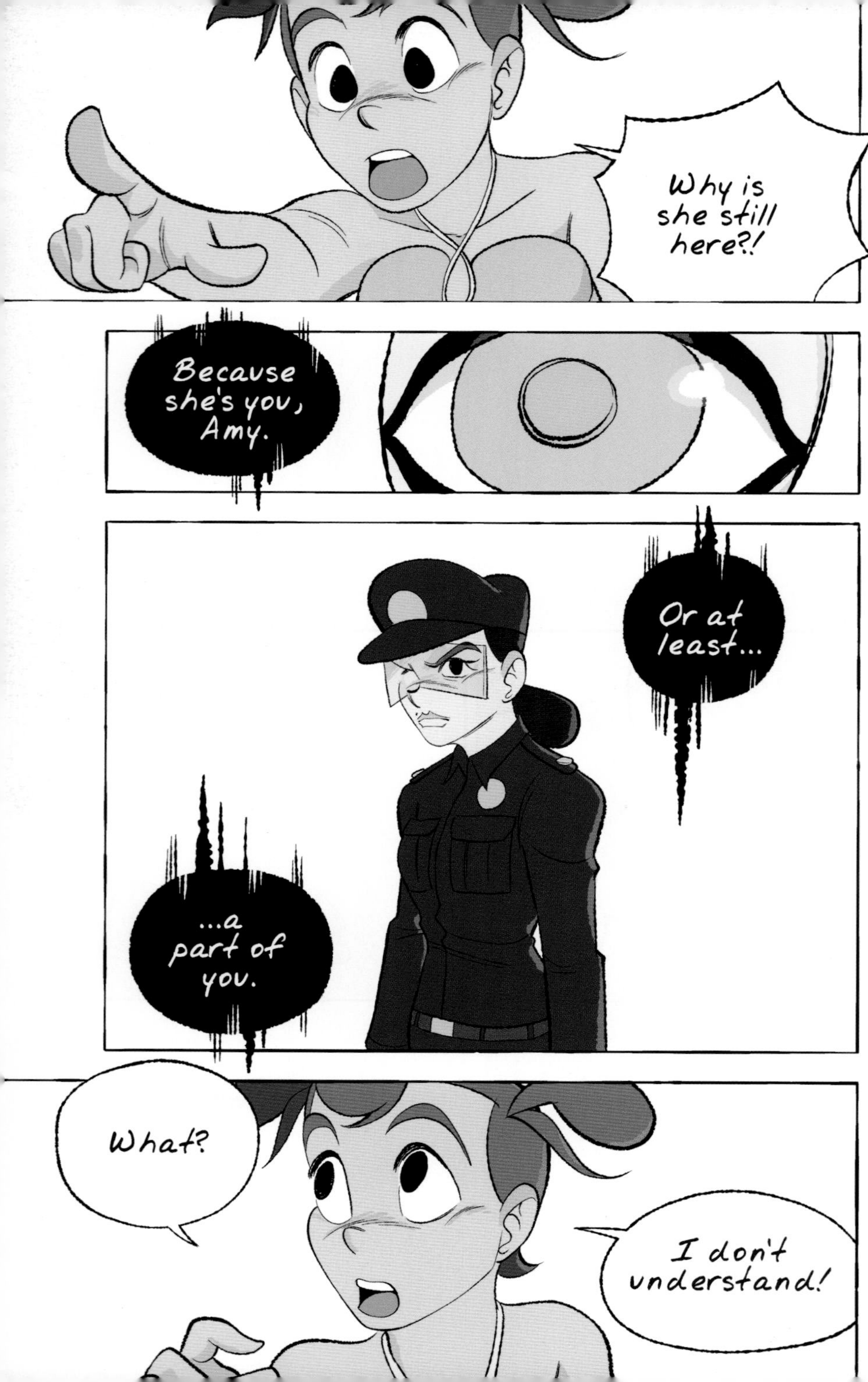
Why is she still here?!
Because she's you, Amy.
Or at least...
...a part of you.
What?
I don't understand!

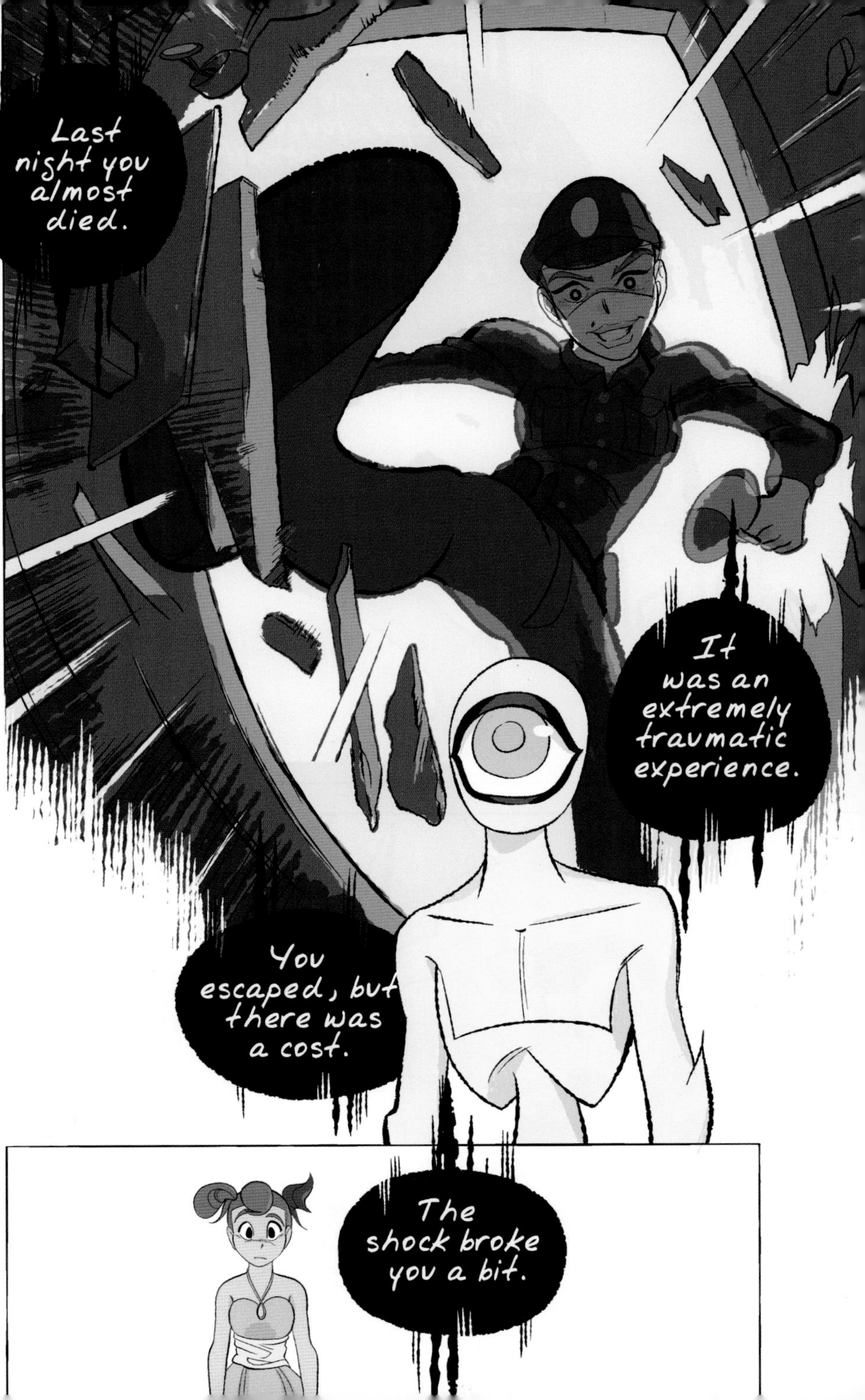

Last night you almost died.
It was an extremely traumatic experience.
You escaped, but there was a cost.
The shock broke you a bit.

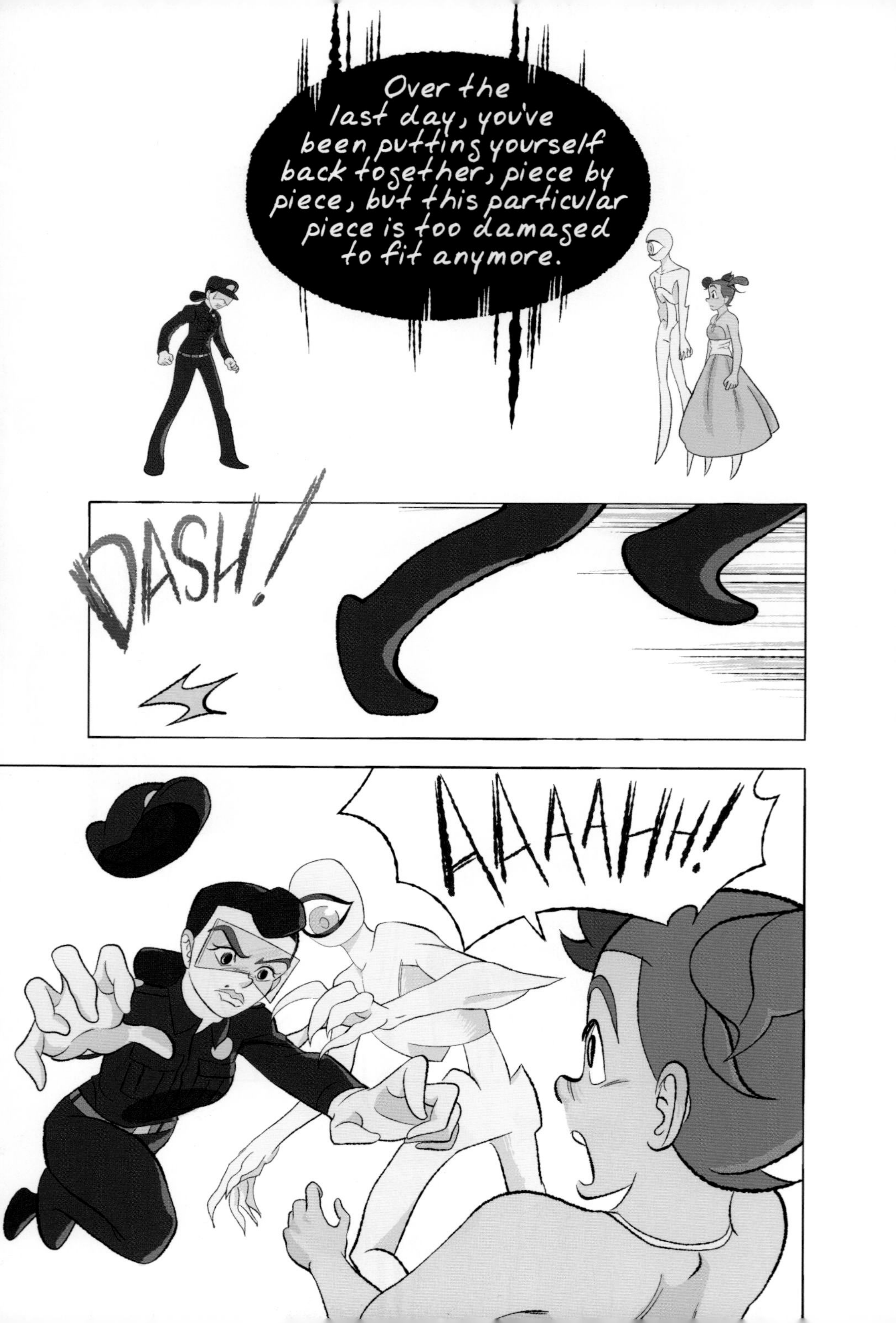
Over the last day, you've been putting yourself back together, piece by piece, but this particular piece is too damaged to fit anymore.
DASH!
AAAAHH!

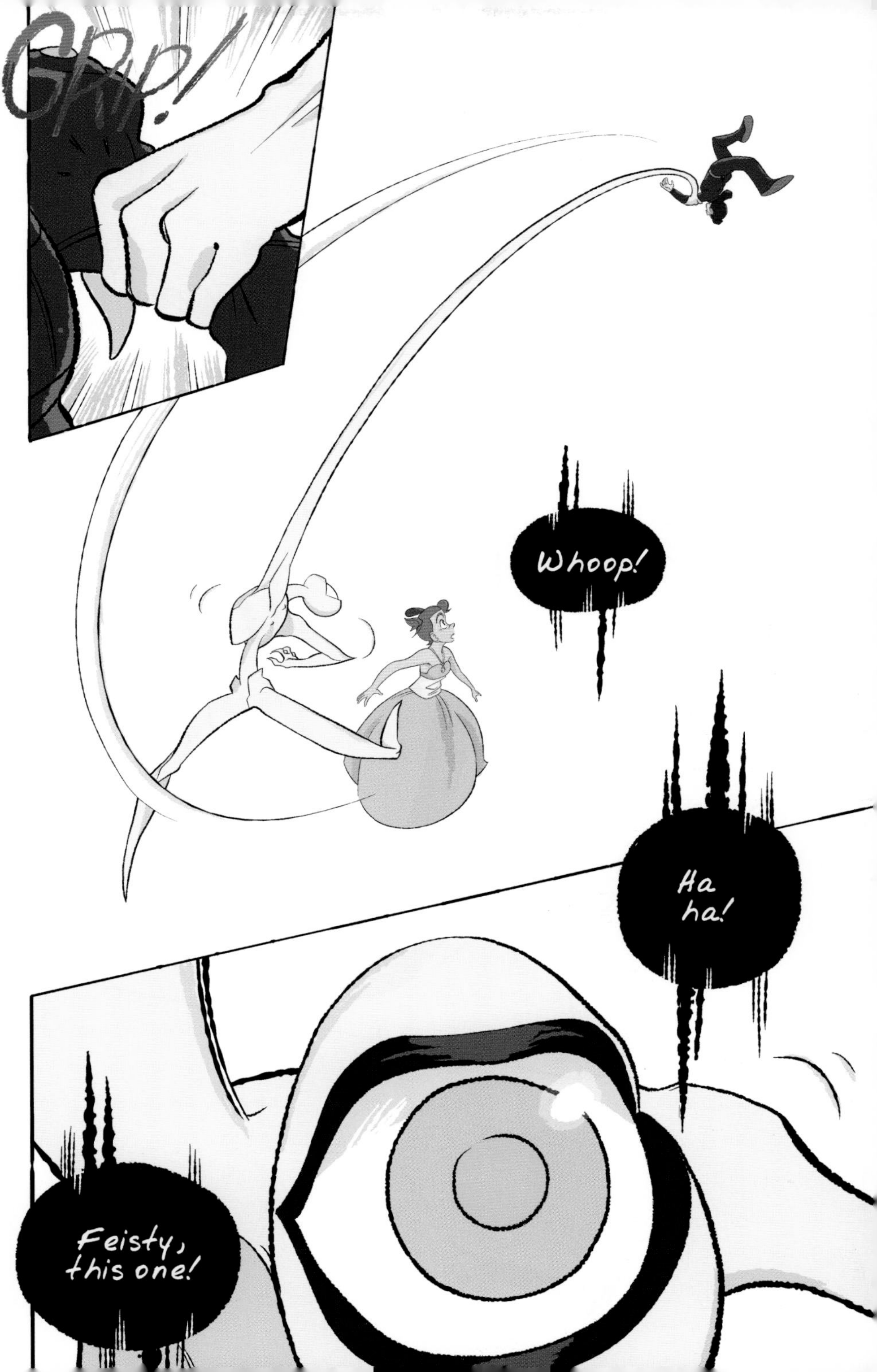
GRIP!
Whoop!
Ha ha!
Feisty, this one!

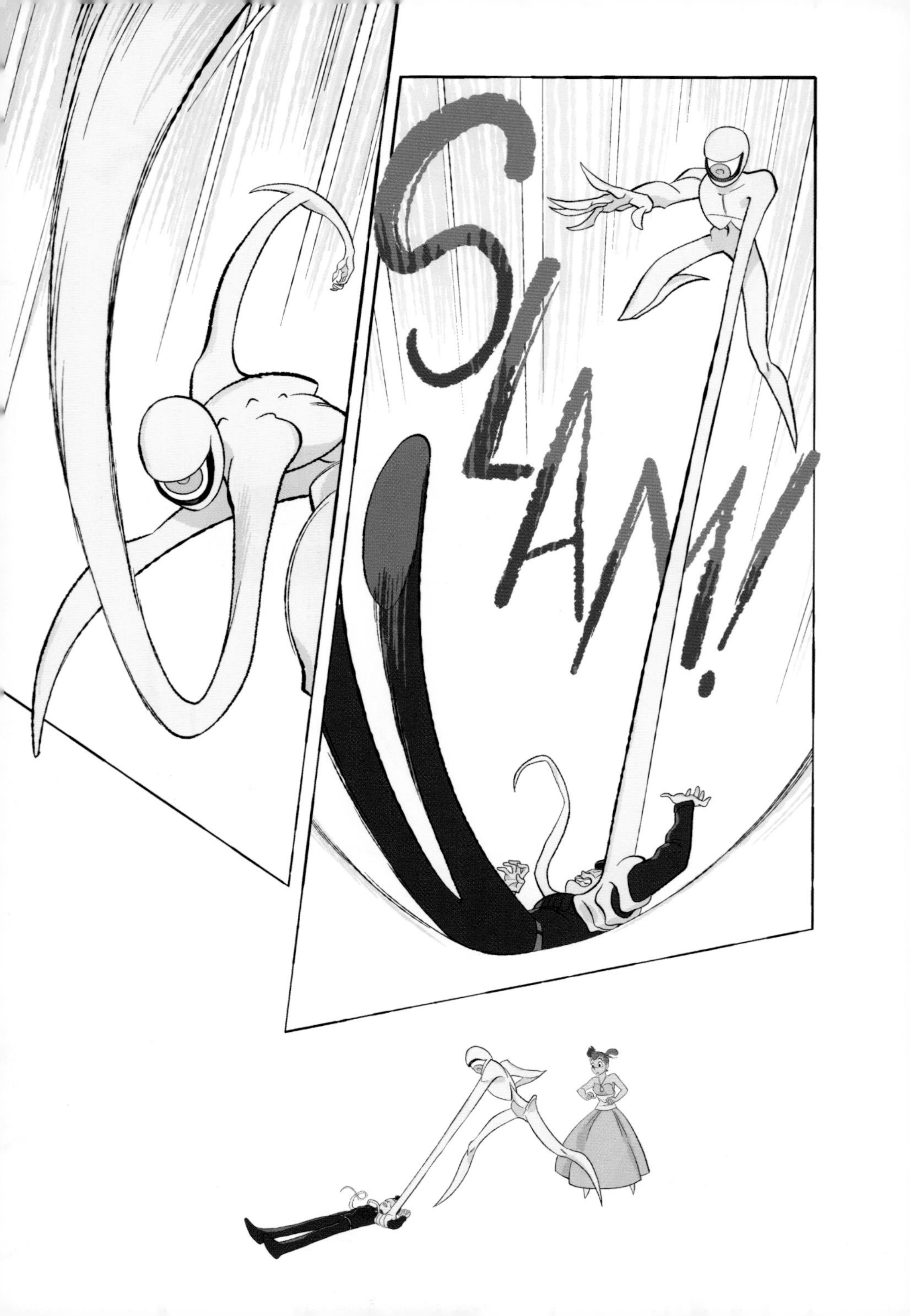
SLAM!!

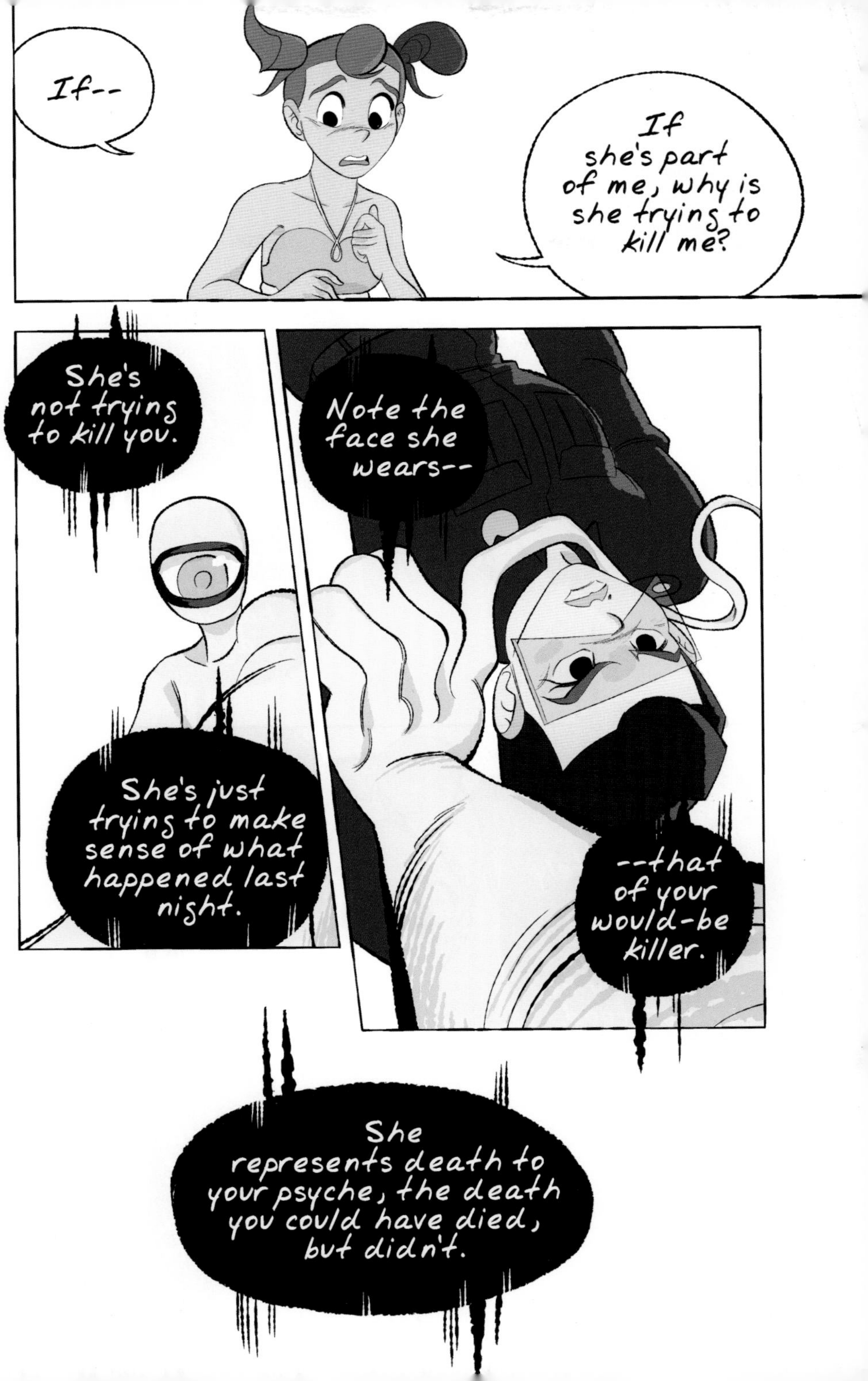
If--
If she's part of me, why is she trying to kill me?
She's not trying to kill you.
She's just trying to make sense of what happened last night.
Note the face she wears--
--that of your would-be killer.
She represents death to your psyche, the death you could have died, but didn't.

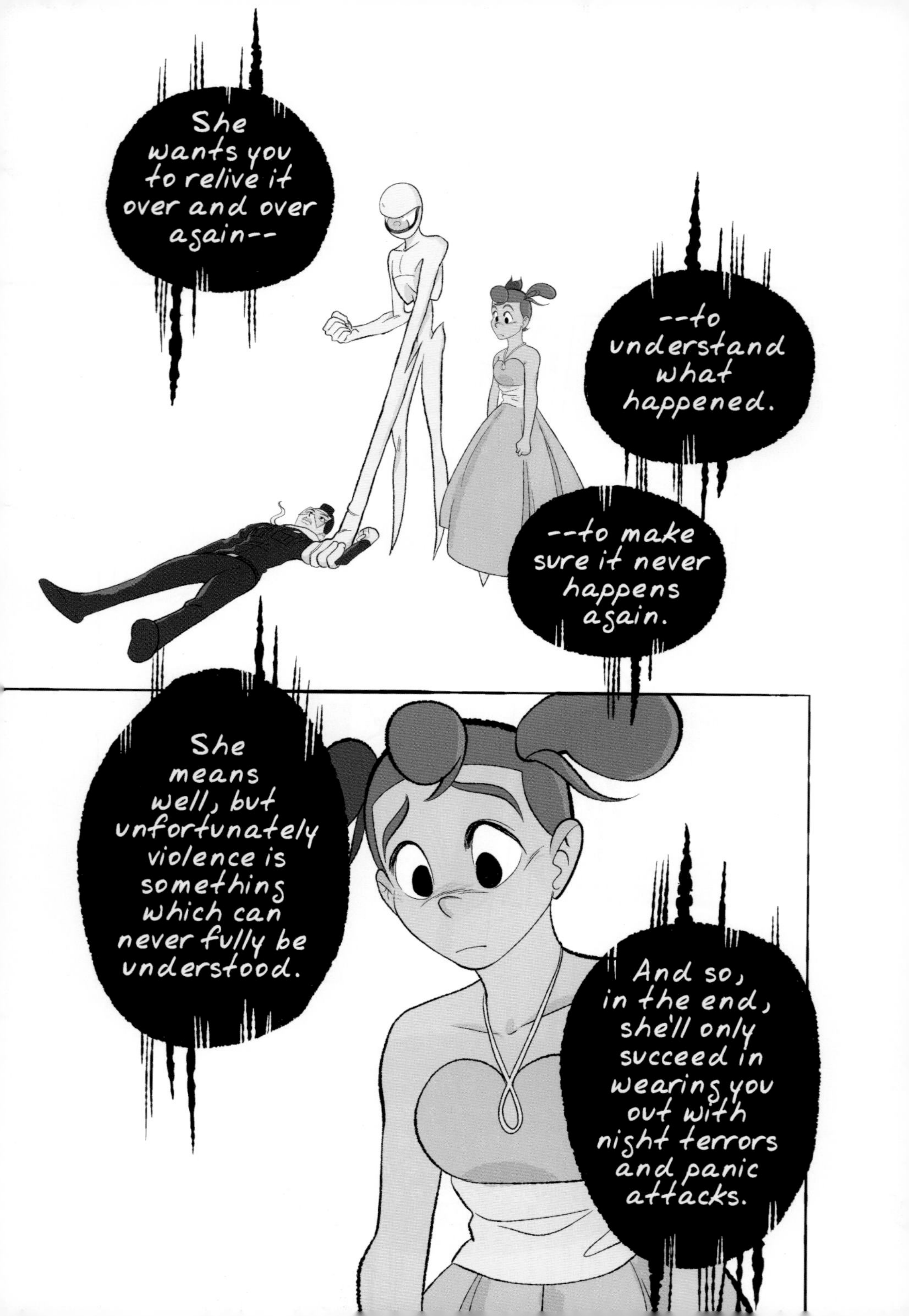
She wants you to relive it over and over again--
--to understand what happened.
--to make sure it never happens again.
She means well, but unfortunately violence is something which can never fully be understood.
And so, in the end, she'll only succeed in wearing you out with night terrors and panic attacks.

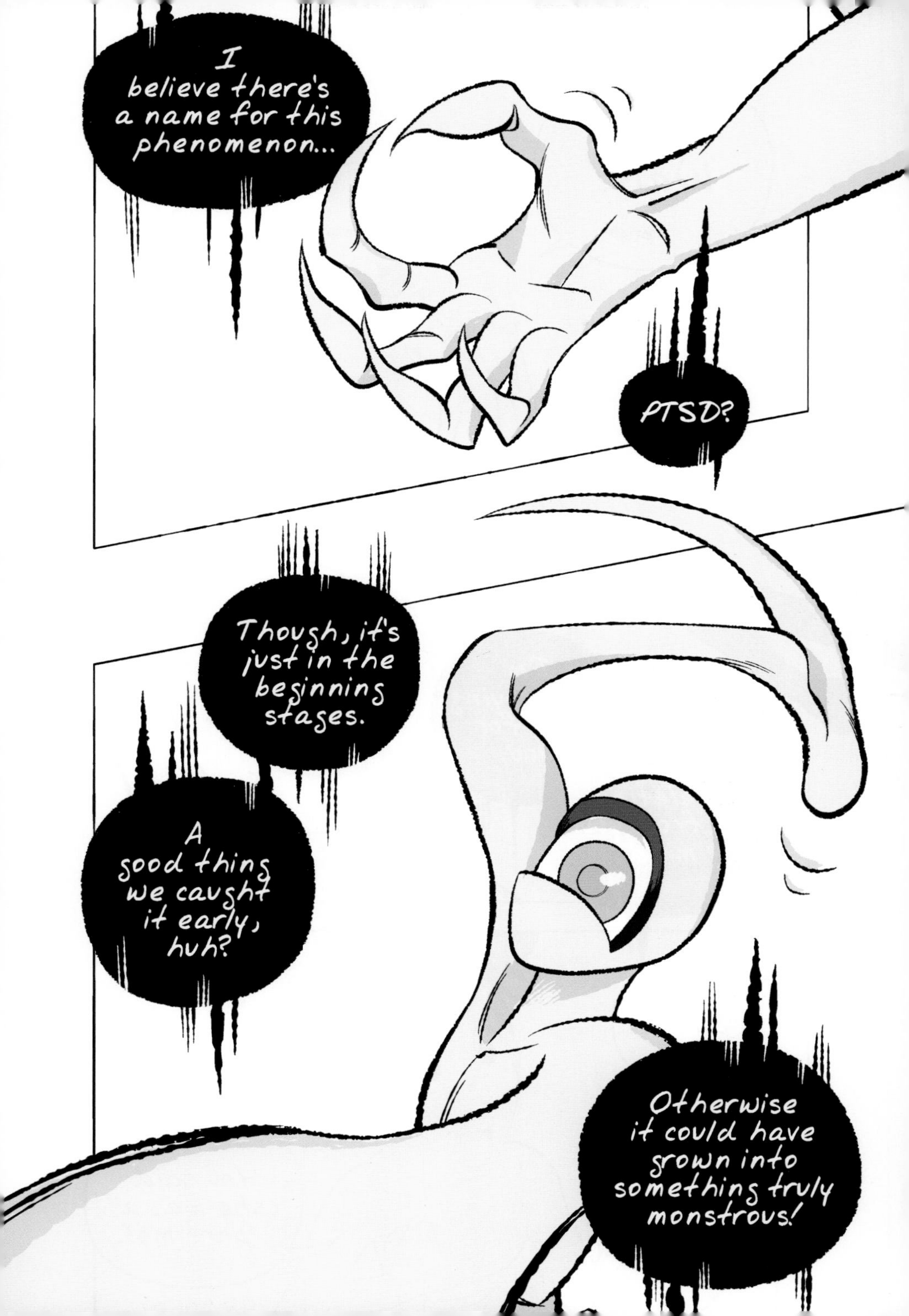
I believe there's a name for this phenomenon...
PTSD?
Though, it's just in the beginning stages.
A good thing we caught it early, huh?
Otherwise it could have grown into something truly monstrous!

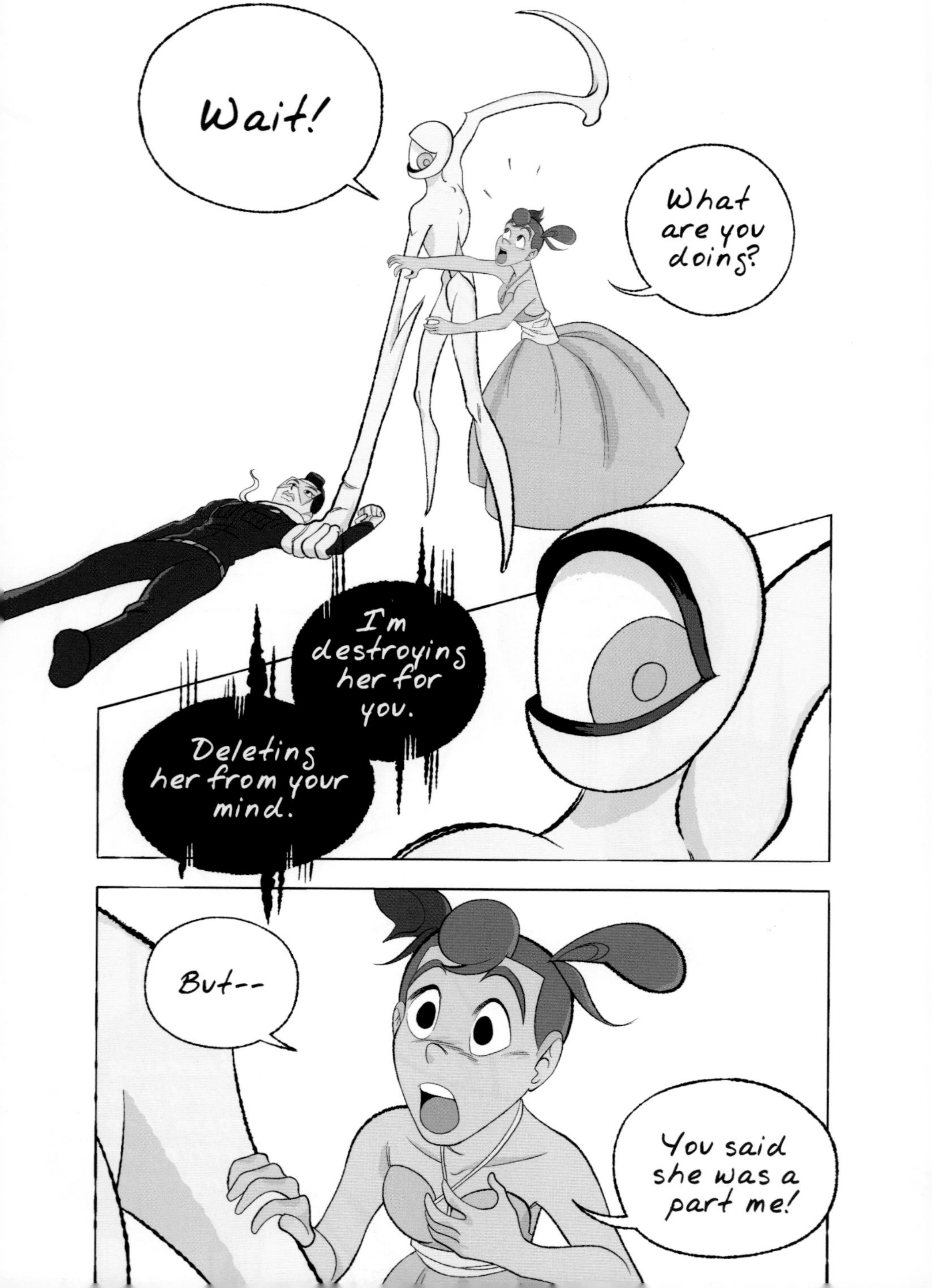
Wait!
What are you doing?
I'm destroying her for you.
Deleting her from your mind.
But--
You said she was a part me!

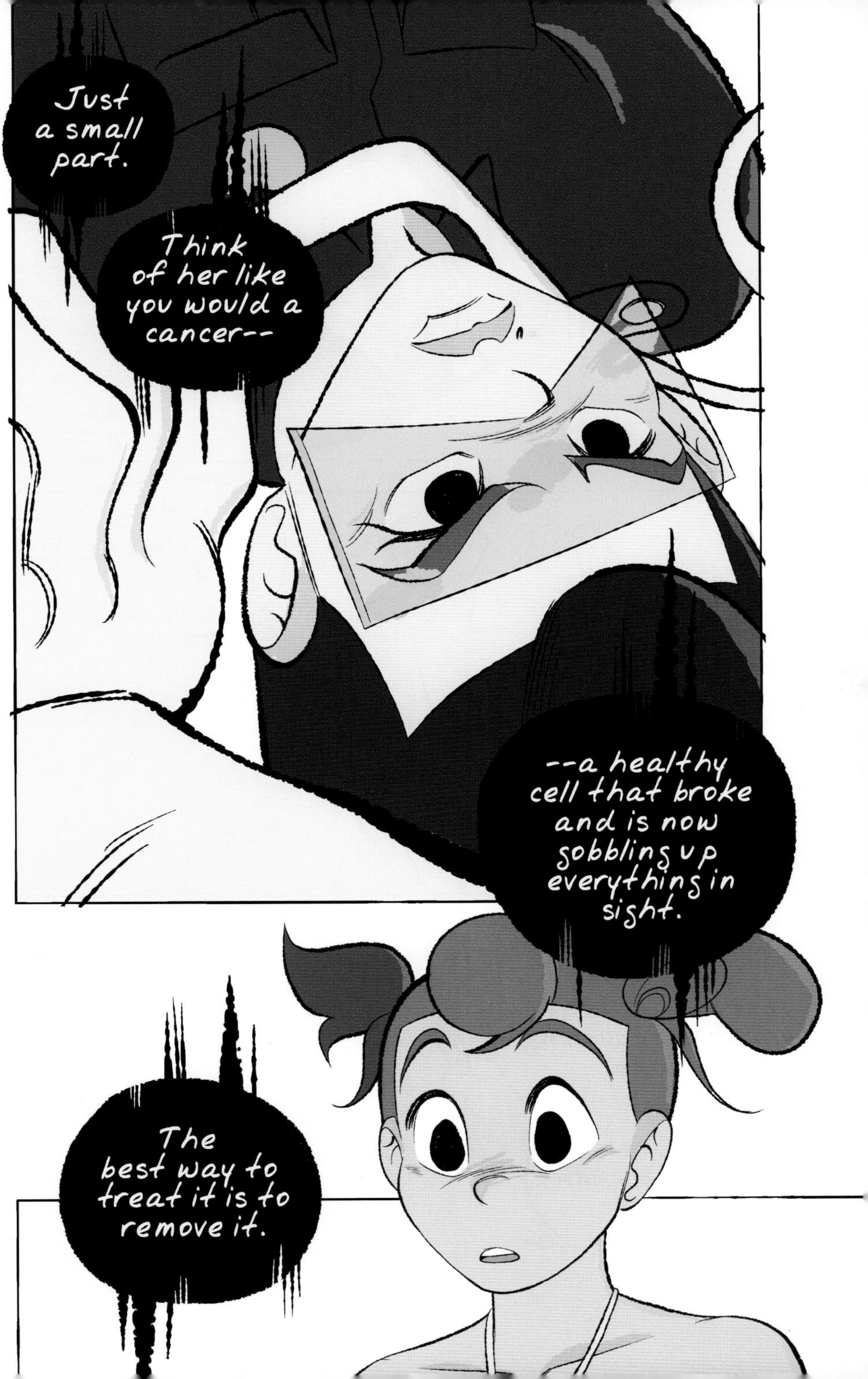

Just a small part.
Think of her like you would a cancer--
--a healthy cell that broke and is now gobbling up everything in sight.
The best way to treat it is to remove it.

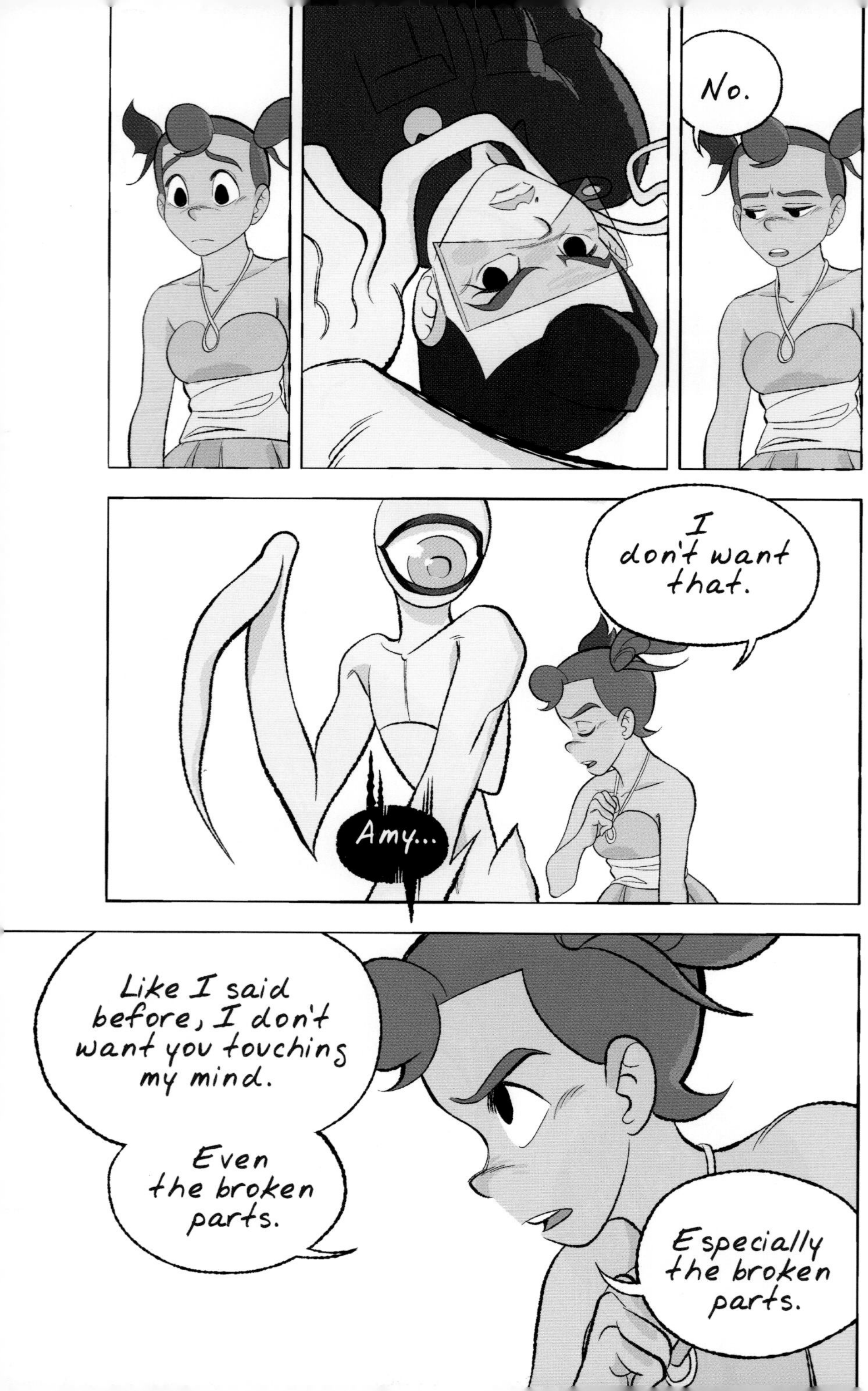
No.
I don't want that.
Amy...
Like I said before, I don't want you touching my mind.
Even the broken parts.
Especially the broken parts.

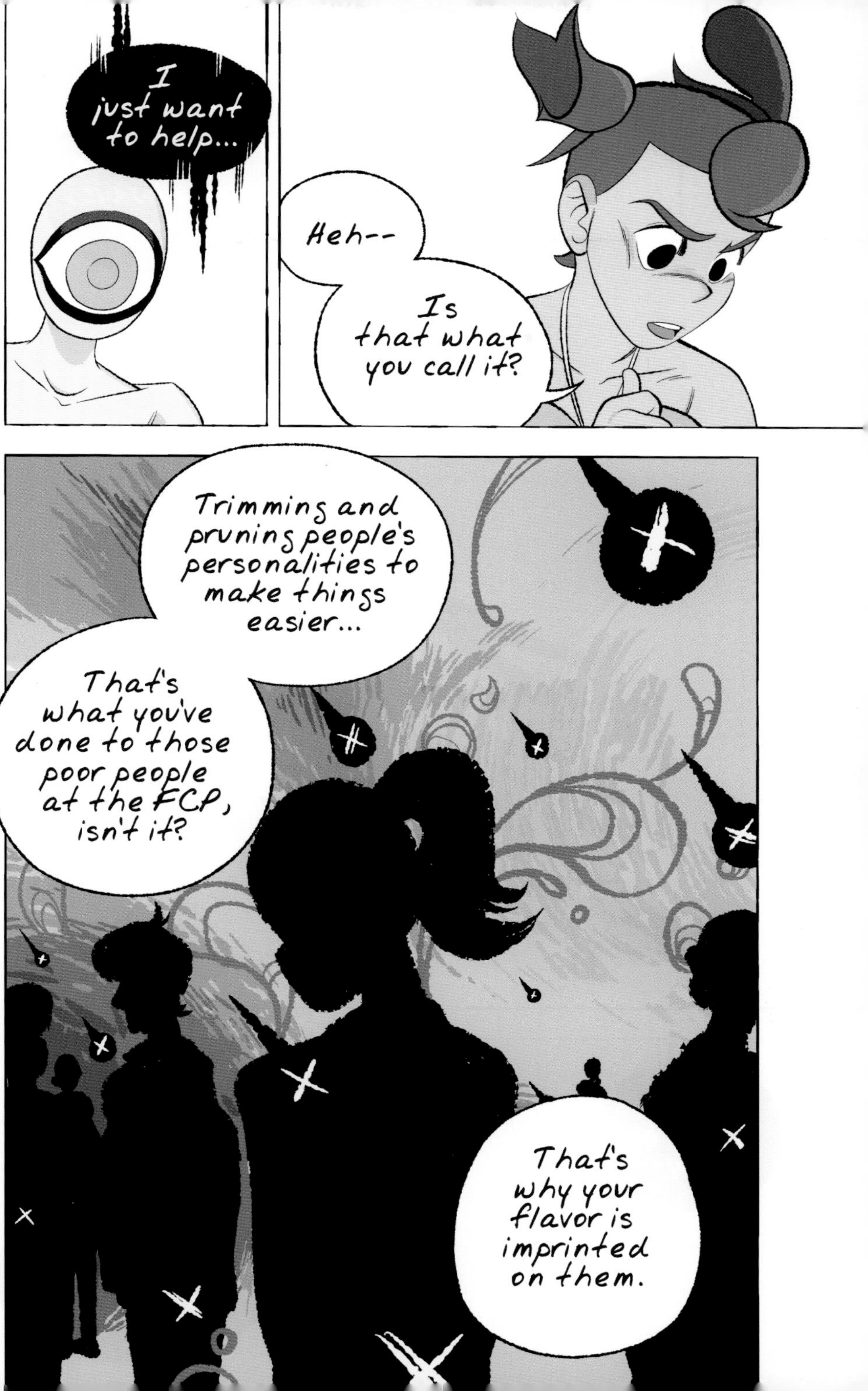
I just want to help...
Heh--
Is that what you call it?
Trimmins and pruning people's personalities to make things easier...
That's what you've done to those poor people at the FCP, isn't it?
That's why your flavor is imprinted on them.

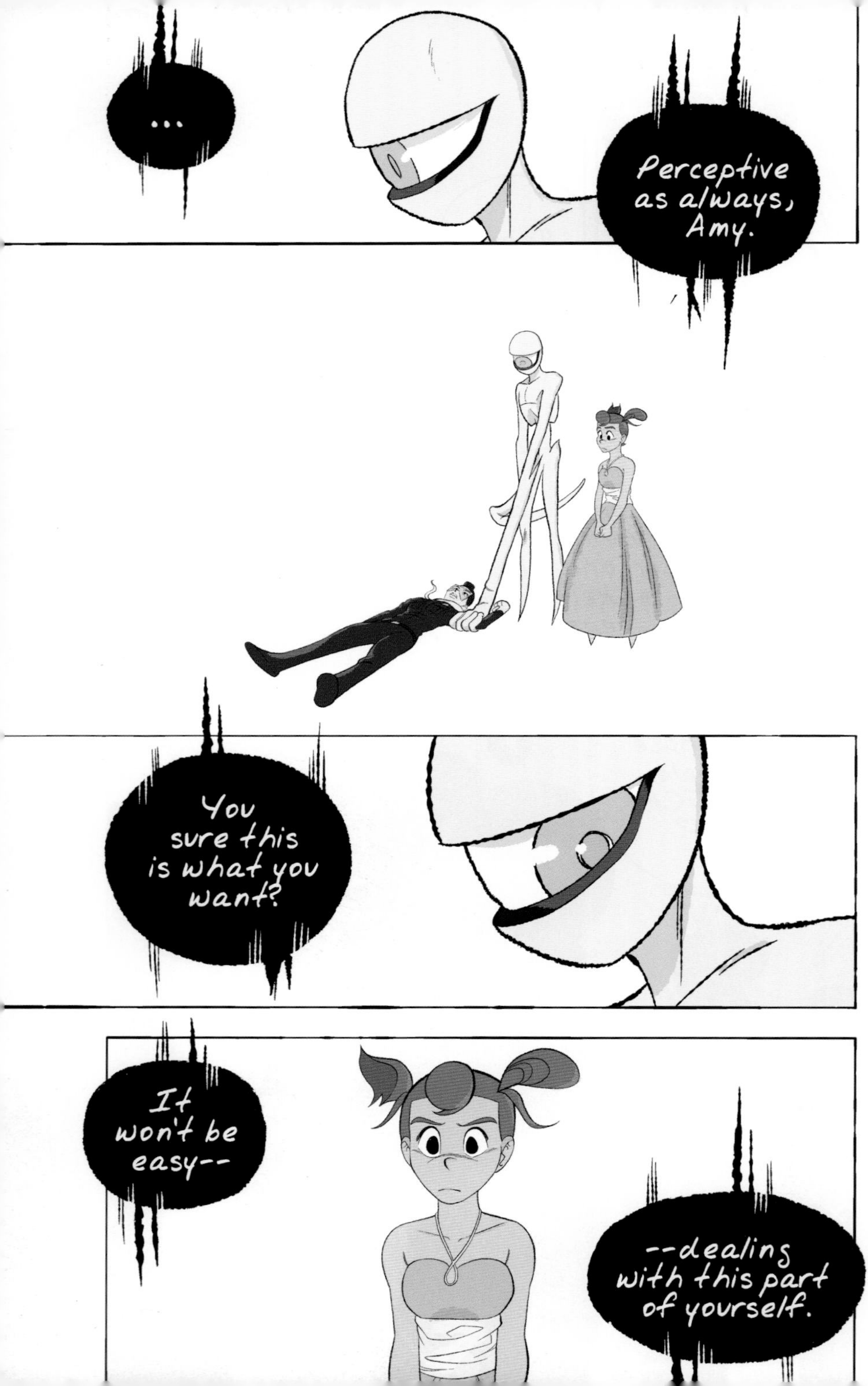
...
Perceptive as always, Amy.
You sure this is what you want?
It won't be easy--
--dealing with this part of yourself.

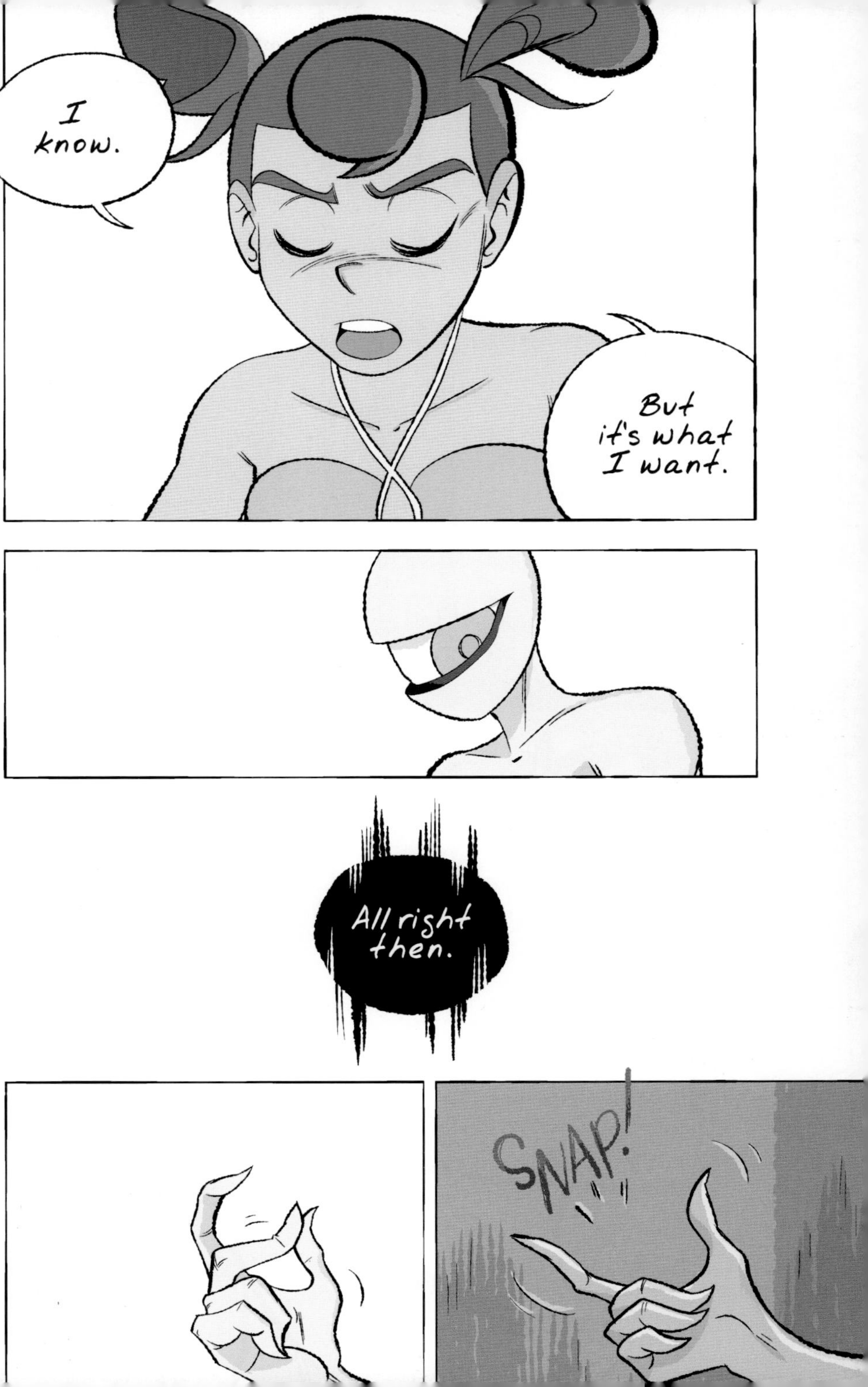
I know.
But it's what I want.
All right then.
SNAP!

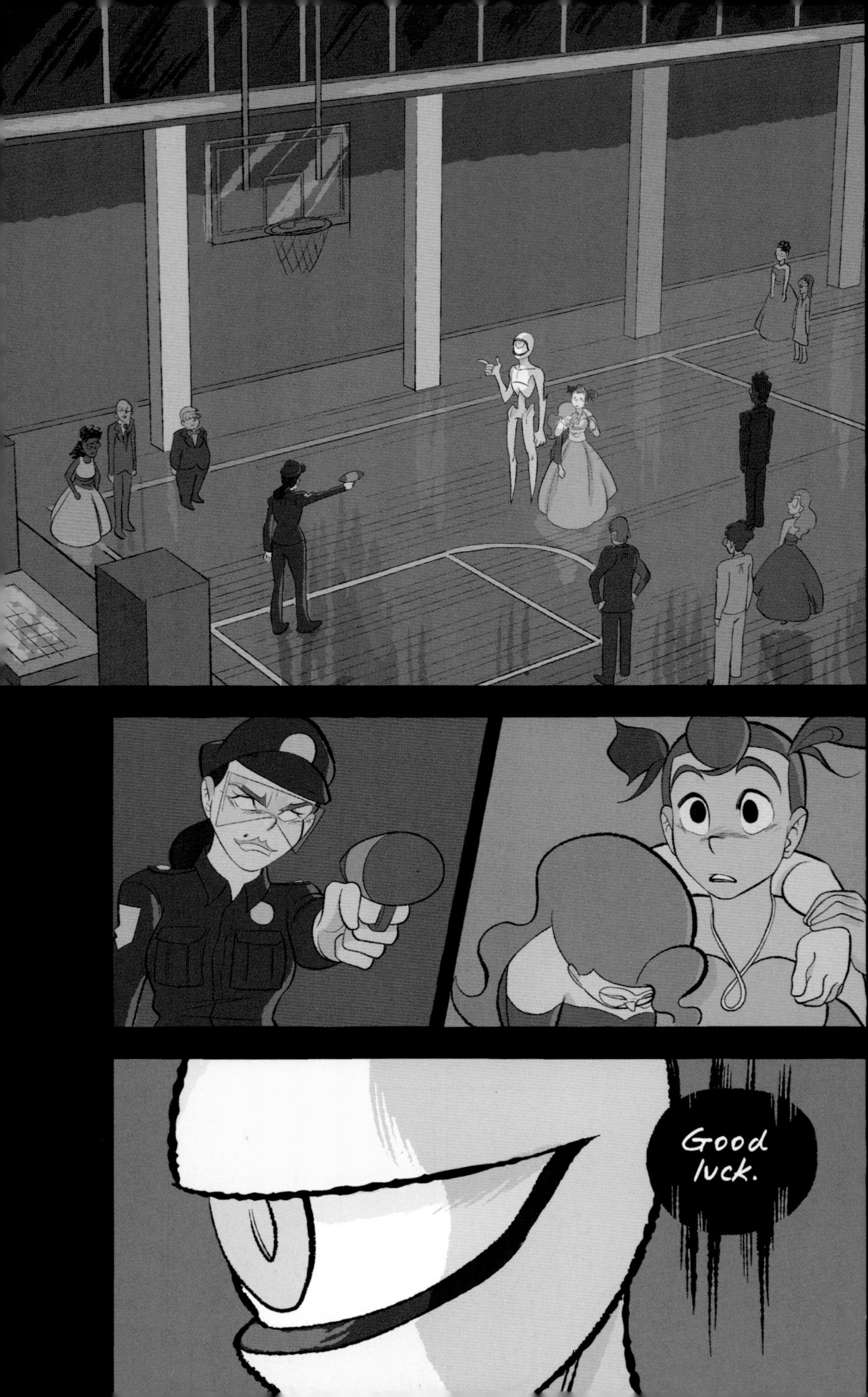
Good luck.

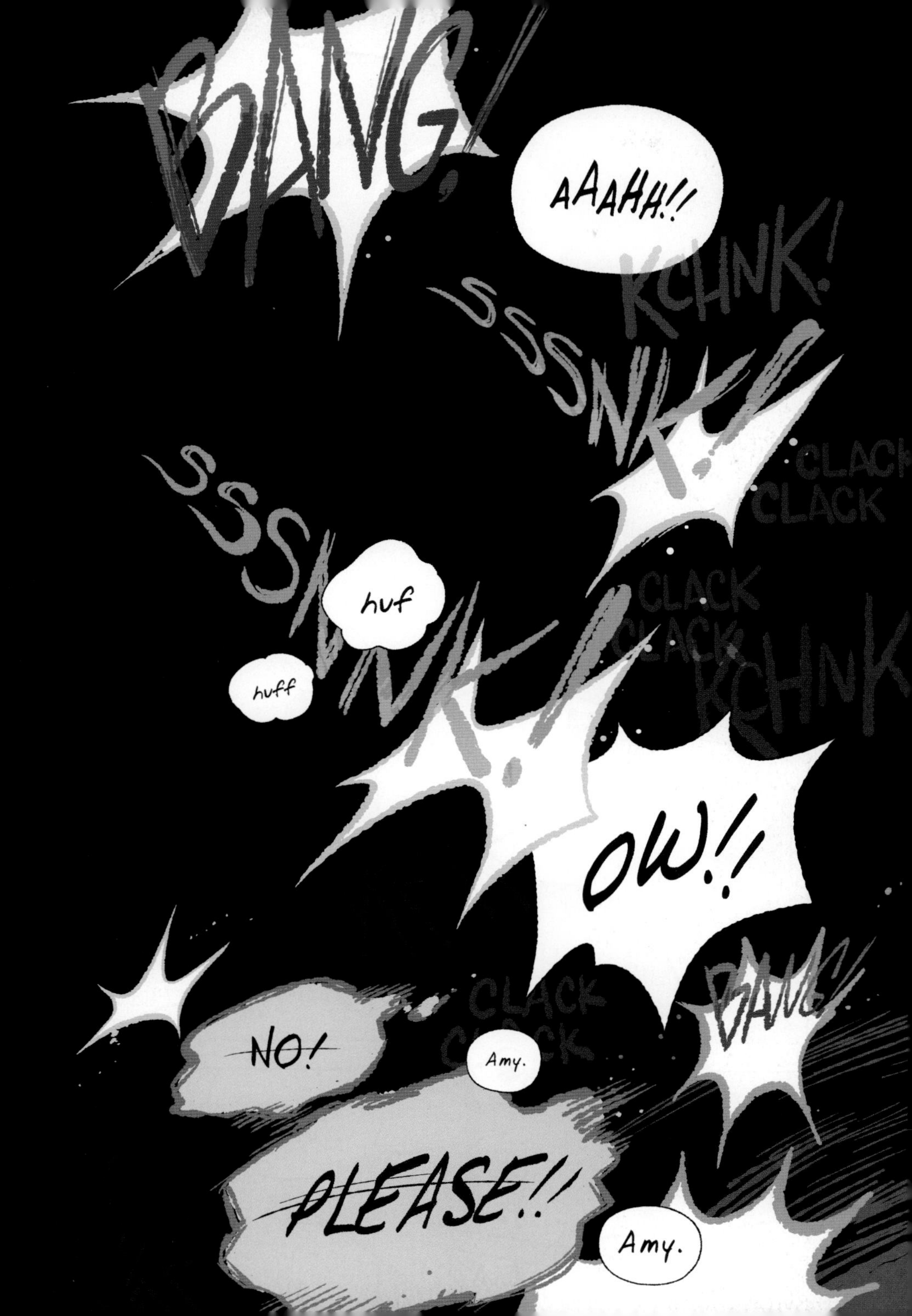
BANG!
AAAHH!!
KCHNK!
SSSNKT!
CLACK
CLACK
SSSNKT!
huf
huff
CLACK
CLACK
KCHNK
OW!!
NO!
CLACK
CLACK
Amy.
BAM!
PLEASE!!
Amy.

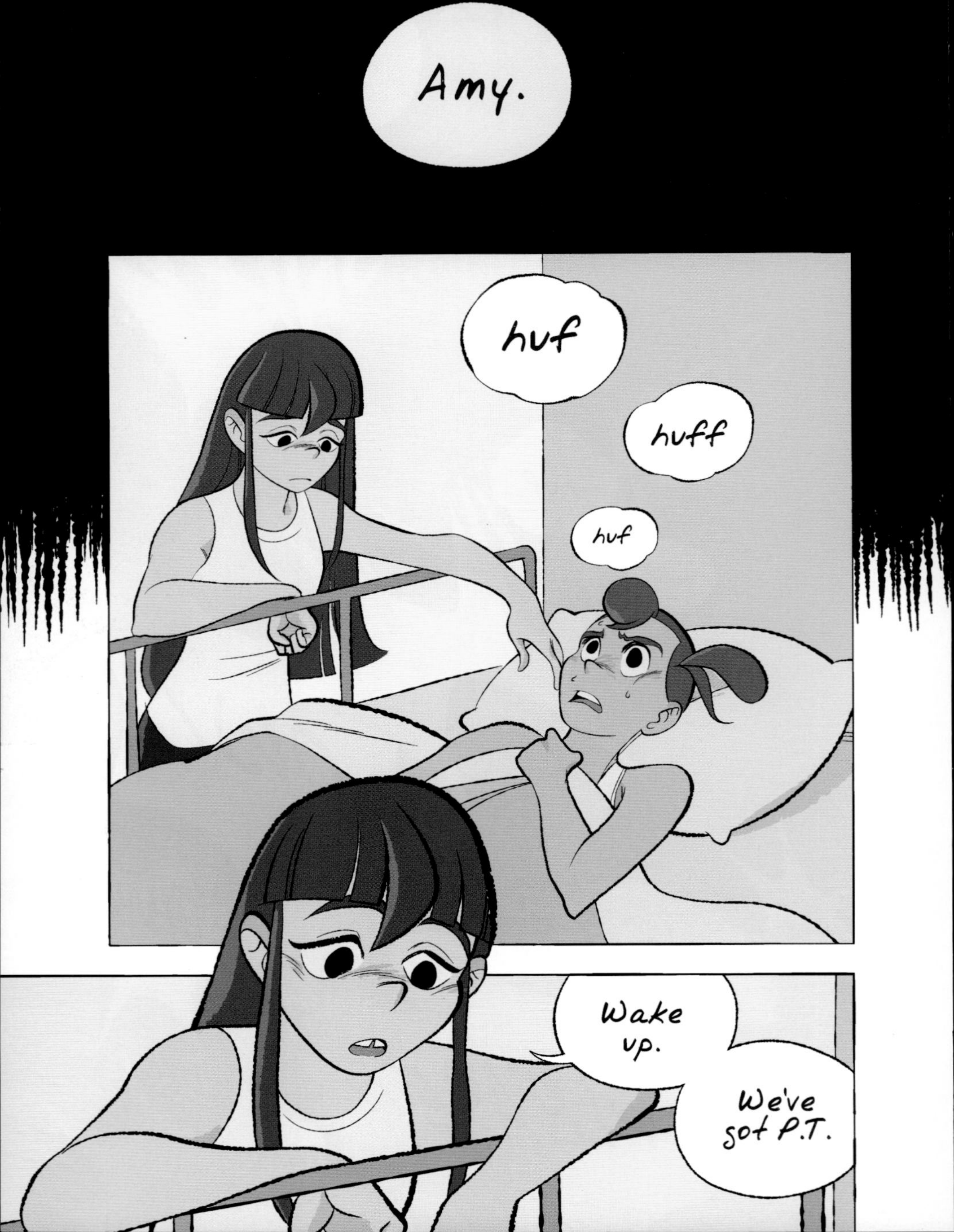
Amy.
huf
huff
huf
Wake up.
We've got P.T.

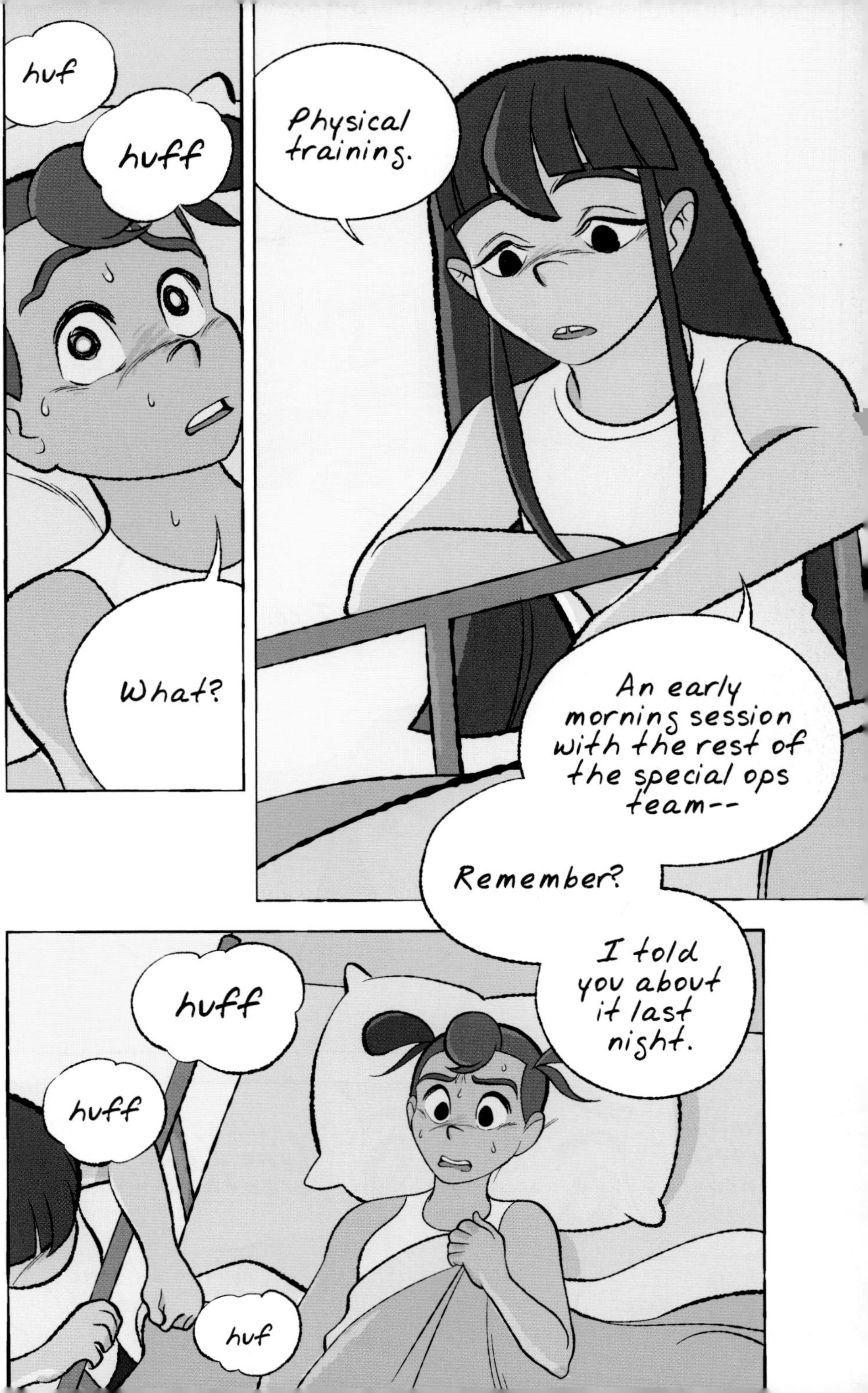

huf
huff
Physical training.
What?
An early morning session with the rest of the special ops team--
Remember?
I told you about it last night.
huff
huff
huf

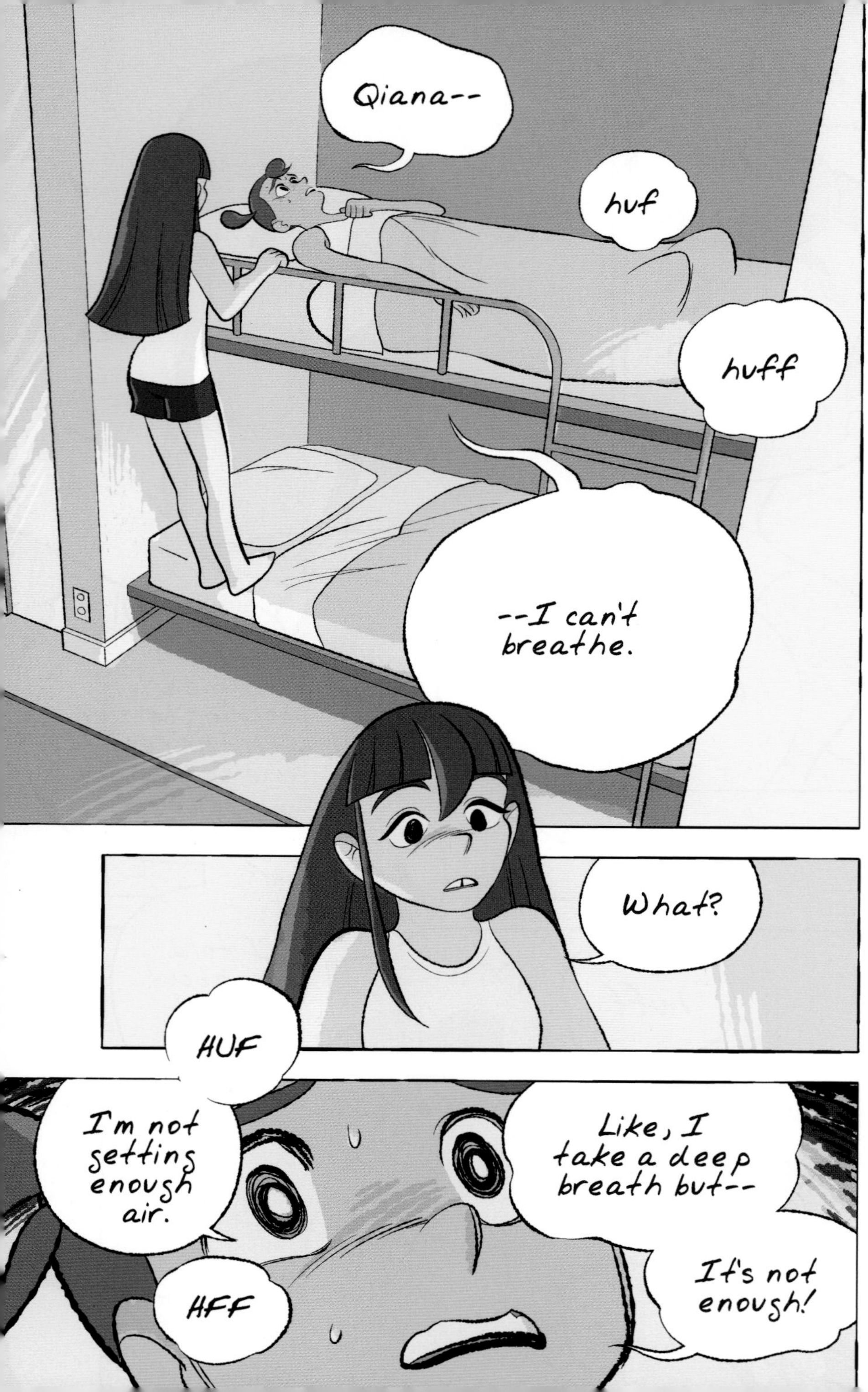
Qiana--
huf
huff
--I can't breathe.
What?
HUF
I'm not getting enough air.
Like, I take a deep breath but--
HFF
It's not enough!

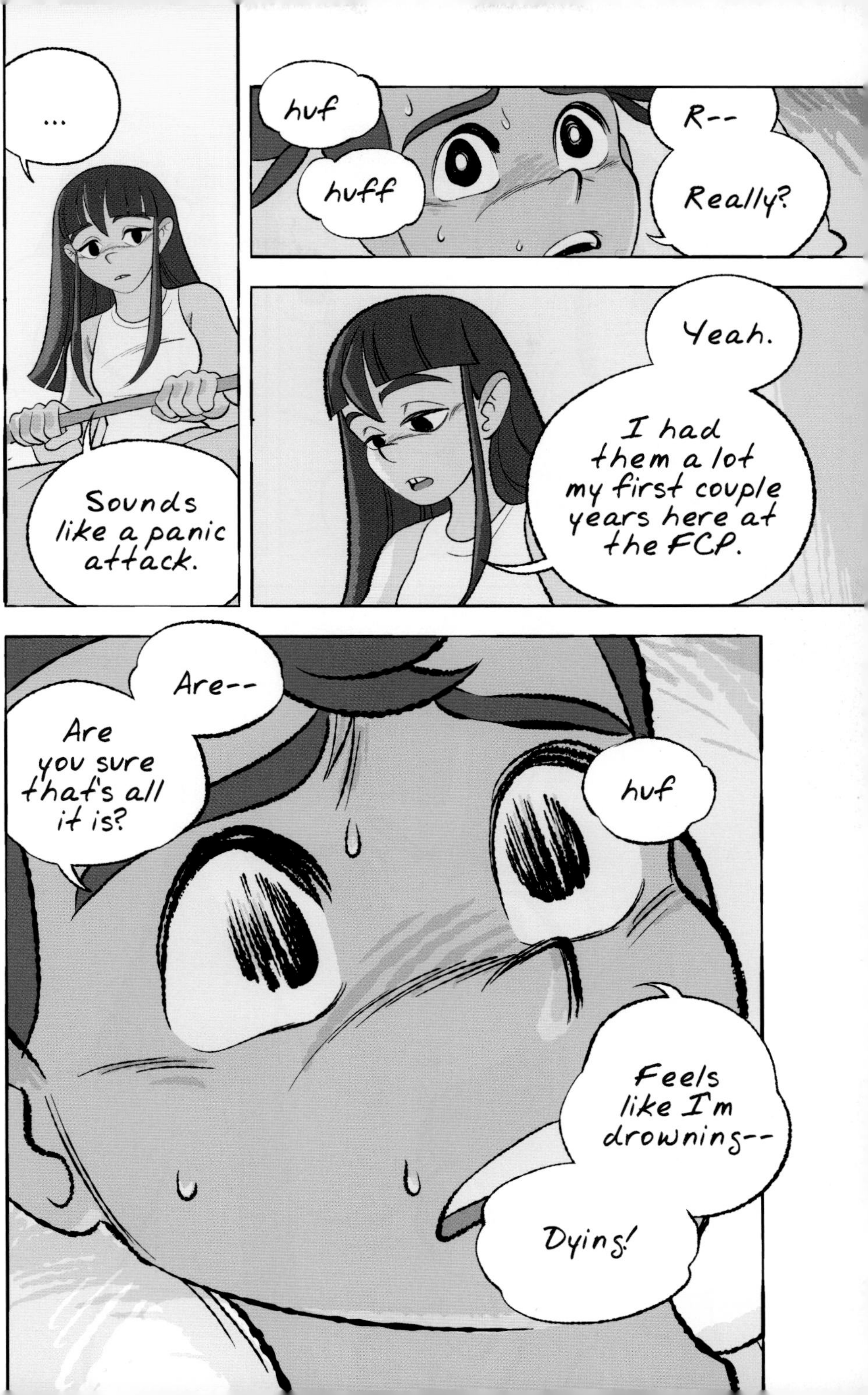
...
Sounds like a panic attack.
huf
huff
R--
Really?
Yeah.
I had them a lot my first couple years here at the FCP.
Are--
Are you sure that's all it is?
huf
Feels like I'm drowning--
Dying!

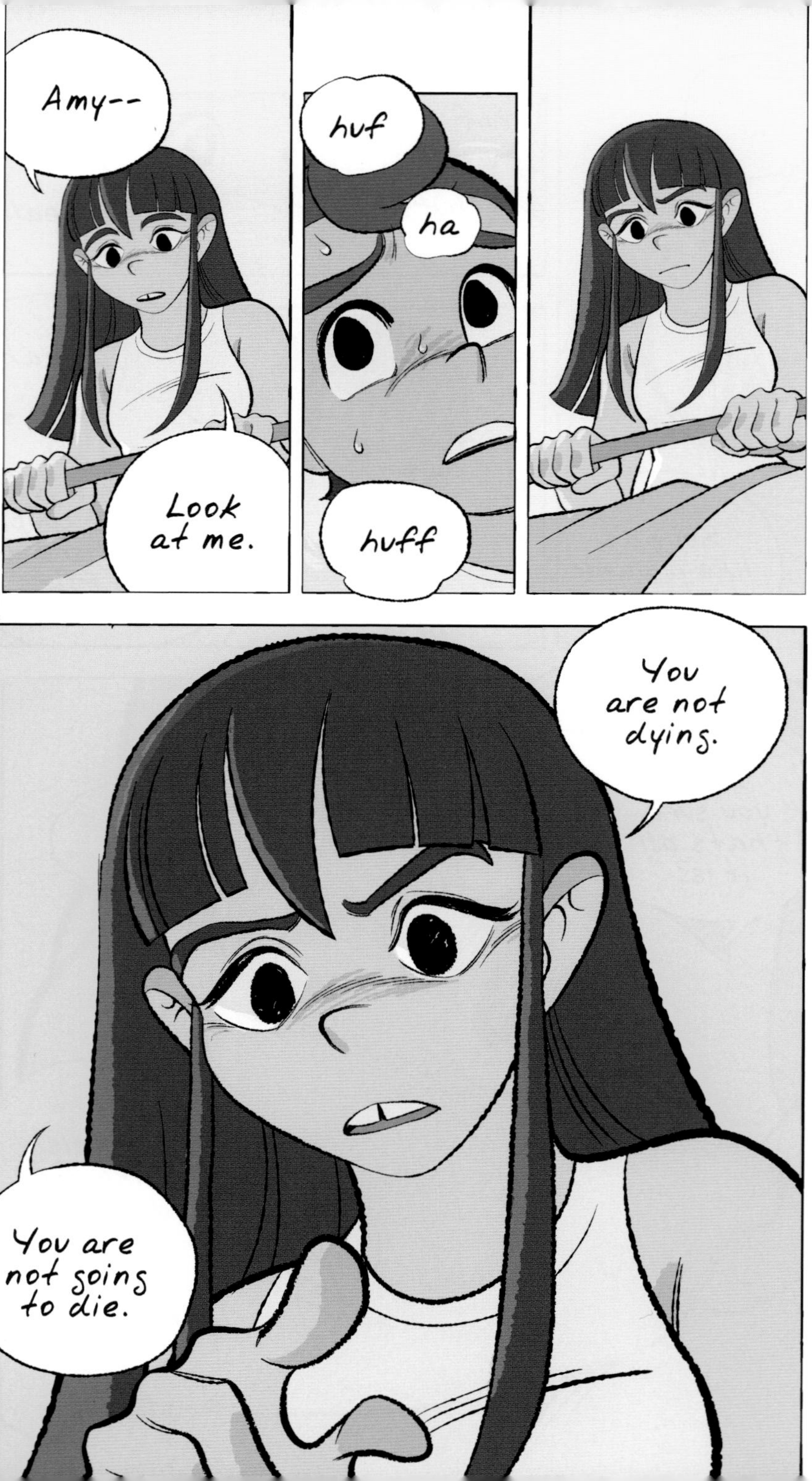
Amy--
Look at me.
huf
ha
huff
You are not dying.
You are not going to die.

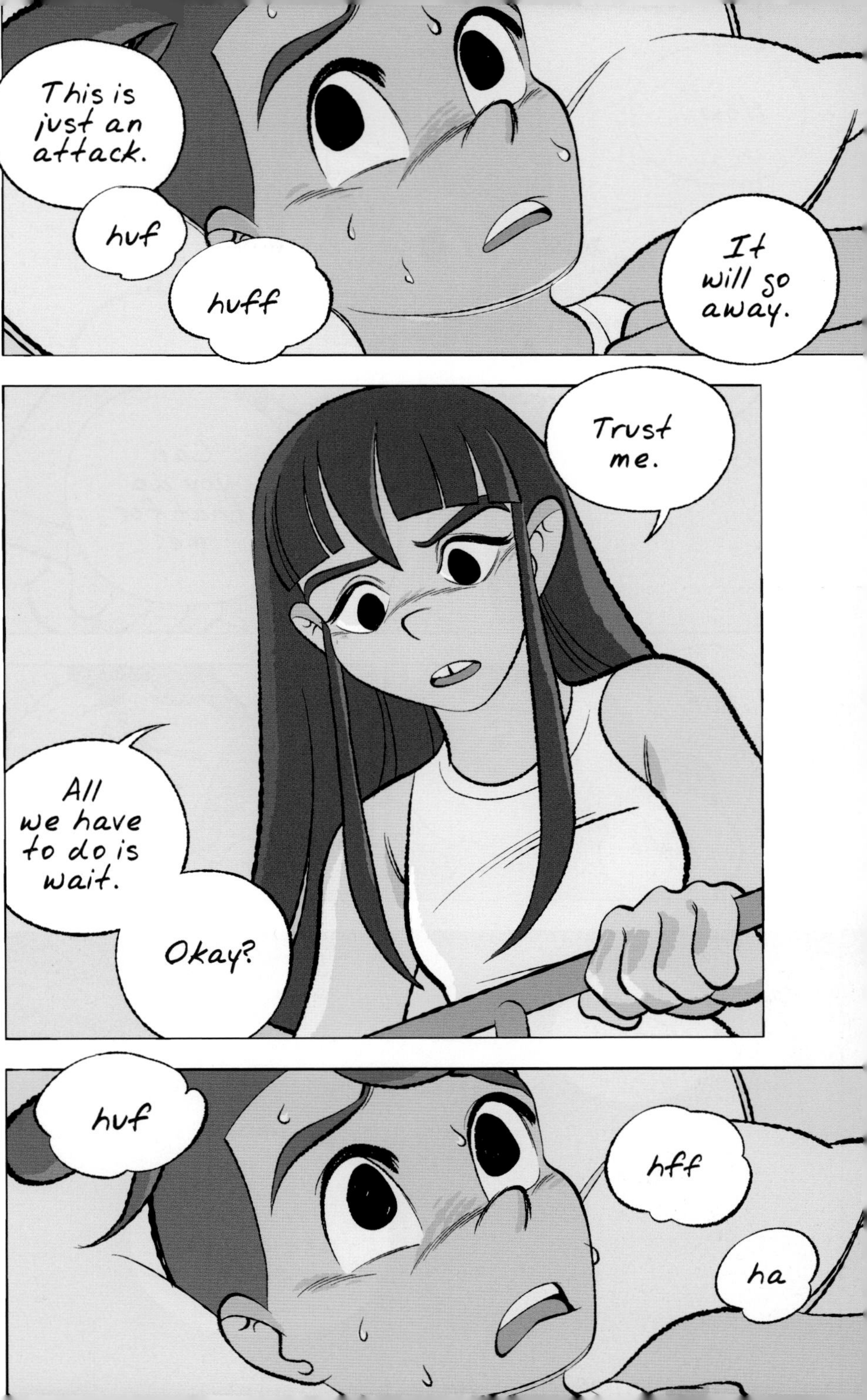

This is just an attack.
huf
huff
It will go away.
Trust me.
All we have to do is wait.
Okay?
huf
hff
ha

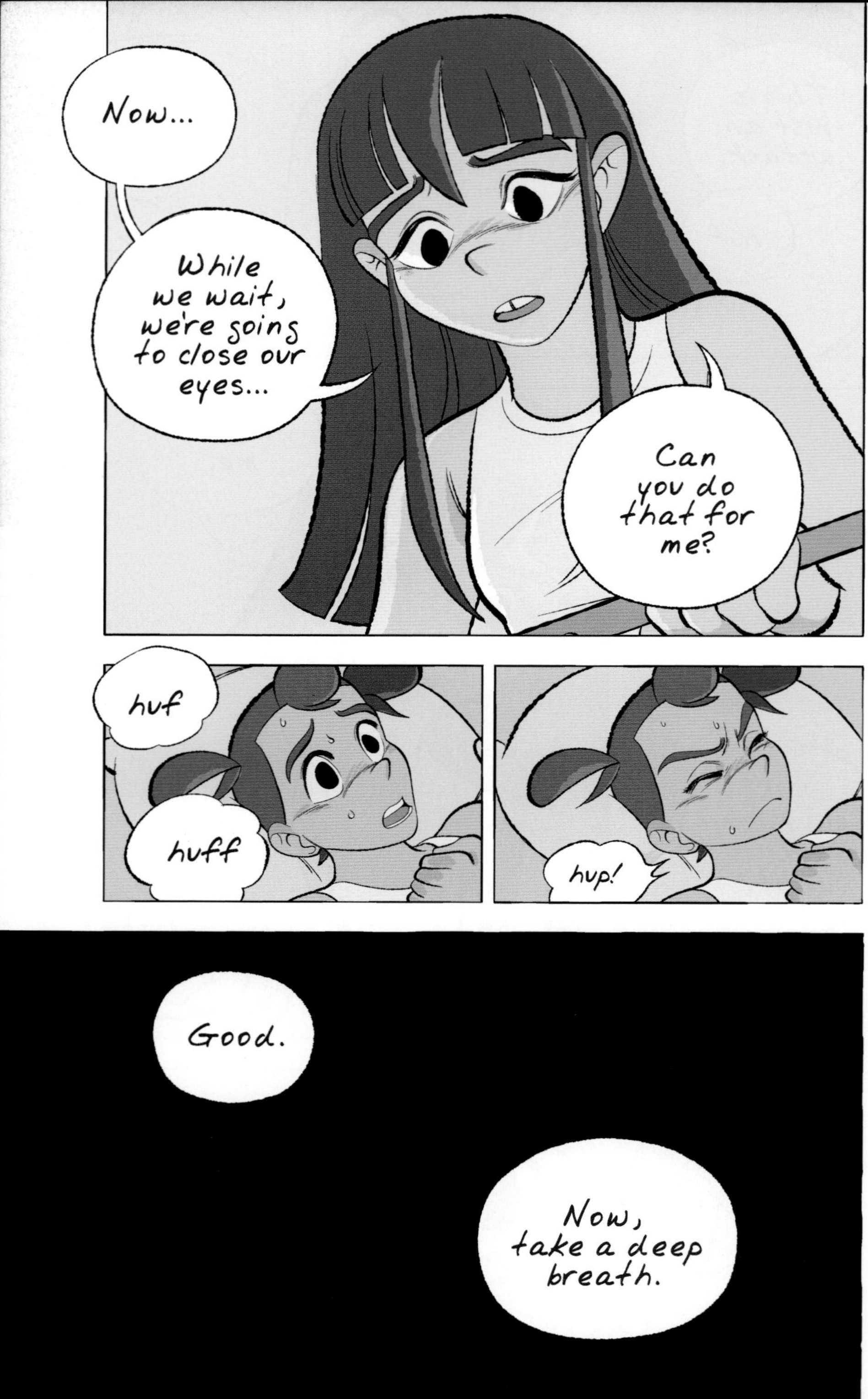
Now...
While we wait, we're going to close our eyes...
Can you do that for me?
huf
huff
hup!
Good.
Now, take a deep breath.

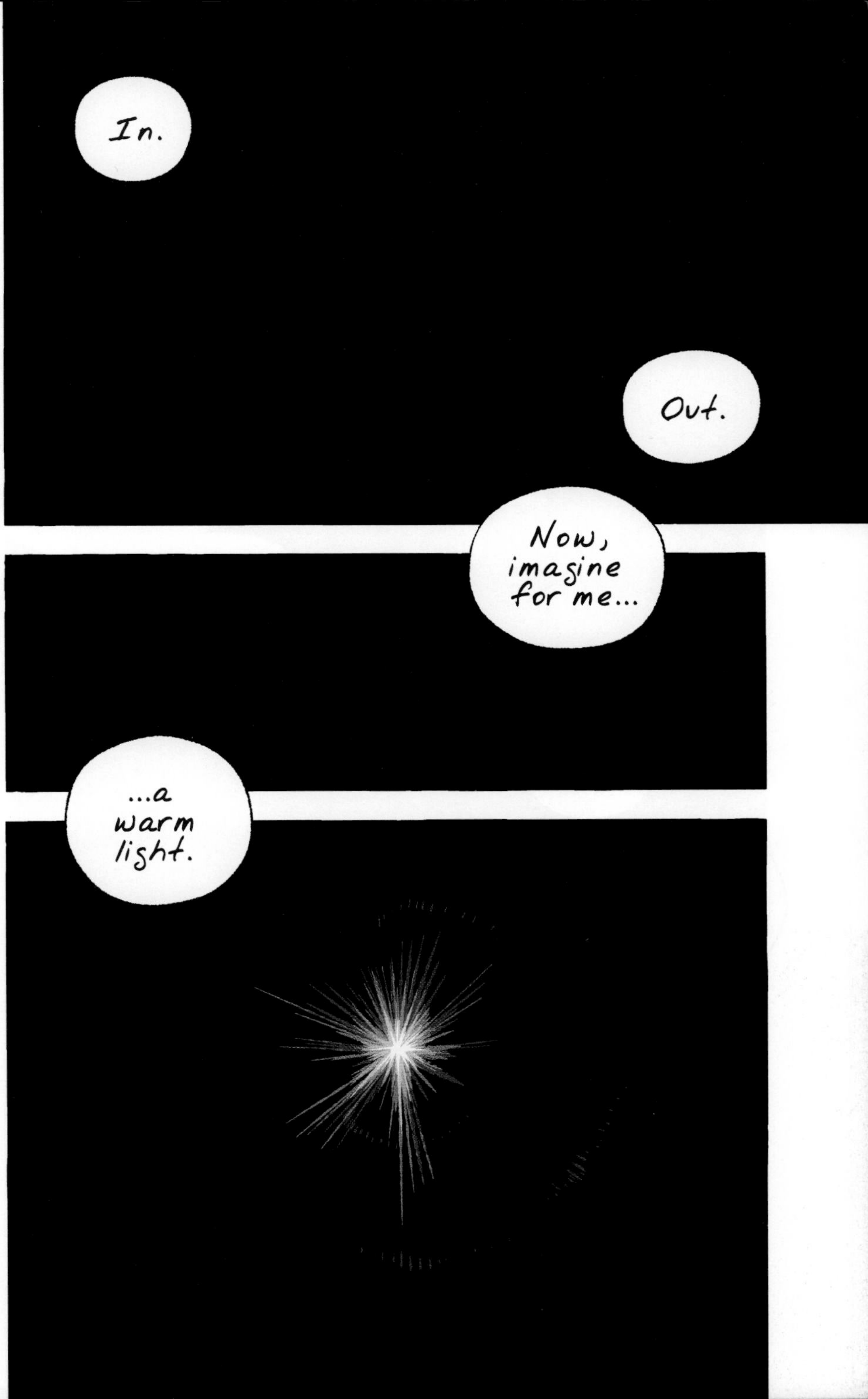
In.
Out.
Now, imagine for me...
...a warm light.

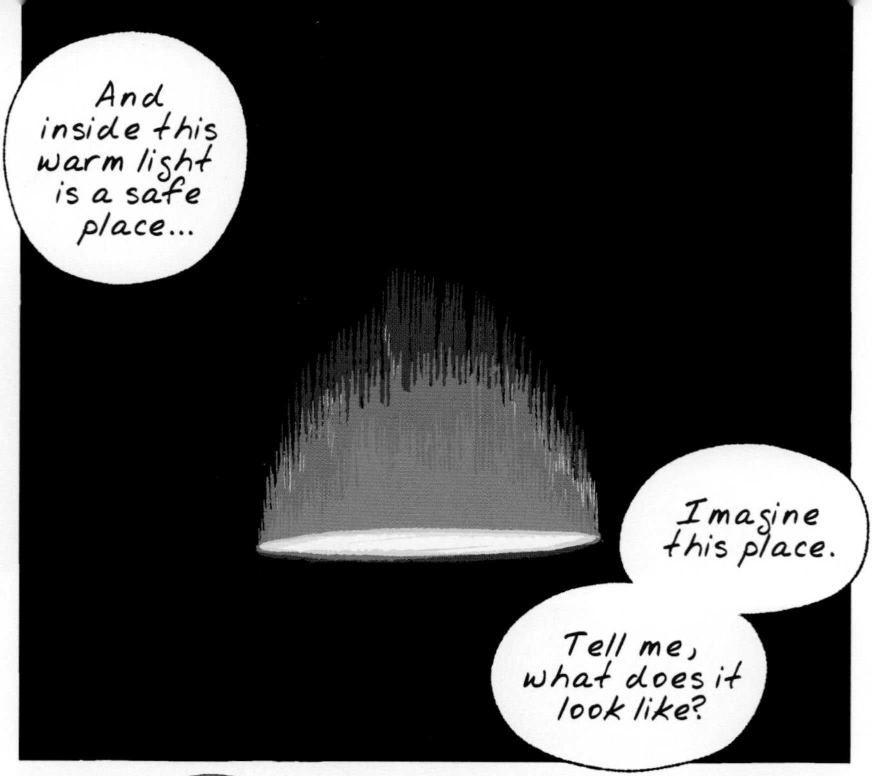
And inside this warm light is a safe place...
Imagine this place.
Tell me, what does it look like?

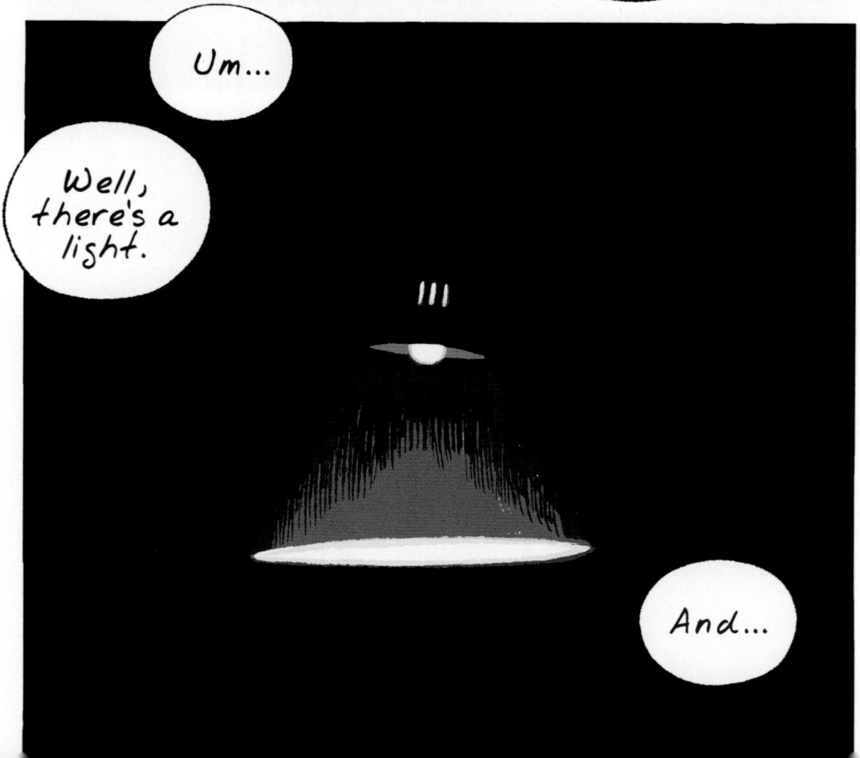
Um...
Well, there's a light.
And...

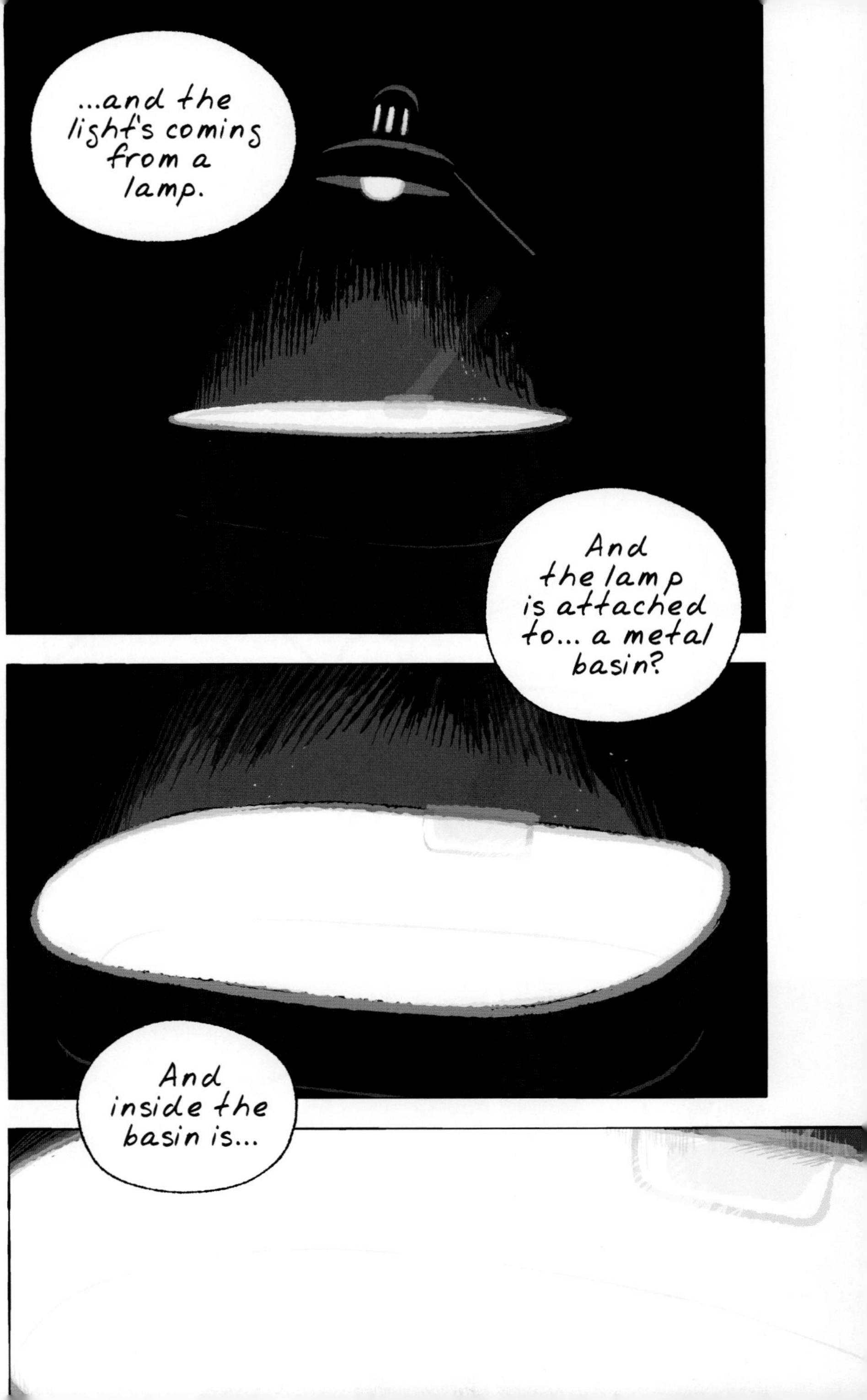
...and the light's coming from a lamp.
And the lamp is attached to... a metal basin?
And inside the basin is...

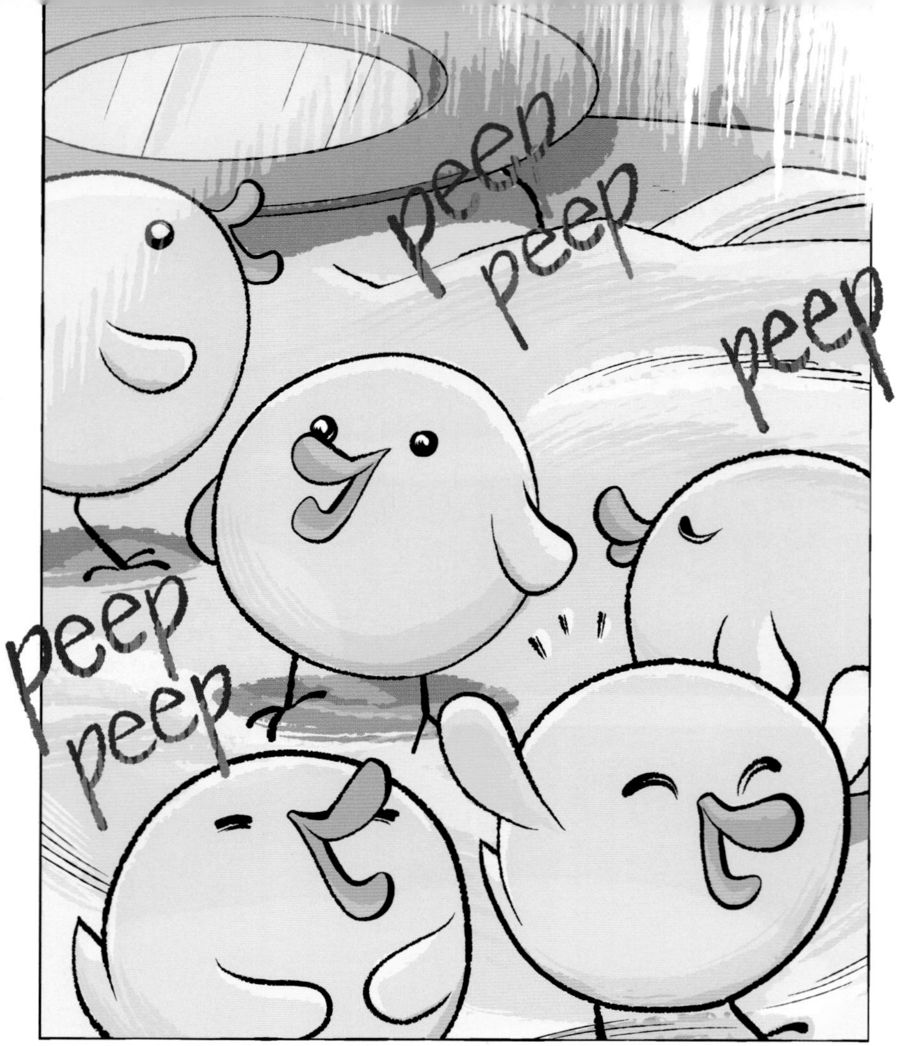
peep
peep
peep
peep
peep

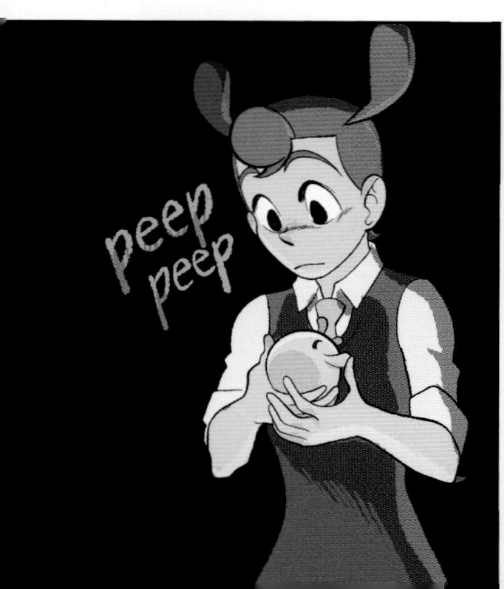
peep
peep

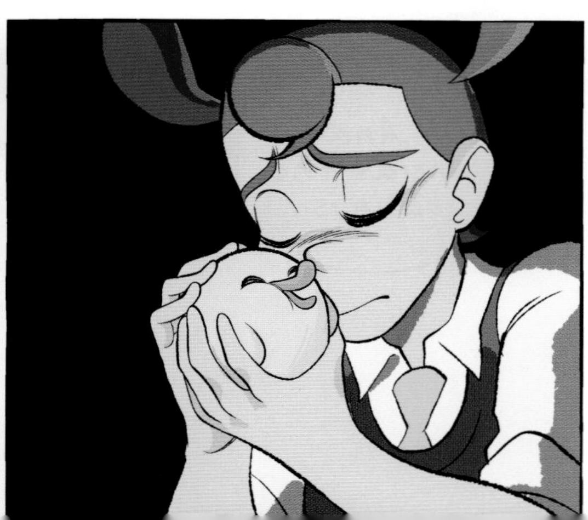

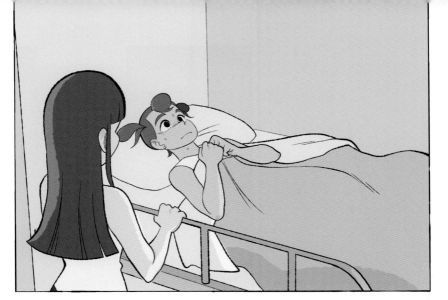

Thank you, Qiana.

It gets better, Amy.

I promise.

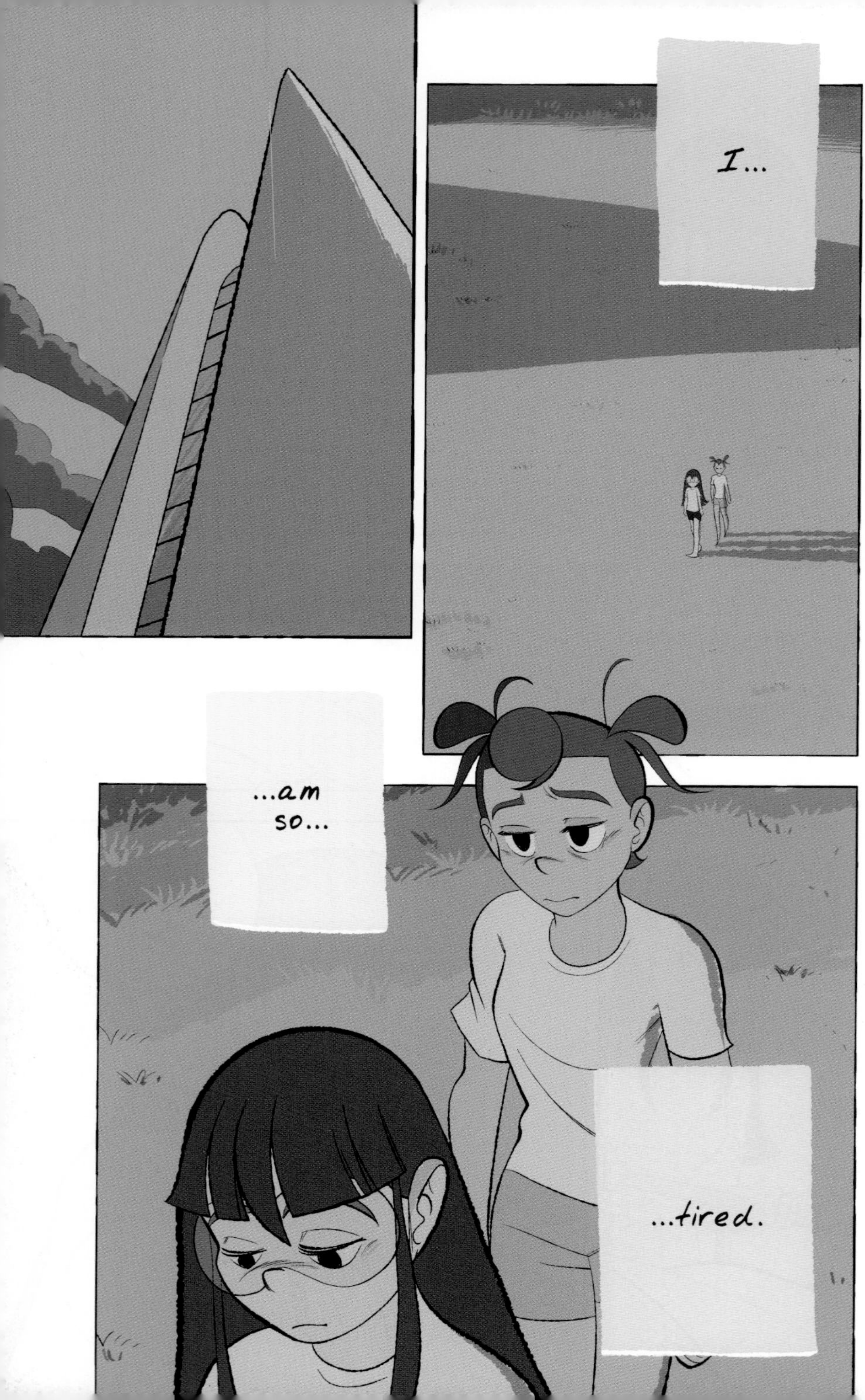
I...
...am so...
...tired.

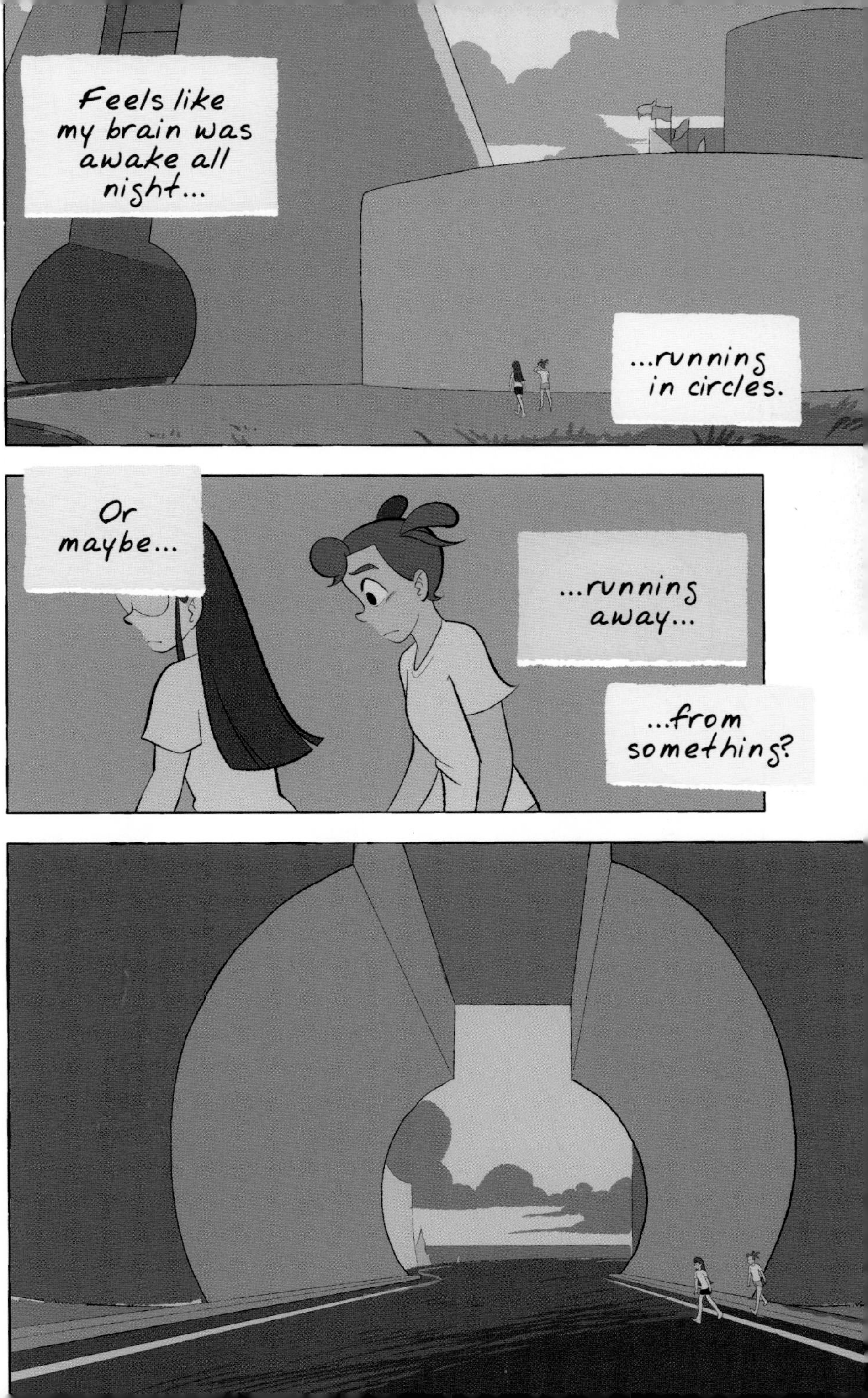
Feels like my brain was awake all night...
...running in circles.
Or maybe...
...running away...
...from something?

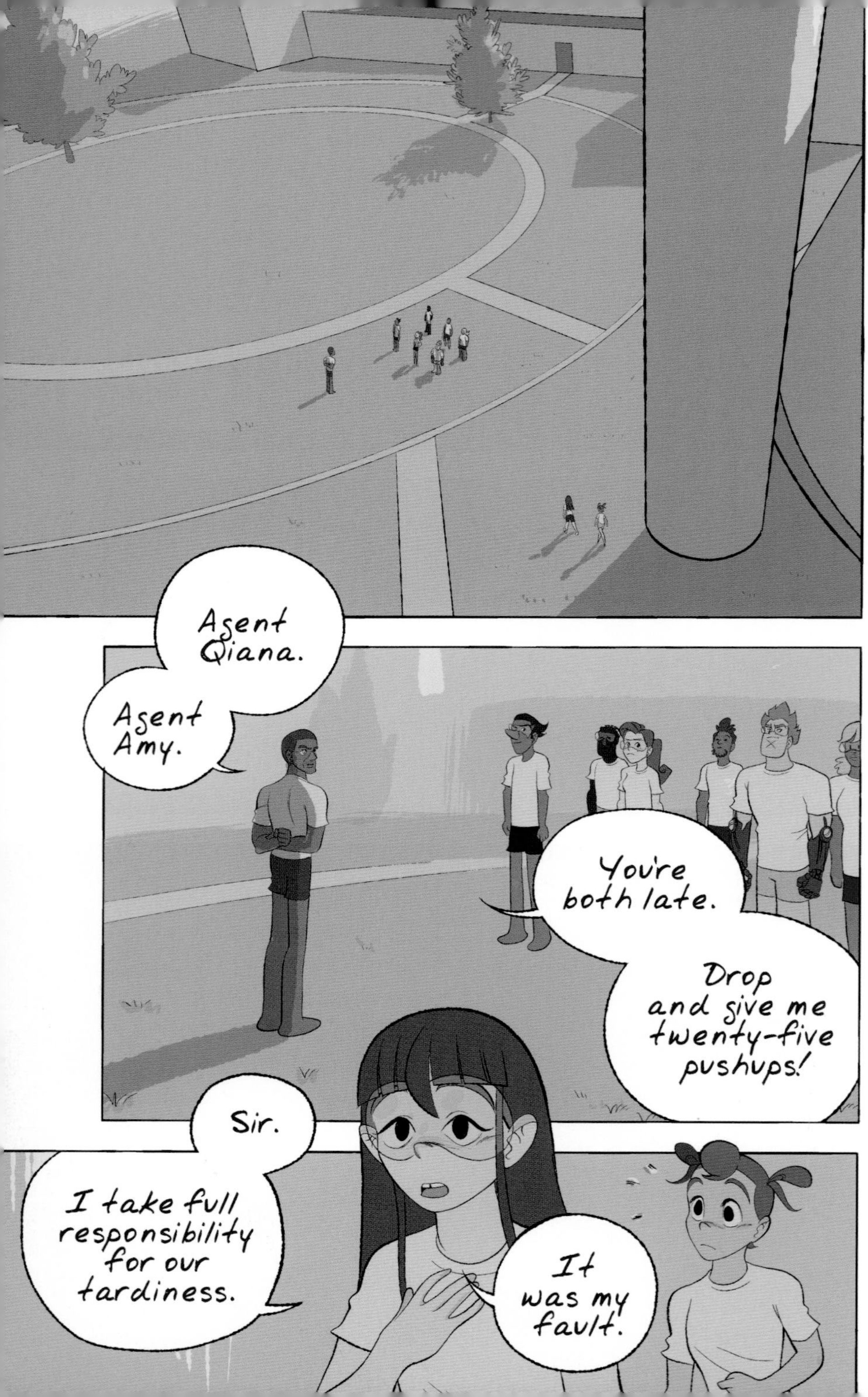
Agent Qiana.
Agent Amy.
You're both late.
Drop and give me twenty-five pushups!
Sir.
I take full responsibility for our tardiness.
It was my fault.

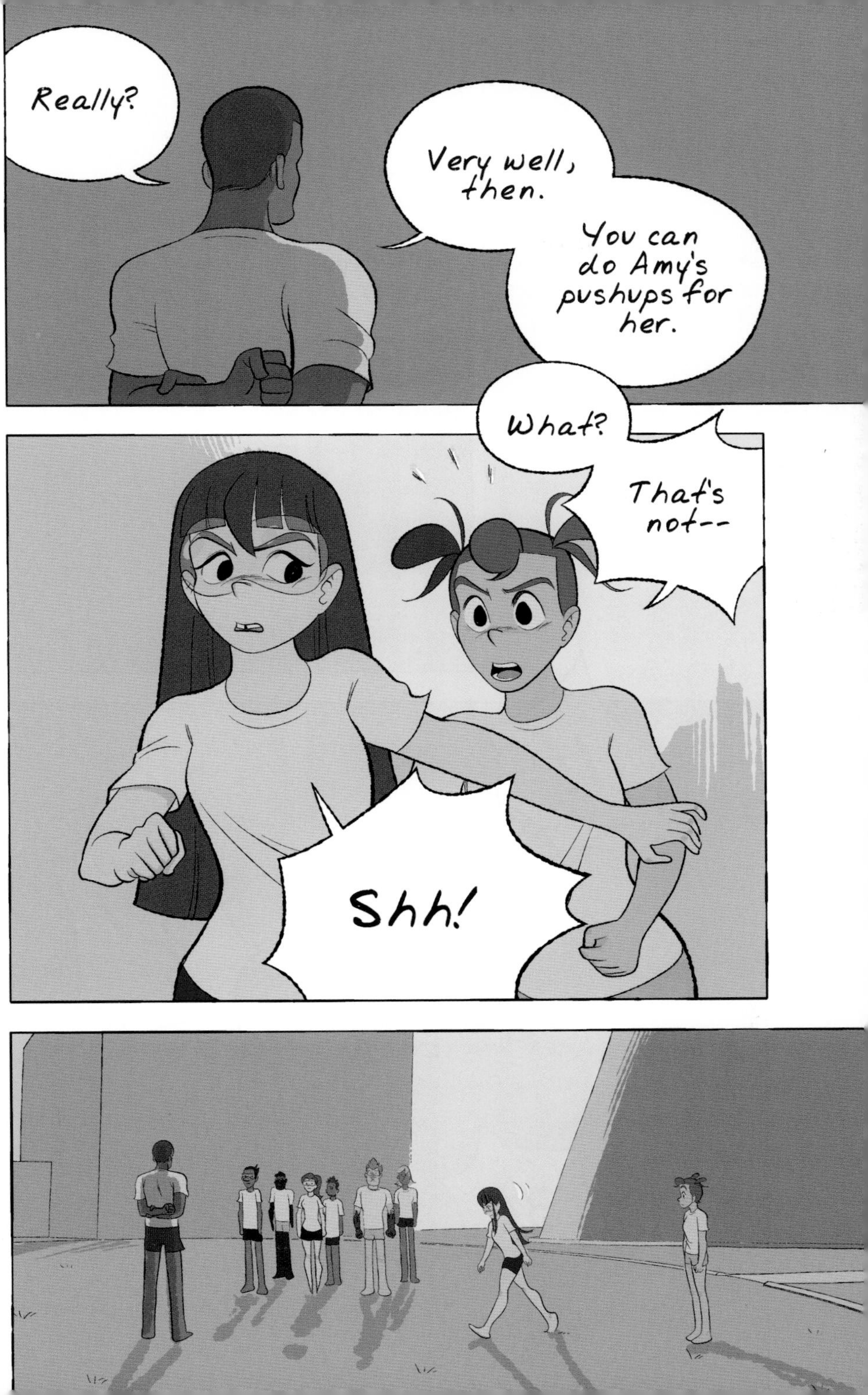
Really?
Very well, then.
You can do Amy's pushups for her.
What?
That's not--
Shh!

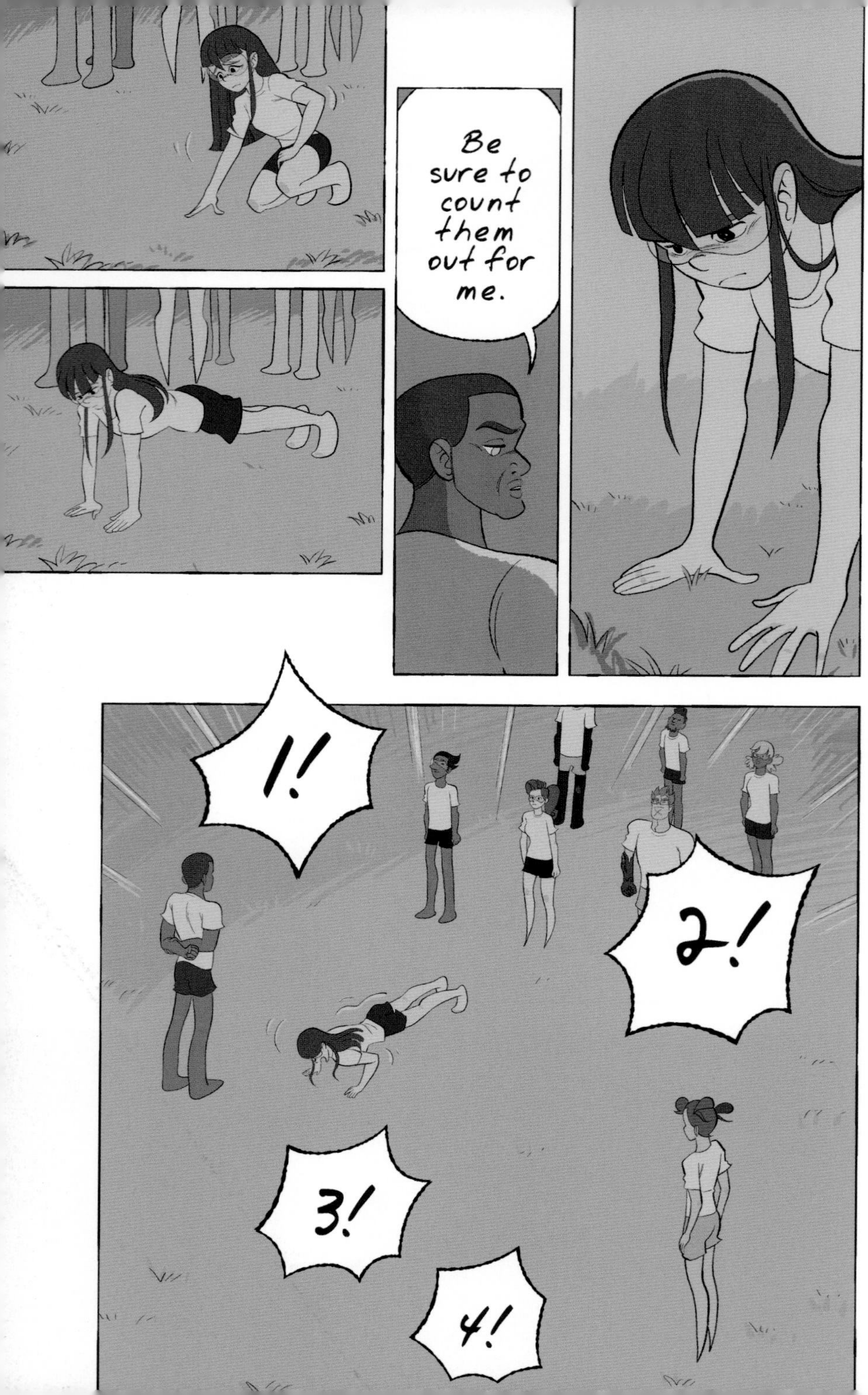
Be sure to count them out for me.
1!
2!
3!
4!

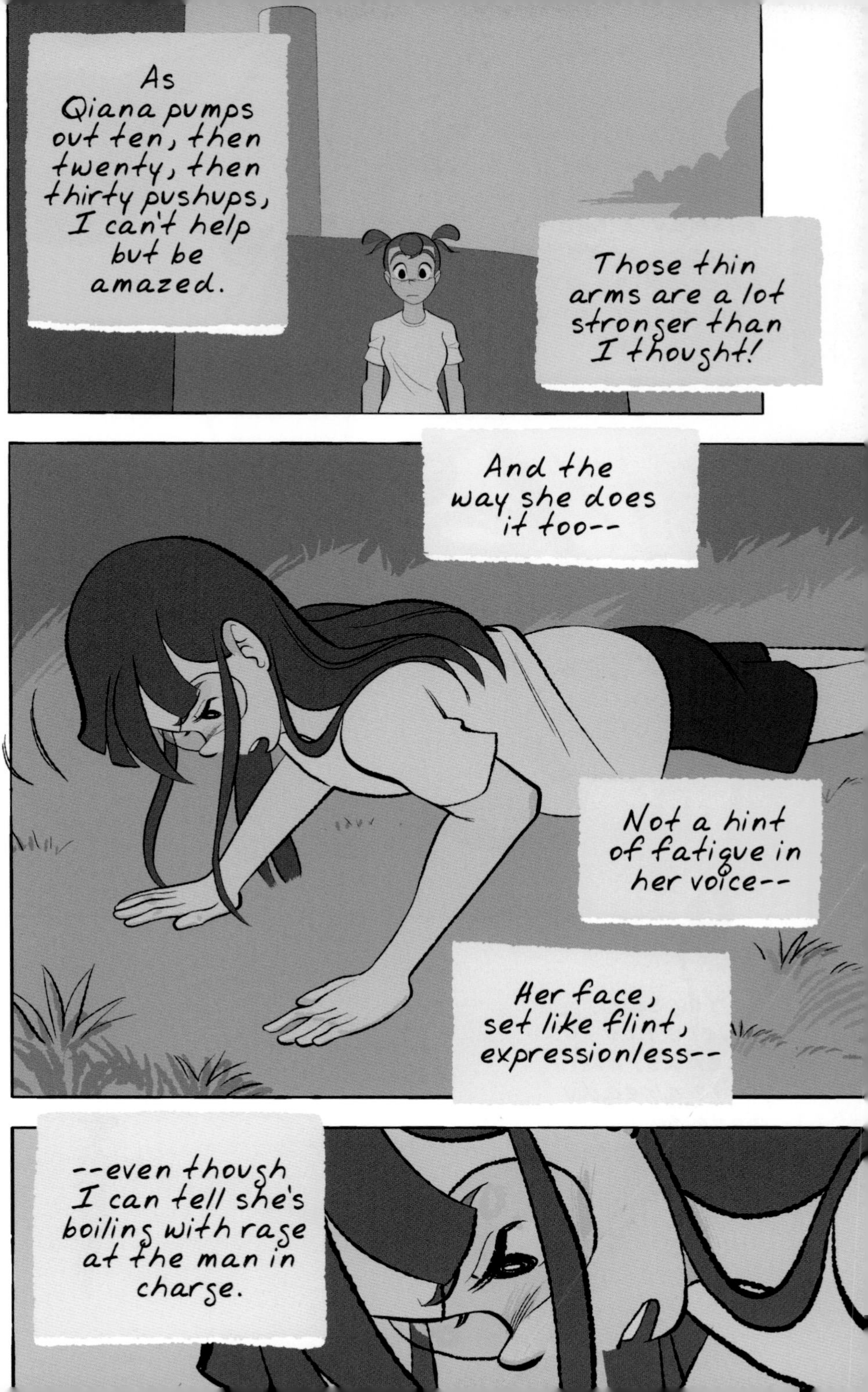
As Qiana pumps out ten, then twenty, then thirty pushups, I can't help but be amazed.
Those thin arms are a lot stronger than I thought!
And the way she does it too--
Not a hint of fatigue in her voice--
Her face, set like flint, expressionless--
--even though I can tell she's boiling with rage at the man in charge.

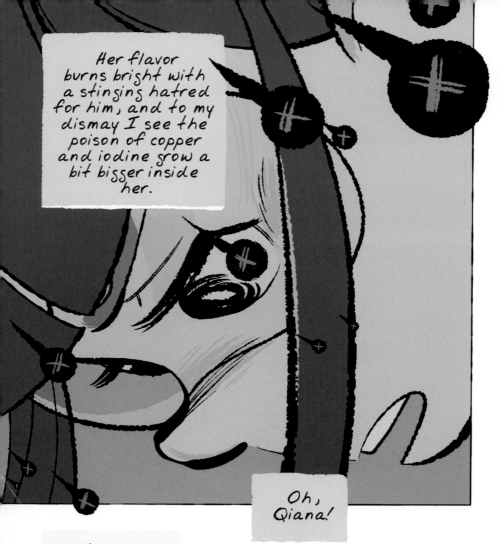

Her flavor burns bright with a stinging hatred for him, and to my dismay I see the poison of copper and iodine grow a bit bigger inside her.

Oh, Qiana!

You say we're not friends, but you've already done so much to help me--

What can I do to help you?

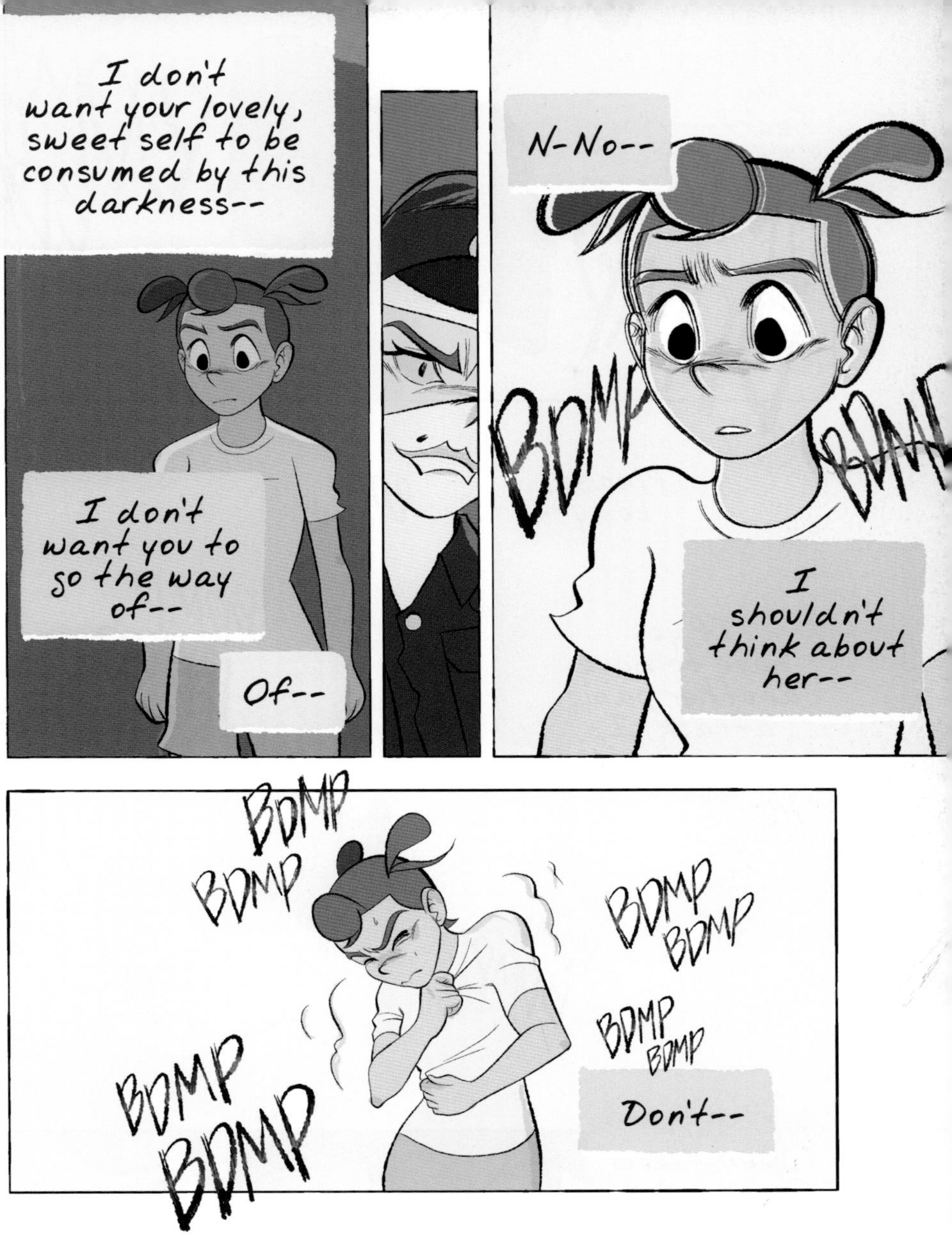
I don't want your lovely, sweet self to be consumed by this darkness--
I don't want you to go the way of--
Of--
N-No--
BDMP
BDMP
I shouldn't think about her--
BDMP
BDMP
BDMP
BDMP
BDMP
BDMP
BDMP
BDMP
Don't--

Please, don't have another panic attack...

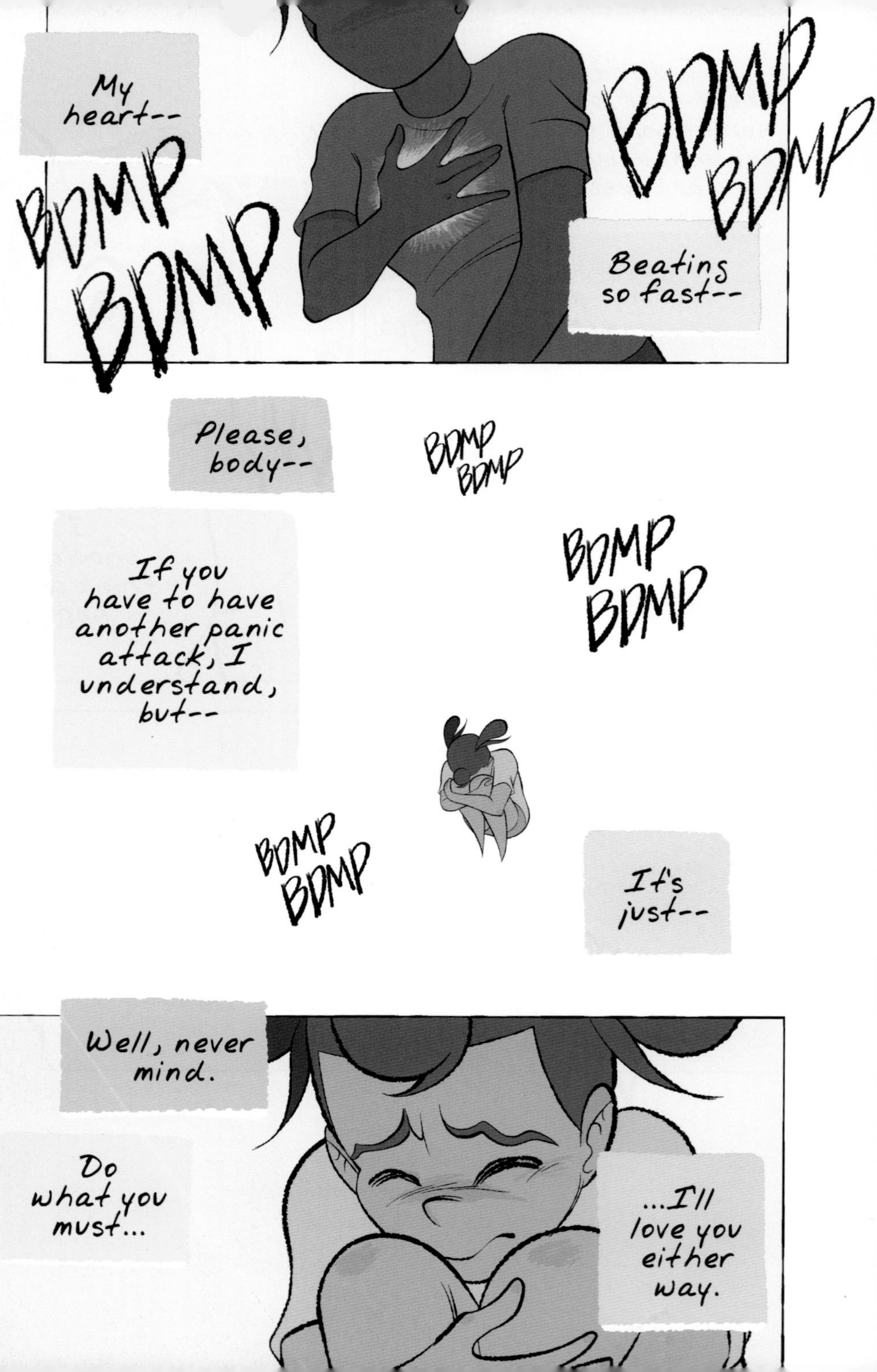
My heart--
BDMP BDMP
BDMP BDMP
Beating so fast--
Please, body--
BDMP BDMP
If you have to have another panic attack, I understand, but--
BDMP BDMP
BDMP BDMP
It's just--
Well, never mind.
Do what you must...
...I'll love you either way.

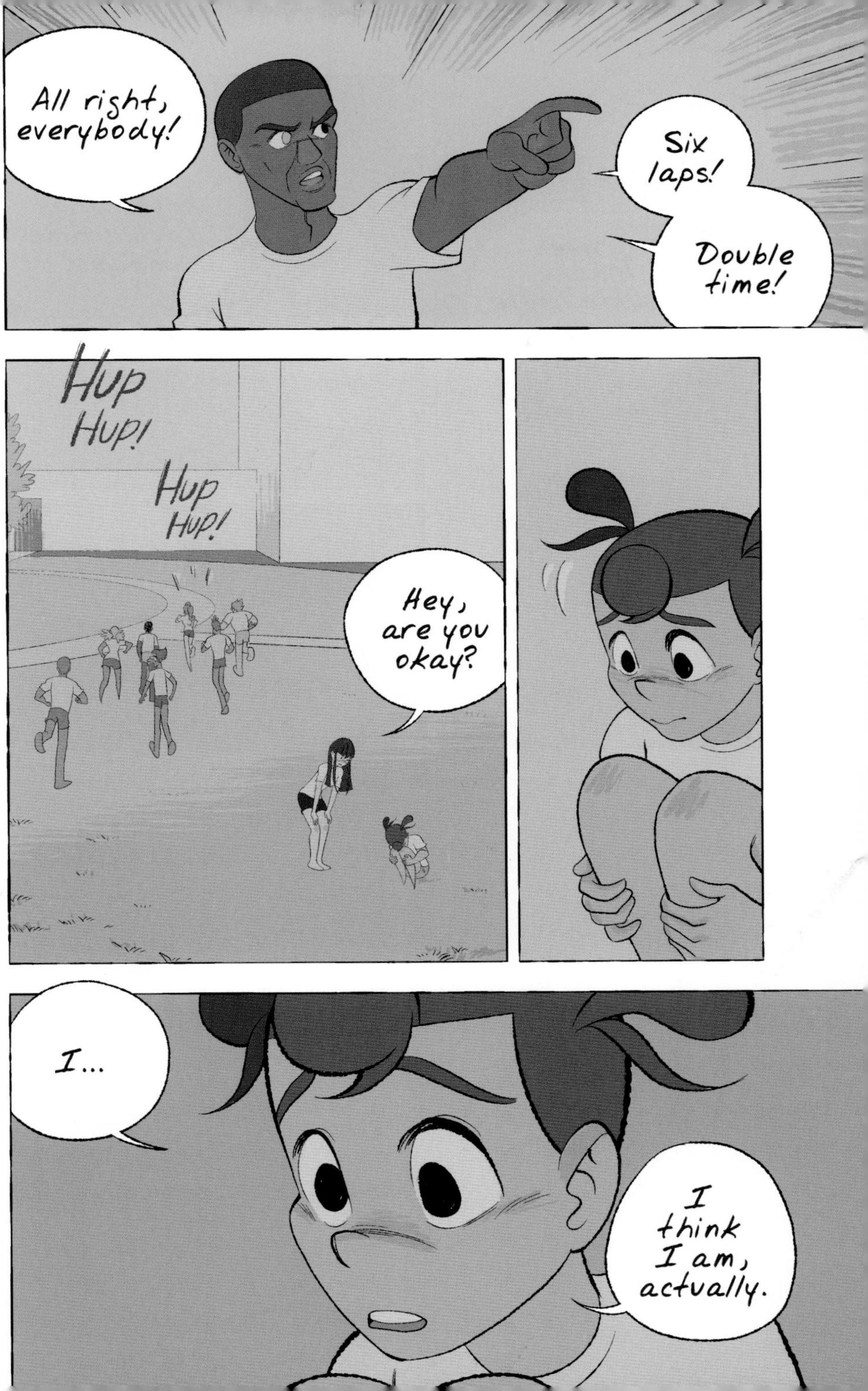
All right, everybody!
Six laps!
Double time!
Hup Hup!
Hup Hup!
Hey, are you okay?
I...
I think I am, actually.

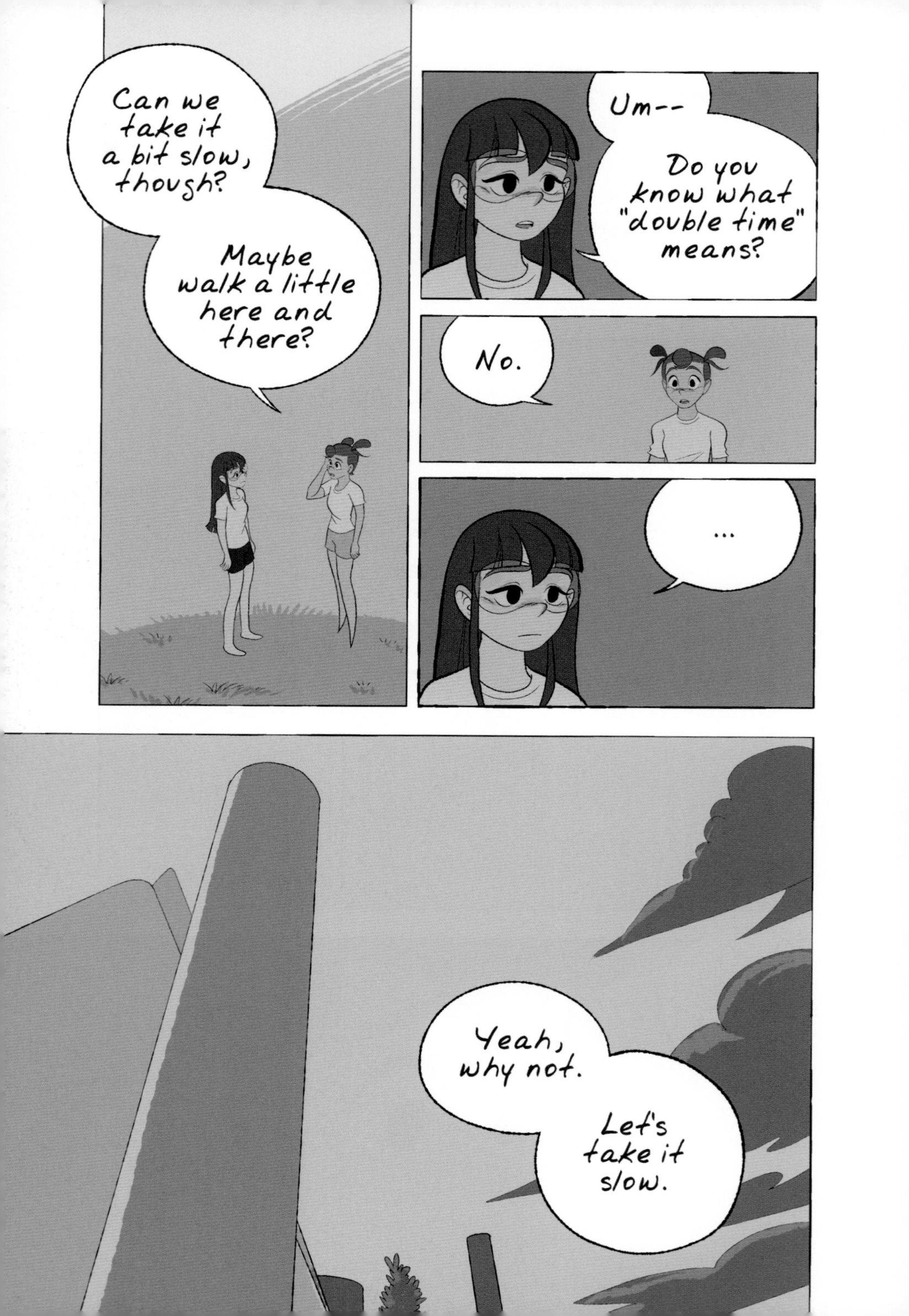
Can we take it a bit slow, though?
Maybe walk a little here and there?
Um--
Do you know what "double time" means?
No.
...
Yeah, why not.
Let's take it slow.

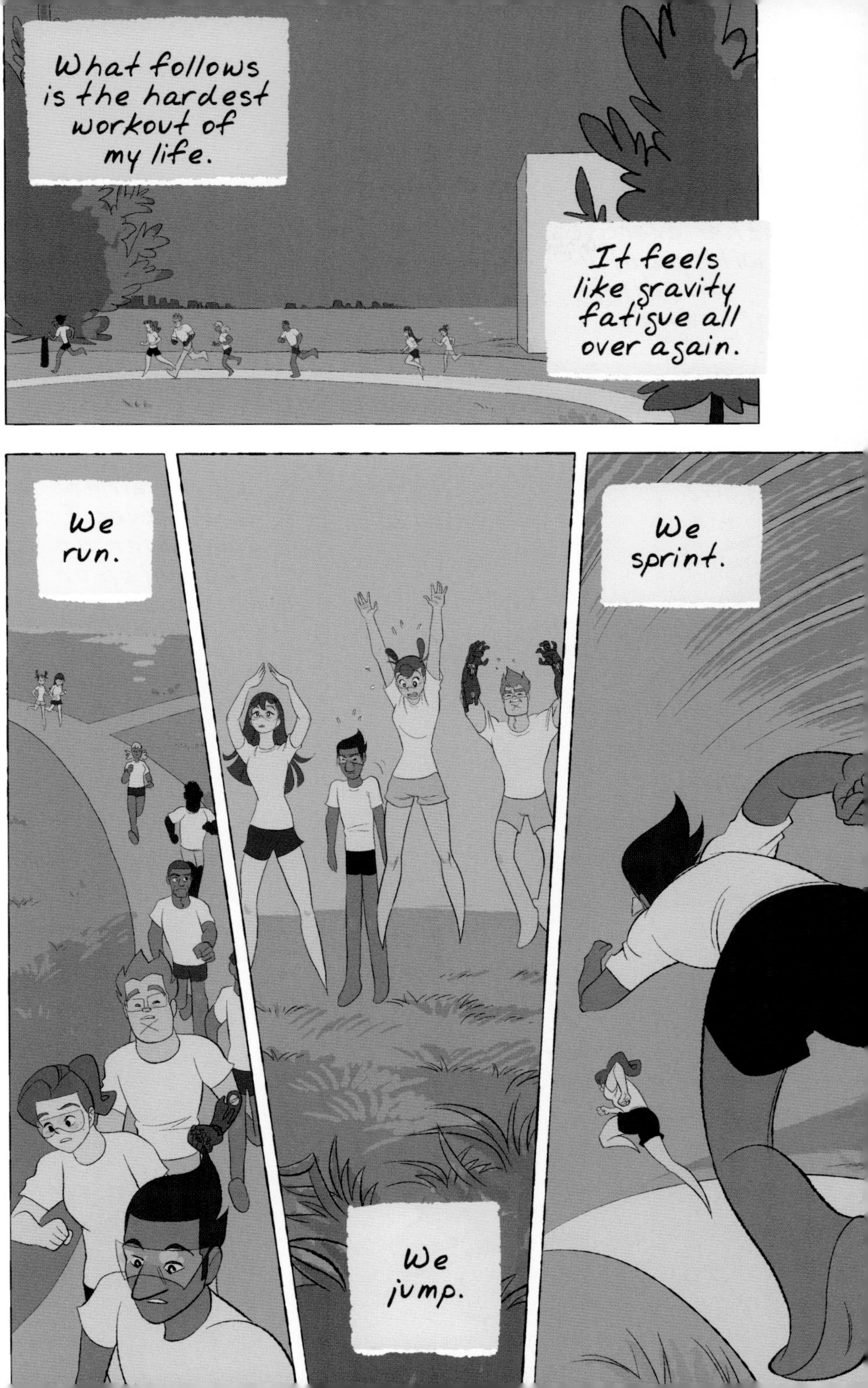
What follows is the hardest workout of my life.
It feels like gravity fatigue all over again.
We run.
We jump.
We sprint.

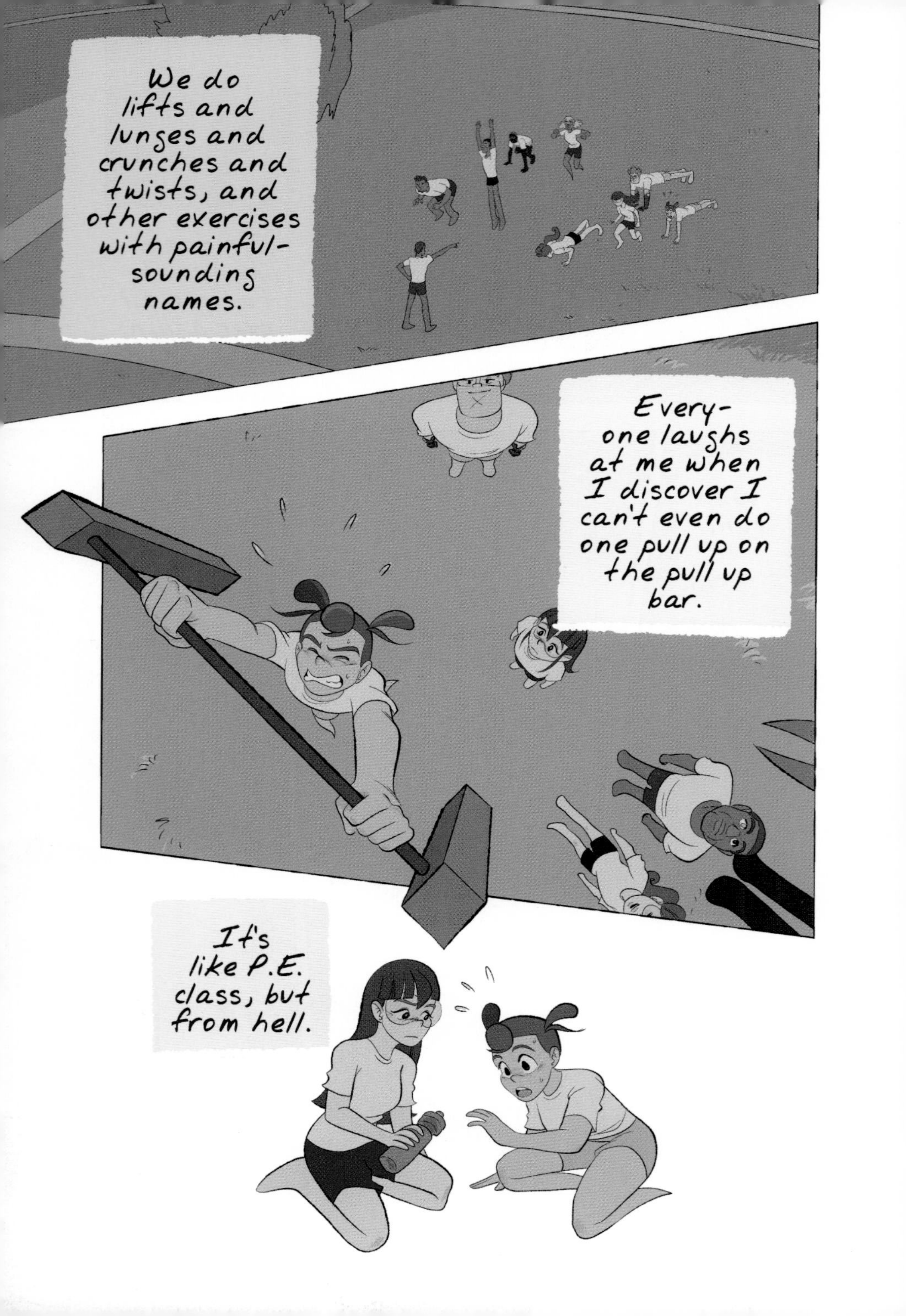
We do lifts and lunges and crunches and twists, and other exercises with painful-sounding names.
Every-one laughs at me when I discover I can't even do one pull up on the pull up bar.
It's like P.E. class, but from hell.

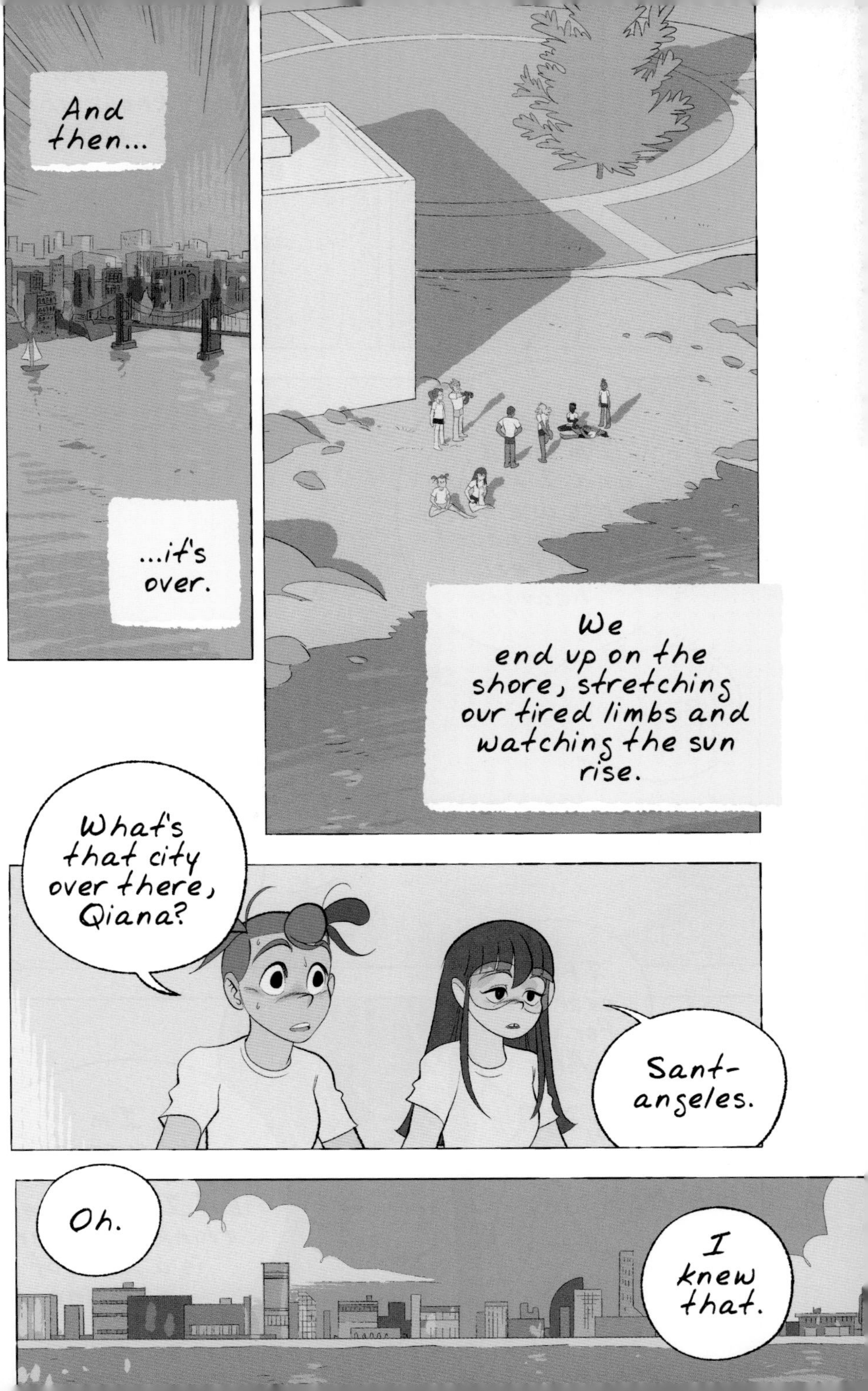
And then...
...it's over.
We end up on the shore, stretching our tired limbs and watching the sun rise.
What's that city over there, Qiana?
Sant-angeles.
Oh.
I knew that.

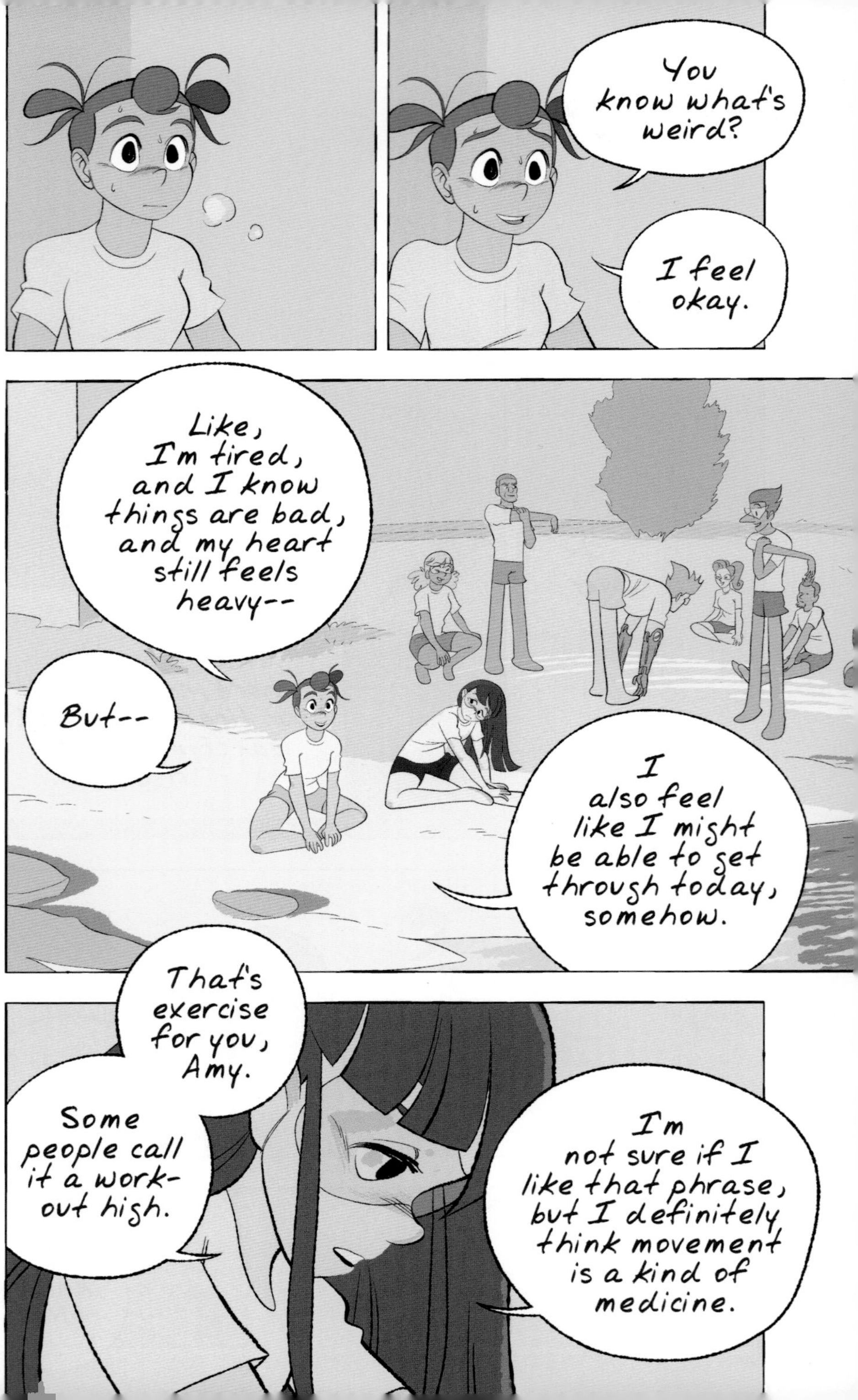
You know what's weird?
I feel okay.
Like, I'm tired, and I know things are bad, and my heart still feels heavy--
But--
I also feel like I might be able to get through today, somehow.
That's exercise for you, Amy.
Some people call it a work-out high.
I'm not sure if I like that phrase, but I definitely think movement is a kind of medicine.

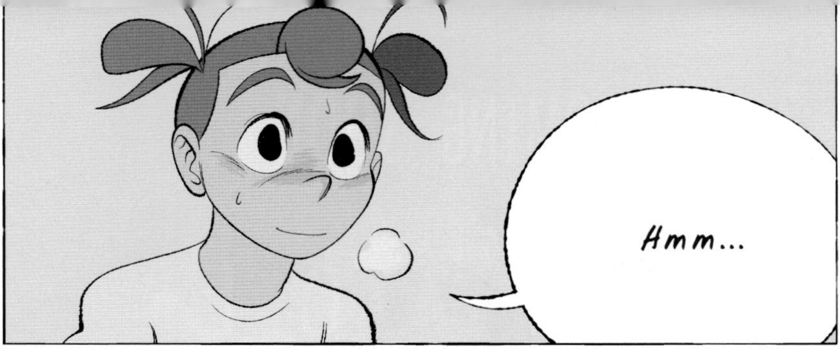
Hmm...

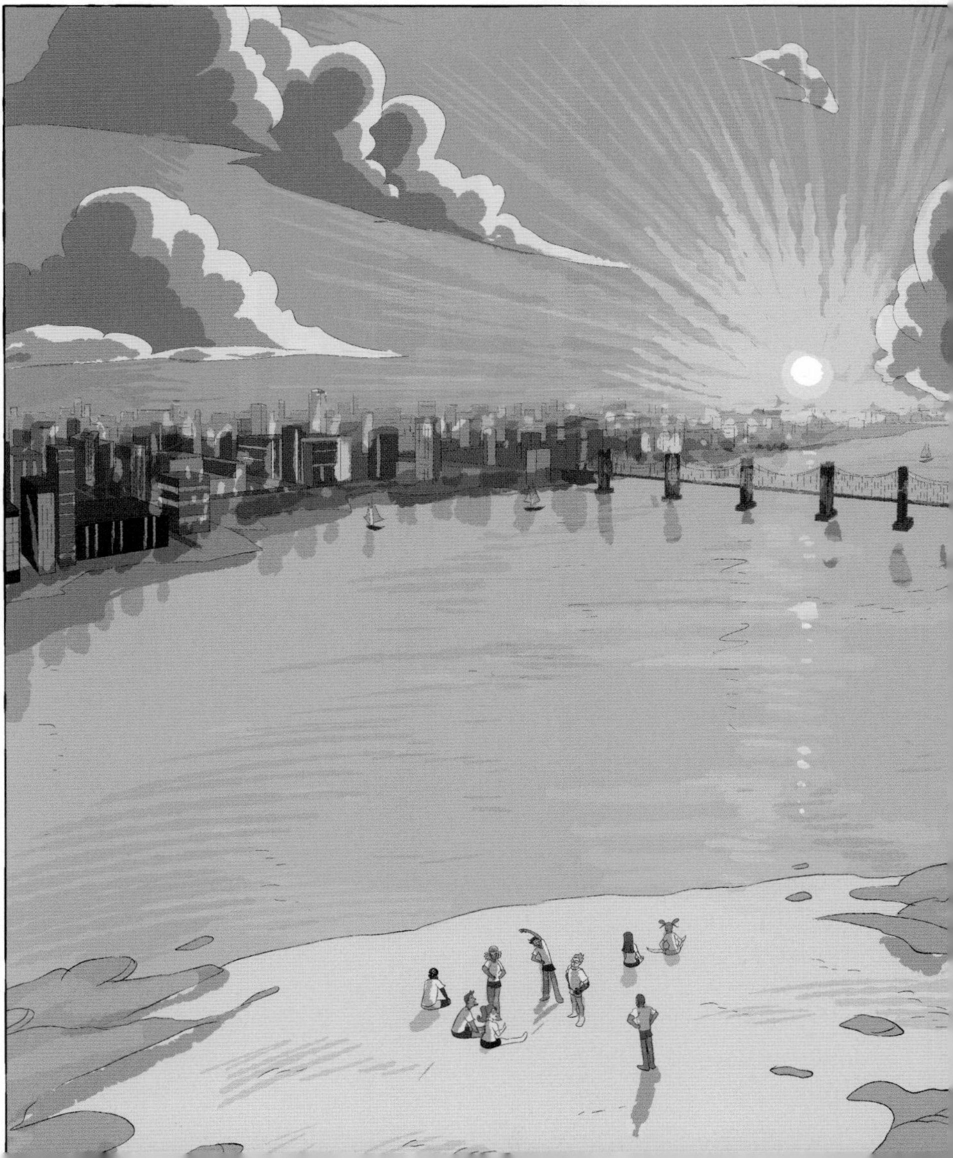

COMING SOON ...

SOMETHING DARK GROWS AT THE HEART OF THE FIRST CONTACT PROJECT.

Amy settles into her new routine of exercise, work, and chatting with Oliver, trying to put the specter of homecoming behind her. But life in the FCP is anything but boring, as she and Qiana begin unravelling the conspiracy within the agency, one which takes them all the way to the office of the Director himself!

Meanwhile in Kokomo, Cassie and Schafer begin to turn up new leads in the case, all the while unaware of the manipulations of mysterious National Security agent, James Silber. And finally, the truth of Tammie's abduction is revealed to the world in the latest exciting volume of Stephen McCranie's *Space Boy*!

Available November 2022!

YOU CAN ALSO READ MORE *SPACE BOY* COMICS ON WEBTOONS.COM!